RISING ASHES

A TRIED & TRUE NOVEL
BOOK SEVEN

CHARLI RAHE

First paperback edition December 2023
First hardcover edition December 2023

Cover Art by Miblart
Chapter Art by Etheric Designs

ISBN (Ebook): 978-1-958055-27-4

ISBN (Paperback): 978-1-958055-28-1

ISBN (Hardcover): 978-1-958055-29-8

Created with Vellum

*I couldn't close out the series without giving you a peek into Brass's mind since
he always gets to see into everyone else's.
Thank you to all who have read Scarlett and her family's journey.
And to my children and husband,
I leave you with my favorite quotes of the series.
I love you. Forever and always. Mine, yours, the world's, for all time. I would
risk the world, defy the Norns, just to keep you.
Because only forever will do.*

Note from the Author

As Scarlett's fantastical story comes to an end, know it follows a woman's journey through her magical heritage in which she encounters several dark scenarios. It is not intended for readers under 18 years of age and includes adult content.

While I'd prefer you to experience it as you go, your mental health matters. Please refer to www.charlirahe.com for a detailed list of possible triggers.

OSTARA
AVES
SUMAR
DAGR
MERFOLK
SUNNA
SJOR
SOLDJOT
SOLS
SANDR
WEMIC
THRIMILCI
FAUNELLE
TROLLS
&
FAIRIES
VIDR
CENTAUR
HAUST
RISAR
LODDA
BLAO
ENOX
MABON

TIDINGS
ELIVAGAR
ITR
REGN
ROT
LYCAN
NATT
BJORN
CRATRODE
VETR
SVELL
LI
KALLA
MINTAUR
SNJAR
KALDR
JOTNAR
GONS
STRAUMR
MOSSUR
TOWN CENTER
TOKER
HVALL
JARN
VALKYRIES
LLA

PROLOGUE

With time, memories become fuzzy. Details were no longer as clear as they once were, but one thing remained the same.

"She isn't hurting anyone," Hawk told Sparrow as they watched Wren through the window.

Tawny and Scarlett played in the front yard while Wren sat on her stool with her easel. Her long hair piled on top of her head with her paint splattered overall shorts on as her brush stroked the canvas. She would be out there until nightfall, sometimes after. In the colder winter months, she would retreat into the storage shed she converted into a small studio. The only time she left was to take care of Scarlett's needs.

"Not yet, but Scarlett starts kindergarten this fall. She needs Wren to be present," Sparrow said.

"Mommy, can I go outside?" Gypsum tugged on her shirt, fixing her with his big puppy dog eyes and dimpled smile.

Resistance was futile.

"Stay in the yard," Hawk told him and opened the screen door so he could climb down the steps to play in the yard next door.

Scarlett opened the gate to let him in and Wren stopped painting long enough to greet her nephew, but hopped back up on the stool and painted again once his giggles joined the girls'.

If someone thought too much about Wren's actions, they could drive themselves to tears. She wasted her years away waiting — hoping.

Hope was a dangerous thing, but no hope was worse. One had to have faith.

Today would be the day Indigo returned to her. Lark was going to come with the boys, or even Alder.

Hawk never had the heart to tell her he had gone back. Closing the portals had taken only a few moments at each stop, and then he'd gone to Valla U and seen the carnage. Lark would never show. He never made it out of the tent. Their father never freed his arm from the Crathode who had caught him.

Reed had seen Hawk briefly, and the two shared a look before Hawk left again. His mother would be safe with Reed's help.

Every time he thought he had worked up the nerve to tell her, he lost it. The pain of her lost hope would be too much for any of them. Hope gave her a reason to get out of bed in the morning and to look forward to the day. He couldn't take that away from her.

Wren watched Scarlett walk down the aisle in her cap and gown. She leaned into Hawk.

"She looks miserable," Wren whispered.

"She *is* miserable. They both are. They will forgive us once we take them to Tidings," Hawk reassured her.

"We pushed them too hard. Tawny goes on a single date with dozens of boys, and Scarlett has stopped trying altogether. They hardly go out; they have no friends other than one another." Sparrow dropped her voice so Gypsum wouldn't hear her. "They'll be the only maidens at Valla U."

Wren smiled at that. "I don't mind that so much."

"Neither do I." Hawk sniffed.

"No? We'll see what you think when they are tossed into that world with no experience, other than their little brother, with the opposite sex." Sparrow gestured to Gypsum who was chatting with a girl his age on Sparrow's other side.

"At least we won't have to worry about him," Wren joked.

"We will, but for different reasons," Hawk noted.

The three smiled and waved to the girls, who gave weak smiles in return.

Brothers. A grandmother. Maybe even a father and a sister. Oh, how Wren prayed that Indigo and Alder had survived the attack. She'd long given up that Lark would come with the boys hanging around his neck and in his arms. Those twinkling grey eyes that had looked at her differently so recently before they were torn apart.

Wren's eyes welled with tears. There wasn't a day that went by that she could forgive herself for leaving their sons. For not finding their daughter. For leaving Lark behind to die. For not having Lark's child before he perished. For not fighting harder to keep Alder. So many deep regrets, she knew, had transformed her into a different person.

She'd wrote those sons at least once a week, sometimes once a day, hoping one day they forgave her. Sending pictures and clippings on things that interested her and Scarlett. Copies of the high school newspaper, which frequently had Scarlett in it for her sports activities or writings. She'd soon find out if it'd helped ease her absence. The mail service was one way. They couldn't risk things getting out of Tidings.

Scarlett *would* forgive her. It wasn't in her nature to hold grudges.

"We aways said when the girls were ready to go to Valla U, we would go back. They have a right to decide for themselves whether they want to stay. If not, they are capable enough to start lives here on their own," Hawk told them. "Gypsum has to go back. Patriarch Sumar has to be a Guardian."

Wren sighed. The ceremony was over. Scarlett would be more educated than most the girls in Tidings but had no fighting skills or outdoor survival skills whatsoever. In some ways, it was like setting a lamb out with the lions.

They all beamed bright smiles at the girls as they climbed down the steps to meet them as they gave reluctant grins.

Everything would change tomorrow and they did not know just how much.

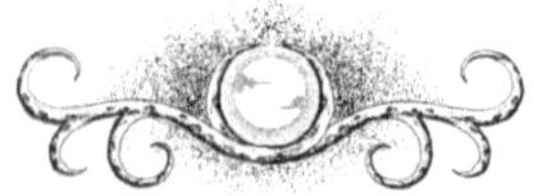

"Little Bird."

Wren's breathing hitched as she stepped from the bushes to their little pond. Alder waited barefoot on the moss-covered stones and shirtless. Suddenly, he was eighteen, and she was in her white dress stained by Jackal's smears.

"Tree," she said in barely more than a whisper.

Her stomach flipped. It'd been over twenty-three years since she'd met him in their private spot. He gestured down to the stone at his feet, which had been freshly scraped of moss. *ALDER VAR AND LITTLE BIRD* was scrawled into the stone.

"I feared you would not show."

Wren's feet hadn't so much as shuffled towards him. Alder jumped over the stones to land right before her. Wren craned back her head to gaze upon him. Maybe he'd changed in twenty years, but she couldn't see it.

The moon gleamed through his short corn silk hair as his eyes memorized her face.

"Of course I'd come. It's this place that gives you doubt. We've seen one another plenty since I've been back," she told him as he ran his fingers through the ends of her long waves.

He bent down and claimed her mouth and Wren's body arched to his. Ostara always amplified his fresh scent. A whimper pulled from her throat.

"Tell me you haven't angered your family, making me the ambassador to the Aves just so you can keep me close to your home so you can have me whenever you wish," she breathed.

She could feel his teeth as he smiled against her lips. "That would be a lie. You needed a career, I need you. You will never escape me again. I set you free, but you returned. I want to be a family, Wren. You and me and our children. Sage could be a part of it, too. I do not wish to exclude anyone."

"And Delta?" Wren pulled away with great effort.

"I have never been in love with Delta. I tried for years, but Natts are not made to give and receive love. Their only love is power. Something I have never had an interest in," Alder said, encircling her biceps with his big hands to pull her close. "Scarlett is breathtakingly beautiful. I do not like Ash Straumr with her. What about lesser family son? Jett seems to have his love life well in hand betrothed to the Prime's only daughter, as well as the Mabon's only ambassador."

Wren beamed with pride as she loosely wrapped her arms around his hips. The only competition for his undivided attention were the croaking frogs and chirping insects.

"He's strapping and so handsome. I wish he had a bit more direction, but Steel seems to have gotten the lion's share of focus and responsibility. Scarlett and Indigo have been drawn together. She's so beautiful. She looks just like you." Alder used his thumb to wipe a tear that had rolled over her cheek.

"Twins. They get along like sisters already. As if they had never been parted. Something innate that causes them to attract like magnets. What of Lark's son? He seems to be vying for Scarlett's attentions."

Alder pushed the straps of her pack over her shoulders so it fell to the ground before he savored undressing her.

"Scarlett and Slate belong together. She'll come to her senses. It doesn't hurt to test the waters before settling down. Ash is charming. He is a good match for her, but there's no fire. No spark. When Scarlett and Slate are in a room, their chemistry changes the charge in the air."

She was bared before him and his thumb traced her curves. "We will help guide her. Indigo needs to find herself a husband. I like Sterling, but they will never let the two of them be together when he had a chance to be with the Prime's niece. Even after I claim her as my own."

He scooped her under her thighs and she giggled like a girl decades younger as he stepped out of his pants and walked effortlessly into the pond. She wrapped her arms around his neck as they floated, losing themselves in their kisses. They had weeks of time together to travel over Ostara, hoping the Aves would treat with them. *Her.*

Alder had readied a cottage, and they were indulging in one another after years of thinking the other was dead and being apart. They had a second chance. Wren wished she cared about Delta's feelings, but she didn't. She wanted everything Alder had promised her — love, marriage, and a family.

"Robin's sons. I think they'd be good for the girls. Brass and Silver? We'll make sure they're introduced. They are very different young men, but both are good boys and close to Slate, Jett, and Steel. It's funny how they've all gravitated towards one another. It also makes me feel impossibly old," Wren said wryly as the cool waters lapped at her skin.

Alder ran his nose along her throat as he nuzzled her. "I do not think I will ever see you as any older than sixteen," he said in his guttural voice.

"You either," she whispered.

"Wren?" Alder pulled away so their faces were just far apart where they could meet one another's eyes.

"Hmm?"

"You cannot ever leave me again. I will not survive losing you a third time. I grow harder and more bitter each time but am helpless to stop it. You are all that is warm and loving in my life, other than our daughter. You would not resign me to becoming like Canis, would you?" Alder tried to lighten where his statement had taken them.

"I won't leave you. Not of my own free will." She sighed. "I swear it. I'd swear you a blood vow if you wish it."

Alder smiled as his eyelids slid low. "I will take you up on that offer. Blood vow to never leave me, and if you do leave, I go with you... but first I will take *you.*"

ONE

All is Fair in Love and War

I woke to shuffling and back slapping. There was the strong scent of vanilla and pine needles where I laid on a mattress stuffed with wool that must have been on tribal lands.

"Try to bed her again and I will break your legs," Slate rumbled in an amused tone.

From the way the bed bowed, I knew he sat at my side. That deep rumble that made my insides coil.

"It's bad enough he is going to have to share her with me." Brass's smooth, deep voice, like a seductive promise.

The first time I heard that voice, he was frisking me in a darkened alley. I was ashamed of myself for wanting him to do terrible things to me in that alley... and then he did.

I squeezed my eyes and widened them as I pushed myself up against the carved headboard. The men stopped and turned to me. Tawny rushed to the bed, pushing past Jett to sit opposite Slate.

"We were so afraid when you didn't come back to the inn. Then I recognized the Lycans with Quick. I thought you were with other werewolves, not with the ruffians from the Dark Dancer. And Brass and Slate! Did you know? What am I saying? Of course you didn't know," she rambled nervously; I knew she was terrified of losing me when she'd lost so much.

I gave her a reassuring smile, trying to ignore the fact that I was stark naked under the thin robe. I gave her a hug and watched Brass move.

Brass's amber eyes searched mine as he sat down on the bed beside Slate. "*Ah*, Love."

He shifted his hand to place it on my knee and I tried to jerk away.

"Come to me in the silence of the night; come in the speaking silence of a dream. Come with soft rounded cheeks and eyes as bright as sunlight on a stream; come back in tears. O memory, hope, Love of finished years. O dream how sweet, too sweet, too bitter sweet, whose wakening should have been in Paradise. Where souls brimfull of love abide and meet; where thirsting longing eyes. Watch the slow door. That opening, letting in, lets out no more. Yet come to me in dreams, that I may live. My very life again though cold in death: come back to me in dreams, that I may give. Pulse for pulse, breath for breath. Speak low, lean low. As long ago, my love, how long ago."

I hissed and scooted to the opposite side of the bed so I could stand next to Tawny.

My head swam again as I stood too quickly and staggered. They all flinched as I righted. I steeled myself and stormed around the bed to Brass and Slate. With every step, I grew angrier. I needed their help. I was on the run. I had never been to Glitra. I was dying when they found me! They said they'd taken vows but would've slept with me if I had pushed! When they saw who I was, they didn't take off their rings and announce their true identities. They were going to trick me into sleeping with them.

Their stupid brows were arched on their stupid faces, as if they thought I was funny. I was just a joke to them. *Worse.* A toy. Their plaything. Maybe they had known all along I was myself and were toying with me. I used both my hands to slap them. I was even more furious that they let me knowing full well what I intended to do, so I slapped them both again.

"Neither of you are allowed in my longhouse. I spend my nights with Quick, as I always do. I've spent more nights with Quick than either of you combined! *He* looks out for me. *He* made sure I didn't die that night when neither of you said goodbye. I could have died. I *should* be dead," I snapped.

"You are cross with us," Brass noted dryly, rubbing his face, which must have stung at least half as much as my hands did.

They had both dressed in padded jerkins. Brass in navy, Slate in the only color he ever wore.

"Cross doesn't begin to scrape the surface!" I turned to Slate. "You didn't tell me Mirage tasted you while you were in your Barghest form." I heard Tawny gasp.

Slate clenched his jaw. "I did not have my memories. What is your excuse?"

"You mean about Ash? I don't have one. He was kind when I was weak. He offered me company, and he is nothing if not good-looking."

Slate's fingers curled as if he wanted to shake me.

"You want to hurt me? I understand, Torch. I have caused you more pain than you knew you were capable of feeling, but if you think you can push me away with your sharp tongue, know I will pull that tongue into my mouth and slide my own across it until it is smooth. You will not win. We will not let you go again," Slate rumbled as he stood and dragged me to his chest, holding me firmly to him.

A hardness pressed against my hips as if he was sitting there the whole time — ready for me. It confirmed that he was not bluffing.

"Hurt you? Like you've both done to me? When I needed your support the most, you abandoned me. I can't possibly imagine what I could do that would come close to how you've broken me."

"Go on. Get it out, Torch. I have never claimed to be the hero, but for you? I would try. I am sorry for all that has happened," he growled, not sounding very sorry at all.

"You may leave. Both of you," I said, walking to the copper tub a few feet away from the fireplace.

Quick followed me and reheated the water. We'd spent enough time together that he anticipated my needs. Jett spoke a few whispered words to Brass and Slate, who shrugged him off. Tawny crossed from where she was watching the scene play out to Ridge, leaning against the wall by the screen that divided the rooms, preparing to make a stealthy get away.

"I should have said goodbye," Slate said to my back.

I turned around and blinked at him in time to watch Jett sneak out behind Tawny and Ridge. "You know what the worst part of you not saying goodbye was? I knew there was a good chance that one of us could die that night, and some of us did. People always say, 'oh, they knew you loved them' to family left behind. Those people are *wrong*. I lived it. I should be dead, and I thought you hated me." My throat constricted as I stabbed my finger at him.

"You hated *me*," he rebuked in a growl.

"I always hate you. Even when I hate you, I love you. I never meant to fall in love with Brass. You must know that. I gave myself to him first because I knew you were too selfish to not rub your women in my face if things got sour. You knew I cared about him then. That's why you made all those stupid plots behind my back. It's always been the three of us. You just never wanted it to be. When we married, those months we were together, he and I were close, but I never let myself take it further."

"It is *my* fault you were fucking my brother?" Slate asked scornfully.

"*Cousin*. No, that's not what I meant," I protested.

"What did you mean then, Torch? You could not stop yourself even when I had been trying to make amends," Slate accused, referring to the night we went to the Merfolk.

"You're right. I can't understand why you want me back. I had Brass's sons. Not yours," I said, knitting my brows. "Balas and Spinel are at the Sumar palace right now with Hawk and Sparrow. I had to leave them to save this horrible world." Tears rose and I blinked, frustrated with myself.

"Because he's hopelessly in love with you and you with him. Thank the gods, you two head cases now have me to clarify for you. The course of true love never did run smooth," Brass said, interrupting our very public fight as he swept my attention away from Slate. "Balas and

Spinel, huh?" You couldn't beat the smile from Brass's face and my lips began to tug up.

"You're not helping, Brass," I said dryly until saw how desperately he needed me to tell him about them. "They're identical. Both have thick unruly hair for newborns and deep toned skin... like their father. Their names were Cordillera's idea. I gave birth at the Valkyrie compound." My chin wobbled. "You should have been there."

"I am going to make it all up to you, Love," he whispered. "Everyone may leave now. I have things in hand, send in dinner. Send our apologies to Donncha, but I have a vow I mean to break *several* times tonight," Brass purred with a lazy smile.

Slate's eyes flashed from winter storm grey to steely silver in a blink. "He has a point."

"I should leave," Quick mumbled, and I gripped his wrist.

"And to answer your earlier questions... I could not let her go because *I* too am hopelessly in love with her," Brass said, scooting up to the wooden headboard.

"This solves nothing. I already know you both find me attractive and enjoy... womanly attributes. It has nothing to do with *love*."

"You believe that we love you, though, don't you?" Brass asked.

"In your own ways," I admitted.

"Ask me," Slate rumbled.

"Ask you what?"

Slate cocked a winged brow at me and gave me a dry look.

I knit my brows. I was addicted to these two men. Suddenly, so much that attracted me to Scarab and Scorpion made sense because they were the same things I'd fallen for in Slate and Brass. Slate with his strong silence and powerful emotions, only for people special to him. Brass, with his honesty and passion, my own tether to what mattered in the world.

"Are you in love with me?" I asked him.

"You are my torch, my light in the darkness. You make me want to live. You are the only thing I have ever needed. Without you, I lose all hope," Slate said, stepping towards me. "I will fix this. For you, for our bairn, and for my brother-husband," Slate said with a rueful smile.

Tender Slate got me every time.

"We'll leave you alone tonight. Go have your dinner," Brass said softly.

Slate looked like he wanted to say more, but he let it go. He and Brass gave Quick meaningful looks before leaving the longhouse. Quick let out a long breath.

"I am going to catch up. I have never believed in fate until today. You were meant to be with those two scoundrels as much as I was meant to be with Indigo. I am sorry about earlier, Scarlett," he said, running his tongue along his lip.

"Forget it. Go ahead. I'll meet you out there," I said, stepping on my tip toes to give him a kiss on the cheek. "Maybe next time you catch me with a man, turn around so I can cover up with a little dignity. I'm only slightly insulted you didn't notice my nudity."

Quick cringed. "Frigga's sweet grass. I am a bastard."

Quick held me with his lips pressed to my head and I sighed. "You're not going to leave me with them tonight, are you? Please don't, Quick. I'm not ready to be alone with them."

"No, I will not leave you to the figurative wolves. See you at dinner, Scarlett," he said, kissing my head one last time and left me alone.

I dipped myself into the warmed water. I used the vanilla infused wash to rid my skin of Brass and Slate's scents soaking in the water and used the cloths the Lycan provided to dry myself off.

I gasped when I saw the furry beast on the big bed. "Tree!" I cried and sat on the bed, urging her to come to me.

She lazily traversed the furs to my lap, her fluffy tail twitching happily as I scratched under her snowy white chin. Her green eyes blinked at me and I ducked down to rub my face to hers. Her purr let me know I wasn't being completely obnoxious.

My pack laid on the floor open and I began to search for the items I hadn't been able to wear since we left Disir. I wanted to feel like my old self again.

I had finished threading through the silver beads into my narrow braids with Pavo and Aeetus's feathers and the pearl Slate had given me. I added the ivory sunburst and the jade love rune to the ends of my braids, then slid the wooden oak leaf comb into my shimmering gold waves to pin back the right side of my hair.

The teal woolen dress they supplied was tube shaped with a flared hem. I was pinning on the white apron-skirt with golden turtle brooches and the gift Niall had brought me when I arrived. Strands of glass beads in blues and greens to attach to the turtle brooches so they hung over my chest. It had a comfortable loose fit and with my chemise the wool didn't itch. Soft fur brown ankle boots with a soft sole were waiting at the foot of the bed.

I slipped my Dagr diamond ring onto my right hand and threaded my stone pieces through my long silver chain with Alder's wedding band. They gently clacked as I pulled it over my head. The silhouette of the mother holding a baby glimmered on my silver torque.

I'd vainly packed a few cosmetics, but then and there, lip gloss felt like the greatest luxury I'd ever felt. A green flash in the corner of my eye drew my attention as the fireplace crackled. On the nightstand was my emerald wedding band. I swallowed hard and slipped it onto my ring finger as it trembled.

No one thinks that the strangers they're traveling with could be their loved ones. It's too impossible to even contemplate. Brass would say nothing was impossible, only improbable, and he'd be right. I should have known. It was only their faces and voices that had changed, not their bodies. Not the undeniable chemistry we'd always had.

Dinner was well underway. It was horribly rude for me to enter late when they'd been waiting for my arrival, so when I entered the mead hall I expected a few stony glares. Instead, I hadn't hindered the festivities at all.

They were a rowdy, boisterous crowd. Men in multicolored tartans over woolen tunics and women dressed as I was in a variety of colors sat on benches at long tables, all looking sturdily made with carvings that must have taken ages to complete. Nothing was polished, everything had a beautiful aged look that was fashioned to fit in with the Lycans' way of life. Simple, but beautiful and built to last.

Laughter rang through the rafters, conversations that battled one another for their rambunctiousness created a cacophony of welcoming sounds. The hall smelled like mead and meat, and I *felt* family.

It was easy to miss Jett, Quick, and Ridge, who were equally drunk and rowdy. Tawny and Amethyst sat near them speaking with a beautiful inky haired woman. Cabhan, the blonde, grey eyed Lycan, was in human form beside her, Lorcan chocolate of hair and eyes, whose dimples resembled Niall's, sat with a brunette who if she wasn't his wife yet, she would be soon. Love wafted from them like fresh-baked cookies out of the oven, and you couldn't help but smile.

There were three dark-haired figures, two men and a woman whose posture was relaxed but authoritative. They smiled and laughed with the rest but held themselves to a higher standard.

A folksy music played from Lycans in human form with a collection of wind instruments. I walked hesitantly into the hall, not confident of where I should be seated. The soft boots they provided were like slippers on my feet. Some women spared me a glance, mostly the younger ones who would consider me a threat, but there was a new look among them. Women with small children gave me knowing looks as if they were ready to induct me into their elite club of motherhood at any moment.

"Scarlett!"

Niall swaggered over to me, his waist long inky waves brushed a tartan of purple and black over his black tunic. His powerful legs were covered in a curly black down of hair that was exposed above fur-lined boots that were wrapped to fit tightly to his shapely calves. He smiled with a twinkle in his Kelly green eyes and dimples popped into his cheeks. Niall was exceedingly handsome and nearly as short-tempered.

"Come. You are at the head table with my father and I." He nodded to where the three collected figures sat at the farthest table was elevated on a low dais.

He offered his arm, and I took it as we walked through the hall. The women's scrutiny changed to curiosity and men showed interest for the first time. It was clear the women here were very possessive, and I was on the arm of one of their men. I really didn't want any problems. Internally, I groaned.

Niall showed me to a hide bound seat at the end of the table that overlooked where Jett and the others sat. Amethyst gave me a rueful smile with a shake of her head while Quick was busy winking at me. Ridge turned around to give me another wry smile. They were clued into something I wasn't privy to, or more likely, Quick had recounted my thickheadedness.

Tawny turned and shot me an exaggerated look of surprise. Tawny and Jett bore matching black eyes. I felt terrible for not having noticed it earlier. Amethyst had told me she had not taken the news half as well as Cherry had and that Cherry would be hearing a piece of her mind as soon as we made it back to Thrimilci. I knit my brows and she tried to mouth me a hint, but Niall had begun to introduce me.

"Caolan, this is Scarlett. The elemental and former Second of the Guardians. This is my aunt and her husband, Tadg," Niall said, gesturing to the older woman with inky waves and eyes that matched Niall's.

Her husband was a silver-haired man whose hair was bound in a tight ponytail down his back and a thick beard, but he had a warm smile that touched his dark eyes.

"Lorcan mentioned you. I am his mother," Caolan said in a lilting voice.

I smiled, having something in common with the apparent matriarch of this tribe. "Yes, Lorcan. I met him first in Elivagar. Is that his wife?" I asked, gesturing to where he sat with the brunette.

"Blathnat. Yes, newlywed and already expecting. My niece has grown fond of your Amethyst." Caolan nodded to the inky haired woman with Cabhan.

"Aoibhe, my sister. I will introduce you later," Niall assured me.

"May I introduce you to Donncha, sagamore of the Lycans and warden of the Igulbjorn Ice Cliffs."

Donncha stood. He was as tall as Niall, over six feet and built like a bull. His hair matched Caolan's, but he had intense midnight blue eyes and a well-kept beard that framed defined pink lips.

"Scarlett Tio, mate to the Grar Dyr, daughter of spring and summer, and night's child," Donncha said in the growl of a voice that held a tone that was used to issuing orders with a rougher brogue than Caolan's.

"Sagamore Donncha." I inclined my head. "Pleased to meet you. I'm sorry for my delay, it has been an arduous journey. Thank you for your hospitality."

My politeness was met with a smile by the sagamore, but the man to his left had a booming laugh that made my eardrums feel as though they'd been popped.

"Listen to her fancy pleasantries. We are looking at our own Helen of Troy. Scarlett of Tidings!"

The man was as wide as he was tall and he was not short. His pitch black hair was plated away from his face. He watched me acutely as he sipped from his mug, ale slopping over his hams for hands. For his rough looks, he had an aquiline nose and soft looking lips framed by a beard that was manicured to run along his jaw line. Donncha and the man wore the same color tartan as Niall.

"I am surprised to find that you're familiar with tales outside of Tidings. And you are?" I asked, trying to maintain a Steel like diplomacy.

He stood with a scrape of his chair and towered over me, at least as tall as Slate and Jett. "Padraig, Niall's uncle." He slapped Niall on the back.

"I am Siobhan," interrupted a high feminine voice.

Niall stepped back to reveal a stunning strawberry blonde. She was what one would call an English Rose. I felt plain standing next to her.

"My father's mate," Niall said flatly, and she inclined her head with a smile.

Not Niall's mother. That much was clear and not the sagamore's wife, but she would make a good one. I offered her my hand, which she shook quirking her lips as she did.

A heavy hand landed on my shoulder and I turned back to Padraig. "Niall has not stopped gloating about having nearly mated with the Grar Dyr's mate."

"A kiss or two is hardly mating," I said, rubbing my belly where butterflies had taken flight.

"How can we be sure you are the woman from the prophecy? It does not look like any pups are in your belly," Padraig goaded.

I narrowed my eyes. He *felt* inquisitive. He was testing me.

"Stop harassing my wife, you bloated whelp." Slate's rumbling bass cut through the conversation like a knife.

Padraig boomed another laugh and fell back into his seat. "A bonnie lass, your mate. No wonder men go crazy or die when she beds them. We all know you are crazy, so you know then you will be cursed on these lands for some time. Aye, I would not mind losing a bit of my sanity myself."

Brass was with Slate, both of them dressed as they were before they'd accosted me as Scorpion and Scarab. They were smiling, if tightly, as they sauntered to the table Tawny and the others sat at.

Brass raised a fresh mug to Padraig. "Careful what you wish for, you don't have much brains to speak of and with your luck you'll die at the sight of her in her skin."

A round of laughs echoed at this and I blinked looking around in disbelief that they weren't tearing Padraig's throat out. Niall leaned in so his lips brushed my ear as he spoke.

"We practice the art of flyting. It is essentially an exchange of insults. The man who receives the loudest laughs is declared the winner."

I pursed my lips. "That's very offensive. Was Padraig trying to engage me?" I asked, hearing more insults being traded between my lovers and Padraig with all the raucous laughter that followed.

"Perhaps. My uncle is our tactician and pot stirrer," Niall whispered into my ear.

"Has Niall told you of his plan to marry you tomorrow? Grar Dyr challenged him for you. Since he is your husband, by our laws, he is legally responsible for you. He can marry you to whom he pleases. This may be a trick, Niall. Do not drink much, Grar Dyr. The Ice Cliffs' Games is no joke, Guardian," Padraig said, and those who were listening *oohed* annoyingly.

"Niall," I hissed, "Don't be ridiculous."

"It is my right. He knows our laws," Niall said simply.

I looked out to Slate afraid my proximity might send him into a rage, but Brass's lips curled. Another inside joke I wasn't privy to.

"She has two husbands, by your laws. I am hand-fasted to her as long as love lasts. Niall may challenge Slate, but he will have to go through me if he wins. Which will not happen, because no one beats the Grar Dyr," Brass said smoothly.

My face was on fire as people made cat calls and began to send jeers about their sexuality to them. This was the absolute worst place to confess being brother-husbands.

"Aye. And does love last, girly?" Padraig asked boldly.

My eye twitched in irritation as I turned to the man ready to use my viperous tongue for a lashing but tried to keep my cool. "It wasn't love to begin with if it does not last."

I held his scrutinizing gaze until his lips quirked within his beard. "I would say it does then, girly. You have your work cut out for you with this one, Niall if it takes two men to please her." His bellowing laugh punctuated his statement, and my face flushed. Padraig's nostrils flared as he took in my scent. "Aye, it is a good time for another husband. I scent your season will be upon you soon."

Tawny and Jett gaped at me with their matching black eyes. Quick stared at Brass, only Amethyst and Ridge looked unsurprised. I wondered if Ridge had some fortune telling talent and that he had predicted this outcome of our reunion.

Niall was still holding my hand, and he led me away from Padraig to my seat at the end of the table, right next to his.

Roasted pork, mashed garlic potatoes smothered in onions and mushrooms, fresh baked biscuits and gravy. I wasn't angry with Niall once he explained that it was Slate who challenged him. He served me himself, mounds of mouthwatering comfort food throughout the night as if he was courting me. I hummed Fernando by Abba as I ate merrily minding my own business. Niall watched me eat, at first this made me uncomfortable, but it was too good to care.

"You take great pleasure in eating. You would never guess from how thin you are," Niall said, encircling my left wrist with his fingers as if to demonstrate.

Compared to the thicker, curvier Lycan women, he was right. I had lost fat when I left Disir. I liked having soft curves and not just in my chest.

"Only when it's this delicious. My compliments to whomever prepared it," I said, flashing him my very best smile after I ran my tongue over my teeth.

"Thank you," Caolan said, inclining her head. "We all hunt, but the women do the majority of the cooking."

"Well, it's very good," I told her.

Tadg rose from his seat to sit beside Padraig and I saw my chance. Excusing myself, I moved to sit next to Donncha. Donncha's twist of lips made me think he expected it.

"Good evening, sagamore —"

"Donncha, please. May I call you Scarlett?" he asked.

"Of course." I pulled my stone pieces from my dress and held up my six pieces of irregularly shaped stones. "I have gone to collect each one of these from all the tribal leader all except for one which I inherited. Two have already been claimed. We know where the project is and with your piece —"

"Did you enjoy your dinner, Scarlett?" he asked with a burr.

I blinked, having a been interrupted again. "Yes. I was just thanking Caolan for her and the other women's delicious work. With your stone piece I would have all seven available —"

"If my son wins the challenge, we will need to know that you can prepare his meals. Are you up to the task?" Donncha asked.

I exhaled, trying to control my sigh. He didn't want to talk about the pieces, I would try a different avenue.

"I can cook. I would love to help the women tomorrow and perhaps we will finish preparations early so you and I can discuss what I need to do to win that piece from you," I said, leaning back in the hide covered chair.

Donncha's lips curled, his eyes twinkled like stars against his midnight eyes. "Make a meal worthy enough to inspire my sated silence and we can talk about discussing it."

I pursed my lips and scanned his eyes. "You know my cousin there is the Matriarch of Elivagar."

"Until this mystery man usurped her," Donncha amended, and I nodded.

"Yes, well, the Grar Dyr is supposed to lead you into battle, yes? What battle do you suppose that is? He is supposed to save the tribes. Help us and the Guardians will sing songs about the Lycans' triumphs. Poets will compete to write odes to your bravery," I told him.

Donncha chuckled. "If you were not so alluring, you could always talk your way into a man's bed. Is that how you earned yourself two mates? One of which is the Grar Dyr? What is Brass to you? Bed warmer when the Grar Dyr tomcats?"

He was leaning in and speaking in a hushed tone, but the Lycans' hearing was impeccable. I laced my fingers on the table top trying to control my scent which would have screamed *Pissed the Fiddlestick Off.*

"Slate and Brass are both good men I am lucky to know, much less have mated with. I have two mates because I am blessed and cursed," I added suggestively. "Want to feel what I could do with my talent alone?"

Donncha's eyes dropped to my lips and slid back up with a nod. I stretched my empath abilities, manipulating them so Donncha's emotions were what I wanted them to be.

Marry... love... wife... I held nothing back.

"Siobhan," Donncha breathed in a rough gust.

The beautiful Lycan turned to us and quirked her thin brows. "Yes, Donncha?"

I gave my manipulations an extra boost and Donncha tore his eyes away from me. "Hand fast me. Tomorrow."

Siobhan smiled radiantly. "*Oh*, Donncha, I love you," she said, winding her arms around his neck.

I got up from my chair and walked from the dais to the table my family sat at before my manipulation wore off Donncha. Quick rubbed the spot next to him and took my hand to help me slide in. Slate and Brass sat across from us and didn't take their eyes off me from the moment I got up to sit with Donncha. I greeted Cabhan and Aoibhe, who was the splitting image of her brother with none of his temper. Lorcan and Blathnat were so *lovey dovey,* envy crept up the way I used to feel when Quick and Indigo were together.

I found Quick's hand under the table and he gave it a squeeze. "Did you get the piece?"

"No. He won't discuss it. He wants me to make dinner tomorrow with the women, then we can talk about talking about it." I sighed, and my husbands chuckled.

"He has been giving us the run around for months," Brass said with a smile.

"I apologize about Niall," Slate interjected.

"My brother is competitive," Aoibhe said with a sympathetic look.

Slate grunted. "Did I hear Donncha right?"

I bit my lip and averted my eyes. Brass chuckled again.

"Manipulating the sagamore into marrying his much younger mate isn't going to make him give you the piece any faster," Brass said, gesturing with his ale.

"She's pure of heart and she loves him. He should make an honest woman of her." I sniffed.

"Oh yeah? Like how you made an honest man out of Brass?" Jett asked leaning past the others to give me a look.

I let go of Quick's hand under the table and he arched his brow at me. "I am offended, Mrs. Scarlett. My sister-in-law and I were not even invited." Quick puckered his lower lip in an adorable pout and I bumped his with my shoulder.

"Now is not the time for weddings. I didn't know what I was doing at the time. I've grown accustomed to the men in my life using my naivety against me," I said peevishly.

"When the war is over, we will have a small ceremony in Ostara," Brass said, and I stared at him. "What? Am I a dirty secret?"

"No. I just... you've already thought about it? Usually you ask a woman and then she has to agree," I stammered.

"I have asked you. *You* have said no. I could take you to lands like these where Slate makes that decision for you," Brass threatened roguishly.

Slate gave me a dry look. "When our minds were not occupied with warring and deliveries, you and family were all we had left," he rumbled.

Quick slung his arm around my shoulders. "We only thought about family and loved ones. It was all we had."

Our half of the table grew silent. We'd lost so many of those loved ones.

"I'm going to go to bed. My idea of a good time is not watching all of you get drunk while I have to sit here sober," Tawny said.

Ridge stood with her lending her a hand as she swung her leg over the bench. "I shall retire as well. It was good to meet you," he said, nodding to the Lycans, Amethyst, Brass, and Slate.

Tawny gave me a hug goodnight and whispered in my ear. "I hate you." I bit my lip to keep from smiling. "You could not leave the handsome eligible ones for the rest of us?" She was joking but that she *could* was a good sign.

I hugged her back and dropped my voice as low as I could, praying Slate couldn't hear me. "You don't toss back a Regn once you've had him," I whispered so low I couldn't hear my own words. "We have to talk. I —"

"Probably why it took you a day longer to get here." She gave me a wink.

A day longer! Another night alone!

Brass ducked his head hiding a smirk and Slate arched a dark brow at me. Quick stood as Tawny walked away laughing with Ridge, the two arm in arm. He looked down at me expectantly and I startled to my feet. I had become the bed hopper, and since Ridge had mostly taken over Tawny's care and Jett had been with Cherry and now he had Amethyst — that left Quick alone.

Well, with *me*.

"Goodnight, all," I said jerkily.

Quick took my hand to help me over the bench. He was drunk or he would've realized how peculiar we looked. I wouldn't leave him out in the wind even though it had been my idea in the first place.

"You were serious?" Brass asked in disbelief as Quick took my arm in his.

"We spend every night together." Quick shrugged with slitted eyes.

Slate looked at Quick like he'd lost his mind. "Last night, Quick. I share her with one man and you are not that man."

Quick waved dismissively at him, blowing a raspberry with his lips.

"I already told you two, you're not welcomed in my longhouse."

"So you say. I want to hear about my sons. We do not mind

convincing you otherwise, Love. There is still the matter of the blood vow," Brass said.

"Blood vow?" I asked.

"Do you think we should let Brass be the lesser partner in this marriage," Slate said plainly, and I spluttered.

"What marriage?"

Brass waved a hand at me dismissively. "She hasn't slept well the last few nights. Take care of our wife, Silver."

Quick saluted Brass as we left the mead hall.

Jett was unfazed by my leaving with Quick. He'd been right, we had spent every consecutive night together for months. I couldn't claim that with any other man.

With the fireplace roaring, I undressed a semi-conscious Quick on the bed. With my handheld pump from my pack, I was back to a normal routine and could try to increase my milk supply.

"You love my brother."

I couldn't tell if it was a question. "Yes." I grunted, pulling his pants off his legs and falling to the floor with a grunt.

"No more games? You want to swear a blood oath?" he asked, lifting his head as I took off my dresses and climbed into bed in my chemise.

My fingers unbuckled his jerkin and rolled him out of his shirts. Quick had put back on the ring Delta had given our father, the one Indi had given him. I pulled the blankets over us and he shifted towards me into our usual position.

His leg between mine with his arms around me.

"I'm still digesting it. I feel like it's going to be a shotgun wedding," I said, looking up at him.

"Niall wants you. Slate said you told him you were a Natt. They were asking questions, but I said they had to get their information from you." He sighed and kissed the top of my head.

"Quick. You're not going to cheat on Indi. In Disir, maybe, but not here where you can barely allow yourself to be happy your brother is alive because being happy means betraying her. It's okay to be happy. I'm going to talk to Donncha tomorrow, make him the best meal he's ever eaten. Slate will lead the Lycans to Elivagar's heart and we'll unite the Lycans with the Wemic and the Faunelle and raid Ostara. I won't let my sister stay with those people," I promised him. Quick's lips were twitching as if he couldn't control his muscles and I placed a finger to them. "I hear you, Silver Regn. I know you're hurting.

"What if I swore you a blood oath that I would not be intimate with another woman until Indigo was free?" he asked in a thick voice.

Free not rescued.

My heart ached for Quick. "You don't have to. I'll stay every night until we get her back if you want, Quick."

He scoffed. "Your husbands will love that." He sliced his hand open and did the same to mine chanting the words of the blood vow and exhaled heavily.

"Feel better?" I asked, stroking his freshly cropped hair.

"Much," he admitted and kissed the top of my head before pulling me closer and putting his chin on my head.

His heavy breaths came swiftly as he fell asleep. Tree raised her head from where she made a home at our feet and gave me a feline look of approval before lowering her head. I nuzzled against Quick. Neither of us could have predicted how close we would get over time.

CHAPTER 2

INDIGO

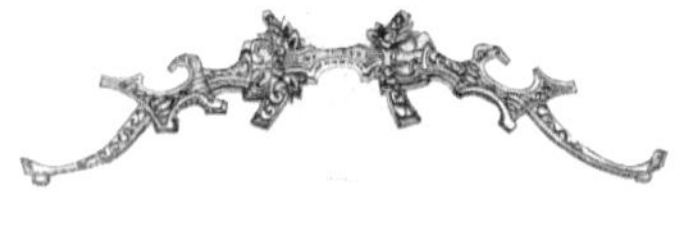

Silver was alive.

His emotions blossomed in my mind. I shot out of my metal framed bed that grew too cold to even brush against on bad nights. I ran to the icicle like bars and wrapped my hands around them.

I screamed incoherently cradling my broken arm. My jaw hurt too much to form words.

"Indigo!"

Thre'ik scrambled to her eight crystalline legs from where she slept in her corner of the ceiling of the Beget Oubliette and grabbed the bars with her human arms. The Jorogumo blinked three sets of eyes on her pale white human face. She had a fan of bleach blonde hair and pinchers that were smaller than most.

I was hyperventilating, I couldn't catch my breath that froze in my lungs under the Frostfell Mountains in the Crathode caverns. I could activate my bond so he'd know where I was... but there was Sterling. He was due to find me any day now. Silver would feel everything I felt.

Sobbing hurt my broken ribs. I'd been counting down the days to when Ash would visit for one of our strange talks where he would undoubtedly leave angry because I couldn't tell him what he wanted to hear. I didn't know what he wanted to hear. He'd been duped, and he had made it clear he didn't like to hear that. Still, he would heal me.

Thrimilci had been overtaken. A woman posing as Scarlett had led the Red Seconds and reclaimed our mother's home island. I had smiled and Sage lost his temper. He said, as he beat me, that Sterling could always plant another bastard in my belly. I didn't know whose son I carried, but if it was Silver's and he had been dead, I had to protect it. I let him rail as I curled into a ball protecting my stomach.

My injuries were tolerable as long as I didn't move much. I still had the son growing everyday inside me.

"*Ma haban,*" I slurred out.

"Husband?" Thre'ik guessed, and tears rolled down my cheeks as I nodded.

"*Awie.*" I pressed my good hand over my heart.

"He is alive?" Thre'ik asked, and I nodded.

"Activate your bond so he can save us from this hell." Vanna'ra said rolling out of her bed across from us clutching a tattered blanket around her.

I shook my head.

"Then shut your mouth! We have two births tomorrow and a score more of our friendly visitors!" one of the females farther down yelled.

Thre'ik gave me a sympathetic look.

"*Ater Ass's misit.*" I swallowed my excess saliva.

"When Ash leaves, you shall activate your bond?" Thre'ik struggled to hide her elation, she didn't dare hope.

Hope was death where we were.

I nodded.

"Thank the Gods." Vanna'ra sighed and slid down to the icy floor.

The Merfolk traitor had a nasty streak. She was a stunning beauty; glossy black curls fell to her waist as her eyes rolled to the heavens from across the narrow hall. Her gills at the sides of her jaw flared as she exhaled.

I crawled under my blankets and shut my eyes. Silver was miserable but had found something to take the edge off his pain. I prayed it was a something and not a someone. I would give Silver a hundred babies if he let me. I'd marry him the moment I saw him.

He fell asleep, and I imagined he was next to me, holding me as I faded into darkness.

CHAPTER 3
SLATE

"What are you two going to still doing here?"

Jett rolled over on the third mattress they had brought over for him when Amethyst told him he was not welcome in her bed. Brass had reassured Jett, that Amethyst was proving a point and that he would be back in her good graces in no time.

That Tawny had bedded Jett, but Quick and Scarlett, the two who could have gotten away with it if anyone could, did not, proved how strange the world they fell into had been. That Ridge Vetr was living there as if only a handful of years had passed was even stranger. They had seen Spinel. Canis didn't have the satisfaction of killing him and from what they had described, there was a chance Brass and Quick may be able to see him again one day. It had brought Brass solace, when we feared we had nothing left to look forward to other than our revenge.

They were alive.

Brass looked over to me. "They have slept enough."

I nodded and began to dress. Caolan had given me an all-black kilt they wanted me to wear for today's Ice Cliff Games.

Fucking Quick. Fucking Niall.

Brass dressed in haste; he did not wash off her scent either.

"Would it be hypocritical of me to say that I do not like to the idea of my baby sister in bed with the two of you?" Jett said folding his arms behind his head.

"Don't worry, Jett. We're not always on the bed," Brass said, smoothing his hair into a knot at his nape.

"Gods, you bastards," Jett said as he rolled away from us on his bed.

The door opened on the single room longhouse and we looked up to see who had entered without knocking.

Scarlett and Quick.

He smiled rakishly and gazed about the room dressed in all black Shadow Breaker gear. Scarlett always wore the native fashions when she traveled in respect to the places she stayed. Something Ash taught her, no doubt.

She looked as lovely as ever, her hair threaded through with her collection of fetishes and feathers. Her turquoise eyes scrutinized the room and then us. Jett folded his arms behind his head as he watched her. Quick ran his thumb over his lips hiding a smile. I felt like a fool in the black kilt and nothing else. At least Brass had pants on.

"Can we help you with something, Love?" Brass asked sitting down on his bed to tug on his boots.

"I'm surprised not to find any traces of women in here. Perhaps I'm not looking hard enough," she said imperiously as she gestured to Quick who helped her down to look under the beds and then helped her back to her feet.

The traitor was still smiling. She wandered over to the dresser and my hackles rose. The first thing she pulled out was the kerchief I carried her braid in and she opened it then set it on the top. Jett slowly shook his head at me, but I could not stand her investigation.

I slammed the drawer shut narrowly missing her fingers and clamped my hands over hers. She didn't move.

"What is it your looking for, Torch? We can point you in the right direction," I growled.

Brass cursed behind me and I sucked in a steadying breath.

Her cool gaze slid over me. "Move your hands. Feel free to inspect my things if you wish. *I* have nothing to hide."

My hands dropped, and she reopened the drawer and looked inside.

Having her so close to my bed was torture when she would not let me touch her. For nearly a year we played this game until *finally* she had given in and she gave herself to me. It was an incomparable experience. She was exquisite from the start. Every day her allure had only increased.

Scarlett held up the few pieces of whittling I had completed. They were not meant for anyone's eyes but mine. I needed something to do or I would go insane and slaughter the Lycans for not giving us the last cursed piece. Carving helped fill the time.

She held up my favorite which was three pieces that interlocked. It was her with arms cradling a child in each arm. One child locked onto the carving around the back while the other child's foot locked to the hand of the mother. It was the only carving I'd painted.

Scarlett placed the carving back in the drawer and saw the other children's toys I made. I could not explain why I did it, but the Lycan pups liked them.

"When I asked Niall about what you'd been doing here for over two months, he said the first month you had many female visitors."

"We put a stop to that. We took vows, I told you," Brass said, sounding irritated.

One thing Brass did not like was being called a liar.

"So you did. He also said you hunt with them, offered council, and... made children's toys. Is that all? No secretive love affairs I should be aware of now that I'm here?"

She turned around. My arms rested on the top of the dresser so she had to crane her neck back to look up at me. So close and yet so far.

"No lovers, Torch. Not a single one of any kind in four months," I growled down at her.

Her superior expression made me want to bend her over my knee. If I remembered correctly, and I did, she enjoyed when I spanked her immensely. Her eyes narrowed, and I knew my scent had changed.

"I still don't want either of you in my longhouse, but... we can have our meals together and... I'll speak to you both."

"Then we had better practice our manners. Would not want to use the wrong fork in front of her majesty," I growled and thought I saw her lips twitch, suppressing a smile.

"Let's start again. Good morning, baby sis," Jett said brightly but neither her nor I made a move.

"Morning, big brother. Rested well I hope," Scarlett said, eyes locked on mine.

I became self-conscious of the silver scar over my eye, at least I had an eye to have a scar over thanks to her. "Thank you for healing my eye and saving me. My bond activated because I had a particularly bloody meal that day. A Crathode whose claw lodged between my teeth." I snapped my teeth to emphasize it, but she did not flinch.

Scarlett looked along the scar and I fought the urge to avert my eyes. Instead she reached up and ran her thumb along its slice, from hairline to cheekbone forcing my eye shut. Her touch was rapture. She skipped her finger tips down to the blazing Nordic sundial and traced the lines, arm tucked in close between our bodies.

"Whose idea was this?"

"Mine. Slate wanted pain; I gave him something to live for instead," Brass told her.

Pain. What an ordinary way of putting it. I wanted blood. To wreak havoc. To raze this earth until all felt the pain I felt. Yes, I wanted pain... to give it.

Her gaze swept from Brass to the side and back to me letting her hand fall back to her woolen tube dress. "I see."

I grit my teeth in frustration and to prevent anything foolish from springing forth. "What else are you looking for? You will not find your missing months here nor a satisfying explanation for why I was such a bastard the months I lost my memories." It was futile.

She bristled at that. "What? I'm just supposed to start swooning because you say it's okay now? Okay to love Brass. Okay to love you. Okay to have things go back to normal?" she hissed, her swollen breasts rubbing against my bare stomach. "There were days I thought I imagined your love for me. I couldn't remember what it felt like to be your wife. Only the object of your disgust and fear. You hurt me on purpose taking Mirage to your bed!" I responded, but her glower stilled my tongue. "Do you remember the day you questioned me about what Ash was doing by your room? How you left me after I begged you to stay? How I *needed* you to dance at the masquerade, just dance with me? You rejected me, left me, stayed at a brothel. The day we opened Vigrid, we made love, and you said you would be there, but instead you went to Mirage." A single tear rolled over her high cheekbones to plunge rapidly down to her jaw where it dangled there as her chin wobbled.

She had begged me. *Pleaded.* Given up her pride and I was a complete bastard.

"I remember it all too well. I am more sorry than I could possibly convey. I must be a better actor than I thought. You were constantly on my mind. You seemed to have involved yourself in every aspect of my life so I could not get away from you," I said emphatically. "You were the first thing I thought of every morning. What I attempted to avoid all day, and what I went to bed dreaming about after I carried you from the bench in the cloister and put you to bed. You consumed my thoughts, my life, and I was helpless to how badly I wanted to be close to you and how much I feared that that meant I would die soon. I never wanted you to leave me. What mistakes I made while my memories were stolen, I did not mean. It was not what I, in my present state, would do. I am yours."

She seemed at a loss for words. I did not like public declarations of affection, but desperate times called for desperate measures and I was dangerously close to losing her for the rest of my short, miserable life.

"I missed you. It hurt so bad... that first day when you offered to pay me —"

"You scared me. I never wanted anything as badly as I wanted you. You were incredible that morning. If I had kept my big mouth shut, I would have fallen for you in that bed all over again."

"Because of the sex?" she asked dryly. "That's not love, Slate."

"Yes, the sex, but because you have that smile, and that laugh, your eyes bright with hope, Scarlett. I had no defense against a woman like you."

"I'm sorry too. I never should have been open to a second husband, I never should have dated Cory, and I never ever should have gone to stay at the Straumr palace... and all things that went on then. All I ever wanted was you back. I was a complete jerk to Brass."

Her confession shocked me. I would not have blamed her for putting the consequences of all of those events on my head. I deserved it, but she was sharing the blame.

"Forgiven. In my mind, Sage and Ash are already dead. Cory was a good man, his night watch was his choice, Torch. He thought you were Freya herself."

She sighed. She had cared about Cory. He was the type of man she would have ended up with in Chicago.

"And sorry for Spinel?" Brass asked.

Scarlett let her eyes drop. "I'm sorry he was your grandfather."

Spinel seduced her, let her believe his name was Balas, but he had been good to her. Better than I ever was, better than she let Brass be. If Spinel wasn't Brass's grandfather, we could have lost her to him. Proof of that was that she named her sons after him.

"I should have killed Peak the second I found out what he had done," I said low so only she would hear.

Her eyes swung up to mine and her brow drew together. They were two shades darker than her caramel hair above those big turquoise almond eyes.

"I'm sorry you'll never be able to erase that from your memories," she whispered.

Peak had nearly killed her. He had forced himself on her continuously. I had not known at first, but I knew she was lying about having a willing affair with him.

"I always want to share your burdens," I whispered back.

"I want to be courted, seduced, something that makes me feel like I'm not just giving in because you crawled back to me with the right words. I need to see effort, not words," Scarlett said loud enough for us to hear.

She wore her wedding ring as well as the Dagr ring I had been wise enough to give her when I had lost my memories. I had few redeeming qualities during that time. I wanted to kiss her, for everyone to leave the longhouse so I could make love to my wife.

Brass cleared his throat and her eyes softened looking past me. "We can manage that, right Slate?"

"I want nothing more than for you to let me prove it," I said, searching her beautiful face.

Scarlett sucked in a shuttering breath.

"Aside from showing me you can be the men I fell in love with, I need one more promise from you, Slate."

"Whatever you wish," I said eagerly, finally feeling like I was making progress.

"Promise you're not going to let yourself die. It's when we're at the project. I think we all know that by now. I want you nowhere near it. Either of you, and I want it in blood. You're now accountable for one another's actions."

... I cannot agree to that...

Brass's amber eyes were molten in the morning's early light when I met his reflection in the mirror beyond her head. His look said, *you had better.*

"I feel like I am getting a raw deal. We swear to be together while you and the others go to the project," Brass said, and the corners of her mouth twitched as if she wanted to smile but fought it.

We chanted the blood vow having slit our palms open against one another's and I felt in sink into my skin. That was a very vague oath. Scarlett was not experienced enough with oaths to know that. Once again, we were taking advantage of her naivety.

"Thank you," she breathed, sounding relieved.

Jett and Quick had a very good idea of just how vague that oath was and we would be having a discussion about it once she left.

"Does that mean you're going to marry me, Love?" Brass asked.

She hesitated, "This is unorthodox." She looked to me. "You're only allowing this because you think you're going to die soon."

She had a point. I had no intention of sharing her before I had lost my memories. Now, I was not sure I could keep her without Brass.

"It began that way, but we can all agree circumstances have changed. Marry the bastard. When I leave this world, I need to know you are taken care of, that you are loved, Torch."

Brass stepped closer. "I won't beg you, Scarlett. I made a few mistakes, namely the night we spent with the Aves, rushing into things with Rosasite, and how poorly I handled Crimson. I am so very sorry, Love. Most of all, I am sorry I did not fight harder for you."

"I don't think we would be in this position if I had never left Slate. Brass, you never gave up on me no matter how hard I pushed you away," she said, knitting her brow.

She always forgave him first. It was an irritating habit I suspected would never end. Now that I knew Scat was Scarlett and Scat had fought daily with Brass, I allowed myself a bit of pleasure out of the ordeal. She had nearly cut off his favorite appendage in the springs, not to mention almost slitting his throat twice.

"We would rather share you than not keep you, Love," Brass murmured, wishing she had let Jett and Quick leave.

She bit her lip and averted her eyes. "Just give me until tonight. I need to process everything that's happened."

Whatever Brass saw in her mind made him smile at her. I wondered if I had never pursued her if she and Brass would not already have a couple more bairn running amok. She tore her gaze away from him and back to me.

"That's a very nice carving. I did not know you had it in you," she said and glanced towards Quick who was leaning against the doorframe. "Balas and Spinel will love the trains you made them."

She had loved those trains when I gave them to Scat. I suspected she had precious little for her sons and the gift from a stranger gave her faith.

"Well, I am starved. Scarlett?" Quick queried, pushing off and offering her his elbow.

We saw now what their game was about. I moved my arm so she could slide past letting my fingertips glide against her stomach. She made no comment about it and spared Brass a small smile before going to the door.

"See you at breakfast, Jett," she said in an altogether different tone than she had been using with Brass and me.

I moved to the door to watch her go, and she stopped and knit her brow at the kilt.

"Why are you wearing that skirt?"

Quick laughed and I let my lips curl. She blushed and averted her eyes. I could not have been happier I was not wearing my distorter ring.

"A kilt, like the tartans the Lycans wear. It is for the Ice Cliff Games. Easy to shift in." I slowly rose, skin darkening, fur growing, until a barghest towered in the doorway made higher than most for shifters like me and the Lycans.

Her brows rose. "You look like one of them in that. Almost like a wolf." She nodded.

"The better to pluck you in, my dear," I teased her with a growl and showed her what I wore underneath.

She turned away rapidly, but I caught the widening of her pupil and the libidinous smile just before she hid it. Quick laughed all the way down the path as I watched them go, shifting back into my human form.

Women were exiting their family homes to start breakfast. Dawn was peeking through the pines as we walked over the dirt paths that led between houses. She was in the longhouse the Lycans used as a honeymoon retreat. They had downplayed their excitement of her arrival. Before this war, only one Guardian had more power than she had.

Then she fucked him.

"You're going to have to let that go," Brass said from behind me chuckling at my jest.

"I will. As soon as I taste his blood."

"If I hadn't witnessed it with my own eyes... death has changed us all," Jett said as he rolled out of bed. "Very classy, by the way. Showing my baby sister your junk right there on the doorstep."

Brass chuckled with me. "She did not seem to mind. I do not have a slow speed, so do not waste your time asking me to wait. I got her going fast and I mean to again. She has already forgiven you; you might as well start arranging your wedding if you plan to do it here," I said, pulling the black tunic Scarlett had been wearing over my head. It still carried her scent.

"She has to say yes first," Brass said with a sigh as he dressed.

"She'll say yes. Scar has a natural aversion to things that don't fit into her plan when she imagined herself growing up. You can bet your ass she didn't see two husbands in her future." Jett washed himself off in the wash basin before dressing. "And you two hurt her feelings. If she needs a little time, it's not to figure out her answer, it's absorbing what she's saying yes to. She's crazy emotional, for obvious reasons. Quick is all she's had to lean on because I am just a big a scoundrel as it turns out."

I went back to the dresser and opened the top drawer with the carving of her and her bairn in it. I took it out feeling the eyes of the other two men burning my back. I let myself feel hope again as I took the stone brushed ring from around the left arm of the carved woman and slipped it back onto my ring finger.

"Looks like she's on her way to forgiving you too," Brass said over my shoulder.

FOUR

I wasn't sure if I should be upset that they weren't more disturbed by the fact that Quick and I had grown so close. They trusted us together. Insulted as I was, they were right. I never would be intimate with Quick.

I sat with Niall at the end of the head table eating my porridge drizzled with honey and sprinkled with blueberries. Niall offered me a basket full of burnt umber colored balls.

"Lucky tatties. I had them specially made for you. You are skin and bones, Scarlett."

They smelled sweet and were warm to the touch. I popped one into my mouth and suppressed a moan. Cinnamon. Who didn't like cinnamon?

"They're delicious, Niall. Thank you."

"What is your meal plan for dinner tonight?"

I'd forgotten all about it. "What would you recommend? What are your father's favorite dishes?" I asked coyly.

Niall's incredibly handsome face smiled knowingly at me. "Why would he want his favorite dish when he can request it at any time? Give him something he has never had before. Surprise him."

A lightbulb buzzed to life in my mind and I leapt up and gave him a kiss on his dimpled cheek before heading down to where my family sat with Lorcan and Cabhan.

"Does anyone have any seeds from Thrimilci?" I asked without preamble as I looked around the table at my allies.

Blathnat pursed her pouty lips in contemplation. "Are you thinking of growing something special for our sagamore?" she asked in their lilting tone.

"Yes, if I can."

Ridge looked at each of us and settled on Tawny. "What do you carry in those packs if not seeds?"

We didn't have to shout at one another over the table as we did last night while the folksy band had played and the boisterous laughter echoed through the hall. The air thrummed with excitement. Few had seen Slate in his barghest form and the children were hopping about our table waiting for him to finish eating so they could run along behind him.

It was hard not to day dream about our children doing the same to him. He was not the kind of man you could visualize bouncing a baby on his knee so seeing him with the little urchins and his treasure trove of whittled toys had made my girly parts positively pulse.

Tawny gave a little shrug. "Clothes, lip gloss, hairbrush, toilet paper. Essentials."

Ridge's brow creased with deep seams as he gave her a wide wry grin. "Seeds. Clothes can be cleaned, food hunted or grown, you never need carry it. See?"

He dug through his pack and pulled out a waterproof metal box. When he opened it I grew positively giddy.

"Seeds," I breathed.

Hundreds of packets of seeds in this four inches high, three inches wide, and about a foot long box. We could eat forever on those seeds if we took care of where we planted them.

"Are they all foods?" Tawny asked in disbelief.

"In my seed safe? No, some are flowers. I always kept a few in case your mother was down. Free tip for you men, always have flowers handy." Ridge gave them a roguish wink and handed the box to me.

"Are you sure you don't mind? I would only need a few." I bit my lip, praying he'd let me take my pick.

"Steal away, Scarlett. I replenish it from what you grow so I am never truly giving them up," Ridge said with a twinkle in his eye.

I dug through the box with Tawny on one side and Amethyst on the other. Tawny still sported the black eye, but Amethyst *was* speaking to them.

"Remember our wedding?" I asked Slate, hoping he would say yes.

His mocking smirk told me he did. "You were going to cheat on Brass that night."

Brass arched his dark brow at me as my face reddened.

"It's not cheating when I'm married to you," I said defensively.

"Who is going to be accountable for *your* actions, Love?" Brass asked, gesturing with a honey laced spoon.

"I will. Anyway, I haven't seen anything, but a few wildflowers here. I have an idea that may help us get this piece," I said, dropping my voice in a conspiratorial tone complete with shifty eyes.

Aoibhe and Blathnat smiled and nodded at my suggestions. They were getting nearly as excited as I was.

"Siobhan would be grateful. You will need all the help you can muster for tonight's meal," Aoibhe said, bouncing her raven haired toddler on her lap.

"I thought the women all helped make dinner together? I assumed I would be giving the recipe and helping of course, but with the usual women."

Blathnat gave me a sympathetic smile tossing a chocolate braid over her shoulder. "*Usually*. There is nothing usual about this wedding. Caolan wants her son to be the next sagamore." Lorcan gave me a dimpled smile. "My husband will make an excellent sagamore, but Siobhan is of child bearing age. Niall will never be Sagamore unless a cursed event should befall Lorcan. If Siobhan has Donncha's son though, that would be another contender to be sagamore. Donncha's has a score or so years left in him at least before someone challenges for his position," Blathnat explained.

"Sagamores are of the same bloodline, but we women have the most sway. Donncha's mother pushed for him to be sagamore the same way Caolan will push for Lorcan. She does not appreciate you coming in and filling Donncha's mind with wishes of marrying a new young bride. You will make that dinner alone," Aoibhe said fretfully, then added, "with mine and Blathnat's help of course.

Amethyst clasped the inky haired woman's hand with an appreciative smile.

I wouldn't let it suck the wind from my sails. I had a good plan. I needed only to execute it with some help from my fellow Guardians. Jett chuckled.

"I've seen that look before. What harebrained scheme are you cooking up, baby sis?" Jett asked.

I had missed his chiseled good looks, even if he was obscenely handsome. "My schemes always work when men aren't involved. Luckily for me, no men are involved in this one. Unless they want to help, I could use some *calling.*" I flashed my very best smile at the four men across from me.

Quick groaned. "Good luck with that one, I cannot take her anywhere flashing that thing around. Men trip over themselves to do as she bids."

I narrowed my eyes at him playfully. "Look who's talking 'Quick' Silver Regn. As if you don't know the power of your own smile."

I threw a roll at him which he plucked from the air and shoved whole in his mouth giving me a stuffed cheeked smile. I held my belly as I laughed, it never failed to surprise me that I wasn't pregnant anymore. The pain at missing Balas and Spinel was so sudden my mouth turned down into a grimace.

Brass and Slate practically flew over the table. Their actions so abrupt, they startled me, almost making me fall over the bench. They shoved their hands at me, forcing Tawny and Amethyst to move out of the way and I fought a smile.

"I miss my... *our* sons." I looked to the others who clearly thought the two men had lost their minds.

"Freya's burly boar, Scarlett!" Quick barked. "I am used to you being pregnant. You nearly gave us all heart attacks with that grimace. Do not worry, Cherry and Katydid are taking good care of Spinel and Balas."

They sat back down, and I righted myself on the bench.

Brass looked to Slate. "How long until she's fertile again?"

Slate looked at me speculatively and I did not think much of his glittering eyes. "Two weeks. In barghest form, I can force her into ovulation."

"What?" I squawked.

"You want me to give you an anatomy lesson, Torch, or will you take my word for it?" Slate asked with a teasing curl of his full lips.

"We can't wait two weeks." I hoped my tone brooked no nonsense because Quick couldn't wait that long for Indi.

Quick seemed to sense why I'd be willing to let Slate do whatever needed doing to force my ovulation so we could end the war and get Indi back once and for all. He gave my knee a squeeze under the table.

Brass's amber eyes softened and I could tell he wanted to kiss me. Right there. In front of everyone. My face tingled with the intense heat I felt as blood rushed to my face.

"You're going to have to get used to it, Love," Brass murmured.

"It's still so..."

"Depraved?" Brass offered, and I shook my head.

"Unconventional."

I went back to shuffling through the seeds. I couldn't believe what exotic items he had in here, cocoa beans, coconuts, pineapples, kiwi, all kinds of squash, sugar cane, the list went on and on.

"I want to marry Scarlett," Brass announced in a conversational tone.

Tawny was bug eyed as she stared at me. "Two husbands?" she spluttered.

I lifted my shoulders in an indiscernible gesture. Jett was patting Brass's back while Quick laughed.

"I'm asking, Jett. In lieu of her patriarch, you are her older brother. Though I could ask Slate who is responsible for her in these parts," Brass noted.

"I would bet my life that neither of you ever thought you would share a wife." Quick gloated.

"You were so against taking them both as husbands and they finally broke you down." Jett teased. "I'm happy for you three. By the Mother, what will you and Slate fight about now that Brass has joined you? Why yes, you have my permission. Without a doubt."

"Nothing. The name of the game is *she wins*. I have learned not to fight her; it only makes her push harder," Slate rumbled.

I stared dumbfounded at the men in my life and vaguely heard Amethyst's excited congratulations.

"Smart man," Ridge said, toasting him with his mug. "You will have to let me know how it goes, the truth," he said in earnest.

Jett gave me a knowing look Tawny only frowned at.

"I know it's nothing like my marriage, but I find having a second spouse inspired. Our life together is never boring. Cherry sees to needs Jett can't and vice versa. It is a well-oiled machine at this point." Amethyst's big almond eyes glanced past me to Tawny. "Despite his single indiscretion."

Single indiscretion my fanny pack. If you call a four month long affair *single*, then yes. Maybe she meant with a single person. Amethyst did not want to know all the sinful things those two did with one another right out in the open.

I should know, I watched them like my favorite show.

Quick's eyes met mine, and we both glanced away. Tawny and Jett would likely take the details of what they did to their graves. As would we. It was all for the best.

"Katydid?" Brass asked and my brilliant idea to have his ex-lover be a wet nurse for our sons to give Cherry a break was not so brilliant anymore.

"She's helping Cherry nurse the boys while I'm away." I pouted.

"She was a good choice. She would have given her left breast or her right to be able to raise Brass's children," Quick said to lift my plummeting mood.

I picked up my fork to poke at my food. I knew it was safer to leave the boys in Thrimilci where we had retaken the island and our family could care for them, but it was hard to justify it in the relative safety of the Lycan lands.

Amethyst placed her slender hand on my wrist. How could I bellyache about being away from my sons when she didn't know where Opal was?

"I thought Katydid broke up with you," I said, trying to redirect the conversation.

Slate and Quick both smirked as they finished their meals. Brass's dreamy amber eyes glittered at me.

"You would think that, but *you* are the only woman to leave me," Brass said.

"Solder was the Jett of their little foursome — Old Jett, not New Married Jett. Stealing women from his roommates when they had a spat," Quick said.

"Katydid frequently thought of Solder. I could not take the relationship seriously until I knew for certain she didn't want him," Brass said giving me a knowing look. "I told her at Jett's twenty-first birthday that we could no longer see one another despite your efforts to force us together."

He had done the same to me with Slate. People weren't meant to know everyone's thoughts. It was cruel and unusual torture.

Tartans of all different colors sat along the benches that framed the grounds in which Slate and Niall would compete. Most of the Lycans stood already drinking as a group of younger girls danced in tartan jumpers, only two wore the same colors and pattern.

I sat on Donncha's left, Brass was behind my seat on the dais. Siobhan had greeted me with all the warmth of a doting older sister, Donncha even spared me a wry smile. Caolan and Tadg sat on Siobhan's side facing the dancers who kicked and twirled in perfect unison. Padraig was to my left and kept one eye on me at all times.

Going in, there wasn't a shadow of a doubt in my mind that Slate would win. Now, doubt frayed my edges making me wish I had a nervous habit to pick at.

"What do those feathers signify, girly?" Padraig feigned drunkenness as he leaned over his chair to me.

"Nothing. They were gifts from the Aves. All my fetishes were given to me the sunburst, pearls, and silver beads from Slate," I told him matter of fact.

"And the jade?" he asked.

I reached into my hair and smiled. Slate and I would have to exchange carvings. I wanted my barghest jade back.

"Slate too. Why aren't you married, Padraig?" I asked, changing the topic as the folksy music continued dominated by the flutes and pipes they preferred.

A flat span of land that reached out over the ocean was cleared for the Ice Cliff Games. I understood now how it had gotten its name. Despite northern tips of any land having a reputation for being colder, these were warmer than the other parts of the island with the exception of the hot springs. The ocean waters were just cold enough to freeze. Sheets of ice formed the land that led directly up from the water. About fifty yards from the lip of the cliff, soil was covered in a thick rough bladed grass. A thin stream of grey clouds lazily floated across the dusky blue sky. There was always a good chance it would snow again in Elivagar.

"No woman can keep up. I should follow your suit. Our women would not agree to be bound with another to a single man," Padraig said, giving me a sidelong glance.

His mission in life seemed to be to make me lose my temper. "My brother is more than enough man for two wives. Perhaps the women have not found a single man who could meet the needs of two strong women."

"Your husband could not meet your needs so you found another?" Padraig asked, eyeing Brass behind me.

"We've been hand fasted for over a year, my husband and I have been married for nearly a year and a half. I worry all the time that *I* might not be enough to keep them happy," I muttered mostly to myself pulling my fur-lined cloak tighter.

I could feel his intelligent Kelly green eyes on me. "I doubt that very much. You did not see them before you came back. Brooding and moody does not cover it," Padraig said and Brass rested his hand on my shoulder as if making sure I was not an apparition.

My thumb ran over the two toned titanium ring I had given him as an access key to the arenas. That was what I told myself. Lera and

Chafer were given pendants they could choose to put on chains, bracelets, or placed into a setting as a ring. I had spent days looking for the perfect ring for Brass.

Of course, we had been on the outs then after he caught me with Spinel before I knew he was Brass's grandfather. Brass had resigned as commissioner from my arenas and taken a weeklong vacation to the Valla cottages with Gharial, his longtime married lover.

"I hear you, Love," Brass murmured in his smooth deep voice.

Gods, something was very wrong with me. They hadn't given me as much flack for kissing Scarab and Scorpion as I thought they would. I knew it was because it had felt right. It was undeniable. We were drawn together.

"You do not wear the beads I gave you," Brass noted in a hushed tone.

... I dropped them from the carriage after I found out who Spinel was. I didn't think you'd ever forgive me...

"You were hardly the first woman that fell victim to my grandfather," Brass said dryly.

... That doesn't make me feel better at all...

The young dancing girls cleared the patch of land and Donncha stood and the silence stretched. He slid the tartan fabric from his shoulder and pulled his tunic over his head to reveal scarred fair skin over a heavily muscled body. Guardian men weren't so bulky with their builds. Slate, Brass, Quick, and Jett were each sculpted with hard muscles and broad shoulders, but they weren't as thick as Donncha. Donncha looked like one of the men I'd seen in magazines competing in banana hammocks. He was enormous. Idly, I thought Padraig would be too.

His skin darkened. Bushy mottled grey fur forced its way from his skin, his limbs stretched, muscles bunched. Donncha's ears elongated as sharp fanged teeth burst from the gums of his open mouth. I wondered if many people knew the Lycans were werewolves. I wondered if they would be beyond annoyed that I mentally referred to them as werewolves.

Once he was done shifting, it was the cue for the others to shift. I was surrounded by wolves and Brass. All shapes and colors of wolves surrounded me. I glanced to Siobhan interested to see what kind of wolf she became and found a slender Egyptian jackal with a red mottled coat and a narrow snout. She was beautiful even as a hybrid.

Padraig howled, and I glanced to him. His thick fluffy coat was white with black tips. His intelligent human eyes shot me a look before he slid his gaze to the wall of Lycans that parted to our far right. I followed his eyes to where a black furred grey wolf strode out into the cleared grass. Slate in his barghest form stood at a height with Niall in his Lycan form. His two sets of off-white horns and tusks caught the dim light of the sun. He was bigger as a barghest hybrid, his muscles bunched and tight. Almost as bulky as Donncha.

Lycans didn't need to wear clothing, their fur was much thicker and longer than the Wemic or the Faunelle's. The Lycan males had removed their tunics, but the women still wore their long woolen dresses having dropped their cloaks to the benches behind them.

Roars and howls resounded through the crowd, the only humans were Brass and me. With the roars, and gnashing of teeth, curled fangs, and taut muscles, we should have been afraid. A red furred wolf that looked to be a cross breed with a coyote stepped into the clearing between the two kilt clad hybrids. Both had long midnight waves that flowed down their backs, Slate's narrow braids threaded with his Celtic etched silver beads.

The three hybrids approached, bodies rippling. A dangerous under-current thrummed through the crowd, excited at the competition between these two champions among men. They stopped in front of Donncha and I, he stood and I thought I could hear the wood planks of the dais creak with his weight.

"Slate, Grar Dyr of the barghest, do you challenge Niall of the Lycans for the hand of this woman, Scarlett Tio, Night's Child, the fire elemental, Second of the Guardians, daughter of spring and summer, and future mother of barghests?" Donncha asked in a deep burr.

"Aye," Slate rasped with a flash of fangs from his jaw.

Future mother of barghests? I had a prophecy to fulfill. The fate of the tribes depended on Slate and I conceiving a son. No pressure or anything.

Niall's green human eyes glittered against his coal black coat. He was enjoying being challenged by Slate for me. It wasn't about me, not really. I continued to be a novelty, only now it wasn't because of my looks, but because of who my husband was.

"Then we begin. To the circle!" Donncha said, and Niall turned around and began to walk to a white painted circle twenty yards away from where we sat.

I looked up to Brass behind me who nodded for me to face forward. Slate had approached, barghest Slate, Grar Dyr.

"I ask my lady for her favor." Grar Dyr's lips curled into a lecherous grin full of finger length teeth.

I panicked. I didn't have anything to give. I nodded absently and removed my silver torque. The silhouette of the mother holding a baby dangled from it. I bent the loop and pried it free from the torque before holding the charm out for Grar Dyr. Instead, he knelt before me and pulled a braid free from his glossy black waves. Brass held out a hand to help me to my feet, and I stood in front of Slate on the semi frozen ground.

I bent the loop around one of his silver beads so it was secure all while he looked at me. He was almost as tall as I was on his knees in this form. I ran my fingers over the braid to the tip and let it drop. Howls rang out around us and Slate stood forcing me back a step.

The Ice Cliff Games began.

Slate and Niall had pressed their feet together with both their fists clinging to a stick between them. Their faces had strained, arms corded until Slate lifted from the ground. I had to keep checking with Brass to see who was winning because the Lycans cheered for them both alike.

"The goal was to raise the man from the ground. Niall won. He's been doing it all his life," Brass murmured, close to my ear.

Slate lost!

I watched Slate closely and saw that he was genuinely perturbed that Niall had lifted him. That made them even. Slate had beat Niall at throwing a big rock attached to a wooden shaft, which I was told was a hammer, and a weight throw, essentially tossing a heavy metal ball on a chain.

Niall was better at the native events; things Slate never would have possibly done in his life like play with some weird stick to lift another man from the ground. Niall had also tossed a weighted bag of straw over a pole with a pitchfork better than Slate. Slate had never used a pitchfork in all his life. Not even when training Safanad for me.

I squirmed in my seat with my hands on my belly. They were doing one last event before lunch and I had to run to check on Tawny and the others. Niall stood in the white circle and cradled a stone roughly the size of my head against the crook of his neck. He moved to the edge of the circle and threw it with all his might.

The Lycans howled and clapped clawed hands. Caolan, shockingly, was a fluffy white wolf I assumed was Arctic by her coat. She gave me a nod as she sat next to her husband, a hulking grey beast that looked more like a bear than a wolf. I pitied the women who had to wear the woolen's while the men got to wear their breathable kilts.

Slate walked to the edge of the white circle, stone in hand, and threw as hard as he could. The stone sailed and fell a good foot further than Niall's stone so he was the clear winner. I cheered internally not wanting to rub in the loss to the sagamore.

The dancing girls came out in their Lycan form and were just as lithe as they spun and kicked leaping like springs were bound to their feet into the air. Niall and Slate spoke for a moment before they headed our way without the red-coated wolf who oversaw the competitions.

"You had better be worth it, Torch," Slate teased in his rasping barghest voice.

"I don't know? Am I?" I asked, batting my lashes at him.

Brass chuckled. He positively radiated a happiness, that would be impossible to maintain, since he discovered my true identity. It put a lot of pressure on a girl.

Slate growled, a real deep reverberating growl that seemed to echo in his inhuman chest before he wrapped an arm around my waist and lifted me from the ground as if I was lighter than air.

"I am going to walk with you to your fellow plotters since Brass has been with you all day," he rasped.

"Watching you," Brass corrected, feigning disappointment.

Slate walked me back down into the village and back into the trees where a few greenhouses were used to grow the Lycans rarer foods. Siobhan had gotten us permission to use a long abandoned greenhouse that we quickly repaired and made use of. I liked how hidden it was and fully intended on surprising Donncha and the others with a superb wedding feast.

Ridge leaned over a bed of purple crocus and iris flowers he'd set in a long planter along the hastily repaired wall. Tawny was busy growing trees she'd set right there in the ground at the back of the big room, while Quick and Amethyst were wrist deep in even more planters nourishing the twenty-year-old seeds.

"Looks good. I can't thank you guys enough," I said as Slate released my hand, now in his human form and shirtless. I tried not to be distracted by his rippling bronze skin.

"No problem at all. Are you married to Niall yet?" Quick chided.

I gave him a dry look and walked over to check on the plants he grew and rubbed my palm along his back. Quick was the kind of man who was more sensitive than you would think. He needed constant attention, which he usually got from an array of avid fans, but he had whittled those numbers down to one and now he had none. Unfortunately, he only had me, a poor substitute for a fiancée, but a loving and attentive sister figure.

"Has Jett come back yet?" I asked, dreading the reply.

Amethyst wiped her hands on her apron and pushed back an ebony plaited lock of hair with the back of her wrist. "Not yet, but Jett would rather not return than disappoint, and if he doesn't return, I'll kill him in truth this time."

Tawny glanced over her shoulder at me and offered me a broad smile. "All my plants died at home. I can grow fiddlesticking trees now. In hours! We have, cocoa trees, coconut trees, lemon trees —"

"I grew the sugarcane and corn and —" Quick interrupted.

"You're all doing a fantastic job. Honestly, I don't know what I would've done without your help," I said giving them each a smile. "Now I only need to prepare all the raw food into something that will *wow* Donncha," I grumbled.

Brass stepped up behind me as I leaned forward breathing deeply over the planters Ridge worked over, his *calling* blooming another purple blossom every few inches. Brass's thumb found the exact spot that ailed me on my spine.

"You'll have to teach me how to pollinate the seeds one of these days," I said to Ridge who glanced up, giving me a wry smile.

"I get the impression fighting and weaponry are the larger focus now for tyros rather than nurture and focus," Ridge said.

"Was it different when you were at Valla U?" I asked.

"Very. Guardians are meant to keep balance in nature. The skill set they teach now is in defense. I do not see how that takes precedent over our true purpose. The Red Kings Massacre changed much," Ridge said and his words were swathed in shame and sorrow.

Tawny moved to her father's side, and they shared a smile making me wonder how I ever thought Hawk could be her father. He raised her and loved her as his own, but she was Ridge's spitting image.

"It is actually very easy," Brass murmured at my ear.

His body seemed to curl around mine from behind so everything he could touch from where he stood he did. "Spinel has a private garden he only shows people closest to him."

Brass paused to see if I would let slip that I had seen this garden. Spinel, as Balas, had laid me down on a bed of flowers and made love to me as petals fell from the trees. It was magnificent. He only grew red and white blooms there, the like of which I'd never seen. Kodupul flowers, campions, ghost orchids, chocolate cosmos, and the Middle Mist red, which was my favorite and the rarest flower in the world. We had no qualms about taking a naked tumble through them though.

I didn't rise to his bait.

Brass gave me a dry look. "That was a foolish of me. I know Spinel would have taken you to the garden. It's where he took his *favorites.* Anyway, he taught Silver and I how to grow the delicate flowers." With his *calling*, Brass began to use a gentle breeze of wind to hop from flower to flower.

I leaned my head back against his chest. I'd missed how effortless our time together was, it was sigh inducing.

"You're not paying attention, Love."

I had shut my eyes and was slowly slumping against Brass. The cold sapped my energy, as did all the pumping.

I opened my eyes turning to give him a rueful smirk. "I was, but then I grew too comfortable," I murmured softly hoping only Tawny and maybe Slate would hear with his sensitized hearing.

"To lunch with you," Brass said, circling an arm around my waist and leading me from the greenhouse with the others.

"Cock-a-leekie soup," Niall replied as I spooned another delicious mouthful down my throat.

The chicken, leek, rice soup had a few onions snuck into it. It was the best kind of comfort food. Hearty and filling, I soaked my buttered flaky bread into the last dregs of my bowl and ate with gusto. I didn't even feel guilty for devouring the caramel shortbread Aoibhe had made herself when it came across the table.

"Pan drop?"

Niall offered me a small dish of disc shaped candies and I popped one into my mouth without further question. It was a mint like Mentos — hard outside but soft chewy inside. I thanked him and slid down the table to Siobhan whose adoring gaze seldom left Donncha.

"Good afternoon, Siobhan," I said politely, keenly aware of Caolan's observant eyes on me.

"Good afternoon, Scarlett," the English rose said with a dreamy look in her eyes.

"I'd like to show you something if you have a moment," I said, dropping my tone.

Caolan forgot herself and turned her head to look at us. I smiled internally as we walked from the mead hall together.

Slate's metal weight narrowly missed the bar declaring him the winner of the weight over the bar feat. Since he also defeated Niall at the weight throw, that put Slate ahead by three challenges. Only three events were left. Niall roared in frustration, which I was told to expect, but it still startled me in flinching at the eardrum bursting sound.

"To win the lady's hand, Niall must win the next three challenges," the red-coated wolf announced.

I glanced about for this supposed *lady* he spoke of.

Niall tossed his mane of midnight locks and raised his head gesturing to the next challenge. I hoped Slate was taking it as seriously as Niall. I thought Slate would pulverize Niall, but belatedly I realized Slate didn't have much experience in his hybrid form while Niall spent half his life as an overgrown wolf.

They were roughly the same size and had similar powerful builds. It dawned on me that Slate *could* lose. He'd never gone up against someone like Niall who thought like a man but was as vicious as the most feral of animals.

Just like him.

Two long logs were brought in by four Lycans and they set them down just outside the circle. By log, I mean it was a skinned tree. When Slate picked it up by its narrower end and rested it on his shoulder, it towered far into the sky above him. The Grar Dyr ran to the edge of the circle and hoisted the tree. I watched it turn end over end and fall. The Lycans stood to see how it fell and approving howls promptly sounded.

Niall had picked up the second tree that stretched high into the sky and rested it on his shoulder facing the way Slate had run. He ran forward and tossed the tree. The Lycans cheered even before it fell a foot away from where Slate's rested and closer to the goal. Niall had won the caber toss.

Slate was still up by two. I was starting to get the impression that if we lost the Games, Donncha would procrastinate further in giving over the last stone piece. Idly, I wondered what would happen to the piece if we took it by force. I had come to the understanding that it must be given and not taken. Otherwise, Canis would have likely taken the piece from the Gorgon *if* he'd known it was there.

Lycans had brought out four stones per man, *er*, hybrid. The red Lycan spoke a few quick words to the two who nodded. The stones were in four different sizes of similar shapes and textures. The red Lycan stood back and gave a short bark, Slate and Niall sprang into action.

They lifted the heaviest stone first, raising it to their waist before setting it back down on the ground, they did the same with the second stone, then balanced it atop the first stone. They were neck and neck with the third stone, and then they placed the final stones that appeared to be the lightest. Slate's last stone wobbled precariously and my eyes widened as it slowly slid and toppled off its rocky tower.

I looked up to the heavens as the Lycans roared their approval. I groaned. Patience was not Slate's strong suit, balancing those rocks must have made him feel like chucking them off the cliff.

"You should have given him some incentive to keep you," Brass teased from behind my seat.

"Don't joke. That'll be you tomorrow if he loses," I said under my breath as he came around my seat. "Where are you going?"

"We're needed for the final task," Brass said, handing me his cloak.

Ridge, Jett, and Quick emerged from the woods and I knit my brows. Jett was back which was a good sign, but what could they possibly be doing to help Slate in his challenge? Lorcan and Cabhan stood. A Eurasian brown wolf with warm whiskey-colored eyes and a grey Arctic wolf with grey eyes gave me matching apologetic looks as they moved to Niall's sides. Tadg was a black-faced wolf with a dark brown coat and even burlier as a Lycan, he stood and crossed the land to Niall. Padraig gave me a knowing wolfish grin before moving to join them.

I slunk back in my seat. It had to be a joke. Slate stood across from Niall holding the rope whose red tie flapped lazily in the cold breeze between them. Each man and Lycan gripped the thick rope, facing off, and at the sound of the red coated Lycan's roar, they tugged.

Slate bore the brunt of the Lycans' strength, but even he couldn't hold up against five werewolves himself. The red coated Lycan spread his arms out in a signal to stop as Slate's boot crossed the white line and the little red flag reached Niall.

I could tell Slate and the others expected to lose, but it was still disappointing. Not as many Lycans cheered knowing it wasn't an even match. Jett gave me a wry grin as he waved with a wink and walked back to the woods with Ridge and Quick. I hoped Quick was staying out of trouble. Brass rubbed his hands together as he moved to stand behind me again. His palms were already healed but I pulled his hand over my shoulder anyway and kissed it.

"Imagine me finally agreeing to marry you and you lose me in a game of tug of war. Maybe I should have given *you an* incentive to keep me as well."

Brass chuckled still breathing roughly from the match. "Ah, Love. That would be the Norns cruelty at hand if it were true."

A little show of affection wouldn't ruin my balance of power. I knew once I gave in, I'd lose the little strength I had mustered to get a show of loyalty and love that I needed to really forgive them. To forgive Slate so I wouldn't care that my heart had been broken too many times to be patched back together by him or anyone. I had to be smarter this time around.

"As a tie breaker, Niall of the Lycans and Slate, the Grar Dyr of the barghest will compete in the Crucifix."

Four Lycans emerged with the weighted balls with chains they had used for the weight throw. Niall and Slate held their arms straight out from their shoulders, their fur chests bare and received one weighted ball and then another.

"The first competitor to drop their arms loses," the red wolf announced and left the two hybrids to standalone in the circle.

Slate's fur was short and sleek like a second skin, he would get colder faster. Maybe he would start to shiver and his arms would fall. After watching the competition for the better part of the day, I was no longer confident Brass would save me from becoming Niall's wife.

The day's events, and my mood, had taken an unpredictable turn.

The first minute was brutal as we held our collective breaths. For following five every slight sway of their bodies looked to topple them over. Then their arms began to shake. I expected an exchange of insults, but it looked like they were reserving all of their energy for holding up their arms.

Slate's silver eyes met mine and held. His furred brow arched and I could almost see his winged human brow doing the same on his hard planed face. We'd overcome so many truly terrible obstacles.

This was nothing.

I pressed the tips of my fingers to my lips and blew Slate a kiss. His canine like lips curled, and I knew he would win. Incentive.

Seconds later, Niall's arms dropped with a growl.

I leapt to my feet and ran to him forgetting all decorum and he immediately started towards me. The red wolf was announcing Slate the victor, but he only had eyes for me. We hadn't broken our gaze since I'd blown him that kiss. My insides coiled at the look in those mirrored silver eyes.

My slippered boots skidded to a stop inches away from him. I couldn't give in yet. Not after everything he'd put me through.

I licked my lips as he stood, looking down his nose at me. He began shrinking into his human form. My lips twitched into a smile. Slate was only in the black kilt and boots. He offered me a hand, and I took it knowing he wasn't going to let me walk.

"There is a break before the hand fasting," Slate rumbled as he slid his teeth along his lower lip and let it spring forth.

"I suppose you have to collect your prize," I said demurely.

Slate lifted me up like a doll and cradled me in his arms. I broke our gaze to glance to Brass.

"Try to keep up," I said with a smirk.

CHAPTER 5
JETT

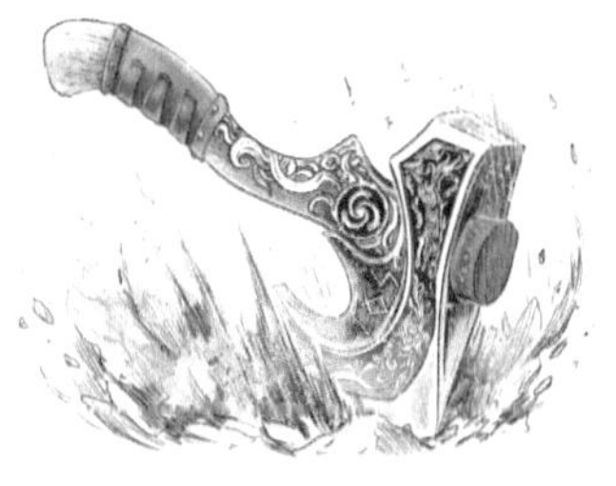

Scarlett was missing the wedding she'd put so much effort into without having been asked. "One guess as to where those three are," Quick murmured, leaning in next to Jett.

Scarlett wasn't a big woman, average height, fit build that some-times leaned towards thin when she was stressed despite her curves. Slate was as big as Jett, a whole foot taller than her. Brass just as broad and only a handful of inches shorter. She would disappear between them. What if they smashed her flat during a blind lust-a-thon? He had gotten carried away with Cherry and Amethyst plenty of times and they were both smaller than him.

"What's that face about?" Quick asked.

They watched on as Siobhan strode between the purple flowered garland Scarlett weaved with Amethyst and Tawny's help. She wore a sleeveless corset dress in the purple tartan that matched Donncha's. Lycans married in either their human or wolf form, they had chosen to perform it in human form.

The Lycan women were bigger boned, thicker in general which meant curvier curves. Since his time with Tawny, Jett had a newfound appreciation for shapely hips and a nice round backside. He looked at Tawny standing on the other side of Amethyst. The curve of her back that led to her firm backside made her dress hang off in a way that more than hinted on what was underneath.

Jett thought he had scratched his itch, but now that he couldn't touch her again, his eyes strayed. Her breasts were pillowy soft, skin creamy and flawless. Slate would call the shade of her peaks kitten nose pink. She hadn't given him that special smile since they spent the afternoon with Cherry and decided their marriage wasn't for her.

"That's a small dress," Jett said as Siobhan's ivory swell of breasts jiggled with her every step into the clearing.

Quick's chuckle sounded like his brother's. His brother who was probably doing all sorts of hedonistic things to his once innocent baby sister. Jett didn't know why it bugged him so much.

Guilt.

While Quick and Scarlett went to go look for a horse that night in Glitra, Ridge had been in one room while he and Tawny had been in a room of their own playing at husband and wife.

"Do you mind if I take a bath?" Tawny had asked.

She'd already taken off her distorter ring so her big hazel eyes peered out from her doll face. "Knock yourself out." He had said, trying to act nonchalant.

She stripped off clothes climbed in the barrel like tub and began to wash. It felt more awkward not watching than if Jett had let himself occasionally glance at her because that was the direction he was going. Instead his forehead had beaded with sweat trying to stop himself from looking.

There wasn't much to the rooms at the Dark Dancer, full size bed, dresser, basin, a trunk, and the tub they'd had to bring up themselves. He washed his shirt in the basin and hung it over the mirror that tempted him with milky skin. He finished washing his face and the essentials with the leftover water in the basin until her fingertips brushed his back and Jett started.

"You can use the tub."

Thank goodness her bath was blissfully short, and she slipped into a taupe cotton shift before climbing into the bed.

"Right," Jett had said brusquely before standing in front of the tub and removing the rest of his clothes before plopping in.

He scrubbed at his skin. Cherry forgave him more easily than Amethyst ever would. Jett knew it and yet...

He had stood grabbing the thread-bare towel off the back of the tub. The Dark Dancer smelled like spilled ale and unwashed bodies. Not her though, she smelled sweet, like frosted Yuletide cookies.

When Jett stood, he felt her eyes on his back. He didn't acknowledge her. He put a fresh pair of shorts on and turned around as she shifted towards the wall.

"Do you care if I leave off my pants?" Jett asked.

"I don't care," she said, voice muffled by her pillow.

She sounded defeated and sad. He crossed the room and climbed into bed next to her under the thin flannel blankets. A small wood-burning stove heated the room.

"Hey. You alright, Tawns?"

"Don't call me that, Jett," she said dryly.

Only Scar, Steel, and Gyps called her that and it was rare when they did. "Sorry," he muttered, and heard her sniffle.

He rolled over so her back was to his front and gently pulled her shoulder so her espresso waves fell over the dingy pillow. She blinked tear-filled eyes at him.

"I'm supposed to be this island's matriarch and I'm staying in stinky motels filled with khorazes and dirty perverts. Someone stole my island right out from under me and I don't have the first clue who it was or what they want. We went to the other inn, and no one had even seen who was in the Vetr castle. Orion never would have let this happen. I lost my father's legacy." She sniffled again, rubbing the back of her hand on the slightly upturned tip of her petite nose nothing like the snub nose the distorter gave her.

"Aside from when it has to do with men, when is the last time Scarlett failed to do something she set her mind to? You think this Lycan village can stand up to her? She'll have them eating out of her palm within hours and at least one marriage proposal," Jett had joked, plucking a lash off her cheek.

She giggled; her wide mouth split into that special smile.

So maybe it hadn't been that long since she had given him that smile. That was only five days past. He'd known Amethyst would be here, and he'd done it anyway. Cherry had made it clear, if Jett could cajole Tawny into joining them, he could use whatever means necessary. He knew *she* would understand.

Then there was Opal. Jett couldn't bring himself to talk about her. Still couldn't. The girls didn't like that.

"Thanks, Jett."

There was pleasure to be found in one another's company, they had certainly found a lot of that in the Dark Dancer's bedroom.

Quick had burst into the room, oblivious of the fact that Jett was tracing the Valkyrie tattoo she had on her back with his tongue.

"Scat was attacked. Two men are taking her to the Lycans. They killed one of the Stygians, it is serious. We have to leave now." Quick left without shutting the door and Lorcan had seen them and promptly closed it, giving them privacy to dress.

They didn't talk about it until Tawny saw Amethyst and she broke down, telling her everything. Including the five clenchers they'd shared three days before arriving at the Lycan village. Amethyst had punched him dead in the eye and immediately did the same to Tawny, only giving her enough time to yelp before she went down.

Now it felt like years ago. Tawny's eyes swiveled to Jett's, and she looked away. *No.* It would never happen again. Amethyst did not want another spouse, and he had done enough cheating to last him the rest of his life. Jett was lucky he didn't have a conventional marriage or he might have found himself out on his ass and no one would have blamed the girls.

"They've started making the food. None of the other women are going to help Scar. Ridge is working on a surprise for the wedding tomorrow. They'll all be in the greenhouse or near the cooking stations," Tawny said. "I doubt Slate is very happy at the moment." She smiled wryly.

Quick grunted. "Not after he went through all that."

The folksy music native to the Lycans started and Jett had missed the whole ceremony. Siobhan beamed on Donncha's arm and for once the older sagamore didn't look like he was plotting something.

Scarlett had done him a favor.

CHAPTER
SIX

I explained everything I could verbalize about my experience in Disir. They wanted me to bring them back to the portal. I went through as much detail as I could about the revolt in Thrimilci and they told me what happened the day we were separated. They had gone to the Lycans first thing after they evacuated as many as they could. Slate didn't seem surprised that the baby Amber carried wasn't his. They knew all about my Natt ancestry and how my great grand aunt had been the green eyed Valkyrie staring at me at all the funerals and my theory on my real great grandma being lost where we were.

We had needed some time to talk without a bed in the room.

Not that Slate needed a bed.

"If you don't stop, sir, I'm going to have to ask you to leave."

Slate had not put his shirt on and while I whipped up dinner for more people than I had ever cooked for in my life, he was more interested in eating the chocolate coconut pudding I was slaving away to make... off of me.

"The other women are being a bunch of catty cows, Torch. Let them starve." Slate's hand found its way under my dress and he goosed my backside.

"If you spent more time preparing and less time fondling her, we could be done sooner and in bed earlier," Brass said, chopping up a storm on a high wooden butcher's table with his sleeves of his tunic rolled up.

A lock of dark hair brushed his cheek as he returned to his chopping. Blades of air came in very handy for mass quantities of food preparation. I grappled free of Slate's hands and skipped over to Brass, bumping him with my hip.

"Thank you for helping me," I told him and he leaned down to peck a kiss to my cheek.

Ridge watched as he grew more flowers in a very inconspicuous way. "You too, Ridge," I added.

"I am forever in your debt, Scarlett. If you had not been adamant about pestering me, I might never of left," Ridge said in complete seriousness.

The thought of him never having left and possibly never knowing Sparrow and Tawny were alive made me so upset I felt tears burn in my eyes. I walked over to him and forced a hug he seemed grateful for. Ridge hadn't been touched by a single person for twenty years until he met me. If Slate and Brass thought they had performed some great feat by going four months without intimacy, they should've had a short talk with Ridge.

"I knew if Wren had a daughter she would be my daughter's closest friend. I am glad for it. You are an extraordinary woman, with equally extraordinary husbands."

Ridge withdrew and looked to the two unbearably handsome, powerfully muscular, Gods among men standing side by side chopping vegetables for my soup and fruit for the salad. They looked wonderfully out of place so domesticated, but all I could think about was getting them back to my longhouse to properly thank them. My will was not as strong as I hoped.

Brass looked up with a smirk and I sighed. Gods cursed mind readers.

"You grew up with Hawk and Sparrow?" Ridge asked, following my gaze.

I nodded. "Yeah. Them, my mom, Tawny, and Gypsum. We were one family. Hawk is the father I never had," I told him, using a sliver of my *calling* to help produce sugar from the sugarcane we'd planted.

Who knew sugar was so hard to make? Or cornstarch or flour? If I didn't have *calling* or the help of my family, I never would have been able to produce the meal worthy of the stone piece and the marriage of the sagamore. It had dawned on me that Donncha was far from stupid and he must have thought my plotting would lead me to where I was now. Preparing a grand feast for his wedding so his people could be off celebrating. I'd have to be more careful around him.

I walked outside to the barrel Jett had put the crabs in and the barrels Quick and Jett had shaped to smoke the caribou Jett had gutted, skinned, and brined. Five skins were stretched and tanned along the outside of the makeshift greenhouse. Ridge had grown hickory expressly for the smokers.

Slate emerged from the greenhouse and his bronze skin prickled on contact with the frigid air as he carried out a man sized basket full of ingredients for the stew. I made my stand today, I had to last *one* more night before succumbing to his lure. By the Mother, it was like the air magnetized from his sheer presence.

"Need a hand?" he rumbled, stacking the logs so one of the massive cauldrons could be placed above it.

"Why thank you," I said, batting my eyes in an exaggerated fashion.

Slate smirked as he began to fill it with water to boil the crabs. There were many perks in preparing large quantities of food with *calling*. It was boiling in an instant and he hoisted the barrel of crabs up and dumped half into the water. He began to set up the second and third cauldrons. One for just the stew.

The chickens for the stew were the only ingredient the Lycans had provided along with the butter and cream. Slate added in water as I used my *calling* to dump in capers, parsley, lemon and green olives into the cauldron. He picked up the man sized basket of chicken we set outside to keep cold and dumped the chopped pieces into the cauldron.

Slate dropped the basket against the greenhouse and dusted his hands off. "Careful not to rub those breasts on the cauldron, Torch."

I rolled my eyes, but watched the twin globes I was unaccustomed to as I used an oar sized spoon to stir the cauldron. Slate came up behind me and lent his arm strength to mine. I ducked under his arms and watched them flex as he stirred.

Slate had such a great profile, I thought dreamily. His straight masculine nose that his full lips could almost touch if he pursed his lips. The hard planes of his face creased as he began to smile. His lashes were so thick and long, his grey eyes looked like the Elivagar skies before a storm.

"You are staring," he rumbled, sounding amused.

"I've only seen you in my dreams for months. Just checking my memory. I was right."

"Right?" he asked smirking.

"Hideous. Just... disgusting. I can't figure out what I ever saw in you," I teased.

He glanced at me from the corner of his eye. I was looking at his left side so his scar shone in the sunlight. He wasn't smiling any longer. Having to wear the distorter and getting his memories back to find the thick silver scar on his face must have been disturbing.

As he continued to stir the cauldron, I snaked my arms around his middle and pressed my cheek to his back. Aside from the few nights he spent holding me as Scat, Slate, a man who bedded at least one woman every day, had been alone for months out of grief for me.

"Is this you taking pity on me, Torch?" he rumbled.

His skin was chilled, but there was an undercurrent of heat flowing through his veins. "Not pity. I could never feel sorry for a man like you. I could feel other things." I purred as my fingers slid over the thick fabric of his kilt. "Be careful. You don't want to rub this on the cauldron," I said, pulling my lower lip between my teeth.

A growl began deep in his chest as I slid my hand under his kilt. "Torch, do not start if you do not intend to finish."

Touching him coiled me so tightly I gave sincere thought to hiking up my skirts right there with Tawny's birth father just inside the greenhouse. Slate had stopped stirring, his breathing deeper. He certainly wasn't cold under his kilt.

"I need to touch you," he growled.

"You start touching me and we'll never finish this dinner," I said throatily.

"That does not seem sanitary." Quick's voice came from behind us, and I hastily pulled my hand from his kilt.

"*Quick*," Slate growled in a rasp, and I realized he was close to losing control.

"We'll finish later," I whispered to him, giving him a pat on his lush backside before turning to Quick, Jett, Tawny, and Amethyst.

Slate's colorful stream of Wemic curses followed us back into the greenhouse where Brass's soft amber eyes looked up to me as he chopped more strawberries for the dinner. I directed everyone to help me finish up. Luckily Blathnat and Aoibhe promised to make all the bread we would need.

All I had left was the cake.

I sidled up next to Brass after washing my hands and tucked his lock of hair behind his ear letting my fingers trail down his anvil jaw. He eyed me with a knowing smile. My will power was absolute garbage.

"Poor Slate," he said smoothly.

"How so? I feel worse for not having a moment alone with you," I said, leaning slightly against his shoulder as I made cocoa beans into cocoa butter and powder with the help of my *calling*.

"*Ah*, Love. You know we have not *relieved* ourselves in sometime. I imagine he is off cursing the day our mother birthed Quick into the world." Brass smirked with his plump, defined lips.

"You're fibbing. I don't believe you." I laughed, but Brass didn't laugh with me.

He grabbed my arm when I went to leave the greenhouse. "I wouldn't go after him now. There's plenty of time tonight when you're not on a schedule."

I bit my lip and nodded. I'd experienced Slate when he was feeling possessive and lustful. I wasn't sure I could handle it right then.

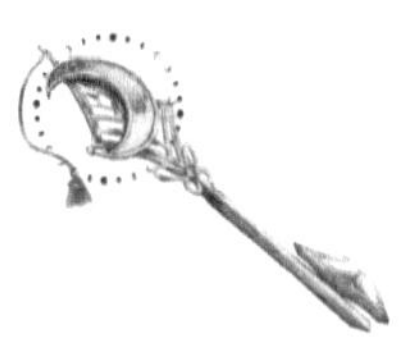

Siobhan was back in human form, hugging me again, as I finally got a chance to sit down to eat. Purple crocus and irises decorated the entire mead hall. Ridge had outdone himself. She looked stunning in the tartan corset dress in Donncha's colors, her strawberry blonde hair plaited around her head with wisps that brushed her shoulders laced with crocus flowers.

We received compliments on the chicken, lemon, and capers stew as we brought in the cake. It was really Quick and Jett who brought in the cake while Amethyst and I fretted behind them. The kiwi, pear, and peach fruit salad sent them into a tizzy. The hickory smoked caribou with pineapple sauce was completely different from anything else they'd ever had. We served it with zucchini, tomatoes, peppers, and eggplant sprinkled with crab meat. Tawny and Ridge were passing out the family style platters of chocolate coconut pudding. Brass was sure we'd have enough cake for everyone, but I was doubtful.

Moist chocolate coconut cake with a strawberry filling and a coconut glaze. It was the best I could do without the internet to search recipes. What I wouldn't have done for internet access.

"I'm happy you got the day you deserve, Siobhan," I told her, awkwardly holding her in return.

"Caolan would have told the women to burn the meal if she had overseen it," she whispered in her lilting tone.

"Really?"

"It is not that she does not like me but wants to keep me in my place as she sees it. Below *her*," she explained. "Did you say something to Donncha to prompt him into asking me to marry him?"

"Merely watered the seed that was already planted." I assured her. "Congratulations, Siobhan. Now, I'm going to go eat because I am utterly famished."

She embraced me one last time before I could walk to the table Slate and Brass sat at with the others. I realized despite its position off to the side; it was the table of honored guests. Lycans seemed to keep their enthusiasm secreted from the sources of their excitement.

Brass offered me his hand as I came up beside him. Slate gave me a cool look and grudgingly made room for me between them. Tawny gave me a conspiratorial smile and held out a slice of cake for me.

"I knew you wouldn't think to grab one," she said pushing it across the table to the three other plates filled with the other delectable dishes waiting for me.

I mustered an exhausted smile. "I couldn't have done this without you guys. Thank you. Sincerely, I love each one of you. Even you, Ridge."

The older man gave me a lopsided grin. It was hard to view him as Tawny's dad, more like an older brother. Especially since when we met him he was Brass's age.

"Can I have a kiss?" I asked quietly.

The music was in full swing as were the dancers. The tables nearest the head table had been pushed back and former occupants found new seats. Barrels of ale were brought out and mugs were passed all around.

"You have to be clearer to whom you are addressing," Slate rumbled.

I had no desire to argue with my husband who was too good looking, more so while dark and foreboding, than was healthy for my resolve. I'd spent the last few hours slaving away in the greenhouse preparing the food and what I really wanted was an easy relaxing night.

"To whomever is passing them out," I said coquettishly.

Slate was in a terribly brooding mood, so I looked to Brass.

"If I start kissing you now, I may not stop."

No kisses for me.

"My compliments, Second." Caolan had walked up behind me and I turned on the bench to try to face her.

Slate steadied me with his big hand and I rested my palm on his thigh. "Thank you, Caolan, but it was a group effort. I am nothing without my family."

Her luminous emerald eyes took us all in. Silver hairs threaded through her inky black hair, I placed her at around fifty years old, but with spectacular fair skin.

"Donncha would like a word," she told me and offered Lorcan, Blathnat, Aoibhe, and Cabhan a warm smile.

I squeezed Slate's thigh. "This is it. A kiss for luck?" I asked.

"You do not need luck, you always win." His lips curled remembering a similar exchange we had before he competed before we had the arenas.

I clenched my jaw as my hand brushed his hair. I'd feel that hair glide over my thighs like silk before the night was through.

"Gods be good, Scarlett," Brass breathed, and my cheeks flushed as I squeezed his shoulder before walking to the dais where Donncha sat.

His new bride was the centerpiece of the dancers stomping and spinning around the wooden floor. Donncha's midnight blue eyes followed me walk along the back of the hide covered chairs. When I came close he stood offering me his hand and pulling out a chair for me.

I thanked him as I sat and noticed the half-eaten piece of cake in front of his seat. "Not a sweets fan?" I asked, gesturing to the chocolaty confection.

"That was my second helping," Donncha explained, taking his seat. His long dark hair was pulled away from his bearded face by a leather throng.

"Sated then?" I asked, pursing my lips in a smirk.

Donncha picked up his mug and hid his pink full lips behind it he watched Siobhan dance. Her milky white skin flushed a flattering rosy hue that touched her trussed up bosom.

"For food, aye."

His insinuation was not lost on me. "May your union bring you joy and many children to come," I said, lifting one of the rare mugs of water to salute him.

Donncha unlaced the front of his tunic and slid the widening gap over his right pectoral. Under the curly black hair above a nipple of a blended peach and pink hue rested a shape just below the skin. Before I could stop myself and recall my manners and people's personal space bubbles, I reached out and ran my finger tip over the shape. The skin moved, but the shape seemed imbedded.

Padraig's loud bellowing laughter jerked me away, and I laced my hands in my lap. Donncha leaned back in his chair and watched me with glittering eyes.

"Your piece, Night's Child," Donncha said, making no effort to tie up his tunic. "It was implanted when I became sagamore. My nephew will make a good sagamore when I am too old and fat to continue. I would rather pass the burden on than have him bear the weight of responsibility the piece entails."

"Would it kill you to remove?" I asked, sobering.

"Nay, less of a chance with your Guardians here to heal me after," Donncha said in his deep burr.

I breathed deep. No wonder he didn't want to talk about giving up the piece.

I glanced up to his new bride. Siobhan was breathtaking. Easiest the most lovely woman in the hall.

"Tomorrow. I don't want to be insensitive since you were just married, but —"

"You need my Lycans and you need the piece. I will give it to you tonight if you defeat Padraig in a friendly round of flyting."

Donncha had an annoying habit of interrupting me. I *would* get what I wanted. What I needed.

"Flyting. Insulting one another?" I asked dubiously.

Donncha chuckled. "Not that simple. You trade insults in verse."

I laughed. "Like a rap battle?"

Donncha arched his brow and scratched at his neck. "Rap?"

He rolled the "R" and I scoffed. "Okay, you're on. Does it have to be me?"

His eyes glittered like a predator about to pounce. "Choose your champion," he said, sweeping his hand out to my table of companions.

Brass's dreamy amber eyes followed me back to the table. He was bent all the way around on the bench, he must have been eavesdropping. He stood when I approached and I cocked my head.

"Don't worry. We'll beat Padraig," I told him, sliding my hand into his.

He held it so I couldn't sit down and rubbed his lips together the way he did when he was hiding something. "Donncha will give us the piece. They want one of us to compete against Padraig in flyting. Amethyst, Slate, Scarlett, and I are out. Scarlett blushes constantly, Slate is quick to anger, and I do not have a sharp tongue. Amethyst is too diplomatic. We leave you to decide on who it will be; we'll be back in a few." Brass left them gaping as he led me from the mead hall.

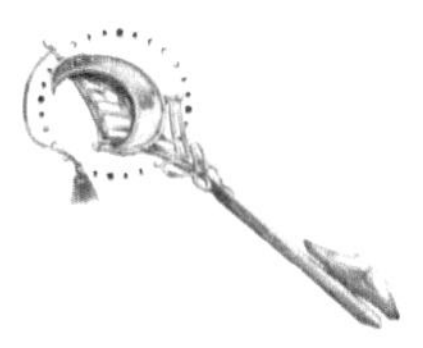

"By the Mother, you know I'm the mother of your children, right? Please don't kill me," I said, huddling against him in the cold as he led me back up the cliff to where the Ice Cliff Games were held.

The spans of land had been cleared so all that remained was the northern lights. Green and blue lanced through the sky as if the Gods had signed their names in the stars.

"I'd be hard pressed to forget something so unlikely." Brass chuckled. "Why do you always assume I am leading you to your death?"

"You'll have to start taking me to nicer places where death isn't imminent," I said playfully, bumping into his arm. He laughed nervously and stopped, turning me to face him. "You're being weird." I took his hands in my own, they were ice cold. "Frigga's sweet grass, Brass. You're freezing. We don't even have cloaks." I pulled at his hands to urge him back down the cliff, but he didn't budge.

"Scarlett. Love. Please, I need you not to talk for two minutes," he said in a clipped tone.

"Okay, Brass."

I knit my brow. He gave me a dry look and dropped my hands. I giggled and mimed locking my lips and throwing away the key.

He dug into the pocket of his pants and a lock of dark hair fell free from the knot at his nape. He glanced to me with a tight smile. The smell of pine needles and tree sap, blending with the cold.

He *felt* tense and skittish.

Brass kneeled in the snow and I slapped my hands to my mouth. Between his thumb and forefinger was a platinum ring. Brass held it up to circle the moon before my eyes. Two crescent diamonds framed a cushion cut Padparadscha sapphire.

"It's called *lotus colored*, but I like to think of it as a sunset. My day begins and ends thinking of you, Scarlett. My sun, the center of my universe."

He took my right hand slipping the pinkish orange ring onto my right ring finger. Our hands were shaking and it wasn't from the cold. Brass licked his lips.

"Coyote gave Butterfly my mother's ring. Spinel was very fond of you," Brass said wryly. "He said if you ever agreed to marry me, you could have the ring he used to propose to my grandmother, his wife. I think if you had let him, he would have been the one to try to give it to you." Despite his calm tone, his heart joined mine in its thundering as he waited for my response.

"Will that make either of you happy? Seeing me with the other?" I whispered. "It's all fun and games while we're in bed, but what about where we'll live or big decisions... what would Slate's children call you or... your sons call him?"

"Say that last part again, Love."

"Your sons?" I asked, my chest fluttering with the idea of him meeting Balas and Spinel.

"Mm-hmm. Our sons, Love." Brass's tone had dropped as his delicious lips lifted into a genuine smile filled with so much warmth I nearly sobbed.

"You didn't answer my question," I squeaked.

"What is wrong with father and dad?" Brass asked.

Air rushed out with my single laugh. So simple. Of course Brass would simplify matters. He was a nurturer, a tender. If my love were a garden, Brass was the one to weed it so it could flourish. Without Brass, I didn't know if Slate and I could mend things. He was the glue that kept us together. It was very strong glue.

"Nothing. You're crazy for wanting to marry me, Brass Regn. I *literally* sleep with your brother. Your grandfather and I had a... *complicated* relationship. Your aunt kissed me! Gods, I nearly forgot about that, and I had a crush on your brother."

"Coyote?" Brass laughed, and I frowned.

"Don't laugh. I've corrupted you — changed you for the worse. I make you a *worse* person."

"Are you working up to a no, Love?" he asked in a joking tone, but the tightness in his eyes told me he feared hearing it again.

"No. I mean, I'm not working up to a no, because it's a yes. *Yes*, you're absolutely crazy for wanting me and all my baggage and a first *crazier* husband. That all being said, there was never a point in my life since I met you that I could imagine it without you. I purposefully placed you in positions to keep you close... I know that makes me a horrible person because I was already married to Slate, but... if I met you first, I would've been with you. I think I'd already be married to you, Brass. Knowing what I do though, I don't think Slate would've ever known love without me. So when I put that access ring on your finger, it wasn't so you'd be my commissioner. I mean, yes, it was, but it was also placing you by my side once again, as long as you were willing to do the job. I love you, Brass Regn. I'm in love with you. You amaze me with your love and compassion and... Are you going to kiss me and stop me from rambling because I don't think I can stop?"

Brass jumped to his feet and cupped my face, pressing chilled lips to mine and laughing. Tears tickled the fine hairs on my face. I was so afraid to be happy. But, happy I was.

So happy, I thought I might explode into glitter and rainbows.

"Marry me, Brass. Don't listen to my crap about waiting until wars are over. I love you. I love you. Gods, that feels good to say out loud." I sniffled.

He laughed again, and I realized he had tears too. Brass kissed me again wrapping his arms around me so my neck so craned back to keep our lips touching.

"I was falling in love with you all over again as Scat. Even after you tried to drown me in the springs and nearly cut off my manhood. I can't promise you it will work, Love, but I know if we don't try we'll regret it forever."

The bright green light above us made me feel like I was in Oz and I would wake up to find myself on Tawny's air mattress the night after my college graduation. I wasn't in Chicago anymore.

"I don't need a big wedding, Brass. I just need you."

"The greater families are cringing where ever they are." He smiled against my lips and I sighed, feeling content for once.

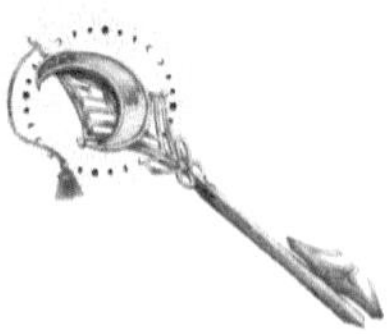

Back in the hall, reality set in and my stomach flip-flopped with anxiety.

"Who has the sharpest tongue?" Jett asked, glittering turquoise eyes watched over his mug.

"Tawny," I answered as Brass helped me onto the bench beside him.

"Hey!" Tawny feigned insult, but she broke into a wide smile. "Maybe, but Jett can quote poetry."

Her cheeks flushed an alarming shade of red as she let her dark hair fall in front of her face. Amethyst sat next to her ignoring the action. Jett's tan face had flushed with hers, and Quick couldn't help but snicker at the two of them as he shared a look with me. He stopped short and reached across the table dragging me back onto my feet.

"Freya's burly boar, I know this ring, Brass!" Quick shouted.

"You seem to be having a slight problem with your volume control. It's grandmother's ring. Scarlett and Slate have agreed to let me join their union," Brass said, plucking my wrist out of Quick's stupefied clutches.

"You have been carrying around this ring since the Purge War began?" Quick asked bewildered.

"Before. He asked Spinel for it when they came back for Keen's wedding," Slate rumbled agitatedly.

I furrowed my brow. "Before I met him?" I asked appalled.

Slate grunted, and I shot him a look.

"Come with me outside for a moment," I said, tugging on his arm.

He pulled it back wallowing in his gloom. "I am happy where I am, Torch."

The table grew silent until Quick cleared his throat. "Well, it is about bloody well time. Does that mean you will not let me keep her?"

"I'm here as long as you need me, Quick. Brass and Slate get me for the rest of their lives," I said, and Slate slammed down his mug sloshing ale over the table and stalked from the mead hall.

I moved to go after him, but Ridge placed his hand over mine from across the table. "Leave him. You have duties here. You can make it up to him later. Besides, the mood he is in, you cannot have him shifting on you."

Ridge's hazel eyes looked at me with empathy and I settled back at the table. Brass leaned into my ear.

"It's a reminder of how little time he has left, Love. Slate thinks he has months... maybe weeks. Now that he's got you back, he's angry about it."

"Jett. You do the flyting. Amethyst, you didn't..." It was an indelicate question but Jett had to know before going up against Padraig in case it came out.

Amethyst straightened, neither ashamed nor annoyed at my question. She nodded to a Lycan man with long strawberry blonde hair and freckles across a wide cheek bones. When the man smiled, his leaf green eyes twinkled with merriment. He looked like he had a good sense of humor and loved to laugh. He bore an uncanny resemblance to the sagamore's gorgeous bride. The man was probably her brother.

Jett's face had gone completely slack as he looked across the table, first past her at the red-haired man then at Amethyst. She met him levelly with her big, dark, captivating eyes.

"I thought you were dead. Cherry left me to have our son in comfort, which I don't blame her for, but I was lonely," she told him plainly.

Brass was rubbing his lips together furiously, and I knew there was more to it.

"You punch me... and Tawny after Cherry gives her blessing. Taking Tawny to bed to back it up —"

"Jett!" Tawny cried face a dangerous shade of red.

"Tawny?" Quick laughed, doubling over.

"You had an affair, Jett. It only ended days ago. You don't have the excuse of not knowing what you were doing, it was after you were with Tawny and Cherry," Amethyst said ignoring the fact that Tawny sat next to her, looking like she wanted to die.

Quick clapped a hand over his mouth. "Frigga's sweet grass, the night Scarlett was attacked. You two —"

"Shut up, Quick," Jett growled through clenched teeth.

Brass had obviously known the extent of the affair, looking the least surprised out of all of us. Ridge had gotten up to refill is mug though a pitcher sat at the center of our table.

"I'm not upset you did it, Amethyst. You didn't tell me. Did you plan to? What is his name? Does he know about me? Does he know I've returned or has he been visiting you at night while I bunk with Slate and Brass?"

Jett grew more upset with every sentence. Amethyst watched with her regal expression never wavering.

"Everyone knows about you, Jett Var. Your deaths, *supposed* deaths, were all we ever talked about because we were in mourning. While you were…" she broke off, clearly upset.

Jett got up from the table and crossed to where she sat, opposite of Tawny, and took her hand in his as he squatted beside her. "I have been a right fool. A bastard of the worst kind. I love you Amethyst, but it hurts to be near you. I miss our daughter who looks so much like you. I can't say I'm not jealous. I don't like other men touching my wives, but I have no room to talk. I am begging you not to bed him again."

Amethyst wiped a tear rolling down her mocha cheek. "If you wanted to sleep with Tawny so badly, why didn't you just ask? You know we would've invited her and Steel to our bedroom. Cerise and I are more than willing to share."

Tawny groaned and slid from her seat, trying to slink her way out of the hall. Ridge intercepted her, and I watched her leaden steps as she leaned on Ridge when they left.

"I didn't know I wanted to. Not really. I only want you and Cherry. That night in Glitra, we had grown used to seeking comfort in one another's company. We were weak. I'm sorry. It won't happen ever again. Promise me, Amethyst. Don't make me fight a Lycan for you," Jett murmured and gave a rueful smile.

"I never slept with him. Never did anything. He walked me to my longhouse when Slate, Brass, and Cherry left this last time and he kissed me at the door. That was it," she said, and Jett beamed at her.

"She slapped him for his troubles," Brass added under his breath, but Jett heard him.

He scooped Amethyst out from her bench and planted a kiss on her lips. "Don't even waste your breath. I am sleeping in your bed tonight. Sorry, Scar. I have duties of my own," Jett said with a salacious grin for his wife before darting out of the hall to cheers from the Lycans who could all catch their scent better than I could.

Brass and I sat across from Quick who was smiling so devilishly I was surprised naked Lycan women weren't stacked in a pile before him. He waved his fingers at us urging us to lay it on him.

"Beg," Quick said, looking roguishly at me.

"You? *Never*. Get over yourself, Regn," I said what Indigo had always told him, and his smile fell. "I'm sorry, Quick. I meant it to make you laugh. I guess that only works when she says it."

"It usually hurts when she says it, too," he said mostly to himself.

I frowned and walked around the table to sit next to Quick. I ducked my head under his arm and held him close to me.

"Please. Pretty please with a cherry on top. I'll be your slave for a day. Foot rubs, back rubs, head, *on your shoulders*, rubs…" That got a laugh out of him and he kissed the top of my head, wrapping his arms around my shoulders.

"I will get this piece in her name. Under one condition," Quick said, looking at Brass.

"No."

"Yes," Quick said smirking. "If I have to be lonely while you get engaged, I get her one last night."

"That's fine," I said, shooting Brass a look.

"You can be the one to tell Slate then," Brass said, folding his arms across his hard chest.

"Yikes. Crap. Okay," I agreed.

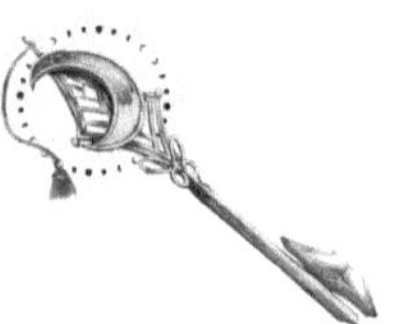

Lorcan and Cabhan wished us luck as Quick ascended the dais to face off against Padraig who looked like he could lift Quick into the air and catch him one handed. Quick was not a small man by any stretch of the imagination.

The music had tapered off and more barrels of ale were rolled out. The festivities would last well into the night. Padraig's mug was permanently attached to his ham fist and he wiped the back of the other of his meticulously kept blue-black beard. His soft looking lips curled in a mocking smile as Quick saluted his mug to him.

Everything about Padraig felt like an act, like he wore a costume for a show each day and nothing of what I saw was really him. Belatedly, I looked for a distorter ring and realized he'd have to wear a barrel binder to fit over those sausage fingers.

"Try not to worry so much, Scarlett."

Brass wound his arm around my shoulders and I laced my fingers with his. Sleeping with Quick offered me the comfort I *needed* for the last couple months. Brass's intoxicating cinnamon scent and strong arms that I melted in offered me the comfort I *wanted*. There were few things I wanted more than to tear the clothes from his body and run my tongue over every inch of him. Unfortunately, getting that piece was one of those few things.

"Have I ever told you how much I enjoy your imagination, Love?" Brass whispered against my ear.

I crossed my legs and uncrossed them. That was not the cure for what ailed me. Brass's chuckle reminded me of what I was doing there.

"Scarlett, Love. They know you sleep with Silver at night. It's all in good fun," Brass warned me.

I groaned as a hush fell over the mead hall. Quick gave us a wink as Padraig held up his mug to Quick and drank.

"Slate and Brass have all had a piece of her ass
except for the eunuch she sleeps with.
So tell us true, what is the matter with you?
It is rumored your staff is a pith."

"Pith?"

"Spongy part of a plant or animal," Brass explained.

"That's not so bad."

"What if you're Silver?"

I could see how insulting Quick's manhood would be unusually upsetting during these times. Quick smiled and saluted Padraig with his mug then drank deep.

"A eunuch you say?
When it is you who is gay,
As if I have not caught you staring."

Quick gripped himself towards the crowd with a lewd expression making several of the women catcall and laugh. My eyes widened.

"He really is gay, isn't he?" I asked Brass in a hushed tone.

"You're just now noticing? It's common practice to insult sexuality and use toilet humor. I don't think Padraig's *out* if you catch my drift." Brass smirked.

Padraig's drank looking at Quick down his aquiline nose and pasted a broad smile on his face.

"Leach, shover, Grar Dyr's manhole cover,
Prettier than a bitch doubling as a drainage ditch.
With all the vigor of a duffer.
Is it any wonder your brother uses you as a fluffer?"

"I did not notice that gem before," Aoibhe said, slicing through the laughter and jeers.

I blinked at her. Lorcan, Cabhan, and Blathnat had slid along the table to sit at the end with us. She nodded her head of inky locks to my ring the color of sunset.

"Oh, Brass gave it to me," I said, returning my gaze to Quick and Padraig.

"You are to join their union in the Guardian way?" Lorcan asked Brass.

I barely heard Brass's response as Quick drank and took his turn.

"Fat with a mother who must have been half naked mole rat. Prattle on annoying as a buffalo gnat, I welcome that. Quail at, rail at, but you will only fail at what you play at. Until I splat that, you overgrown house cat."

I laughed and covered my mouth. Padraig's smile looked a bit more authentic.

I turned to Brass to see if he'd heard Quick's rebuke and found Cabhan and Lorcan had left us, but the women were laughing.

"Where are your children?" I asked Aoibhe.

"In bed, their cousin is too young for flyting so she watches over them for me in exchange for my beadwork. I teach her so she has a skill to trade." She smiled and looked back to the dais.

"Baby brother, no power or lover. Shit of smell and shit for brain cells. The Mother should have smothered you, one after the other."

Padraig singled out Brass and my fury blazed. Blathnat squeaked a cry, and I saw smoke. I was on fire. *Sugarfoot.* The table burned where I sat and I got to my feet.

"Love. You okay?" Brass asked in a hushed tone not trying to worry anyone else about the human inferno that stood inside what was essentially a tinder box.

Padraig and Donncha spotted me and their eyes widened. Siobhan looked like she wanted to dance with my flames, her green eyes wide with wonderment.

"Have something you want to say, girly?" Padraig's voice boomed across the hall.

Quick saw I had gone full elemental and leapt from the stage to my side.

"I didn't mean to," I whispered my voice echoed inside my flames before being sent out to their ears.

"Mother's children, you are arresting." Tadg spoke to me for the first time since our initial greeting.

His adoration wouldn't win me any favors with Caolan. He looked younger gazing down at me despite his silver pulled back hair. His expression mirrored Niall's who sat beside him on the dais. Niall, Lorcan, and Cabhan had seen me in my elemental form before.

"Wrap it up, Silver," Brass said from behind me.

Quick licked his lips and nodded.

"Tongue as sharp as a butter knife. In your fantasy life, you are wife. End your strife. My words are the elixir of this quality life."

Padraig stared at Quick as the hall waited on bated breath. He lifted his mug to his pink lips and drank deep, his Adam's apple bobbing beneath his manicured beard. Before he lowered his mug, Donncha laughed.

"Such a boast, Silver Regn," he said, clapping, and the room broke out into laughter. "Stow your whist, Second. Come get your piece," he teased.

I slowly winked out and sat back down feeling shaky. "Quick and Brass can handle it."

"I am afraid they cannot." Donncha nodded to the door of the hall.

Cabhan and Lorcan burst through the doors with a troop of men carrying baskets and jars. For a horrifying moment, I thought they were attacking us. Brass placed a hand on my shoulder smiling.

"It's a Blackening," he said, smiling.

They'd roused Jett, Ridge, and found Slate from where ever he was off punching rocks. They were all smiling.

"Seeing as your bride is recovering from a birth, we will spare her. Unfortunately for you, Brass. You will be doubly insulted," Donncha said with a loud cheer.

The Lycans exploded into movement and Brass was yanked into the clear aisle between the tables. His shirt was stripped from him as he laughed.

"Oh no, my molasses," I muttered as they dumped the jars over his head and chest.

Flour, feathers, and dirt was mashed into the molasses making him look like a giant dirty chicken. Aoibhe and Blathnat each took one of my arms and forced me forward as they held our heads and forced our lips together. Brass laughed at the face I made as we came apart. My lips and nose covered in his muck.

"To the tree!" Niall called joining in the festivities and hoisted Brass up with the other Lycan men marching from the hall.

"Do they always do this?" I asked Aoibhe.

"They did my father last night after you left the hall. They do it to us all unless the women are not the kind who would appreciate it." She nodded with a smile to her aunt Caolan who watched Tadg join the men outside.

Donncha waited for me at the dais with Siobhan. Aoibhe and Blathnat joined me as he handed Siobhan his discarded shirt to reveal his curly hair covered bulkily muscled chest.

"Get on with it," he said, taking a swig out of a skin I assumed contained something harder than ale.

I gave him a reassuring smile as I placed my hand over his skin with the misshapen form underneath it. I wouldn't lie about it not hurting, it would. I *called* a blade of air and made a shallow incision along the side of the shape. Blood spilled over my fingers; it was thin from all the drinking.

It was lodged. I couldn't wiggle it free. I used a bar of air to pry it from the muscle that had formed around it. Donncha gritted his teeth as a sickly wet sound came from inside the cut. Acid churned in my belly as his skin shaped around the piece as I pulled it from his skin. I gagged as the skin closed with the removal of the piece and Donncha's grunt of anguish. I healed him immediately and washed his blood from the piece.

"Come. We will walk you to the longhouse," Blathnat said offering me a rosy-cheeked smile and with her the skin Donncha set on the table.

SLATE

"Leave them." Jett gave an arrogant grin as Brass was passed on to Niall's shoulders.

I grunted but ignored them. I stalked the undulating dirt path to her longhouse. If Quick was going where I thought he was going, I was putting a stop to it.

Before I entered the house, I could hear the music. Hide covered chairs, a dining table, and tapestries hung in the unlit front room. Screens separated the single long narrow room and the bedroom; she had all the comforts of home. Thick squat off-white candles were lit giving off a vanilla aroma. A fireplace to the left made up of stones that built the larger longhouses blazed.

They were laughing. I should not feel like a peeping Tom with my own wife. I stood behind the screen as she placed Quick's hands on her hips and began to sway.

"Dance with me, Silver Regn." Her gravelly voice shouted over the lyrics and she sung to him.

She wore Quick's loose white linen shirt and nothing else as she danced barefoot with his arms around her waist as he threw back his head and laughed. Quick did not have a problem matching the way her body moved against him.

"You are drunk."

Her high cheekbones rounded as she gave him a smile full of mischief. "I haven't been drunk since... Slate's wedding to Amber when I was still with Chris. Cut me some slack. Is that how you dance? Show me your moves, 'Quick' Silver! Oh Gods, we missed Tawny's twenty-second birthday!"

"Oh, I have got moves, Natt. You cannot handle these moves."

Quick grabbed her... *his* collar and pulled her close before spinning her around. She laughed as he pulled her arms up around his neck as he wound around her waist, bunching his shirt in his hands. I sucked in a fortifying breath. I should not have been in the shadows while they practically made love in front of me.

The song changed and Scarlett turned around in Quick's arms and pushed his shoulders before starting to sing again.

She swayed her hips until she was low to the floor and Quick took off his shirt and threw it at her face. She fell back laughing, and he scooped her up under her arms to set her back on her feet. I caught sight of where her long tan legs curved to her supple backside. She was not wearing under garments.

She walked over to the bed and turned down her device on the nightstand. Quick undressed as he filled the copper tub that stood next to the Arctic fox fur rug by the fireplace.

"Is Brass still in one piece?" she asked, pulling his shirt over her head and tossed it on the floor.

Her caramel waves fell down her bare back. Quick walked to her side and handed her a thin thistle robe which she took with a small lazy smile before slipping it onto her bare shoulders. It had been months since I had seen her completely undressed without the distortion ring on and Quick had acted as if he saw her nude daily.

"He is. The same cannot be said for your husband. He is sexually frustrated." He laughed.

My anger simmered until Quick stepped out of his undergarments and got into the bath. My anger flared.

Scarlett cocked her head, but crawled into bed leaving the front of her robe open as she placed the plastic gadget against her breast. She let out a little groan as her milk spurted into the container. It was a myopic device for nursing, I realized.

"I know the feeling," she said wryly.

"I offered my services," Quick joked, and she rolled her eyes.

"Right. I'll sleep with my sister's husband because that is so in character for me."

"You slept with my grandfather. Brass forgave you for that. Tell me, for future purposes, what was it like making love to a man four times your age?" Quick cupped his hands in the water making the water squirt to the opposite side of the tub and she made a face.

"Don't be a cache hole."

"I am serious. I will likely inherit those genes and if Indigo leaves me to become Sterling's second wife, I need to know if I will be able to handle the Vigrid champions I will undoubtedly be bedding."

Scarlett's good humor faded, and she set aside the device and covered herself before sliding off the bed. She let the robe fall to her feet and *calling* his shirt back into her hands to tug over her head. She walked to the bath, turquoise almond eyes glassy as she slid her legs into the tub and sat across from Quick.

"I know what it's like to sleep with someone to hurt someone who hurt you. If Indigo slept with Sterling, it wasn't to hurt you, Quick. She probably thought you were dead. If Ash slept with her, it's not because she wanted to. Sterling could hardly stand it when you two were together, you're crazy if you think he'd be okay with Ash doing it," she said softly.

"What if she has married him?" Quick asked.

"She wouldn't." Her eyes searched his face before she dunked her head in their shared water and wiped her hand that wore the ring Brass gave her over her face to her narrow chin.

"You should not be in the bath with me. This is not Disir, Scarlett and you are drunk… and I want to hurt her," Quick said in a low tone.

Scarlett's too full lips curled as she floated nearer Quick to rest her palms on his bent knees and my hands balled into fists. "You never would. That is the only reason I can so inappropriately climb into this bath. Come to bed, Quick. I owe you a massage."

She stood. The white shirt clung to her skin so nothing was left to the imagination as she climbed out and Quick followed, using a towel to dry himself before going to his pack and pulling on his boxer briefs. Scarlett switched back into her robe and set his shirt on a chair before the fire before getting a jar out of her pack and gesturing for Quick to lay on the bed.

He laid down on his stomach and I started as a hand rested on my shoulder. No one snuck up on me. It was the second time it had happened it two days.

Brass had washed off all the molasses and grit. His eyes looked golden in the firelight.

... He wants to fuck her...

Brass inclined his head and nodded to them again. The music played softly in the background as she straddled his hips and began to rub her hands along his back. Quick's hair, which was meticulously styled every other day, was drying in a disheveled manner. I knit my brow. In all the years I had known him, he never let anyone touch his hair or see it out of place.

Scarlett's hands slid over the black jagged Celtic tattoos that covered the entire left side of Quick's body on the front as well as the back. Quick made a choked sound and Scarlett cooed softly to him.

"I took it from her room when we stayed there," she whispered to him.

"Fuck, Scarlett. What are you trying to do to me? It smells like Indigo, honey and freesia. *Fuck*. It was easy not to bed another woman because you were with me, but now you will sleep with Brass and Slate and I will be alone," Quick said in a thick choked voice.

She slid off his back and sunk down against the pillows pushing her robe between her legs and parted them. "Come here." She beckoned with her hands and Quick weakly crawled between my wife's legs where she cradled his head against her breasts.

"Fuck you, Scarlett. Are you purposely torturing me with her?" Quick wrapped his arms around her waist as he wiped salty tears on her robe.

She stroked his hair and kissed the top of his head. "Hate me all you want, Regn. You'll hate yourself more if you sleep with some hussy because you're lonely. I'm here. I'll stay here. I wish someone had done this for me when I was at rock bottom. When all I needed was affection. If you want me to withhold myself from Brass and Slate until we get

Indi back, I will. I'll swear you a blood oath right now. I love you, Quick. I want you and Indigo to be together."

"Truth." Quick sniffled and rubbed his face against her robe which happened to be where her breasts were. "You are a khoraz, Scarlett. So is Slate. It is a miracle you are not tearing your clothes off as it is. I would not do that to him or Brass. Spinel tried to do this for you, but it was not in his nature to be platonic."

Brass smiled at my side as did Scarlett as she stroked Quick's head. "If he was fifty years younger, maybe I could have had a third husband," she joked, and Quick strangled out a laugh.

"That old devil. I knew he must have had some secret talent in order to get all those younger women. Are you going to answer my previous question?" Quick rested his chin on her ribs and she used her thumbs to wipe his tears.

Her lips curled, and she quirked her brow. "He was a very good listener and had a wealth of knowledge he didn't mind sharing. He didn't let me make stupid choices. I got so sick of making decisions as Ash's Second, it was nice to relinquish control to him. He also had a very talented mouth." Quick chuckled, and she licked her lips. "I'm sorry, Quick. I know the only reason they went after him was because he was my lover." She sighed and averted her eyes.

A tear rolled down her cheek as her throat worked.

"Have you noticed that when you take a lover, it is part of the initiation process that they must fight with another one of your lovers? Brass *still* fights with Slate, Slate fought Ash and Chris and killed Peak, Chris fought Ash and Slate, Ash nearly killed Spinel. It is a serious gamble bedding you, Scarlet Natt. Ash will probably be killed by Slate too."

"You're not making me feel better," she said dryly.

"Oh, I was thanking you for never giving in to me. Though I wonder if it is worth a good death." Quick shifted, lightning fast, burying his face in her breasts and tickling her ribs as she squealed, trying to push him off.

"Gods curse you, Regn! I'm ticklish!" she said through her breathless laughs.

Quick quit his onslaught and rolled onto his back as she straightened her robe. Not once did their scents spike. There was a simmering attraction when two good-looking people were close, but nothing that made me think they would bed one another.

He tucked her damp hair behind her ear and wrapped an arm around her waist to pull her to him so their stomachs touched and she lifted her knee so he could slide his leg between hers. His chin rested on her head and she hooked her arm around his.

"Goodnight, Scarlett. Thank you."

She shifted her head to look up at him through slitted lids. "Activate your bond, Silver. You're not going to bed anyone. I promise you won't regret it."

Quick looked down at her and cupped her face. "Do it for me," he whispered.

She worked her mouth, and I felt her emotions blossom in my mind. Her EH rune activated. She took her own hand and pressed a kiss to the tiwaz rune over her ring finger and Brass sucked in sharply, she was letting us know she wasn't bedding Quick. Love and warmth and longing stemmed through our bonds. Scarlett took Quick's hand from her waist as they locked eyes and she pressed her lips to the EH rune he had with Indigo on their rings fingers.

I could smell the salt of his tears before he buried his face in her hair.

Brass brushed my arm and nodded back to the door. Scarlett was using her *calling* to blow out the candles as the song about star-crossed lovers played on her speaker.

EIGHT

"We could douse them with ice water." Brass's smooth deep voice roused me from my slumber.

"Fire," Slate rumbled.

"She'll just absorb it. Ice water is better," Brass reiterated.

Quick chuckled, and I struggled to open my eyes. By the Mother, I was hungover. What was in Donncha's skin? I vaguely remembered forcing Quick to dance with me and climbing into the bath with him. He had cried most of last night. The first time since he went to rescue Indigo and Ash had carried her off.

The furs were drawn up over our lower halves, but Quick and I slept in our usual position which may have been a bit too intimate for Slate and Brass's eyes. Quick's hands slid from my waist and I rolled onto my back.

Slate and Brass stood over my side of the bed fully dressed and I knit my brows at them. "Gods, what time is it?"

"Early. You drank much last night," Slate said matter of fact, and I nodded.

Quick touched my elbow and stilled my roiling stomach and cured me of my headache. "Thanks," I said in a sleep thick voice and turned to him.

Quick's hair was more disheveled than I'd ever seen it other than when he first came out of Disir. I laughed and ran my hand over it to smooth it down.

"Gods be good. Do not let my sons inherit your brother's nest of hair. I'm guessing Indi agreed to marry you before seeing your hair like this."

Quick gave me his patented panty dropping smile, and I returned it. "*You* look ravishing as always, Ms. Scarlett."

"Why thank you," I said playfully, and heard Slate's growl begin in his chest.

"I hate to leave you to the figurative wolves, but I fear I have reached the end of their patience," Quick said rolling onto his knees and pressing a kiss to my forehead before sliding off the bed in nothing but his navy boxer briefs.

I sighed. I could see how it would be an issue. I had activated my bonds last night so they would know without a doubt nothing ever happened with Quick and me. Quick dressed as Brass took his spot and I scooted up to lean against the headboard.

"Look what I got from, Donncha," I said, shimmying my shoulders as I held up the seventh stone piece on my silver chain around my neck. "While you two were off doing manly things, I got the last available piece." I beamed at them and Brass pulled me over on the bed so Slate could sit next to me.

"So you drank in celebration?" Brass asked, and I nodded.

"It has been a long time since I've gotten good and drunk," I said defensively and let the stones drop between my breasts.

"Thanks for the massage," Quick teased before leaving and took the jar of Indigo's lotion with him when he left.

My face heated as I sat between Brass and Slate. "He had a rough night," I said, folding my hands in my lap. "I was trying to cheer him up."

"We didn't come here to talk about your and Quick's newfound affection for one another," Brass started. "It will take a few days for the

Lycans to rally their people to travel so we are going to make sure deliveries are taken care of."

"What?" I asked, sitting up and looking at each of them in turn. "You're joking. You must be joking. I just got you back and now you want to leave?"

Fury raged in me. I shrugged off their hands in their attempts to keep me in bed and slid down to the foot of the bed and crossed the floor to the tub. It was still filled from Quick's rinse off last night so I began to heat it.

If they left, that meant they would go to Thrimilci.

"You activated your bonds last night," Brass said with a hint of humor.

"And you're Brass Regn, the mind reader. I think my feelings are fairly transparent on the matter," I said, lighting the candles in the room with a lance of fire that came from my finger tip and wound around the squat vanilla candles.

"Was that sarcasm? You will have to explain it to me, I am not that bright."

Slate got up from the bed wearing a woolen tunic that ended over his trim hips still undone so his bronze chest shone from within. I returned my gaze to the rapidly heating tub. My own particularly insane brand of jealousy welled up over me like a tsunami before it crashed.

"Well, I only married you for your pretty face so I don't expect much."

We hadn't spoken about Mirage or his time at the khoraz brothel. For him, it was this past winter. For me, it was a couple weeks ago. I wished I was past it.

He stood beside me and ran his fingertips along the swell of inside my breast. I shifted to remove his finger.

"What about me?" Brass asked, rolling to Slate's side of the bed.

"You're pretty, too."

Brass seemed proud of himself for coaxing a smile from me. "She married Rikke," he said dubiously, "I didn't see that one coming."

Mirage had married the Wemic scout. The black panther hybrid was a good man, and I begrudged Mirage her happiness. If I ever saw her again, it would be too soon.

"Mirage? That is what is upsetting you?" Slate scoffed.

My insides boiled, and I shot him a look that could curl paint. *Upsetting me.* I sniffed. Slate grabbed me by a fistful of my hair and spun me around. My robe fell open as I reached for his wrist. Internally, I was thanking Amethyst's foresight in helping me to do some routine grooming. A muscle in his jaw leapt as he clenched his teeth leaning me over the tub.

"Torch. I am only going to say this once —"

"Don't tell me —"

"You jealous creature —"

"*I'm* jealous?"

"You are the only woman, my mate, future mother of my bairn. Torch. *Everything.* You are everything, without you I was lost. Would be again," he growled.

"You seemed to find yourself just *fine* when Scat came along," I snapped.

Brass chuckled from the bed and Slate lips quirked. "You *are* Scat."

"Yeah, but you didn't know that," I rebuked.

"Gods be good." He looked to the heavens. "You are an infuriating woman!"

I opened my mouth to argue, and he slanted his mouth over mine. My hands dropped from his wrist and slid up his chest as I deepened the kiss. It was like attempting to climb a mountain naked. I bounced on the ball of my foot and used my arms locked encircling his neck to wrap my legs around his waist. Slate's growl sounded like it came from deep within a cave as he squeezed my backside in his big capable hands.

That was what got me into trouble in the first place.

I was that man's khoraz. I never saw his pupils dilate like mine until he had worn his distortion ring and his eyes were blue, not barghest silver. I was a ticking time bomb of lust and debauchery. My needs had not been met for too long.

He kept leaning lower and lower until I felt water against my backside and yelped. Brass chuckled, and I felt Slate smiling against my lips. We sunk down deeper into the copper tub.

"You're getting wet," I breathed.

"Are you getting wet, Torch?" he teased.

His kisses were deep, our whole bodies were involved in each mind numbing press of our lips.

"You can't distract me with your talented tongue," I said as he pulled me into his lap.

The water was dangerously close to spilling over the sides. "We shall see."

Slate slipped his hand between us and rubbed his calloused finger tips against me. My head fell back as I inhaled sharply. Gods, it'd been so long. I didn't want Ash to be the last man to pleasure me another day longer.

My damp robe clung to my shoulders as I straddled Slate's lap. His mouth was on my throat as I tried to keep from passing out from his skilled touch.

"By the Mother, this is strange," Brass said roughly from the bed.

Slate's teeth grazed my throat, and I curled my fingers in his wet hair as my insides coiled. His fingers moved faster against me. I expected pain since I'd so recently given birth, but there wasn't any.

"Give me your pleasure, Torch." Slate growled as he buried his face in my chest.

His voice did spectacular things to me.

"*Ah.*"

A low moan poured from me and I felt my let down. I couldn't stop it.

Slate and Brass both laughed as Slate pulled away from me and wiped his hand across his face. I slumped against his shoulder.

"Sorry. I can't control it. I felt them start to tingle," I murmured, puckering against his corded neck, strands of his hair stuck to my lips.

"You're falling asleep," Brass noted, getting to his feet.

I could hear him walking over the floorboards. He had caught his seed with his *calling* and sent it into the flames. Brass poured water over my head and with their combined efforts, washed me and brought me back to bed.

"You stay. I'll start looking over the supply claims," Brass murmured as he dressed.

Slate didn't even put up a token protest as he slid into bed with me.

After I woke up from my nap and Slate watched as I relieved my aching chest with the pump Katydid lent me. He rested his head in my lap as I worked.

"Happy, Torch?"

"I don't want you to go. I'm terrified that I'm too happy and something terrible will happen."

He rolled his head in my lap and looked up at me, letting me admire how handsome he was. I ran my finger down his scar.

"Hope, Torch. It is all we have at times. Luckily, I also have skill and cleverness to help." His mocking smile fell and his eyes softened to winter storm grey. "My heart... and appendages belong to you, Scarlett. I am back. Really and truly. I will never be with another woman as long as I live."

"What if you get sick of Brass and me? Or so jealous you seek comfort —"

He pressed a finger to my lips. "Never. Brass is my brother, we had many, *many* discussions about what we would have done differently. What stuck out most was our tensions over you when we could have been happy with you instead."

"Are *you* happy?" I asked him.

"Scarlett Natt, you have given me what I never dared to dream. I have a beautiful wife to have children with and I am the patriarch of a greater family. There is nothing left for me to want for. You have done that. If I had not met you, I would have continued my half lived existence until my death." He ran his fingers over my cheek and into my hair.

"Does that mean yes?"

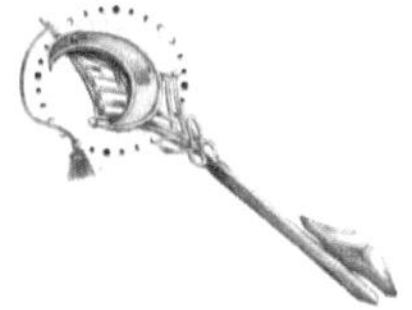

"But why white?"

I couldn't understand why I was being laced into a corset. I had to admit, it made my waist look fantastic... not to mention my new plump milk dispensers.

"Would you quit whining? You've slept all afternoon. Time to get out, get some fresh air and see the world. You look gorgeous. If my body does not bounce back like yours, I'll secretly feed you weight gaining supplements until your feet are too fat for your boots," Tawny said playfully as she held my hand so I could step into the thick skirts.

Amethyst and Aoibhe pulled the dress over my outstretched hands and began to lace up the sides. I ran my fingers over the lace long sleeves.

"This is lovely. Where did you get it?" I asked, looking to Blathnat who cooed to Aoibhe's baby snuggly wrapped in a carrier against her chest.

"'Twas Caolan's," she said in a baby voice.

It was sheer embroidered lace that fell over the A-line skirts and corset. Tawny sat me down in a chair and I knit my brows.

"Your hair is a hot mess."

"Jeez, thanks."

She smiled at me and braided it with her calling with Amethyst's help, leaving my fetishes in. They wove a lace ribbon through my hair wrapping it around the top of my head twice and pulled my thick waist length braid over my shoulder. Aoibhe had a basket full of flowers I hadn't noticed before.

I pointed to the flowers feeling speechless. Aoibhe wound a crown of white wildflowers and placed it atop my braids. I noticed the peonies in the basket and pointed again.

"What? I?" I broke off as the girls giggled like a bunch of drunken tyros.

Aoibhe tied a lace trimmed kerchief to the bundle of peonies and thrust them into my hands. "You are getting wed. Off you go."

I looked at each of them finally understanding what I'd missed. They were all dressed up, no apron-skirts, and softer fabrics than the usual wool. I patted my Yggdrasil necklace and squeezed both of my torques. Slate kept the silver charm, for luck, he'd said. He had traded our jade pieces; he wore the love rune in his hair again.

"Go on. Go on. Your husband awaits. Whoops, *husbands*," Aoibhe teased, giggling with Blathnat.

Their good humor was contagious, and I found myself smiling without any clue as to why. Slate hadn't tried to make love to me after our bath and I thought I knew why. He was letting Brass have his day with me untouched... for the most part.

So far, things between Brass and Slate hadn't changed. They were content to share me and didn't get in one another's way. They joked about our complicated relationship, not letting anyone else's jests bother them. Those who dared to jest.

We walked up the dirt path like a procession. White wildflowers with the occasional peony were looped in pine garland that trimmed the trees leading up to the cliff top. Lycans lined a flower petaled path, a curtain of strung together flowers blocked my view of the circle Slate and Niall competed in.

The cold didn't bother me. My powers were returning.

The other women wore furs, Aoibhe and Blathnat hid Aoibhe's babies inside their cloaks safe from the wind. They were all constantly having children. Another reminder of what I needed to accomplish before I could save the world.

Their traditional folksy music played; a cacophony of wind instruments fought against the frigid breeze to reach our ears. I blinked at Ridge who appeared from nowhere.

"It would be my honor if I could walk you down the aisle seeing as you are a Natt and we are related," he said, offering me a lopsided grin.

Despite the cold, it was a clear day with only wisps of clouds lazily streaming across the sky. I nodded in a daze. I couldn't believe I was marrying Brass. A thrill shot through me as I bit down on my lip and took Ridge's arm. We started down the petal covered aisle.

"You grew these flowers didn't you?"

Ridge gave me a mischievous grin as we reached the curtain of flowers. My heart leapt. Slate would be up there. I questioned whether I could say the vows in front of him. I swallowed hard.

"You love them?" he asked.

"Yes," I rushed out in a breath.

"Then smile, Scarlett. They are your husbands, not Karkinos."

The curtain parted and at the end of the path stood Slate. Quick and Jett stood off to the side, smiling like loons. The two smuggest men I'd ever met giving devilish grins. Slate's eyes found mine and his lips quirked.

Then Brass stepped into view. I never thought I would be one of those weeping women on their wedding day... but my nose burned the second I walked under the curtain.

This was not how I thought my trip to the Lycans would go.

Brass wore a white kilt with a white woolen tunic. An Arctic fox fur was pinned to his shoulders by silver brooches. His bearded anvil jaw was trimmed, dreamy amber eyes lifted as those glorious lips pulled into a bright warm smile.

As I walked with Ridge, the music took a slower tempo. Smiling faces blurred except for my family's at the end of the path. While I smiled, I cried. I blamed it on hormones. No one had a right to be as happy as I was.

Ridge passed my hands into Brass's and placed a kiss on my cheek.

Slate began to speak, and I started, jerking Brass's hands and yanking me out of my trance.

"Scarlett and Brass, know now before you go further, that since your lives have crossed in this life, you have formed eternal and sacred bonds. As you seek to enter this state of matrimony, you should strive to make real the ideals that to you, give meaning this ceremony and to the institution of marriage. With full awareness, know that within this circle you are not only declaring your intent to be hand fasted before your friends and family, but you speak that intent also to the Mother. The promises made today and the ties that are bound here greatly strengthen your union and will cross the years and lives of each soul's growth. Do you still seek to enter this ceremony?" Slate rumbled and I gaped at him.

He was performing our wedding ceremony?

"Yes," Brass answered and arched his thick masculine brow at me.

"Yes," I stammered out.

I had been married before. My husband was acting as an officiant. I'd never heard these words before. They were not the same ones from when Brass tricked me into not only bonding him with our tiwaz tattoos, but hand-fasting him. I hadn't even known what hand-fasting was then.

Slate continued and my tears had finally dried. "Blessed be this union with the gifts of the East and the element of Air, for openness and breath, communication of the heart, and purity of the mind and body. From the east you receive the gift of a new beginning with the rising of each Sun, and the understanding that each day is a new opportunity for growth."

The Lycans turned towards the east with his words.

"Blessed be this union with the gifts of the South and the element of fire, for energy, passion, creativity and the warmth of a loving home. From the fire within you generate light, which you will share with one another in even the darkest of times."

They moved again as one to face the south.

"Blessed be this union with the gifts of the West, the element of water, for your capacity to feel emotion. In marriage you offer absolute trust to one another, and vow to keep your hearts open in sorrow as well as joy.

"Blessed be this union with the gifts of the North, the element of earth, which provides sustenance, fertility and security. The earth will feed and enrich you and help you to build a stable home to which you may always return."

Slate finished speaking after the Lycans looked west and then north and back to him. Siobhan walked up with lace and white ribbon in her hands and gave us a megawatt smile as she passed the ribbons to Slate.

"I bid you look into each other's eyes. Will you honor and respect one another, and seek to never break that honor?"

"We will," Brass and I replied, and Slate draped the ribbon over our hands.

"Will you share each other's pain and seek to ease it?" he asked, looking down at our joined hands.

"We will." The response came naturally to me and Slate draped the second ribbon over our hands.

"Will you share the burdens of each so that your spirits may grow in this union?"

"We will." He draped the third piece over us.

"Will you share each other's laughter, and look for the brightness in life and the positive in each other?"

"We will."

Slate wrapped the fourth piece over our hands. "And so the binding is made. As your hands are bound together now, so your lives and spirits are joined in a union of love and trust. Above you are the stars and below you is the earth. Like the stars you love should be a constant source of light, and like the earth, a firm foundation from which to grow." He sliced his hand open, and I whimpered in surprise.

Brass sliced open my hand and then his own beneath the ribbons. Slate had taken my other hand and now both bled out in the cold.

"My name is not my own, it is borrowed from my ancestors. I must return it unstained. My honor is not my own, it is on loan from my descendants, I must give it to them unbroken. Our blood is not our own, it is a gift to genera-tions yet unborn, we should carry it with responsibility."

We chanted our blood vow in unison. I felt it tighten my skin as it settled over me. Brass could never marry another with the traditional oath now that we used blood. Slate put a hand to both our shoulders, and I felt the heat of his healing flow through me.

Brass didn't wait before pulling me to him and slanting his mouth over mine.

"Wife," he whispered against my lips.

"Husband," I squeaked back.

Cheering broke into our bubble and we parted smiling. I looked over my shoulder to Slate to find him checking out my fanny pack. He raised his eyes to mine and waggled his brows. The lech.

Brass and I trotted through the shower of flower petals until we reached where the path met the trees just before the village. Brass pulled me against him again and kissed me in a way that made me wish I wasn't wearing so many layers or that there weren't so many people around staring at us.

"I hear your mind, Love," Brass said in his smooth deep voice.

NINE

Garland hung from the rafters of the mead hall and each table had a beautiful centerpiece of snowy flowers. There was so much white in the hall I almost missed Tree-gold sitting on top of the head table. Two chairs were covered in more flowers and Siobhan snuck up behind us and removed our ribbons and ties the two chairs together as we entered the hall.

The band followed us all the way from the ceremony and continued to play as we sat. I found Slate and beckoned him forth. Brass waved him up to take the undecorated seat next to me. It wasn't like Jett's wedding to Cherry and Amethyst at all.

The benches filled and women began to bring out platters of roasted grouse piled high with *rumbledethumps* after a soup they called *cullen skink*. In spite of their strange names, I found it all mouthwatering. Last, but not least they brought out tipsy lard and toffee. The first a fruit filled trifle with a hint of liquor I couldn't identify and the second a boiled sweet.

I fed both my husbands with my fingers and they did the same for me. Caolan had done a superb job for our wedding feast.

I went out onto the dance floor with my new husband. The traditional Lycan dances incorporated a lot of choreographed dances in lines that involved the whole of everyone spinning around the dance floor. I traded dance partners dozens of times. Dancing with Niall, Lorcan, Cabhan, Padraig, Tadg, and even Donncha himself as well as Lycan men I had never seen much less spoken to.

Siobhan caught me heading to the privy. "Need help?"

I looked down at my skirts. "Sure. Thanks."

Siobhan held up my skirts as I fit into the privy. Her rounded cheeks were flushed from dancing, strawberry blonde braids had long since fallen from her head.

"Slate and Brass have never smiled. Now they cannot stop. They are dancing!" She chortled. "If I had not seen it with my own eyes…" She laughed again. "They are different men with you. The women are grasping why they never stood a chance. You know some tried to catch their seed. A barghest pup would be a great honor as would a talent like mind reading," she said as I stood, helping me straighten my dress.

Trust. The basis of any relationship and mine wavered for Slate on a day-to-day basis. I knew women had tried to sneak into their beds, but not that it was common knowledge. I wondered which women they were trying to steal my husbands from me and felt my insides boil.

"Your love brings out the best in them," Siobhan said as she looped her arm in mine walking back to the mead hall.

"Brass brings out the best in everyone, it's not me."

Her pouty lips split into an indulgent smile. Fluffy snowflakes had begun to fall while we feasted and they matted our hair, her head steamed from the heat of her body in the cold.

"No love, it is you. They were empty shells. Shadows. They walked through their joyless lives waiting for death to claim them until three days ago when you walked into our village and they vied for your affection with everyone else. Donncha would never say this, but he was a bundle of nerves about your arrival. Padraig has been giving you a hard time because of it. Niall has spoken of you for over a year."

Brass carried me off to the longhouse to the jeers of the Lycans and my own family. I wound my arms around Brass's neck giggling like an imbecile as he kissed me everywhere his lips reached drunkenly stumbling as we went.

They had decorated the longhouse with the wildflower garland.

We fell into the doors and tumbled onto the floor with a cry from me as I smashed him beneath me. Brass let his head fall to the wood panels and laughed as I pulled myself up his body, weak with laughter.

Slate was giving us time alone though I wondered if he fully intended on interrupting us. Four months in the world of Slate might as well be four years.

Brass ran his hands over my back and hips. "I never thought I would see you, much less feel you again, Love," he said in a hushed tone.

I was pulling on the laces of his tunic, in a slow methodical manner not quite believing he and I were married. "I was not sure you *wanted* to see me again."

"Are you tired, Love?" he asked, sitting up with me in his lap.

"Nervous? *Why do you tremble? Relax, Love. You can trust me.*" I repeated the words he said to me after we made love the first time in a mocking deep whispering voice.

Brass laughed and stood taking me with him. He tossed me onto the bed with a rustling of my many layers skirts and began to remove his tunic.

"You were determined to compromise my honor in that alley," Brass teased.

His thick dark hair came down to his pecs as more strands fell free of the knot at his nape. It was longer than I'd ever seen it, almost as long as Slate's.

"I knew that I wanted you, I just hadn't realized how badly. You were right about me being afraid to feel passion. You broke down a very dangerous door that night. *Mmm.* Slower," I purred, rolling onto my stomach.

Brass gave me a wry smile as he arched his thick masculine brow letting his tunic fall back to his shoulders.

"I'll make it worth your wile," I promised as I *called* my device over, scrolling through to find one of my favorite songs.

I was rewarded with his dreamy amber eyes sliding low as he heard the song begin. Its slow sensual beat was perfect for what I had in mind. It wouldn't be the first time we made love to its tune.

"I should have known it was you when you sang this song in the spring."

They'd caught me singing and dancing as Scat, I'd been mortified and angry at the time. Their scents had been like trumpets in my ears declaring their desire. I smiled knowingly at my husband.

"Be careful with that smile, Love. It's a heartbreaker." His voice dropped, and the candles whooshed out with his *calling*.

"I'll spare your heart if you strip, slowly. I want to see you *move*." I bit my lip as I waggled my brows at him.

Brass kicked off his boots and gripped the end of his tunic. I didn't think my eyes could get any brighter. His trim hips rolled as he moved, slowly pulling his shirts up over his hard dark honey muscles. Each one flexing as he teasingly swiveled his hips. As he pulled it over his head, his dark locks fell down to his sculpted shoulders.

Licking my lips, I watched as he let it fall to the floor. He ran his teeth over his lips and the heat rose in my cheeks. His eyes never left mine until he turned around and his corded arms moved to give me an optimum view of his sculpted back. He shot me a smoldering look over his shoulder that caused my insides to pull directly from my loins. There was something deliciously naughty about the whole dance with my first husband nowhere to be found.

He pushed his kilt over his hips, the arrow shaped muscle of his lower back seemed to point down to his taut backside. I bit my lip again and brought my eyes back up to his. When he turned around, those magnificent "V" muscles at his hips stood out against his hand that he had wrapped around himself.

I crooked a finger at him and his thighs flexed as he took short steps to me with his kilt sliding down thighs dusted with dark hair. His head fell back with a moan as I pulled him into my mouth.

Women in the myopic world had to wait a month and a half before being able to lay with their husbands after giving birth. It had been two weeks since we fell out of the portal from the sixth little known island and four months of growing my identical twin sons caught up with me all at once. I'd gone into labor on the shore, terrified I was having a miscarriage, but really, my womb could not accommodate the space needed for my boys and forced them out. I had barely looked pregnant before we escaped Sage and the Jorogumo in the portal, my body had gone through a frightening amount of changes in a short period. I did not look like I had twins two weeks past.

My hand gripped his hard backside to bring him close to me. My tongue swirled against his satin skin. His own hands gripped in my hair guiding the speed of my motions. Brass and I had not made love alone since I acquired the stone piece from the Merfolk six months ago. Not once after he caught me with Spinel and I'd broken his heart.

Was he thinking about what I'd done with his grandfather?

His dance made my lady parts scream in fury. He knew exactly what to do, though he could've done anything and I would've melted into a puddle for him. He hadn't even balked at my request. Brass was an alpha male, his confidence well-earned and deserved. Jett had said they were a pack of alphas with Slate making a good case to be alpha of the alphas.

Still, it nagged at me.

Brass's rough moan punctuated his clenching fists in my hair. I waited until I felt his hard muscled backside stop flexing and carefully pulled away rolling onto my back.

"You've done this before."

"What?" he breathed.

"With the patrons, right? I bet those women did *exactly* what I just did. That is, unless they waited stark naked for you to bed them. I could imagine Gharial waiting nude for you on one of Lera's velvet couches."

I rolled away from him and *called* the blankets over me, hearing the flowers in my hair crunch.

"You've got to be joking, Love," Brass said, incredulous.

I didn't answer. I felt sick to my stomach thinking of the women who had tasted him, been with him. Brass had been with well over twenty women in his short twenty-six years, which wasn't even half as many as Slate who left me feeling like I needed a shower with his hundred plus women. A half-life indeed.

I felt the bed bow as he climbed behind me and wound his arm around my middle. "Please. I don't want to be touched," I said sliding his arm off me.

"Not by anyone?" Brass asked.

It was so easy to forget the things we'd done when we were here away from it all, but he was going back. We'd all go back. Our past was there waiting for us.

"What do I have to do, Scarlett?" He gently pulled me onto my back and I looked stubbornly up at him. "You need to bedded. You are *non-compos mentis*. It has been too long. You are a khoraz — it is an unfortunate side effect."

His tone held no note of mocking which made me even more furious. He believed it.

"I'm in my right mind! *Dicks* are not the solution for everything," I spat.

"It has worked before," he said with a curl of his plump lips.

I growled at him. It did not have the desired effect. Brass was fast, he and Slate had both trained me to fight. We knew one another's moves well. His hair framed his face as he caught one of my wrists and we fought for the other. I'd only ever made love to Brass. He was a deeply compassionate man with more heat in his little finger than other men had in their entire bodies. Losing myself to him was the smartest thing I'd ever done concerning my love life.

He caught my wrist and held them so one of his big calloused hands gripped both of mine. Brass cheated, using his *calling* to lift my skirts as he climbed between my legs.

"I never saw the appeal of being rough, but now I know it is because I was never with a woman who enjoyed a good fight." Bass said throatily as he hooked his finger in the lace of my underwear and I felt it tear away from my skin.

Watching Brass act in a way I so seldom saw him do, did traitorous things to me. He slanted his plump defined lips over mine and I tugged his lower lip into my mouth to stroke it with my tongue. He made a sound deep in his throat and my body responded accordingly.

I said those two words I had used only once before with Brass. Then I begged him. The response in Brass was visceral. I loved watching my warm, gentle husband lose his reserve and use the raw strength I knew he was capable of.

Brass drove into me without preamble and my body arched on the bed as I sucked in a sharp breath. "I am so angry with you, Scarlett," he ground out.

I knew he was. He had every right to be.

"I'm sorry, Brass. I love you. I never meant to hurt you," I whispered as he moved, driving harder and faster into me.

"You pushed me away. Rejected my marriage proposal. Bedded the man who raised me. Acted like carrying my sons was a horrible secret and other days acted like it meant nothing at all," he said roughly.

His breaths came short, punctuated by rough gasps as his skin slapped against mine. His hand squeezed my wrists painfully as he grit his teeth.

"I hurt you?" I asked, feeling his anger and frustration through my empath abilities.

"Yes," he said, simply plunging deep enough to make me gasp.

"I'll never do it again. I swear it. My love is yours for the taking. Do with it what you will," I breathed.

His trimmed beard rubbed against my cheek as he moved. "You are not allowed to come, Scarlett."

Easier said than done.

My dress was bunched up around my hips and flattened beneath him as I tried desperately not to enjoy his loss of control. He so rarely let his anger slip. Disapproval was the most I ever got from him, but he needed to be angry. He needed to get it out so we could move past it.

Brass's chest heaved as he shuddered and I had to bite down hard on the inside of my cheek to keep from joining him. The pain brought tears to my eyes but did little to hamper how perilously I balanced on the cusp.

He released my wrists, and I slowly brought them down to hold him. He pushed off the bed leaving me bereft of his warmth as he walked nude to stand on the Arctic fox fur before the crackling fireplace.

I scooted off the bed and straightened my dress. Flower petals fell from my hair that we'd smashed during our interlude. I pulled the remaining flowers from my hair and set them on the end table before unlacing all the layers of my dress.

With my wedding dress over a hide chair, I walked to Brass where he stood with his arms folded across his chest.

He seemed molded of burnished copper in the flickering flames. I gently placed my hands on his shoulders and pressed my lips to his spine where I could reach it. Brass's chest rose and fell with a sigh as I trailed my kisses down over the curve of his backside.

"What are you doing?" he asked brusquely.

"Marking my territory. I want under your skin, Brass Regn. Husband, father of my sons, my most guilty pleasure," I whispered as I dragged my teeth over the back of his thighs and crawled around him to kneel at his feet. "I never should have gone to your bed. I knew you were Slate's friend, but I couldn't stop thinking about your lips made for kissing and how inviting your eyes were whenever you looked at me. I knew the night I manipulated you in Lera's office what kind of man you would be in my bed and I wanted it. I wanted *you*."

He looked down his nose at me, eyes gleaming. I'd hurt my sensitive Brass so badly. I began kissing up the insides of his thighs and everywhere in between as he stood there watching me. I ran my tongue along the corded muscles of his hips and up the silken trail of dark hair that gradually spread out over his chest. I took his hands away and placed his palms against my backside so I could step on my tip toes and kiss along his collar bone.

"I am so sorry. I was never ashamed of you. I only rejected your offer because you have always been too good for me, Regn. I knew I was in love with you both but married to Slate. I thought it would tear you two apart. I hated what I did to you. I hated that I wasn't ashamed to carry your sons, that I had to pretend they were his in order to save them. I would've done anything to keep your sons," I whispered.

I had. I gave into Peak and let him use me so he wouldn't force me to carry his own seed.

"I know. What you did to keep my sons, no woman should have to endure." He slid his hands over my curves and back down again. "You were not the first of the girls I was with that Spinel seduced. I was in love with you."

"Was?" I asked, feeling a crushing weight on my chest.

He sniffed as his lips quirked. "*Am.* I did not marry you today only to tell you I no longer loved you, Scarlett."

"It does seem uncharacteristically cruel," I said chuckling at my own ridiculousness. "Tell me, Brass. What can I do to make things right?" I coaxed and slid my hands down his back.

"Ash was the last man you were with."

I nodded. "Crimson?"

He gave a curt nod.

"I would say we could make another child tonight, but the prophecy demands I carry Slate's," I said with ludicrous jealousy flaring inside me over his last lover.

Brass looked back to the fire and let his arms go limp. I knit my brows as I turned his back to me with his fingertips.

"What's wrong, Brass? What *else* is wrong, I should say."

"I am sterile. This was the first time since I lost my fertility and I couldn't please you," he said, clenching his jaw shut after he spoke.

Internally, I groaned. I heard when Guardians lost their fertility there was a period of depression afterwards. It was a small price to pay when you received the powers we had.

"You told me I couldn't. I tore a hole in my mouth trying not to. I don't care if you can't have children, Brass. We have two already. My gods, how many do you and Slate think we're going to have?" Insecurity crept into me. "It's the first time I've made love since giving birth."

I understood now why he said it. My supposed skills in the bedroom were rusty and after having two babies — maybe I couldn't please two husbands.

Brass's brows drew down as he met my eyes. "Don't be ridiculous." He scoffed. "It doesn't feel real. You being here telling me we have twin boys."

"It's real. I have a vivid memory of the pain to prove it." I smiled, getting an idea. "Sit with me. I'll show you. Every second of every memory I have with them, I want you to share."

Brass allowed me to pull him down to the floor, and I straddled his lap as I closed my eyes and wrapped my arms around him so our heads touched. He smelled like cinnamon and morning dew over a field of wildflowers.

Quick carries me into the guardhouse with the Valkyrie Lily kicking at her beige robes as she throws more robes on the floor. Her tan brow and shaved head glistening with sweat as she tells me I'm going into labor. My pants are damp with my womb's fluids. The pain feels like blades are sliding down my spine and through my hips.

Tawny holds my hand as Quick cradles my head. She is sobbing for having slept with Jett. Tawny is having a daughter Ridge tells her. Quick and Jett are whispering prayers as Lily tells me my body cannot handle the twins.

I curse ever having laid with a man as I push.

Jett wraps a dark-haired boy in the torn robes and wipes him down before offering him to Quick to cut the cord with a dagger from his boot. I hold my first-born son, Spinel with a green band, Balas in blue. There is so much love.

*Q*UICK AND *I* IN BED, *it's the middle of the night and he falls asleep with Spinel on his chest while I nurse a fussing Balas.*

*Q*UICK AND *I are in bed again, Lily tells me the boys are already showing signs of growth and asks if their father is a big man. He says he is the same size. Jett tells me the boys look like Brass and Spinel and Quick laughs.*

*T*HE WAY *C*ORDILLERA *looks at my sons makes my heart swell. She is their aunt, but she looks at them like I do. She tells me the boys look like Spinel and trails off. She wants me to name our sons after him. Brass will hate it, I tell her. It suits them, she tells me and coos down to Balas.*

"Do you like that name little Regn?"

I HAND *over Balas and Spinel to Sparrow and Hawk as Cherry assures me she will take care of them with Katydid. I can't stop crying and Quick tucks me to him as we leave.*

· · ·

I DIDN'T KNOW when I started crying, but so was Brass. His fists are in my hair, kissing me as he crushed his arms around my body.

"Thank you," he said roughly, and I nodded unable to find my voice. "I need to meet them. *Gods.*" He groaned and lifted my hips to slip into me. "Curse you, Scarlett. No man stands a chance against you. I could not stay angry with Spinel. I knew Slate was in love with you and I took you, anyway."

Brass's powerful arm banded around my back into my hair while the other banded around my hips making me move in his lap. Shadows danced over his skin, catching on his tears. His lips were soft, so unbelievably soft and they're mine.

"I'm sorry," I whispered against his lips.

"Stop apologizing. I have been in love with you since our first kiss, I knew you would be dangerous for me and I could not stop myself. I love you. Cursed woman. I love you."

"I can't stop myself," I said throatily as I felt my insides coiled despite his curses.

"*Good.* Now you know how I feel," he said, pulling my hair so my head tilted back and he had access to my throat.

It was the first time of many that the venerable Brass Regn wielded his mind reading abilities as a weapon in the longhouse bedroom.

CHAPTER 10

JETT

"What the fuck do you mean she was gone when you woke up?" Jett shouted in stilted words.

Jett had never gotten into an argument with Brass. Not in all the years they had been friends. Brass was not backing down and Quick and Slate were gently pulling them apart.

"Did you get into an argument last night?" Slate asked, and Brass turned his molten gaze on Slate.

A lesser man would've taken a step back.

"It doesn't make any sense," Tawny said, wringing her hands. "She knows better than to do things on her own now. I'm positive she wouldn't go out on her own without one of us."

"We fought, but we mended things. She was not the one who was upset," Brass ground out.

Jett dry washed his face. His eyes burned. They had hardly slept; the sun was beginning to peek over the horizon. Brass had gone in search of Scarlett when he woke up not thirty minutes past and when he didn't find her in Slate's bed they roused the rest.

The gods cursed frozen land was too damn cold not to have furs on.

"Amethyst, go back inside. I don't want you catching a cold," Jett said, sparing her a look and instead of ignoring him, she listened for once even though the prospect of catching a cold when he could heal her with a touch was ridiculous.

"I suppose it is a foolish to question how she was able to sneak out on you without you noticing," Quick asked.

Brass slid his gaze to Quick giving him a dry look. "I knew she would want to say goodnight to Slate. I felt her get up. I thought nothing of it until I awoke and she hadn't returned. She wouldn't let me wake up alone. Not after last night," Brass insisted. "I can't lose her again." The air of hysteria to that single sentence made Jett's mood change entirely.

"She would not go willingly. We will check the paths from the longhouse to where I slept and look for signs of a struggle." The muscle in Slate's hard jaw leapt as he started out.

"What was she wearing?" Quick asked, guiding his brother back to the longhouse to dress him.

"Her wedding gown. All her blades are still in the longhouse."

Jett's stomach dropped. Scar definitely didn't go willingly if she left all her blades behind. Ridge put a reassuring arm around Tawny as he led her to the house they slept in. The women were starting to exit their homes to prepare breakfast for the tribe.

A roar tore through the dawn and Jett bolted in Slate's direction. Flashing silver eyes made him skid to a halt as the seven foot tall barghest hybrid's corded throat loosed another ear bleeding roar. Jett ducked his head involuntarily and covered his ears.

"Drugged," Slate rasped in his barghest voice.

Wickedly sharp horns stuck up from his scalp. He pointed to a tree. Jett leaned in to see three tiny pin pricks that could have been made by an insect. Slate gestured to a clawed hand to the dirt path. Some of the dirt was spilled over onto the rough frosted grass. Someone running could have kicked it up. Hardly concrete evidence of a scuffle. Then Slate held up what he'd fisted in his claw, a single white peony.

It was the things of nightmares. The worst case imaginable flitted through Jett's mind. The Stygians got her and now she was in Ash and Canis's clutches. Rational thought didn't come until Brass and Quick barreled into where they crouched looking at the imprint on the ground.

"That looks like her skirts brushed it. Like she collapsed," Quick said in a gruff tone. "This is my fault."

"What?" Jett asked dubiously.

Quick ran his palm over the trimmed hair at the back of his head. "She convinced me to activate my bond with Indigo so she would know I was alive. She thought it would give her hope... and prevent me from doing something precipitous."

Jett's head swam. If Indigo was brainwashed and told Ash and the others where Scarlett was, then he'd lost both his sisters.

"I will get her back," Quick rushed out.

"We knew. It was not a man who took her." Slate shrank back to his man size.

"You knew I activated my bond?" Quick asked.

"Who took her?" Brass asked, ignoring Quick.

"The Bjorn. It is their poisoned darts. A heavy dose of marawacian." Slate gestured to the ground again. "They shoved her in a sack. I can smell her blood and theirs."

Niall came running in his wolf form bright green eyes glittering as he sniffed the air and howled. Slate held up his hands to stop him.

"Do not be rash. We will get my mate back. If they wanted to kill her, they would have," Slate said in a surprisingly calm tone.

"They invaded our lands," Niall spat in a harsh voice.

"We already have a war to fight and it is not with the Bjorn. We need their numbers. Your two tribes have always riled against one another," Slate finished, and Niall howled.

Brass grit his teeth. "Careful, Lycan. I do not like where your thoughts lie. Scarlett has made her choice. She is ours."

Niall narrowed his eyes but backed down letting himself shift back into his human form. Tawny ran up with Ridge holding her belly and looked at each one of their faces in turn.

"What did you find?" she asked, her heart-shaped face tilting up towards them as she gripped Ridge's hand.

"The Bjorn took her. *How* did you know my bond was active?" Quick asked again.

"We spied on you with Scarlett that night," Brass said dismissively.

Tawny tried to ignore Niall who had run out of his longhouse in the nude. Her fair cheeks red from the effort. Niall's nostrils flared, and he whipped his head to her.

"So when are we going to get her back?" Tawny asked, fisting her hands on her hips.

"Quick and I will go. You will stay here. Slate has deliveries and Jett has a son to check on," Brass answered.

Jett protested and looked to Slate who hadn't said a word.

"You think you can convince them to release her and follow you to Elivagar's town?" Slate asked, looking at Brass.

"If we can't, she will awaken and make them sorry they thought to take her. They could not have known who she was when they took her," Brass said.

"You are both bastards. I never slept with Scarlett. You did not trust us," Quick interrupted.

Slate and Brass gave him mirrored wry looks. "A womanizer with a khoraz, neither of which had laid with another in months. You will have to pardon my skepticism. I would prefer if you refrained from bathing with my wife from now on," Slate growled.

Quick had the decency to look away. Jett looked to the heavens as he counted to ten. How much could one brother take?

"You are the Matriarch Vetr?" Niall asked.

Jett spun to them and held up his hands stepping in front of her. "No. Don't even think about it. You can't have her."

"Jett!" Tawny admonished.

Jett cringed. He hadn't meant to say that out loud.

Niall was hot tempered. Fair skinned as most the Lycans were with black curly hair down to his hips. Not many Lycans ever cut their hair. Jett supposed women found his roguishness attractive.

"You cannot catch her scent when she looks at me," Niall said in a deep brogue.

Jett squeezed his eyes shut. He was going to regret this.

"We've invited her into our marriage. By rights, she is ours to claim first. Unless she says otherwise." Amethyst had returned probably because of all the shouting.

Tawny was dumbfounded and touched her black eye remembering the sock Amethyst had given her despite her pregnancy. Amethyst offered Tawny her slender mocha hand. Jett held his breath. Gods be good, he thought.

Niall stalked off and Jett looked back at the girls who were walking hand in hand back to the longhouse Jett had joined Amethyst in. Silence fell over their group and Ridge ran his hand over his dark close cropped hair.

"Can I join you on your rescue mission?" Ridge asked.

"You'd be welcomed," Brass said, and Ridge nodded as Jett opened and shut his mouth trying to find any words at all that would comfort a father knowing his daughter was about to participate in a coupling of the best kind...depending on your stand point.

Ridge offered a tight-lipped smile and walked off using his staff as a walking stick.

Slate, Quick, and Brass stared at Jett. Quick shrugged.

"If she had let me, I would have."

"Be glad Steel is no longer here to see how you look at his wife," Slate said, watching Tawny disappear into the longhouse.

Jett licked his lips. "I could stay out here."

Brass rubbed his trimmed beard. "Slate and I agreed to share Scarlett because he preferred to know she would be cared for. His children, should they have any, looked after. What do you think Steel would want?"

"To fuck his own wife," Jett said without thinking.

"She won't marry you," Brass told him soberly.

Jett nodded distractedly as he started towards the longhouse. "Right. I better go check and see if they need any help."

Quick chuckled as he walked away and Jett cursed himself for an immoral rake.

Jett ran his hand down Tawny's tattooed back. She'd fallen asleep on top of him, her head of dark waves against his chest, her pregnant belly between his thighs, smelling of frosted Yuletide cookies and tasting twice as sweet. She'd been more confident with Amethyst than she had been with Cherry.

Amethyst ran her nose along his jaw as he shifted his head to her. "I see now why she is so hard for you to dismiss."

Jett gazed into those depthless dark eyes and spoke, but she pressed her finger to his full lips and her wide mouth pulled into a smile.

"Let's keep her. I know her and Cherry get on very well. She is less hostile towards you than any man I have seen her with other than Steel. I could grow fond of her. She is very easy to please." Amethyst smirked.

"Three heirs in one marriage won't work," Jett said, running his thumb over Amethyst's mocha diamond shaped face.

"Then Matriarch Vetr will be our paramour. She is already."

Scarlett's bond had flared to life at noon with Brass the day before. Brass, Quick, and Ridge had gone first thing that morning. Tawny had stayed all day and all night with little convincing from Amethyst.

The spitfire gave Jett someone to appreciate her pillowy breasts with. Amethyst had been obsessed with them.

"You'll be all right? You could always come with," he asked her again.

"I'll stay with Tawny. It's only two weeks, right?" She sighed.

Jett scoffed. Amethyst wanted Tawny to herself. It was only a matter of time before Scarlett won back her island and Tawny would leave them. She was lonely, but she'd soon have enough suitors to fill her days once they righted Tidings.

Amethyst guessed his line of thinking and cupped his face to kiss him. "Once we take Elivagar, all we have left is three more islands to check for Opal."

Jett sighed and Tawny stirred. "By the Mother, what time is it? Pregnancy is exhausting."

"Late morning. He's going to have to go soon, but you can stay here with me until the Lycans mobilize," Amethyst offered graciously.

Tawny rested her chin on the crease between Jett's abs and gave a lazy grin. Jett felt his own lips tug. It wasn't her special smile, but it was the one she gave when she was feeling lustful. She pushed herself up and Jett licked his lips unwittingly as her breasts swayed. Tawny straddled his lap as she reached behind her head and lifted her dark waves over a shoulder.

Amethyst reached up to run her thumb over a hardening kitten nose pink peak and Tawny flashed her that special smile. Jett nearly gripped his chest it was so stunning. He shifted her and her eyes widened fractionally as he slid inside her. He had no intention of doing more, but Amethyst sat up and placed her mouth where her thumb had rubbed Tawny an instant before. Her mane of sable hair fell across her back.

Tawny's arms fell from behind her neck and her head lolled. Amethyst had a skilled tongue. Her slender leg lifted and Amethyst slid behind Tawny. She ran her hands over Tawny's ribs and firmly cupped her heavy breasts as she kissed along her neck. Soft moans squeaked from Tawny's open mouth.

Jett let the girl's do their thing. Content to sit back and watch for the moment until he saw what Tawny had taken from around her neck. The auseklis portal key. The sigil of the Vetr dangled from the silver necklace next to her cheek now that her mouth melded to Amethyst's.

"Tawny, what are you going to do with the portal key?" Jett asked roughly.

Amethyst was guiding her hips to rock him inside Tawny and it was terribly distracting. Tawny blinked down at Jett.

"Hmm?" she asked and looked to the necklace in her hand. "Oh. Take it. It will take less time to complete the deliveries without having to wait for each one to open at their designated time so you can come back to us sooner. Ridge has one, so I won't need it for now." She sucked in sharply as Amethyst slid her fingers between her legs.

Tawny leaned forward and Jett lifted his head so she could clasp the necklace around his head. She managed to surprise him constantly. She trusted him. Amethyst caught his expression and laughed as she pushed Tawny forward. Her breasts smashed against his face and Amethyst took her place in his lap. Tawny laughed until she caught the expression in Jett's eyes.

"You can't keep me," she whispered, scanning his eyes.

"Give me what I can have then," Jett said, and pulled her thighs up until they framed his face.

They were all shit when it came to goodbyes. It lasted an eternity and a half before Slate and Jett finally started out. Tawny and Amethyst held each other as Jett left. At least Amethyst wouldn't be alone even if Jett felt a spike of jealousy at the two of them indulging in one another's wiles while he was away.

Jett eyed the fluffy white cat that trotted along with them, less of a cat and more of a Samoyed. Even Tree's stark white coat resembled the dog's.

"Tree goes with every month. I am surprised she did not want to go with Brass. He is her favorite," Slate rumbled as if reading Jett's mind.

Slate looked like a lumbering mountain beneath all of his furs. Scratch that, *Scarab* looked like one of the Minotaur covered in marbled black furs. Jett would have to remember to answer to Jawfish. Jaw for short while they wore their facial distorters.

Descending the cliffs was not nearly as difficult as climbing them. "How was Scarlett?"

Jett saw his lips quirk.

"Good. Brass said she was irritated and determined. Is Amethyst's bond active?"

"Hers, not mine in case Cherry's healed and feeling salacious. Though I may regret that since Tawny stayed behind." He smiled rakishly at his adopted brother.

"I do not think I can go to Thrimilci, even with our sons there. If I set eyes on Mirage again during this turn of the wheel, I will peel the skin from her face so she will have to project another's for as long as she lives so other people can stomach to be around her."

"That seems *hostile*. She didn't exactly force herself on you and we all told you what a bad idea it was." Jett rubbed his jaw, wishing he still had a beard to hide the horse face the ring gave him.

"You do not know how badly it still hurts her," Slate murmured.

Jett stared down at the snow, sliding every so often, his gloved hand keeping him from slipping all the way down. Slate taking back up with Mirage had shattered her. It's what drove her back to Ash, why she thought for one horrible moment that bedding that cocky bastard would make her feel better.

"You've forgiven her for Ash?" Jett asked guardedly.

Slate stopped dead and turned to him so abruptly, Jett's boots flew out from under him as he fell on the seat of his pants. His eyes flashed; the cold made his dark skin dry. He hadn't shaved this morning and blue black stubble shadowed his hard face; with the scar it gave him a sinister look.

"There is nothing to forgive. He spent two years trying to get her to lay with him and succeeded after tricking her. Not for a heartbeat did she enjoy herself, that is why she ran from him…back to me that very morning. Even the bastard I was, she still preferred me over him. I should have said goodbye." He turned and walked again, pulling his hood over his head. "She would have forgiven me if I had said goodbye."

Down at the bottom of the cliffs, a polar bear and her cubs crossed the ice. Jett had never seen polar bears before. He got to his feet to watch them, completely oblivious of their observers.

"If she slept with you, she's forgiven you." Jett scoffed.

The bears cubs kept lunging onto one another's backs playing. Garden variety bears, not the Bjorn. Slate gave him a wry look.

"We… did not. Your sister is a khoraz, her needs must be met. She can put her anger aside for a few hours, but it *always* returns."

Jett gave Slate's back a dry look. "You let Brass scratch that itch then? Aren't you worried he'll bugger her up again?"

"He lost his fertility while you were away. She is *my* khoraz. She will let me know when she is ready to welcome me back," Slate said without a hint of recrimination.

"Why did you leave her? Why not have Brass come with me instead?"

Brass losing his fertility was a big deal. Thank the gods Scarlett had Balas and Spinel no matter all the issues they went through to have them.

"You do not want to know. He would prefer not to meet his sons without her," Slate answered.

Jett exhaled gustily pressing his lips into a firm line. He'd always tried to be lenient with Slate when it came to Scarlett. He lost his mind whenever it came to her. From the moment he'd set eyes on her, the game had changed.

"Are you hoping she'll miss you or something?"

"Along those lines. You know what they say, absence makes the heart grow fonder. She will be —"

"I get the picture. She'll have missed you. Got it. That's actually clever," Jett said with grudging admiration. "Just how many kids do you plan on bestowing upon my baby sis?"

"A dozen. We plan to keep her pregnant until she catches on. Does she not look beautiful with all those soft curves?" Slate asked with genuine affection.

"She always looks beautiful. It's the curse of our family. Damn fine genes." Jett jutted out his chin as he smugly grinned at Slate's back.

"Tawny seems to be enjoying them well enough," Slate said slyly, and Jett shut his mouth tight. "How did you finagle the auseklis away from her?"

"She offered. I never asked," Jett said petulantly.

"That good, huh?" Slate shot him a look over his shoulder and Jett glanced away.

Discussing Tawny in bed was not something he would ever do with anyone outside of his wives.

INDIGO

My singing voice wasn't as good as Scarlett's, but my fellow prisoners were hard up for entertainment. The women caught on quickly, I tried to pick songs that wouldn't leave us feeling worse after we'd sung them.  Most of them couldn't carry a tune. Some of the other tribeswomen were speaking their first English words in Beatles' songs.

One of the Gorgon women hissed and our singing cut short. I hopped back in bed watching the other hybrid women scramble to hide, though no place was safe. I wondered what kind of male they would bring down and who would be forced with him. Some of the men were forced as they were and beaten until they submitted. I'd seen a dusky blue Merfolk man beaten until he couldn't stand and then he was dragged away leaving a trail of blood behind him. The Crathode woman he was supposed to lay with was shouting for him to do it so the beating would stop. Eight different tribes and one human made up sixty prisoners in the ice dungeon.

Footsteps approached. I rarely had a visitor outside of Ash. The Guardian Prime had healed me a few days past after my half-brother's beating. Ash's celadon eyes had been wild when he saw how badly beaten I had been left. Part of me thought my sister's former fiancée was trying to develop feelings for me to justify making me a khoraz, but so far, he'd never tried to touch me. I would have let him. I was drugged with a rousen/marawacian cocktail that left me devoid of emotion and leaden all day long.

He was still infatuated with Scarlett. He spoke of her often even though she was dead. Silver was alive though. I felt him far to the North through our bond. He went through bouts of utter despair to over-whelming joy. He was experiencing more joy as of late and I wondered if he'd met someone new. I quickly discarded that theory because I would feel it when he slept with her, and no woman could resist "Quick" Silver Regn for as long as he'd been happy. It was something else.

"Indi! Indi, answer me! Where are you?" It was Sterling's raspy voice that called through the dungeon.

"Sterling?" I sat up in bed. "I'm here!" I called, getting to my feet and hurrying to the bars so I could wave into the hall for him.

My mind swam. Showers were a luxury in the Beget Oubliette. I frantically tried to remember if I'd showered since Ash's last visit, if not, Sterling's heightened barghest senses would catch the scent of Ash on me and grow angry the Prime was visiting me while he couldn't. He might even be able to smell the rousen.

Sterling's violet eyes found me inside the icicle cell. His chocolate brown hair was even more disheveled than usual, his thick brows pulled together in distress.

"Indi! By the Mother, they told me you were at the Natt's. All this time?"

"I've been here." I cried in relief as he gripped my hands over the bars.

"Gods, did they hurt you? Did... did they touch you?"

He dropped his eyes blaming himself for my predicament. Maybe it was his fault, but I had to believe that the boy I fell in love with a decade ago had loved me enough not to want me in that hel. Sterling was going to shift or cry, his wide tan cheeks darkened. I raised my hand to his face.

"Can you get me out of here?" I asked searching his eyes unable to answer his questions without risking him losing it.

He seemed to snap out of it. "Cygnus is coming. He is going to let you out."

"Sterling, they're breeding an army. They're using these women to birth these monsters." He looked away as I spoke and I realized he knew about it; he knew it all. "Oh... Sterling," I said, feeling loathsome, and retreated to the metal bed.

Sterling shuffled his feet as he tried to keep me at the bars. "Indigo, I have nothing to do with any of this. Please believe me. I found out they were doing this the night before the Purge War started. They have been breeding them since we were born."

"Then free them. Use your *calling* and let them go," I said, standing with my blankets wrapped around my shoulders.

"No need for the dramatics, Indigo. You and your father."

Cygnus walked into view. He wore his green velvet Var patriarch robes with the golden tree of life emblazoned on the back. He was tall and broad like Jett and our father had been. His blonde hair had gone white at the wings and was carefully combed away from his square jaw. My grandfather had classic Var looks, as my father, Jett, and I did.

"Are they not feeding you, granddaughter? You have always been thin, but you are wasting away. You are growing a Haust son, you need to have your strength up."

His blue eyes glittered as he unlocked my cell and I stood frozen, touching the nix torque that rendered me helpless. It was so cold, pain lanced through my fingers to my elbow.

I looked to Thre'ik. I never thought I could be friends with a Jorogumo, but the crystalline spider hybrid was just that. She spread her pinchers and curled her human lips. I wanted to tell her I wouldn't forget her, that as soon as I got the chance, I'd come back for her.

"Are you coming Indigo or have you grown fond of the Crathode?" Cygnus asked.

He had a way of sounding like he was always in good humor but managed to insult you. If you got upset, it was your fault. You were overreacting. He had done it to my grandmother, making everything he asked or said seem perfectly reasonable no matter how outlandish.

I didn't answer. My slippered feet were moving before my brain registered what was going on. Sterling pulled me to him. He was an even six feet and several inches taller than I was, his lean muscled body held me firmly as we walked over the ice floor. I buried my face in Sterling's chest. My body was much weaker than I had anticipated. The few weeks of being malnourished paired with the drugging cocktails had taken their toll.

There were so many winding icy staircases, Crathode were everywhere. Ice stalactites and stalagmites met to form towering icicle columns. The Crathode had carved designs into the columns so the caverns were like one enormous shared home. The higher we went, the brighter the blue shone through the ice like a naturally formed stained glass ceiling.

"Here."

Sterling swept me into his arms and I didn't waste my breath fighting him.

My body jerked as we moved. My head swiveled around in confusion. Sterling had piled furs on me and I could barely see with the sun reflecting the snow. In a sled being pulled by four strong Norikers, Cygnus sat facing us with Cassiopeia in the seat beside him.

She made my blood run cold when her frosty eyes took me in. Her black furred trim on her navy matriarch robe rustled as we spend over the ice, brushing the curled under ends of her honey blonde hair. It bore the star inside the circle on the back. You could tell she was a Natt; blue eyes and fair skinned only came from Elivagar.

"Look who's awake," Cygnus said as my eyes adjusted to the brightness.

Sterling held me close to him and I began to drift back to sleep. One black cloaked Guardian with the silver valknut embroidered on the back held the reins while another sat on the bench behind us.

"This son you carry, they tell me it is Sterling's. Is it?" Cassiopeia asked point blank.

I couldn't remember another time she'd addressed me without Delta in the room. "I don't know," I said in a sleep thick voice.

"She was in season the first time we were together," Sterling said defensively.

"But she had lain with the youngest Regn — Silver, that night?" Cassiopeia continued with her inquiry.

"Yes," Sterling answered and glared at his grandmother.

Not many would stare down Cassiopeia Natt. She pursed her lips; lines were more defined around her mouth. Guardians didn't age the same way other humans unable to *call* the elements did, so while she was over seventy, she looked around fifty as did Cygnus.

"What will we do with you then?" Cassiopeia slid her chilling gaze to me, and I shivered despite the furs.

"She is *mine*. My bairn or not, she will eventually have mine. You have lied once to me; I will not have our deal reneged again."

Sterling's violet eyes flared as he snarled. Sterling was a Haust son, a barghest like Slate. He had claimed me and a bond existed between us that would last until his death. Barghests could only mate with one human, one for life. Slate had chosen Scarlett and Sterling had chosen me.

Lucky us.

"Relax, child. It is a legitimate question. Play with your toy but think before you place another babe in her belly. Your wife is a Natt," Cassiopeia warned.

They spoke as if I wasn't there. I had no say in my future. Diamond Natt wouldn't have cared who Sterling was with if she could be with Gypsum. The animosity between Natts and Tios went way back, the Sumar were caught in their sticky web. It was a miracle they let Ash be with Scarlett, but no one told Ash what he could and couldn't do.

"I can have two wives," Sterling told her, pushing my hair from my eyes.

She laughed. It had a cruel edge that made me cringe instinctively.

"I should think not. Natts do not share."

"Diamond will have to. I will not give up Indigo again and she is a Tio. There is no need to treat her like a peasant. Her children will be elementals."

"I will discuss it with Dahlia, but do not get your hopes up. You may keep her as your paramour. Give her a cottage outside of Mabon's heart, but for now, she comes to Valla," Cassiopeia informed us.

"What's in Valla?" I asked as fear spiked in me at the idea of going to the Straumr palace where Ash would have unlimited access to me.

My best bet was Sterling. I didn't know what Ash's end game was with me, but I suspected he was waiting until I birthed my son so he could take me and get himself an elemental child in his line. On the pleasure inducing rousen I would let him and love it.

"The war, dear Indigo," Cygnus answered. "Your cousin needs some incentive to surrender. Seeing you in good hands should provide him with it."

If I wanted to stay in good hands.

The threat hung there. He was supposed to be my grandfather. My father's father only cared about what others could do for him. I was a pawn in his game of chess, always finding the best way to use me. Sometimes, you had to sacrifice your pawns to win.

"There is a camp there. I will help you get cleaned up; you will have your own private accommodations. A hot bath, clean clothes, a large, warm meal..." Sterling soothed.

"*Whoa!*" The sleigh slowed as the Guardian in front navigated around one of the snow drifts that textured the land like waves frozen in time.

Two men, the biggest men I'd ever seen, held their hands up as they rose from behind the snow drift we'd dodged. The two Guardians jumped from the sleigh and came towards the men. They didn't look familiar, but anyone that didn't bear a resemblance to the fair skinned natives of the island of perpetual winter were pressed for traveling papers. Sterling had told me that before they'd taken me from the Var castle and put me in the Beget Oubliette, so I understood why we made frequent stops.

One had hair as black as pitch and deep tanned skin, with eyes so blue the sky would shed silver tears with envy. His look was spoiled by his weak chin and beak-like nose. Those eyes though, the fierceness behind them was undeniable. The second man was just as tall, with close cropped dark blonde hair that did nothing to flatter his long homely face and buck teeth. The cant of his jaw was one of challenge. These two big men were fighters and probably part of the rebellion.

Their coloring made them stick out like sore thumbs.

"Papers? What are your names?" The Guardian drew his long seax from his scabbard.

The man with long black hair reached into his pack and pulled out a sealed scroll and handed it over.

"Scarab and Jawfish," he said in a voice much higher than his broad chest would suggest.

The long-faced man scanned the sleigh and clenched his oblong jaw. He wasn't doing a very good job of hiding his contempt.

"Ice fishing?" the Guardian asked, looking over the paper.

"Aye. To feed our families," the black-haired man answered in the dialect of the people who lived on the northern outskirts of Elivagar.

"Does he speak?" the second Guardian guard asked, circling around the horse faced man.

"I do... when asked a question," he responded coolly in a scratchy voice.

"What is the delay?" Cygnus turned his head to look upon the traveling men.

The furs slipped from my head and both men went rigid. They recognized me, but I had never seen them before.

"You know these men?" Cygnus asked, noticing their reaction.

"I've never seen either," I answered honestly, but Cygnus looked dubious.

"Come. Take a closer look." Cygnus opened the short door of the sleigh and held out his hand for me.

I had washed yesterday. My plain woolen dress wasn't as rumpled as it could have been. Sterling had clasped a white cloak around my shoulders so I looked somewhat presentable even with my slippered boots.

The men's breathing quickened. I must know these men if my presence caused such a reaction from them. They were head and shoulders taller than I was when I stood before them. Sterling held me tight to his side glowering at the men.

"Do I know you?" I asked.

"No, miss..." Jawfish asked.

I looked to Sterling. "My pregnant mate. Her name is none of your business. She does not know these men."

"Pregnant?" the black-haired man asked, nostrils flaring. "You look far too thin to be with child."

I glanced away. There were no mirrors in the Beget Oubliette, but my woolen dresses had begun to hang off me like sacks while my belly had a swell to it.

"Just over four months," I answered.

"I have twins. Step children, identical boys," Scarab answered. "Her well-being is a priority, as is the safety of my children."

I knit my brows.

"I will take better care of her. Thank you for your unsolicited advice," Sterling said stiffly.

"And you? Do you have children?" I asked.

"She does not know them. If their papers are authentic, let them fish for their families." Cassiopeia hadn't bothered to spare them a glance.

"A little girl and a newborn son," Jawfish answered.

"May I offer your wife a small gift, sir? In honor of her pregnancy?" Scarab asked, his eyes hitched on the nix torque around my throat, but quickly brought them back to my face. "I have a soft spot for beautiful pregnant women." His lips curled at me into a mocking smile as if we shared a joke.

Sterling looked to me and sighed with a nod. "I do not have a problem with it."

Scarab dug through his pack as Jawfish seemed to be memorizing my face. They couldn't arrest them for walking on the ice. They were more than likely members of the Red Seconds, but two men were not going to make a difference.

"For your child —"

"Son. I'm having a boy," I interrupted.

He smiled and something nagged in my mind. They were both smiling. He handed me a carving of a toy train, hand whittled and unpainted. I felt something cool beneath it, but the way he pressed it into my hands made me think I shouldn't look at it in view of the others.

"Good day. Take better care of yourself, ma'am," Scarab said, pulling back up his hood and taking the scroll from the Guardian.

"You are... okay?" Jawfish asked, furrowing his brow.

His question astonished me. The Guardians had returned to the sleigh and Sterling had turned me away. I stopped and looked over my shoulder.

"I wasn't, but..." I looked to Sterling.

"You are with me now. Safe," he reassured me.

Sterling led me back to the sleigh, but I couldn't stop staring at the two men. My mind nagged. I traced the cool piece beneath the train in the pocket of Sterling's cloak. It was a jagged key shape, a love rune. I knew one man who would have a love rune on him and had reason to hide it.

My breath hitched as we glided past them. They hadn't moved from their spot. I pulled my single narrow braid into my fingers under my furs and quickly untied my braid. I reached over Sterling as if to hold him and tossed my turquoise tree of life fetish into the snow, praying they saw it.

Jett and Slate.

I buried my face in Sterling's chest. He held me, comforting me, but for the wrong reasons. Sterling wanted me safe. He would shift if they tried to take me away and if Slate and Sterling fought, it would be to the death. I was certain of it.

"Get some sleep, Indi," he murmured.

His fingers worked into my hair. In the ice caverns, the Crathode captors pushed a heated water basin into my cell with a cloth and I stripped down and washed until the water grew too cold to stand. The bath at the inn was a luxury spa compared to that cold basin.

Sterling kneaded my shoulders and back, massaging my aching muscles. He was still their puppet; he wouldn't take off the nix torque. Cygnus had removed it briefly to check on my health and my son's but had quickly put it back on before leaving me alone with Sterling.

It was a merchant inn designed with wealth and status in mind. Grecian columns and polished granite floors with vaulted ceilings. Crinkled silk was swathed in every entranceway as if we were sleeping in a theater. The bathroom had heated flooring, and the bath had jacuzzi jets whirring that was big enough to sleep in.

"Are you hungry?" Sterling asked, running the tip of his nose along my ear.

"Not anymore." Our trolley full of half-eaten food sat in the sitting room where we'd gorged ourselves on an array of different foods.

"They told me you were with the Natts. If I had even the slightest inkling…"

"Help me escape, Sterling. My life is in jeopardy while behind enemy lines. They will renege again." I leaned back against his chest and blew the bubbles from my nose.

"Where do you think you can go to be safe?" he asked rubbing his hand over the swell of my stomach.

A horrible fear welled up in me. What if Slate and Jett told Silver I was pregnant with Sterling's son? Slate said he had two children? Had Scarlett already had the twins? Sorrow like I hadn't felt in months pulled me back into the abyss.

"Sterling." I choked out. "They will never let anyone with Sumar blood survive this war. They are going to wipe out my family from the face of this earth. Your sisters, your mother, your grandmother… they've manipulated you. You have to get out of here, we both do. We could go to Valla U. Gypsum would take us in." I swallowed repeatedly, but the lump was lodged.

"Indigo, you are upsetting yourself." He stood, lifting me up with him and *calling* over fluffy terry cloth robes.

He wrapped me in one as if I was made of glass and led me into the bedroom. The plush bed was a far cry from the metal framed mattress at the Beget Oubliette.

In my cloak, Cygnus had slipped the murky blue vials of marawacian and rousen cocktails. I was an addict. Sterling's own khoraz and he did not know. I couldn't go a day without my dosage and no one cared enough to wean me off except for Sterling who would be heartbroken if he found out. There would be nothing he could do. He'd have to live with the guilt. Sterling wasn't a bad guy, I knew that in my gut and in my heart, but he never had the stomach to stand up to his mother and grandmother. Not even his father, before Scarlett killed him.

"Don't let them take me away from you, Sterling. I can't survive that again."

As Sterling walked to the sitting room to bring in the trolley of leftovers, I downed a vial of murky blue fluid.

CHAPTER

TWELVE

I smiled, slipping into my wedding dress tucking a flower behind my ear and giving Brass's cheek one last kiss before I hurried out into the cold morning. I thought it *must* be morning despite the dark skies, it dawned late on Elivagar.

Brass and I had made up, then we made up again. Make up sex. *Mm hmm...* If he wasn't sterile, we would've conceived. I was sure of it. I'd have to fight with Brass more often.

My feet practically floated over the dirt path as I hurried to Slate's longhouse. He deserved a kiss goodnight and maybe I could find something else he would like to do with my mouth.

I was giggling like an idiot something stung my arm.

I slapped my hand to the spot and pulled out tiny dart that had pricked my skin. Burly shadowed figures detached from the tree trunks and I heard something whistle past my ear. I fell to the ground and collided with a set of legs. I aimed for what I could reach and was

129

rewarded with a groan when my fist connected with a man's sensitive bits.

My vision spun as I tried to stand and I fell back on my hip unable to straighten my eyes no matter how I widened them. Another shadow came at me and I kicked my legs in the heavy skirts and caught them off guard so they fell onto their back. I threw my body in the general direction of the body unable to aim and searched it for a blade.

The shadow was revealed as the cloak fell away from its face. A muzzle snarled at me. It needed no blades, and I didn't find any. It was a bear. I felt another sting at my neck and opened my mouth to scream but fell face first into the Bjorn.

Light peeked through the threads of the sack I was carried in. The Bjorn had indelicately stuffed me into a bag like a load of garbage. My dress and knees crowded my face and I tried to calm myself to take even breaths. I didn't like being bound. It reminded me of Non're when the Merfolk prince had drugged me with rousen and I was his prisoner for four days. He trained me with his sister and their subjects in pleasure and when I was rescued, Slate had to wean me off rousen. It was the beginning of a snowballing of problems for me.

My breasts were leaking and ached painfully. My hands were bound behind my back, but I wasn't wearing a nix torque. It didn't make any sense. I could get out of the sack with a sliver of my *calling*. I sliced my ring finger to activate my bond with Brass. They had probably woken up and wanted to burn down the woods to find me.

I was safe and unharmed, for the most part. They both activated their bonds immediately, and I smiled. Brass was much clearer with his emotions understanding what it was like to deal with other people's minds and emotions. He was feeling guilty and worried, *ugh*, and so afraid to lose me. I sent him happy thoughts letting him know I was irritated, but not concerned yet. Slate was another story. I wondered how he was behaving with them. He seemed to be holding his breath, like anything would make him explode into a fury. He needed release desperately. It was easier when we were apart because the temptation wasn't there, but reunited and knowing I had consummated my marriage to Brass last night was driving him right into crazy town.

I'd been there. It was not a good place to be.

I'd had just about enough of bumping against some bear's back when I was unceremoniously dumped on the ground. I grunted in surprise as I kneed myself in the nose. Light poured through the hole at the top of the sack and I was temporarily blinded as I was dragged to my feet.

There wasn't a one of us who had been to the Bjorn lands before. In the distance, I could see the edge of the ice cliffs near the cave Brass had shown me the northern lights when he was going by Scorpion the Red Seconds rebel. He had told me he was falling in love with me then as Scat, the blade wielding, milk leaking psychopath.

We stood between towering snowcapped rock formations, as if the shifting glaciers had taken several twists and turns carving a haphazard pattern through the land. There was no straight shot to the Bjorn, apparently.

I couldn't speak Bjorn. Another failure on my part, to Jackal's endless dismay. Their language was harsh with an emphasis on consonants, rolling "R"s and the complete absence of "W"s. I ducked my head, trying to get my eyes to adjust.

"You are not red-haired," one said, and I blinked until a brown faced grizzly bear came into focus.

They all wore varying monochromatic shades of fur lined vests over wide tunics that fell past their hips and billowy pants cinched at the ankle. Some wore boots whose toe curled that was similar to the curled hats they wore all trimmed in fur.

"Good to know bears see in color," I spat as I scoured them all with my deadliest gaze. "A half-dozen men for one woman?"

One man seemed to be guarding his lap from my gaze with a black furry clawed hand. Another with a brown grizzly face and pale blue eyes too human to be a bear's had a splint on one of his legs.

"You were described as a soft feminine *katyonak*. Not this... *blud*."

The grizzly man obviously had a dislike for me for breaking his leg. I didn't know what a *blud* was much less a *katyonak*, but I knew one was worse than the other. Another stepped forward in brilliant shades of yellow and olive-colored eyes in a white face with black ringed eyes. He bent his knees to look better at my face and I glared defiantly before he let his eyes fall down to my chest.

"You are not the sagamore's new wife. You were in the honored longhouse, in a wedding dress, but you have cubs?" He gestured to my frozen chest, and I gave a curt nod.

"I'm a Guardian. You wanted to capture Siobhan. Why?" I asked, demanding an answer in my most official sounding voice.

"We received word he was hosting Guardians. The wolves are short-tempered." He shrugged. "We meant them no harm. Only goading them. I am Gennadi," the panda faced man said with a quick smile of his short muzzle.

It was a strange combination, the bear faces with fur covered man like bodies. Chests were deeper like the Lycans with long fur like theirs and they were mostly over six feet. While being bear like in appearance, the Bjorn didn't have protruding muzzles like their full-blooded brethren.

"Why did you not try to free yourself?" The black bear gazed at me with human hazel eyes. His hands still covered the front of his pants.

"I haven't been awake that long," I said, giving him a dry look.

The black bear wore a color scheme of greens and pointed to himself. "Klim."

"I'm sorry for punching your manhood, Klim. I'm guessing you tranquilized me thinking I was Siobhan so she wouldn't shift?"

I was postponing giving them my name. They had undoubtedly heard of Scarlett Tio, the Khoraz Seductress and I had to find out what side they were on before I revealed myself. Regardless, I needed them to take me into their lands so I could speak to whomever was in charge and convince them to join my cause.

I was facing Klim when I felt the sting of the dart bite into my arm again. I hissed and yanked it out as a second hit me.

"Demyan!" Gennadi barked.

The golden furred grizzly came from my side and his deep set pale blue eyes glinted with disdain. "Give me the notices from the Guardians. I have seen this blud's face before."

My eyes fluttered, and I staggered back. Klim darted out and caught me before my head hit the stony ground.

"*Ah!* Here she is... impossible." Demyan shoved the scroll of vellum at Gennadi who snatched it out of his hands.

Gennadi's head whipped up, and he held the vellum next to my face. "The Seductress."

Words faded with my consciousness.

"What if her milk is poison?" hissed a voice near my head in the harsh tongue of the Bjorn.

"He is my cub, I decide. What if her milk has magic?" countered another higher feminine voice.

I heard the tiny growl of an animal and felt teeth latch on around my breast. I gritted my teeth and opened my eyes groggily. My wedding gown was unlaced at my side and I was no longer wearing my corset. Someone must have undressed, then redressed me. My arms were bound through the bars of a cage so I rested on my knees and the toes of my slippered boots.

At my bared breast where my dress had been pulled askew, a bear with a tawny face and black fur suckled. My head felt heavy, my mind thick, I thought I was hallucinating until I saw what was a female Bjorn with a pure white coat and white hair bound back by a swath of red fabric hold up her polar bear cub to my other breast that the mother had pushed aside. I blinked groggily until it's little sharp teeth bit into my skin as it began to suckle.

"Frigga's sweet grass, that smarts," I gritted out.

I'd startled the two women, and they nearly dropped their babes. The tawny faced bear cub resembled it with long black hair that parted down the center and was tucked behind her ears which were placed where any humans would be. Their dresses were long tunics with modest necklines and thickly trimmed in monochromatic colors. They were split to the upper thigh to reveal a thinner dress beneath that matched the trim of their collars and hems.

I sensed the apprehension through the bonds of Slate and Brass and I sent reassurance.

Other than my nudity, I didn't have a reason to be upset. On the contrary, I would've thanked them for relieving my aching chest.

They looked at me like some dangerous animal, which I found ironic. My cage was set in the center of a stone hall. Long banners of graduating color hung from the cavernous ceilings to the floors and in between each banner was a succession of stone steps to throne-like chairs. Torches lit the enormous room as well as the braziers that circled the room.

My cage sat in the center of the room; a black sheet was puddled on the floor which must have covered my cage like a bird. From where I kneeled it would've been impossible to touch the bars.

"Careful, khoraz. This is a nixing cage we fashioned out of torques delivered by your own people."

The dark-haired bear had a tawny chest as well I noticed as I focused my eyes on her. They weren't taking their cubs away from my chest even though they seemed frightened by me. I wondered if they truly believed they could absorb my powers through my breast milk.

"I'm Scarlett *Tio* — Natt. Are you who disrobed me? How old are your babes? I have twin boys, only two weeks old. My thanks for letting me feed them, I haven't been able to tend to myself since... what time is it?"

I used my most patient tone even though I could tell darkness had set in outside and from the rumbling my stomach was doing, I hadn't eaten all day. Slate and Brass would feel how hungry I was. The women had their arms extended as far as they would go so they only had to lean into the cage slightly in order for their urchins to steal my so-called abilities.

"We undressed you. We would not let the men see you so you could seduce them," the white-haired woman with jade eyes said, with her "W"s sound like "V"s.

The urge to scoff teetered my pleasantry scales dangerously. "I'm just a woman and a mother, like you both. I allowed your men to bring me here so I may speak to any man or woman that may lead you because the current Prime and his regime does not have your best interest in mind," I said in a calm tone. "I am very hungry. Would I be able to get a bowl of stew or something simple either of you could feed me?" I had to start small. "If I don't eat, my milk supply will dwindle and I have two babies to feed at home. Please."

The Bjorn I recognized as a sun bear hybrid nodded and carefully broke suction from her cub's mouth and my chest then covered me back up. She swaddled the cub and put it on her shoulder as her curled booted feet scraped the surface of the stones.

The polar bear woman was the more apprehensive of the two and she eyed me warily. My shoulders hurt from the awkward position and I thanked the Gods I was an elemental so I couldn't get frostbite, but I was chilled.

"What is your name?" I asked after a few moments.

She raised her skeptical jade eyes to mine. "Zlata. I will cover your cage once you are fed. No one will disturb you so you may sleep." She eyed the bonds around my wrists. "If you can. They say you broke Demyan's leg. That you are a very dangerous blud."

"You defend yourself when you're attacked, don't you? What is a blud? I'm not very good at languages," I admitted and her mouth quirked.

"Not a flattering term for a woman. What do you think you can offer us that others —"

She whirled around, pulling her cub away abruptly as footsteps approached. It was not the sun bear. She growled and stepped out of my cage. The woman slammed it shut as she pulled a cord and my black sheet was pulled over my cage like a curtain, but not before I saw a speckled bear. It looked like someone had thrown bleach over its dark furred face discoloring it, leading a troop of Bjorn towards me.

I was cut off from view.

"She is a known seductress. You should not speak directly to her," Zlata said in a stern voice laced with obvious disapproval willingly meeting a woman of ill repute.

"Step aside, Zlata. I will not set eyes on the khoraz. I want to speak to her and my advisors will take measure of her powers," barked a harsh voice gruffly.

The black curtain tugged and I mustered as much dignity as I could manage as my temper flared. I felt my skin heat and fire churned under my skin, white hot, as flames licked up my arms. The bonds around my wrists were not the pewter nix material and on the toes of my boots, none of my skin was touching the nix torque metal. The binding melted like mercury to slither over my sleeves and drip off my elbows, hot coals instead of eyes burned in my skull and my hair writhed around my face.

At the last second, I winked out. I had a plan.

I dropped back to my knees and waited as the black sheet was drawn back to reveal Klim, Gennadi, the speckled bear, and Zlata. Zlata moved to face the three male Bjorn, Klim was the only one whose eyes rested on me. The other two kept their eyes shut as if the mere sight of me would seduce them into freeing me.

"I am Lyov, tsar of the Bjorn. Do you know they say you are dead? Have you been hiding on Lycan lands since Yuletide?" he asked without taking a breath.

Klim had never seen a human woman's side boob. He stared blatantly at the unfastened lacing, but not in a lewd manner, out of fascination. On a different day, I would've been amused.

I sat in silence hoping to aggravate them into acting. The curtain lifted and the dark haired Bjorn held a stone bowl that steamed from the heat. I could smell the meat and potatoes and my stomach rumbled.

"Gennadi!" she accused.

The panda man took a step back and whirled whom I assumed was his mate or wife. "Faima, go back to the baby," he said, radiating embarrassment.

"Drop your eyes Klim or I will get your mother and tell her how you are treating this woman." Faima gave them scathing looks that skipped over Lyov as she opened the cage door and leaned in to tip the bowl back. "They do not see human women often. No matter your station, they know better than to disrespect you so."

She shook her head as she poured he stew slowly down my throat. I gulped greedily as I decided whether to rush the door. I decided not to after she'd defended me.

"If you lace my dress, I could speak to them plainly," I said hopefully as she drew back the bowl.

"We searched you for weapons, I do not see why not," Faima said, closing the cage behind her and shooing away Gennadi and Klim.

Zlata had disappeared and Lyov refused to move or meet my eyes. "I arrived a few days ago in Elivagar. Last night I married the father of my children. I was planning to come to your lands to persuade you to join us. I am Scarlett, the Prime's former Second. I am an elemental and one of my husbands is the Grar Dyr. I'm not asking you to fight in something you don't believe in but take your lands back from the Crathode and the Minotaur."

Lyov's dark eyes flared, and he forgot to keep his gaze away. I'd hit a nerve speaking of the Minotaur. Zlata lifted the curtain and brought in a woolen robe for warmth. She lifted her hands to unbind my wrists and found them free. I got to my feet crouching and offered her a smile as I slid the robe over my shoulders while she was still stunned.

Lyov cursed. "You released her?"

Zlata denied it, her head of white hair shaking fervently. "I broke the bonds. No one helped me."

Faima said a few harsh words in Bjorn I couldn't understand and Zlata ran from the cage with Faima in her place.

"How long have you been unbound? You could have used your *calling* and escaped, but you did not. Why?" Faima asked, lacing at my side.

"You should know, I activated a bond I have with my husbands. They know where I am. While I am at risk in this cage, I am not helpless. To think so would be a mistake. I've already told you all. I planned on coming here. Now, I can stay in this cage of my own free will or you could release me of yours."

I ran my fingers through my waves to tame it and faced the tsar as Faima retreated from the cramped cage.

"She stays inside until we take a vote," Lyov said, and slammed the cage in my face before letting the black fabric fall back over the bars.

Having given up all pretenses of being bound, I sat in the corner of the cage and shut my eyes. The drugged sleep hadn't helped me rest and my head still felt thick and dim-witted. After having eaten the large bowl of warm stew, the cold seeped out of my skin and I fell asleep in minutes wrapped comfortably in the robe.

The cage crashed open, and I blinked at the bodies crowding the entrance. Faima and Zlata were back with their cubs and Demyan was with them.

"You would let your babes, drink from the teat of evil?" he snarled, pointing his clawed finger to me.

"If your leg ails you, I can heal it, Demyan," I offered as I stretched my limbs hoping to ease some of the stiffness.

He made some gesture over his chest as if my mouth saying his name cursed him and he warded off my evil. "When your children die because of her poisoned milk, do not seek to find comfort from me."

"As if we would," Faima said combatively.

He turned to me as if it was my fault that they were going to let their children nurse from me. His pale blue eyes held something that disturbing. I saw torment and disheartenment. He cursed and drew his eyes away as if I would draw him into hypnosis and he hurried away, his limp pronounced with the splint.

The two women looked at me warily where I sat cross-legged in the corner. "I don't bite. I promise. Thank you for thinking of me."

I began to unlace my dress unbelievably grateful to nurse the babes killing two birds with one stone. The moment I woke, I felt Brass on the move so my time was limited. If he saw me in this cage our chance at cajoling the Bjorn to our side would be over.

I sat bared for the women and didn't offer to hold the cubs, worried that might be too much for them to bear. They shifted closer in their long dresses and I watched the two root at my chest. My heart ached for my sons worse than I had in days. Brass's immediate worry made me shove it in my lockbox of emotions to save for another day.

I hissed a sharp intake of air as they latched. The Bjorn must have teats made of leather to withstand their cubs needle-like teeth.

"Breakfast will be brought in once we are done," Zlata said in a soft voice.

"My thanks. What is the vote for?" I asked watching the cubs purr and paw at my chest. "By the way, I don't think there's any way for your cubs to receive powers through me. I do appreciate your help tending to myself. Thank you."

"It was worth the risk," Faima said wryly. "We will vote on whether to return you to the Guardians or let you be on your way. Natts are not an esteemed family in our lands."

My body gave an involuntary shiver. I hadn't lost faith I could convince them to our side, but the idea of being given to the Natts made me feel sick. I'd never see my sons again if they did that. Would they give me to Ash as a boon for all his cooperation or would they force Sterling to put a baby in my womb?

"Are you okay?" Zlata asked cautiously.

I nodded and wiped at a rogue tear. "It's been a very long year. I had been fighting with my husbands, we made up only a few days past. My sister is in enemy hands and I'm trying to keep her betrothed from losing hope. I miss my sons whom I had to leave behind because these lands aren't safe yet and they're so little. Their father hasn't met them yet. On top of which, my uncle, my grandmother, my parents as well as countless friends have all been killed by the people you want to hand me over to. At some point, I thought people would see what was in their best interest and want to fight for themselves."

I sighed and handed Faima her golden faced babe before wiping my tears. The Bjorn didn't seem like the type who appreciated frailty in their leaders. Zlata leaned forward to take her cub who had fallen asleep in my lap. They had let their babes lay in my lap and during my mewling, had sat back and listened.

"We have heard of your prophecy," Faima said, running the back of her dark furred hands along her babies cheek. "When the Grey Beast chooses a time, the day and night will blend as one against the rising flood. Together, they will stop time and decide the fate of the world. It is an old prophecy about the twins of the spring and summer who carry the pieces. Tio means time. The rising flood is the Tide, or the Straumr."

"Salvation comes from the love of the shamed daughter's babe. Temptation takes shape, her love lights the flame. The son of the beast is finally claimed. In his blood, destiny takes aim," I finished, and they looked up wide eyed at me. "My first husband, the Grar Dyr, is the beast's son. My mother was shamed, as I have been." Slate had only told me his prophecy once, but I would never forget it. "I dream of the works, the project of Storm Dagr and of the battle to come. I know how it ends... with the death of my first husband."

The women sat silently, and I sighed. I hadn't found a way to save him yet. I wished Slate was there so I could make love to him. It had been too long for us.

"Why do you still seek to fulfill the prophecy if it ends in his death? Why not take him and your husbands... your sons, and leave?" Zlata asked, her white hair was in loops pinned to her head that shook as she bounced her babe.

"They say it's the only way for our world to survive. I don't think we have to do it the way it specifies. I think that it has to be me and it has to go a certain way for the outcome to be the best. That the tribes would suffer and... I spoke with the Prime. He wants to go back in time and give the Guardians domain over the entire world, even those without *calling* who know nothing about tribes and being able to *call* elements. They're entitled to their world as much as you are."

I felt overwhelmed. I had no business trying to take on all of this responsibility. Faima rested her black furred paw on my hand.

"We know the story of Dagr and Natt. Will your mate sacrifice himself? Is that how he dies, like Wind Dagr?"

I shrugged weakly and ran the back of my hand over my nose sniffling. "I have no idea. I just know we're supposed to be together. I love him. I don't want to lose him." I raised my head and gave them a teary smile. "Sorry. I'm missing a lot of people these days and my heart feels like I have a permanent hole in it when we're apart." I heard myself swallow.

"I will make sure we free you."

A breathy voice startled the three of us before the curtain lifted. A squat woman with longer dark fur than the other Bjorn I'd seen and ringlets that stuck out wildly around her face. Her muzzle was cream as well as her buxom bosom. It was difficult to discern her age, but I assumed she was older than the other two women I placed around my own age.

"Asya!" Faima cried, getting to her feet.

"Relax, Faima. I believe what she says."

She turned cobalt blue eyes to me and I saw the bowl of porridge she carried. I took it with an inclination of my head.

"I am Asya, the tsar's wife. You met my husband yesterday. Allow me to apologize for any... impropriety on his part. Gennadi and Klim should know better."

"Scarlett," I said with a smile. "Gennadi and Klim have been kind when they are able, as have Faima and Zlata. My thanks."

"My son was the liaison to ambassador Natt. You will have to excuse his... bias," Asya said as I tipped the cinnamon sprinkled porridge bowl back to eat.

"Willow Natt, correct?" I asked.

Asya inclined her head of curls. "Come. We know now you will not try to escape before the vote. There is no need for a cage."

THIRTEEN

Through the long high-ceilinged halls, Asya, Faima, and Zlata led me to an unpolished wood plank door. The Bjorn built a castle out of one of the rock towers I'd seen on my way there, the few minutes before Demyan tranquillized me a second time. Braziers lit the halls; painted murals were the only decoration throughout the light grey walls.

The scent of tea and jam filled the halls which made me think of mornings with Pearl the Sumar palace. I wondered when the ache in my chest would ebb. I could forget for a short time, but it always came back.

The Bjorn didn't have much for furniture. Everything was carved directly into the rock. The shelves, the beds, steps, and garderobes — all a part of the castle. The woolen blankets they gave me kept me toasty warm after I moved the brazier close to the large alcove that the stuffed mattress rested inside.

I hadn't slept all night while I made up with Brass. The drugged sleep in a sack left me feeling stiff, as did the nap on the freezing nix torque bars. With my belly full of porridge and Brass's comforting presence in my mind, I thought about activating my bond with Slate. I was nervous he might come to my rescue and lose his temper. I knew his control was wavering.

I decided against it and curled up on the mattress content to wait for lunch when Asya assured me they would take the vote and she would speak in my favor.

When Zlata brought in a plate of gravy soaked meat and carrots, I ate with zeal. I hadn't known what to expect with the cold weather tribe and I hadn't seen any farms to speak of. They must have had a greenhouse hidden in a part of the castle I hadn't seen yet.

"Your mate, he is near?" Zlata asked, her "S"s sounding like "Z"s.

"Very. I'm surprised he didn't leave last night or once he found me missing. It was the morning after our wedding after all. Perhaps he's grown tired of me already," I joked and coaxed a tight smile from the nervous woman.

Even the chairs were carved stone pieces, I hadn't seen a single tree for wood when I'd been released from the sack. The Wemic got by with their clay and mud, I supposed the Bjorn used what they had as well.

"I am to lead you back to the gathering hall. It is a good sign Asya wishes to join you. Lyov will not like it. He digs in like a termite when Asya pushes him. I hope for your sake she is subtle."

Zlata's dress was a cerulean blue with thistle trim and a thinner dress that peeked out from the slits near her thighs that matched the trim. Her snowy looped hair had a twisted headband through it. It looked like a comfortable style and begged the question, where did they get the dye?

She caught me admiring the dress she wore and beamed proudly. "At the highest point of the castle, we have a greenhouse. I grow many flowers there for dyes only found in Ostara. We sell or trade with the tribes. The Lycans bring us the wool from their stock, we dye it. The Minotaur used to trade with us even though they are on the other side of the island, but over the last few years they have grown more reclusive as the Crathode have." She grimaced, running her white furred hand over her thighs. "The mines are what fuels Elivagar's economy. Not much for mines this far. Crabs, whale, wool, most of our males fish."

Zlata explained the Bjorn council. There were seven figureheads since Klim was unmarried. Faima, Klim, and Demyan were the tsar's children, naturally I would break the leg of the equivalent of the Bjorn prince. Gennadi was on the council as Faima's husband, and so was Zlata since she had married Demyan. Asya and Lyov completed the seven.

"The assembly is usually split and the last remaining male will decide between the male or the female side of the vote," Zlata said with a sigh.

"So the men side with Lyov and the women with Asya? Who is the swing vote? Klim?" I asked.

She nodded. "Klim is the only one who could get away with siding between parents. He can read truths in people; his parents accord him much leeway."

"Why is there so much tension? I feel like the air is thick with it."

So Klim was like Quick — an interrogator. That was news. As was their council like assembly. I got the impression Zlata was not a huge fan of her husband. I could empathize the sentiment.

"The Lycans are left alone. They rarely leave the Igulbjorn Ice cliffs, so they would not understand the pressures of dealing with the Natt and Vetr. We have been threatened for years. Now with our closest neighbors being a favored tribe, we fear for our tribe's safety. That is why Demyan is so hostile. He would rather turn you over to the Natts and be done with you than suffer their wrath. We had hoped with the new Matriarch that times would change, but then they killed her too. No one is safe," Zlata said, holding her babe close to her chest.

"She's alive. She's my cousin and she's hiding with the Lycans. Zlata." I placed my hand over hers. "My first husband is a patriarch, my cousin is a matriarch, my brother is the heir to Ostara, and my sister-in-law is the heir to the Geol. We are not weak. We are only divided in the physical sense. We need bodies to even the odds against the creatures the Stygian Knights bred."

I'd seen the hybrids of hybrids myself. They'd used the tribes like the Jorogumo and Gorgons who bred in numbers to hatch a tribe of brainwashed supplicants. We had all agreed that it must have happened in Elivagar. As soon as we won back the island, I'd make sure we found the breeding nest and returned those captive to their native islands.

Zlata was silent as she stared at our hands. "They have my sisters.

My three younger sisters in order to keep us out of the war. They threatened their lives."

It wasn't the first time I'd heard about hostages from the tribes to keep them compliant. The Stygians had taken the son of the Gorgons' king.

"We'll get them back. They have my sister too," I said, feeling the despair wash over me.

Brass was suddenly so prominent in my mind I sprung to my feet and looked around as if I'd find him somewhere hidden in one of the carved alcoves. Zlata's jade eyes rounded.

"What is it?"

"My husband. He's here, and he's angry."

Since I woke up for lunch, I'd felt Slate slowly moving south. He wasn't with Brass. I couldn't understand how Brass had gotten to the Bjorn so quickly, it should have taken him a full day.

"What time is it?" I asked, and Zlata shook her head.

"Around two in the afternoon."

"How would a Guardian enter the castle? We need to meet him or —"

I cut short. I'd been gossiping with Zlata for two hours and not paying attention to our bond. I wondered who all he had with him and started for the door. I could find him myself with him being so close. Zlata got up and followed me as I swept from the room.

I picked up my skirts and began to run, my sweet husband was growing dangerously wrathful. As it turned out, our bonds worked more like a compass than a precise locator especially when there were multiple levels so while I could feel him directly below me, I had to wind down several flights of stone carved steps in order to get to him.

Arguing in barked words and a smooth seductive voice snapping curt replies reached my ears and I knew it could only be one man. I didn't stop my running when the stairs gave way to the gathering hall and I saw Brass's broad shoulders piled with marble fox furs wearing his Elivagar traveling gear. A thick padded heather grey jerkin buckled to his throat and matching woolen pants were tucked into fur-lined boots that came up to his calves. He turned and his defined lips curled as I smiled. Bodies of Bjorn lay at his feet. Sleeping, not dead. I could *feel* their contentment.

Brass was alone. He opened his leather clad hands for me and I threw decorum out the window as I hiked up my skirts and launched myself into his arms keenly aware of the Bjorn who were already seated on the stone carved thrones between banners.

"I went to say goodnight to Slate. I know him letting you have me first was such a big concession. I didn't want him to feel left out. They thought I was Siobhan and were trying to irritate the Lycans, nothing more. He didn't come, is he angry? Are you okay?" I asked in between kissing his face and everywhere I could reach as he tried to gently pry me from him.

I began searching his body for signs of wounds or bleeding. He was perfectly perfect, as I'd always known. He grabbed my face and slanted his mouth over mine. I sighed. He wouldn't be kissing me if he wasn't well.

I melted against him and he left a possessive arm around my shoulders. "My goodness, wife. It has only been a day. Try to control your urges," he whispered in that smooth deep voice that sent my body into shivers.

"You're never allowed to leave my side again. I'm going to start following you into bathrooms. I wouldn't ever expect any privacy for the rest of your life, Brass Regn. Is he angry? He isn't here," I said again.

"Later, Love. They tried to tranquilize me as they must have done you," Brass said as he looked down to the slumped bodies at his feet and then took in the seated figures.

Zlata ascended a stone seat swathed in blue and purple banners that stretched from the high ceiling to the floor. Brass squared his shoulders as he looked over the figures in their seats and faced Lyov. His mind reading abilities must have been in full effect because abruptly he gritted his teeth.

"My wife tells me it was a case of mistaken identity. Yet you stripped her and caged her like some beast. My *wife* who has given birth two weeks past and who only sought to defend herself from your people. The mother of my children treated like a rabid animal. She spared your lives. I hope you know that. Her power is greater than any Guardian who lives, but she chooses words not force to persuade you even after how you've treated her." Brass ground out.

"Brass, it's fine. I'm okay, but I'll take a little healing if you're offering," I said, giving him a grateful smile as warmth flooded through me.

"It is most certainly *not* okay. You people are terrified. As you should be, if the current regime is not overthrown you will never get your hostages back. Did they ever seek out your assembly to speak as equals or did they make demands and give you ultimatums? Discuss what you need to. We will be leaving this place at first light and you may join us and the Lycans in taking back these lands or you may sit back and wait and pray that they don't make slaves of you all when there is nothing to stop them. She offers you peace, they offer you nothing. They only take. Join the Red Seconds or not. It is your choice, but make no mistake, we will not come to your aid if you do not aid us now."

Brass gripped my hand and strode from the room as an explosion of voices called questions out after us. My feet skidded over the stone squares as he dragged me through the halls.

"Brass! We have to convince them. They'll be caged themselves if Ash and Canis have their way. They don't care about the tribes," I chastened as he pulled me towards the stair ways. "Do you know where you're going? Where are you going?"

"Back to your room. They've already made up their minds, now they need to go through their bickering and get over their fears. Nothing you could have said would have made a difference, Love. Sometimes people need to figure it out for themselves. They have until morning, then we must get back to rally the Lycans. Slate and Jett are going to the safe holds to make the last round of deliveries before we give the Stygians the war they've been asking for. Elivagar will not be easy to take. Silver and Ridge have gone to the Niflheim to make sure the evacuated people and the Breakers there are ready. We're going to hit them from both sides. It was Ridge's idea. He thinks we need to lock the Natt portals so they can't retreat there and hit us from behind."

Brass knew exactly which room I'd been in and opened the door as soon as we came to it.

"I'm not complaining, but why wouldn't Slate want to come after me? He could've shifted into a full barghest and been here in hours. How *did* you get here so fast?" I asked.

Brass took off his furs and boots. "There is a long forgotten pass between their lands that I found because of your bond. It would be impossible for the tribes to take without a Guardians *calling,* but with a little work it can be restored. Bridge work and the like. Slate was being strange. I thought he would lose his temper if they had done something *unnecessary* to you... for example if you had still been stripped in that cage."

I cringed. If Slate had seen that, he wouldn't have been happy until someone had died. Still, I couldn't help, but be disappointed. Brass caught my mood and smirked.

"I didn't want to meet our sons without you and one of us had to go on deliveries. He wanted to be here. How easily you forget how had we've fought to get you back, Love."

Brass's jerkin laid over his furs and he prowled over to me hooking a finger in the leather strap that bound his hair and pulled it free. He shook his mane of hair like a lion and I gave him a questioning gaze.

"What are you doing?" I asked, unwittingly backing up.

Brass broke into a run catching me around the waist so quickly I let out a cry in surprise before I could stop it. "I haven't bathed in days," I protested as he kept reversing me to the wall.

"Have I told you how very much I like you in this dress, Love?"

My dress crunched and crinkled as he pulled it up to get to my hips underneath. He made a contented sound in his throat when he found I hadn't procured undergarments.

"Is there something I exude that turns normal men into animals or has your time with Slate turned you partly into a beast too?" I teased.

Brass's smile was sigh inducing as he gripped around my thighs and lifted me up against the stone wall. "No more words unless they're dirty ones. Feel free to cry out my name as well," Brass purred as my ankles locked around his waist.

Brass chased off a young Bjorn girl who tried to bring us dinner and then another Bjorn who wanted us to come back to the hall to discuss the vote. Brass was unabashedly nude and both Bjorn would've been left blushing if their fur had not covered their cheeks. Guardians had no modesty whatsoever.

Not until Lyov and Asya themselves came did Brass allow them in. A little heads up would have been preferred before he held the door open for the tsar and his wife. Pants also would have been nice.

Brass held the wooden door open for the couple who did not drop their eyes over his naked body as I pulled the woolen blankets over me like a cloak. I drew my brow down to look at Brass who looked expressionless at the pair as they moved to stand within the room and faced me. I exhaled heavily and got to my feet.

"After much debate, we have decided to join you if —"

Brass cut off Lyov as he moved to stand behind me offering a little covering for his gloriously nude body. "No *if*. You are or you aren't."

Asya's eyes stayed on mine. "Zlata's sisters were taken as hostages. She says they have been bred."

I knit my brow giving them a sympathetic look. "As has my sister. I hope not, but from what I've seen outside the walls of Valla University...there is a good chance they may have been bred against their will. I promise to find the place they're being held and free them if they're there. We won't leave them, Asya. You have my word."

She searched my eyes and nodded. "I believe you, Second. We will be ready to march come dawn."

Lyov glared at Brass. His dark eyes against his lighter furred face intent on searing his face off if he could. The two males stood at the same height and girth and I waited for the tension to pass.

"Thank you, Asya. May I ask how many tribal members will be joining us?" I said in my most diplomatic voice.

"Two thousand men, women, and children. Like the Lycans, we leave no one behind. We dare not risk the Crathode attacking those who remain. We all go or we all stay," Lyov said brusquely.

"Other than cattle, there is no need to bring other stores for food. Our people have been growing what we'll need for the march. Your contribution to our cause is appreciated." Brass smiled warmly at them for the first time and I watched Asya's brows quirk.

"Until morning. There is a spring at the lowest level inside the castle. Should you wish to bathe," Asya told us and to my surprise, looped her arm through her husband's.

Lyov looked down at the squat curly haired woman as if she'd lost her mind until his nostrils flared and seemed unable to leave the room fast enough. I leaned back against Brass and tilted my head back to gaze up at him.

"Sometimes it's easier to keep fighting than be the first one to make up," I said throatily as he ran his thumb along my neck.

"I am always the one to forgive first. What do you know about losing a little pride, Love?" he teased.

"Did you know they would join us?" I asked as he looked down at me.

"I thought they might or they would not have taken care of you. The women liked you from the start. You have that effect on people. It's hard for them not to fall for you wherever you go. That may be why you have two husbands and a dozen suitors praying you'll consider a third." Brass gripped my chin firmly between his rough fingers and pursed his lips. "I speak for both of us when I say, not a chance will we share you with a third, Love."

"Not even Pavo?" I asked, biting down on my lower lip.

The peacock hybrid Aves was the most handsome being I'd ever laid eyes on. Brass wrinkled his nose.

"Especially not Pavo."

"Or Sear're?" I asked, smirking.

"Really? Sear're? You like them older, do you?" Brass asked dryly.

Sear're was the shark hybrid Merfolk who was advisor to the king. He was also long lived so was over a hundred years old.

I gave Brass a rueful smile, and he slanted his mouth over mine before turning me around. "No tribes. No men. Only the barghest hybrid and the mind reader and you. Come, as much as I love when you smell of sex and dirt and sweat, baths are mandatory once every few days."

I pulled my lips into my mouth feeling embarrassed as Brass chuckled. His pants flew to his outstretched hand as he pulled the blanket up tight around me.

Brass led me down through the multitude of levels to the bowels of the castle where a spring poured from the rock in a cascading waterfall. The halls were empty. The vote had gone on for hours and it was well past dinner.

"I am glad you didn't activate your bond with Slate." Brass purred in my ear.

We hid under the falls against the smooth rocks the water had shaped over the years. A small ledge fit us both when I laid on top of him. I sat up and looked down at my glistening husband. My skin long since turned *pruney*.

"I hope he didn't mind. I just thought if he knew how angry I was or if something went wrong, that you were less likely to murder them all. Should I activate it tomorrow morning?" I asked, biting my lip.

I definitely wasn't going to activate it then. Brass chuckled, his stomach muscles flexing, and I squeezed my thighs to his hips, smirking.

"He will not be back for a few days," Brass said, letting his head settle back against the ledge.

I pursed my lips unable to stop my wriggling. "Maybe I'll wait until he's on his way back."

Brass's mouth curled and his dreamy eyes hinted at his approval in my decision.

CHAPTER 14

GYPSUM

If Slate and Jett had not come with Cherry and my mother carrying three babies in their arms, we would have thrown all of our *calling* at them the instant they appeared a week earlier than usual. It'd been the same routine for four months, their sudden appearance boded ill or it should have, but when they'd strolled the marble floors into the dining hall of Valla University for Guardian Mastery like they owned the place, it was hard to think about the war outside the sprawling yellow stone castle walls.

Since Ash was not with the good guys and Scarlett was with the Lycans, Sky Tio and Crag Straumr sat at the head of the hall in front of the fireplaces on a dais before the other provosts. The provosts were wearing their robes, black with a thick gold trim, sleeveless with the university sigil on back in silver. Only the headmistresses and masters wore black robes with gold trim.

Fern Rot was the only headmistress since Dahlia was outside the walls with Ash. The curvaceous red head was the mother to everyone inside Valla U, sometimes in the literal sense since her children and grandchildren dominated the population. Even *I* was related to her. My great aunt had lost her husband the in first few days of the war.

We sat towards the middle of the hall and were told the left side facing the provosts was for first years, right second years. I stood up from the bench when I saw them approaching. Yellowed stone sculpted pillars lined the room and sculptured people lined the edges of the ceiling looking down at us. Chandeliers were on each side of the hall, two by two all the way down. Between the chiseled rafters were circular stained glass mosaics depicting the phases of the moon as a nod to the Straumr family, I guessed.

My mom was going to cry. I could tell right away from the way her tilted dark eyes gleamed. She picked up her pace when I stood, her long dark waves like Tawny's fanning out behind her.

"Gypsum!" she cried, and I sucked in a deep breath before I could start crying in front of the other tyros.

"Mom," I said stiffly as she clung around my waist.

My mom was tiny like Tawny and looked at least a decade younger than she was which never bothered me before that exact moment with all my perverted friends watching my mom hug me, who by all rights looked thirty at most outside of Tidings. She tilted her olive face up to me and put a strong hand to the back of my neck to force my head down so she could kiss my cheeks.

"Mom. I'm okay," I said, looking to Cherry for help.

Cherry, or Cerise Enox, as she was truly named, was Jett's second wife. Technically they married Amethyst at the same time, but Amethyst was a Geol heir. Cherry had the tall slender frame as her wife, but with fair milky skin bright cobalt eyes and a pouty red mouth.

Her fox-like face smirked at me as I managed to get an inch between my mom and I. Jett's chiseled tan face was also smiling as he held up the bundle in his arms.

"Balder's brow! You had your son!" I finally noticed the other two dark-haired bundles. "By the Mother, are those Scarlett's sons? Balas and Spinel?" I asked, checking with Slate to be sure he had okayed those names since Brass's grandfather had been her lover for a short time.

Slate and Jett were like two walls of solid muscle. Only Hausts and

Vars were that big. My mom was placated with letting her hold on to me as I greeted the other three. Slate's silver scar stood out over his left eye against his deeply tanned skin. He was smiling. I could count on one hand how many times I'd seen him smile outside of Scarlett's presence.

"Junior," Jett said in his deep smug baritone, jutting his square jaw proudly.

His son was totally bald, his blue eyes had already started to get lighter. They would probably end up the same turquoise Jett shared with Scarlett. Junior's skin looked fair and would likely end up like Cherry's milky white skin. There was no mistaking Brass's sons. I peeked into the swaddled baby in Slate's corded arm not even as long as his massive forearm.

I guffawed. "Gods, there was no way she was going to be able to play these two off as anyone else's but Brass's."

Slate chuckled with the others and my mom finally stopped weeping. "This one is Balas. Balas is always in blue Scarlett says, Spinel is in green so we can tell them apart." Slate's voice had a growl to it as he held up the amber eyed baby with dark hair.

"Their eyes just changed. It's because of their *calling*. Guardians mature faster, but it'll stop at your age," Cherry chirped.

I'd be twenty at midsummer. I looked like I was in my mid-twenties.

"How did you guys get here? Aren't the portals locked?" I asked, and Jett sucked his lower lip into his mouth.

"Your sister lent Jett her portal key since Ridge has a spare."

I leveled my eyes at Jett who gave me a look and shrugged. "She's good. In case you're wondering. Not great. Amethyst is taking care of her."

"Why didn't anyone else come? Not that I'm complaining, but Brass hasn't met his own kids yet, has he?" I asked as Drill-tooth scampered up the center aisle to my leg.

There was nothing particularly special about the grey squirrel other than the fact it had chosen to become my friend and didn't mind running errands for me. I was a zoolinguist. Animals of all kinds got a kick out of the fact that I could understand them. I had a Northern Goshawk named Storm-pale that delivered messages for me since the war started. My friends were used to it. My roommates didn't mind our unexpected guests.

"Brass and Scarlett's sons?" Crimson Rot had slid up beside my mother.

Beryl Sunna, one of my four roommates and Sunna heir had his arm around her waist. She was one of the many red heads that came from the Tio/Rot family. There was no end to their fertility it seemed. I'd gotten to know her well since Scarlett introduced her to Beryl the night the war started. Her grandfather was my great uncle and had been executed with my grandmother at the beginning of the war.

She fixed sapphire eyes on the little bundles rubbing her nonexistent baby bump. She had the signature milky skin of the Rot. I wondered what their child would look like. He was her opposite with pin straight sable hair trendily styled like any guy our age you'd see in the States and dark up tilted eyes. He wasn't as severe as his father Boa, the first year headmaster, but he had the deadly grace of one intimately familiar with a long seax as I was.

"Scarlett managed to get herself kidnapped. Brass, Quick, and Ridge are saving her," Slate said nonchalantly as he looked down on his stepson. "Brass joined our marriage. We are blood bound."

"*Uh*... congratulations?" I said skeptically.

I expected his eyes to flash, but they stayed a pale grey as he lifted them to my face, confusion written all over it. "My thanks. The Bjorn took her. No doubt she is making their life difficult as we speak."

"You're not shifting or going crazy or anything? Everything is... good?" I asked still dubious of this scarily relaxed Slate.

"Forgive my saying so, Sparrow, but he needs to get laid," Jett interjected. and my mom smacked her lips in disapproval. "You know it's bad if I said so!" Jett said in defense.

Slate's head swiveled to the table, and I looked with him where Jade Kaldr and Rosasite Sol sat and gave them both a flat look when Jade waggled her fingers. Ro and I were currently *on* in our odd relationship though we were mostly friends who enjoyed one another's beds. Her exotic honey-colored eyes were set off by her creamy coffee skin and black shoulder length ringlets. She was a Shadow Breaker and deadly with her blades. I'd met her while Brass dated her for a short while. Come to think of it, Brass had dated half the girls I sat with though Slate was the renowned womanizer.

Jade had the classic good looks of Indigo with Scar's fighting skill set and that same toned look without losing her curves. The blonde looker could have her pick of any man in the building, except Slate and Jett. Even I would be amenable to a romp if she was halfway pleasant for an hour.

One of the two girls must have said something to make Slate pay them any mind. His hearing was unparalleled as was his memory being a prophet.

Jade's cousin was Zircon Snjar who had killed his own brother Hunter on the night the Stygians tried to take Valla U and saved my life in the process. He was the Snjar heir now, and I still hadn't figured him out, but he'd set his sights on Mica which made it difficult for me to warm up to the guy. He wasn't as tall as Slate or Jett, no one was, but he had a big build like they did with dirty blonde hair pulled back away from his tan skin. I'd heard the girls talking about his aquamarine eyes like they were something special. I supposed they found him ruggedly good looking through all that stubble.

Mica.

She turned from where she had sat with Malachite between us. She hadn't spoken to me since the night of Crimson and Beryl's wedding. I'd technically gotten back together with Ro that night after Mica more than hinted that she wanted me to make love to her for her first time.

It was a bad idea. I had Diamond. Even though Diamond was married to Sterling, she wouldn't be happy if I hooked up with Mica. Mica wasn't the kind of girl you slept with once. You kept her and endeavored to make her yours. You married a girl like Mica. I wasn't looking for marriage. It was better that Ro found me.

Hair that fell to her hips with blunt cut bangs, Mica's svelte figure twisted as she smiled at Crimson who had taken Spinel from Cherry. She didn't have the sapphire blue eyes most the Rot had but brown and soulful like Butterfly's. She did have the porcelain skin all of them shared with a smattering of freckles, that I could see well, standing as I was, between her breasts of her black v-neck caftan that all the tyros women wore. She had on the red belt of the first years, like all of us first years wore.

Malachite wrapped his arm around Mica's slender shoulders. He was as close as I had to a best friend now that Steel was dead. Another Shadow Breaker I'd met through Ro. As tall as Zircon, but with a build more like mine broad shouldered and chiseled instead of being a brick house. He was easy to overlook unless you caught the mischievous look in his crinkling dark eyes. His brown hair was always disheveled which went well with his lopsided smirk that belied just how cocky he was.

Ever since Scar came back from the Merfolk, she could catch the scents of people attracted to her and their pheromones caused her own to react since the pleasure center of her mind became more sensitive. Her eyes always dilated with Malachite Blao, heir to the Blao of Mabon. She would call him *cute*. If she gave him half a chance he would've bedded her or Indigo. He had a major crush on my cousins, but any girl was his type. He was probably trying to make Celestine jealous by leaning on Mica.

Celestine was the only one not tied to any of the greater of lesser families being from a common family in Valla. The ebony skinned fourth roommate of the girls was quiet and contemplative but could play the lute like nobody's business. She ignored Malachite's blatant attempt at her attention and continued her conversation with Zircon, running her fingers through her long braids. It would take more than a few well-timed jokes and cocky smirks to melt Celestine.

I heard footsteps behind me and knew the provosts had finally gotten sick of waiting patiently for them to approach. Butterfly led the group. She and Mica looked a lot alike. Coyote Regn, Brass and Quick's older brother had three children with the petite red head.

"Brass's sons?" she asked, clasping her hands to her chest as she approached Slate and Crimson.

Slate nodded and held out Balas for her to take. "*Oh,* blessed Mother. Thank the Gods he had children before he lost his fertility. They look just like him, don't they?"

Butterfly didn't ask where he was or if he was okay or anything about Scarlett. She delved deep in the baby world and was lost with her two sisters with her. Wisteria and Magnolia huddled around the twins being twins themselves with their daughters. Mica got up to lean over her mother's shoulder while Magnolia took Spinel away from Crimson to coo and awe.

My mother held me tighter. "Tree stayed with Bee-gold at the palace. I think all the traveling is finally starting to wear on the fat cat."

Tree was my insider with Slate and Brass, but I guessed I wouldn't need her now that Slate seemed more like himself.

Sky and Ford Tio were not far behind their sisters. Ford, a rougher, taller version of his older brother with a prominent forehead and wider face, and Sky with his beard and shoulder length hair her kept tucked behind his ears. He'd always reminded me of a wizard and it wasn't just because he taught Counter Calling. Sky had been up against Ash when he had been elected Prime. The five siblings had all lost their father when Reed Tio had been executed right outside the walls of the castle.

The three Straumr brothers bypassed the babies and went directly to Jett and Slate. I could see the back of Crag's shaved, ebony head as he spoke to Slate who stood a head taller than he was. The stern eldest brother stood with his stocky shoulders bunched as he faced Slate. River looked the most like Amethyst with her skin tone and dark eyes. He and Fox both had goatees that framed their wide mouths and tight curled hair. The youngest brother had been doing a little extra late night training with Jade. His sky-blue eyes slid past her as he stood between his brothers. Fox's wife was Novaculite Natt and rumor had it that the baby she carried was Ash's because Fox was around thirty and had lost his fertility ages ago. She was also the twin sister to Ash's wife Quartzite and on the wrong side of the war.

"How is my rambunctious niece? Oh dear, do those urchins mean I am a great uncle again? Gods be good. I am far too young," Jackal said, sidling up to place his head on top of my mother's.

Scar's uncle rarely took life seriously. He taught Languages at Valla U in spite of his family's wishes to marry and become an ambassador as all greater families should, in their opinion. Too bad Jackal didn't play by anyone's rules and had risked his ties to his Var family to live with Crag at Valla U. He had to bend to rest his chin on my mom's head. She smiled as she looked up at him.

He gave her a sly smile with glittering blue eyes, his blonde hair always wound up having a floppy style to it no matter how he combed it. He was a Var. Tall, broad, blond, and blue eyed with tan skin. Just like Indigo, though my slender cousin would never be called broad.

"Captured by Bjorn. I'm guessing she has at least one marriage proposal by now and the women are cursing her very existence," I joked.

My mom gave Jackal a hug. "Sparrow. You have your hands full these days. How *did* you welcome your husband home after twenty years?"

My mother's face turned bright red despite her olive skin and I slid away from her. I didn't want to hear if my mom had taken back up with her first husband. I didn't even know what that made me since that meant my father's marriage wasn't legal in Guardian eyes. I was still heir to the Sumar, but illegitimate? Freya's burly boar, did my mom sleep with her first husband when he came back? How did my dad feel about that?

"They are building siege machines. It is only a matter of time before they attack," Crag said in his croaking rough voice.

"There is more." Asp Sandr appeared as if from the thin air.

She looked so much like Shale it hurt. I couldn't stand to be around the provost with her pin straight dark hair and dark up tilted eyes. We'd lost Ama and Shale before we even knew we were fighting a war. They had both been my occasional lovers and good friends.

"What's that?" Jett asked.

Asp and Boa were brother and sister. He placed a hand on her shoulder stopping her from continuing. He had a way of looking down his nose at everyone. A severe face made more so from the way he swept his hair away free of any softness.

"It is better if we show you. They will parade her out after dinner," Boa said in his usual clipped tone.

"Parade. What an apt choice of wording," Jett said as his nostrils flared.

Indigo wore a pale blue caftan with heavy white lace trim with a small bump just below the white lace belt that cinched her otherwise trim waist. If you asked Scar, she'd say Indigo was beautiful, and that *she* was sexy, now that she had experienced more of life than she had wanted to.

Indi was beautiful in an obvious classic way. I could agree with that sentiment. Light blonde hair to her elbows and powder blue eyes that glittered when her mole on her right cheek lifted and her pink lips parted. Cygnus escorted her around camp tonight sometimes it was Sterling. Though I had watched for a long time and saw that Ash frequented her tent.

"We saw her in Elivagar. She has been here a short time?" Slate growled and ran his fingers through something at his shoulder.

I caught a glimpse as he released it and saw Indigo's turquoise tree of life fetish Scarlett had given her. How Slate had gotten it was a mystery.

"Four days," Jackal answered somberly as he watched his father show Indigo the siege machines. "She is pregnant. If I had to guess, I would say it is Sterling's."

Cygnus wore his green sleeveless robe trimmed in gold with the golden tree of life emblazoned on the back as he walked between tents. He was a Var, other than the white wings of his side combed hair, Cygnus was blonde and built like Jett. Where they walked was just the tip of the iceberg. Behind them over the lawn of Valla U were the abomination army they'd bred.

"Thank the Gods Quick didn't come with," Jett breathed. "She looks better since we saw her. Sterling must be fattening her up."

Cherry cradled Junior in her arm as she pulled Jett's waist to her, away from the long window.

"I had a bunch of tyros up here —"

Jackal laughed remembering the first time I saw her out there. "He demanded we try to levitate her into the building."

Jett and Slate both turned to offer me wry smiles that made me feel like an idiot all over again. "Scar can levitate people; she can even form a step out of solid air a foot high to give herself a boost. We only needed to stack those steps so she could reach the windows, but she always has a nix torque on. It could've worked," I said defensively, and my mom stroked my long hair, rubbing the copper beads I wore through the narrow braids that reached my shoulder blades.

"If anyone could, Scarlett would've done it. We'll see if we can get her here soon," my mom soothed.

Spring in Valla meant caftans in the Ostara style. My breath caught as Diamond Natt came into the torchlight riding a dappled mare with her chestnut hair bouncing off her back. She favored pink. It looked good with her celadon eyes and caramel skin. If she was in Mabon, she would've been in one of their taffeta bustled dresses. That meant she was at the Straumr palace. It was the first time I'd seen her in over four months. Without her help, I would've been dead. As would my father and countless others. She'd been blood sworn not to reveal the Stygians plans but had asked me to walk her to the portal doors and right into Dahlia Natt plotting away with a contingent of the assassin's guild.

I grit my teeth when I saw Sterling emerge from the tent Indigo stayed in. He was there while his wife was away. Diamond had all the softness her brother lacked. He was riding beside her, but Diamond consumed my world.

"Mother fucker," Jett cursed as Ash swung off his horse.

He turned right towards the window they stood in knowing we'd be watching Indi. His eyes like Diamond's, that pale green with caramel skin and chestnut hair, his cropped short like Jett's. Ro had told me that if I was asking, which I wasn't, the best looking man in Tidings was Jett, but that Ash was a close second.

He smiled at the window and Jett stepped back into the shadows. My stomach burned with anger.

They didn't know Jett was alive, but they knew Slate was. He crowded the narrow window looking ready to leap from it. He could if he shifted into a full barghest. Slate could even get to Ash before they swarmed him with their army.

Sterling was helping Diamond down from her mount as Ash bypassed them to Indigo. Slate gripped the window sill so we couldn't see.

"She is a khoraz. Sterling's khoraz," Slate growled.

Not his usual growl, deeper somehow and with a vibration that I could feel in my throat. Jett fought for a spot in the window and I bent to peek beneath his elbow. Indigo's body language had changed. Her spine curved to Sterling, her fingers curled as if she itched to touch him and it took an effort to restrain herself in Diamond's presence. I'd seen

Scarlett do that with Slate when he'd lost his memories enough times to know what it meant.

I held my breath until the feeling of desperation passed. So close, but so far. It was more than any man could take. Jackal put his hands on Slate and Jett's shoulders.

"At least we know she is alive and well. I know it is not ideal, but Sterling will make sure she is looked after. If nothing else, the dupe loves her. Has, as long as they have known each other."

I watched Crag and wondered if he felt anything at all about siring Diamond and Ash on Delta only to give them up to his uncle and Dahlia Natt to raise as their own because she was infertile. Did Diamond hurt since the only man she knew as her father had been killed the night they tried to take Valla U?

"We are leaving. We are going to take my sons back to Thrimilci with Sparrow and Cherry, then we have to go back to Elivagar after we see Viper at Folkvangr. It is time this usurper pried from Tawny's seat," Slate said, turning away from the window.

Viper Enox was temporarily running the Mabon arena Scarlett built, her Vigrid competitions were the furthest thing from the minds of the people.

I walked alongside them in silence until we reached the long portal room. A multitude of vine carved arched doors were locked. Tapestries hung at either end with sconces in between each door lighting the room. Jett hung back, giving Junior to Cherry.

My head ached. My chest ached, though maybe it was my heart. We were prisoners in the castle while they had free rein over four of the five islands that made up Tidings.

Jett and Scar could've been twins. His hair was blonder than hers, but that was it. He had full lips and those turquoise almond eyes that should have been too pretty for a man's face, but Jett's chiseled features made up for it.

"*Uh*, I just wanted to say that if Tawny lets me, I'm going to take care of her and Steel's daughter. The girls have agreed to make her a wife... if she wants," Jett said with an unusual amount of awkwardness.

I furrowed my brow at him. "Bro, I don't want to know what you and your two wives want to do with my sister."

Jett chuckled nervously as he ran a hand over his short hair. "No kidding, chief. I just don't want you thinking she's alone or we're... you know, using her or something." He licked his lips, and I wished I could rewind time and erase the conversation from my mind.

I took a deep breath. "I already knew. Scar, Tawns, and I don't keep secrets even though some secrets *should* be kept. I'm glad she's not alone. I don't think with Steel being... gone and her dad showing up out of nowhere, that she would've been doing all right if she hadn't had some help. Add being pregnant and I'm sure we would've had to have her committed. As long as you don't hurt her, we won't have a problem," I said with a shrug, but I met his eyes so he knew I meant it.

Tawny had always taken care of herself, but she was more sensitive than she seemed. Jett was a giant, a full six inches taller than I was and possibly six inches broader, but maybe I would be faster. I would *try* to kick his ass at least if he hurt her.

"Chief, man. I don't think I'm going to be the one to end this courtship. Trust me," Jett said before he pulled the auseklis portal key over his head to open the locked door.

"Yeah, well I know Tawns and if she gave you that key, she's thinking about something she wasn't thinking about the last time I saw her," I said before they were swallowed by the white light of the portal.

My mom hugged me until I thought I heard my ribs crack, and Cherry planted a firm kiss to my lips with glittering blue eyes. "Your lips are as soft as your sister's," she said with a purr and I groaned as she left through the portal.

Slate ran his hand over his unshaven jaw and I quirked my brow. "I am going. I need to steady myself. Mirage is at the Thrimilci palace and it takes a great deal of effort not to tear her throat out."

"You're not..."

"If I had not lost my memories, I would not have taken up with her again. She knew that and has avoided me since I regained them."

"Probably because she knows you're going to kill her. What about Lynx? All done?" I asked.

Slate's eyes took on a gunmetal sheen. "I burnt down Shadow Breaker headquarters, I burnt down the brothel. Everywhere I betrayed my wife is ashes like those memories. Scarlett will never have to set eyes there and relive those memories."

I shivered as he stalked through the door.

CHAPTER 15

GYPSUM

There were pads on the combat section of training room floor. I practiced throwing the short axe Scarlett got me for my birthday into the straw dummies across from me next to the archery targets. A track spanned the tiered stone seating of the dome capped room. Someone had left the Gauntlet out in the center of the room and River would tear whoever it was a new one if I didn't put it away for them.

My sister becoming a polygamist, Indigo a khoraz, my mother possibly not being married to my father, and Scarlett being captured *again* even if Slate didn't seem concerned. I wouldn't be able to sleep. I sure as hell wouldn't go back to dinner. I could've gone to Ro's room, but I couldn't distract myself in Ro with Mica in the room. She always came to my room, or we found an empty classroom.

The thunk of the axe in the dummy, the flex of my body as I threw, that's what I needed. I should've asked Malachite to spar with me. I drew my long seax over my shoulder and attacked the dummy. I stabbed Ash through the heart. I gutted Sterling. My blade slid across Sage's throat.

My black linen shirt stuck to my body, and I unbuckled my modified scabbard to remove it. It used to buckle around my hips, but I liked how Malachite's looked and we had little else to do trapped in the university as we were. I had a sheath for my axe at the center of my back as well that fixed with a button and that was when *calling* came in handy.

I buckled the black leather around my body again when I spotted Mica walking out from the women's prep room. I tried to ignore her, sliding my grandfather Flint's blade back into the scabbard and took up the axe again.

"Does it owe you coin?" Mica's high falsetto penetrated my concentration, and I turned to her.

I was distracted by my grief and my fury for her to sneak up behind me without me noticing. Her scent of orchids and loquat should have alerted me at least.

"What?" I asked too curtly, and she glanced away and gestured.

"The dummy. It was a joke. A stupid joke, obviously. You are especially distracted," she said, sliding her fingers over the handle of her whip.

She wore the snug black pants and a black cotton tank top that the female tyros sometimes got away with wearing during battle training. Her red hair fell loose to her slim hips.

I grunted. "I am distracted," I said as if it wasn't obvious.

I walked back to the dummy and pulled my axe out as an excuse to move away from her. She was distracting. She was still standing there when I returned and I glanced down to where I'd thrown my shirt. I should put it back on. My hair was sticking to my back and my chest, the beads slapping with each throw.

"Your mom is beautiful. She looks too young to have a son your age," Mica continued.

"Malachite was quick to note it," I said as I threw my axe again.

Mica tittered nervously, and I cocked a brow at her. Her porcelain skin flushed, and I sucked in a deep breath. I just wanted to be alone. I couldn't have her being sweet and innocent and beautiful while I was trying to envision killing people.

"Malachite notes whenever he sees a pretty woman," she said wryly.

Had he come on to her? What was I thinking, of course he had. I pressed my lips into a firm line and *called* back my axe. Maybe I could propel my axe into Ash's face from the window.

Mica finally got the hint and unfurled her whip. Her slender arm flew as she cracked it against the dummy's throat tearing straw free. It was good for an opponent unable to draw close to you, but not for close combat.

"You should train with a spear or the quarterstaff," I said absently as she let it crack again.

Her big brown eyes slid to me. "Maybe you could show me how to use a short seax. I have heard Ro grudgingly say your cousin is the best female blade fighter the university has seen in two decades and her husbands are both master assassins," she said with a tone of awe.

I'd seen Brass and Slate spar and mean it. It was fast and bloody. I'd seen Scar spar with them both and it only slightly less bloody. I nodded. I had picked up a few tips before I decided to specialize in the long seax.

I pulled my short seax from the sheath at my back and gripped it to show her. "Fox taught Scarlett the basics, like holds and stuff. He'd be best to show you, but I can teach you a few things."

I showed her the most common holds for a short blade and she pulled her short seax from her thigh sheath and mimicked my actions.

"Like this?" she asked, and I shifted her hold with a nod.

"Good. You could use your whip with the blade," I told her and stuck my short seax back in its sheath.

"You do not want to spar?" she asked, blinking those soulful eyes at me.

I lifted my brow. "With you? I don't want to hurt you, Mica. You're a hundred pounds with your boots on."

She seemed taller since she had long limbs, but she was probably Indigo's height and shorter than I was by several inches. She was also about a third of my width. I'd crush her if we tried to spar.

Mica's delicate brows drew together as she squared off against me. Gods blasted Guardian women always think when a man was being chivalrous it's a personal affront or a challenge. She stepped back, and I reached for my short seax behind my back.

My eyes widened as her whip cracked out around my elbow and the sting of its tip that had drawn blood. I cursed and ran my thumb over the wound.

"Two out of three, first blood drawn. I think that one goes to me," Mica said as her bright pink lips pulled into a knowing smile.

Frigga's sweet grass, that coy smile could do serious damage. I stalked around her as she slowly spun in a circle, whip at the ready. I lunged rolling over my back and heard her let out a charming little giggle as she cracked her literal whip and it coiled around my throat as sprung onto my feet. I'd managed to get my hand between it and my neck, but the tip had cut into the side of my jaw.

"I guess I win," she said, loosening its hold until it fell off my shoulders.

"You're talking to me again. I was getting used to your silent treatment. Are you always so stubborn when you don't get what you want? You're not quitting already are you?" I goaded.

Her eyes widened and her cheeks reddened. "I was not giving you the silent treatment. I was giving you a chance to explain why you left me on the dance floor and wound up with Ro again."

My ears burned. So she'd heard about that. Not exactly like it was a secret, and I hadn't chosen Ro over her — Ro chose me and I gave in. That was how it went every time we got together. I couldn't think of a single time I'd ever chased after a girl. I never got the chance.

"I'm sorry for leaving you on the dance floor. I thought my sister was dead, and she appeared in the middle of Crimson's wedding. I was shocked," I explained, and her eyes narrowed.

"Best out of three," she said with a nod and began to circle me.

I turned to follow her form that moved so smoothly it was like she glided. "That's it then? We're all good?"

"Are all men as blind as you or are you especially oblivious?" she asked peevishly.

I stared at her stunned. She'd never been anything, but sweet to me or anyone else.

"I'm sorry. I don't know why you always seem to be upset with me," I stammered, and she groaned in frustration.

"Go on then."

I blinked and pulled my short seax before dodging the first crack of her whip. She was fast, and her narrow nose was wrinkled as she cracked her whip. Time was slowing again as it had at Crimson's wedding when I walked to Mica on the dance floor. I slipped under the curve the tip of the whip made and crashed into her legs taking her feet out from under her.

She clenched her small jaw as I held the blade to her throat. Her chest rose and fell heavily beneath me as I pinned her to the training circle.

"You have to draw blood for it to count," she said in a strained voice.

"I think we've already established that you've won, Mica," I said wryly.

Her porcelain skin was red down to where it disappeared under her shirt and I dragged my eyes back up to her face. "I don't get why you're always ignoring me. I get along with nearly everyone. I haven't done anything wrong, have I? Tell me if I have — because I didn't mean to. I like you, Mica."

I liked saying her name.

Her lips parted and she shouldn't have been able to get any redder, but she did. "Freya's burly boar, Gypsum. You really are blind. You can get off me now," she said, and I wondered why I hadn't done it already.

I slid my blade into its sheath. "You're spending an awful lot of time with Zircon. Are you together?"

Her brows twitched. "He asks me to walk to classes together and to eat meals with him, but I have not let him come to my room," she answered.

He hadn't brought her to our room either. Malachite would've told me. Gods, why was I even asking her? I didn't care. Did I? Maybe a little.

Maybe I could kiss her a little. She wasn't making any move to shove me off. Ro would only be upset if I wasn't honest with her or if she found out through someone else. *Yes.* I would kiss her.

Mica was watching me intently as I held my inner debate and took a shuddering breath as I canted my jaw to hers. She exhaled right before my lips took hers and I caught the hint of mint from dinner and smiled.

She wrapped her slender arms around my neck, fingers slipping through the sweat and beads that clung to it. I used my thumb to angle her jaw just so and kissed her deeply as she squirmed. I loved her eager little wriggle.

Her soft pants came with her constant moans as I trailed down her throat. I could keep kissing her, there was plenty to kiss as long as I didn't do more. Mica kept her hands on my face or at my shoulder reminding me of how uncomfortable she was putting them anywhere else.

I wouldn't be a lech this time. I wouldn't push her limits.

I hooked my fingers in the sleeves of her tank top and bra and pushed them over her shoulders kissing the freckles that always drew my eye. I wished I could kiss each one of those freckles one at a time. I pushed her top even lower until her dusky pink peaks hardened with my rough breaths.

Just a little more kissing. She didn't seem to mind. On the contrary, her legs were shifting, and I lifted my hips so she could bend them to either side of me. By the Mother, I fit perfectly against her. Her moans grew higher and I let my tongue probe lower.

Her breasts fit snugly in my hand. Not too big or too small. Her back bowed off the ground as I slid my tongue around one of those pink peaks and sucked gently on it. Her fingers had curled in my hair as she held my head in place, it grew harder against my tongue before I shifted to the next.

It was still only kissing. Some of the best kissing had a little tongue. I wanted to kiss lower, so the shirt would have to go. I slid back and pulled her up by her arms as I tugged the shirt over her head and let her red hair fall around onto her milky skin. I brushed her bangs away from her face as I pulled her close sensing her insecurity and her calves slid over my thighs as I held her to my chest.

We were skin against skin as I ran my rough palms over her flawless back hoping I wasn't leaving scratches in their wake. Her hands stayed on my shoulder driving me insane.

"Mica, *Gods be good*, touch me," I breathed against her mouth.

"Where?" she asked throatily, and my head just about exploded.

"Wherever you want. There's nowhere you can't touch."

I wanted to scream it, shout it, but instead I busied my lips with hers as I pulled her tighter into my lap and began to move my hips against her.

Her moans grew even higher as she splayed her hands on my chest and worked her way over the hard ridges of my abs. I leaned her back and ducked my head to kiss at her chest and she ran her nails along my shoulder blades.

Oh, thank the blessed Mother. About time.

More. I wanted to kiss more of her. I laid her back down and her breaths came shallow as I ran my tongue along her belly.

"Kissing. More kissing," she breathed, and I couldn't have agreed more.

I practically dove back to her mouth stealing her moan as our hands unbuckled one another's belts then pants. Just kissing. Kissing and touching. It was hard to give a good kiss if you didn't touch the other person.

She whimpered as I sucked in sharply when I sprung free of my pants. I clasped her hand over me and felt her wriggling change as she melted. She was opening up to me and all I had to do was take it.

No. *No.* Just kissing and a little touching.

I guided her hand over me until she was confident enough to do it on her own. My stomach tightened as she ran her thumb over my ridge and I cursed internally. No, she couldn't touch, only I could touch. I had to change the rules or I was going to break mine. I gently took her hand away and pulled my lips away from hers.

Her sweat mingled with her sweet floral scent blended with the citrus smell of the loquat. I wondered if her scent would be even stronger if we were in the greenhouse or in the shower.

Her pants slipped easily over her hips as I moved south and shoved them down to her knees. Her skin prickled against my tongue as I followed the curve of her pubic bone to the thin trail of fiery red hair between her legs.

"Oh, Gypsum!" Mica's cried with her head tossed back as my lips met the apex of her thighs.

Ama and Shale hadn't been shy about their preferences when I kissed them there and they had been very good teachers, so I'd been told time and time again. I was kissing. Just kissing and a little nudging, maybe with a bit of touching.

Mica's slender thighs kept trying to close around my head and I settled on my chest to tilt her hips up. She let out a number of gasps and curses as I did more kissing until the pants that were attached to her legs around her boots strained as she gripped my hair even tighter.

"Ah!" she cried out louder than I probably should've let her, considering we were on the battle grounds — but my cock was pressed to my stomach and the blood flow was not getting to my brain.

Her body jolted as rubbed above her little bud and her body continued to tense. "Wait," she begged, but I knew I could do better.

I was relentless as I strummed her into a frenzy. Her back bowing, her breath hitching, as she held my mouth in place against her until the shocks subsided. Mica went limp as I dragged my kisses back up her belly. Her fingers unfurled from my hair to slide down my back until she gazed up lazily through her lashes.

"Make love to me, Gypsum," she said softly as I kissed her swollen pink lips and my hips settled between her legs.

"Don't tempt me, Mica," I told her roughly as I ran my fingers over her cheek.

She was stunningly beautiful.

Mica's hands slid lower over my back to run over my backside and I slid my eyes shut. I could get up now, take a cold shower and leave her alone. She'd date some worthy guy her mother approved of and give herself to him for her first time.

Or some commitmentphobe could spar with her on the battle grounds, strip her to nearly nothing, and take her right there in the grit... at least once before bringing her into the men's prep room to find out if her scent really would be stronger in the shower. I'd have to find a room where we could spend the night together because I wouldn't leave her after her first time and I didn't want it advertised that she'd spent the night with me. I was a Sumar/Tio, and I had no delusions of what my reputation or my family's would do to her.

There wasn't a moment where I decided that I was going to take her. There was only kissing her and then she was tilting her hips up to me. I rocked against her knowing she would be as ready as she could be for me to take her. She met my movements with her own and I felt myself sliding between her legs.

I lifted my head to those depthless brown eyes, and she gave a little nod with parted lips. I kissed her again. She was so damn beautiful. I leaned back, putting my weight on my elbow, as I gripped myself to guide slowly into her.

"Tell me to stop or go slower, or —"

"Gypsum. I trust you," she said, and my heart nearly exploded.

I watched her expression as I ran myself against her, testing the waters so to speak, and she eagerly tilted her hips again almost rising onto her feet to urge me inside her. She stiffened as I began to slip inside, anticipating pain and I stopped.

"Mica?" I said, feeling shaky as I withdrew.

"What's wrong?" she asked, and my stomach dropped.

"Do you like chocolate? Slate and Jett brought ice cream with them from Elivagar," I said, grasping at straws as I scooted back trembling as I began to *call* her clothes over to us so she wouldn't feel exposed.

She stared numbly at me as I took her wrist and pulled her into a sitting position before I tucked myself away and pulled my shirt over my head, awkwardly fitting it over the seax still strapped to my back.

"Ice cream?" she asked in disbelief and I nodded stupidly. "No, I do not want to get *ice cream* with you, Gypsum Sumar," she spat.

A kick to my manly bits would've been just as good as she got to her feet and yanked her pants up before pulling over her shirt. She shook as she shoved her bra into her pocket and stalked over to her whip.

"Wait, Mica. Let me explain," I started, and she shot me a scathing look.

"Save your breath."

"You're too good for me, Mica. You are now, you were two weeks ago, you were four months ago. You'll always be too good for me. You don't wait until your nineteen as a Guardian and sleep with some asshole who can't appreciate how fantastic you are," I said, chasing after her as she strode to the women's prep room.

She whirled on me making me stop in my tracks. "You are just like Crimson. You think everyone does not know but they do. I know the real reason you do not have a relationship or a betrothal already is because you are sleeping with Diamond Natt. The entire university knows it. You are not fooling anyone."

I felt like the air had been sucked out of the room.

She shook her head. "Straumrs are born into privilege, they are raised knowing people will want to be close to them, marry them, and they will have power no matter what. They never have to be nice to a single person *ever*. She is using you. You make her letting her parents choose her life for her tolerable, but you do not get to have one in return. You will always be her toy when she needs to do something rebellious."

I balled my hands into fists. "You have no idea what you're talking about, Mica. Diamond loves me and I love her. If she hadn't been betrothed before I came to Tidings, we'd be married by now. I am no one's toy. I am with her because I want to be."

"To what end? What happens next?" she asked, and my lips parted but no sound came out. She gave me a sympathetic look, and I grew even angrier. "*Nothing*, that is what. You will never be more than what you are right now to her."

"If you already knew all this, then why am I here? Why do you want me so badly, Mica? When you could have a dozen other men who wouldn't turn you down. Who would take what you're giving and not think twice!" I shouted at her, and she took a retreating step.

I never shouted. I never lost my temper. Why was she getting under my skin so badly I wanted to shake her?

"Because you are a good man and I have hope for you. I thought maybe you had feelings for me too and that they might grow into something special to help you forget about her. That eventually you would want me as badly as I want you," she said, dropping her eyes.

I couldn't think. I couldn't speak. I felt like a total numbskull staring at this beautiful woman who had tried to give herself to me not, once or twice, but three times and I kept screwing it up. She was right. She was right about all of it and it hurt like nothing I'd felt before. Different from the deaths of my Aunt Wren or grandmother, Pearl. I felt used and stupid.

"You're right," I said, suddenly feeling leaden and heavy. "But, you're wrong about one thing, Mica. I care very much about you and that's why I don't give in. You *do* deserve better. You don't want to feel... how I feel."

My feet couldn't take me fast enough. I wished I could fly with Storm-pale and we would get far away from there. I pushed past the prep room doors and tore off my shirt punching the walnut cubbies until one cracked. I unbuckled my scabbard and let it fall to the floor.

I wasn't a bad guy. Diamond was beautiful and lovely. When Scarlett asked me to join her in going to the Straumr place I had seen Diamond once before and became infatuated with her and I couldn't resist. I'd had two semi-serious girlfriends before coming to Tidings, but they were nothing like Diamond.

It wasn't even an hour into our first quasi-date and she had seduced me into her bed. I didn't stand a chance. I knew about Sterling and hadn't cared. Then we had taken it a step further and there was no going back after I'd made love to her. I'd fallen in love with her that very day and had been wrapped around her finger ever since.

I woodenly disrobed as I walked to the showers and hit the energy plate so the warm water would cleanse me of my sins. I knew how people had looked at Crimson. I'd gotten to know her pretty well since she dated Beryl and she was a very innocent girl. Ash had been her first and she his, and he'd broken her heart repeatedly. Brass was her unfortunate second and now she had Beryl who at first saw her as his in to a greater family daughter, but after a few weeks of being trapped in the university with her, fell in love. The baby in her belly was intentional, not a happy accident. We all thought he was crazy until we gave her a chance. Ash had destroyed her reputation, and that was why she threw herself at Brass for the chance to have an honorable marriage even if that meant tricking him into getting her pregnant.

Was *I* Crimson?

I rested my forehead on the warm tiles as I tried to collect myself. It'd been a trying day though it had started as boring and dull as the last hundred. My feelings were hurt like some adolescent boys and it irked me to no end. I growled in frustration and punched the tiles.

"Does the shower owe you coin too?" came Mica's falsetto voice from my right.

I blinked water out of my eyes and wiped my face with my hand. I couldn't move. I stared, gaping as I tried to think of something clever to say and found wispy clouds in the place of my brains. Mica nude in the men's prep room was not what my tongue could find words for.

"Anyone could come in and see you." I cursed myself for a wool head.

"And if they did?" she asked, taking a bold step forward though her skin was as red as her hair.

"Then I'd have to poke their eyes out for setting them on you and that wouldn't be right. They don't expect you to be in here after all," I told her and tore my eyes off her flawless porcelain body to face the tiles again.

I squeezed my eyes shut as she wound her arms around my middle and pressed her cheek to my back. Gods, what did I do to deserve this? I wasn't sure if I was cursing them or thanking them.

"Mica —"

"Please. I am losing my nerve. I do not have much to begin with, but if you reject me a fourth time, I might have to go crawl into Malachite's bed," she whispered through the fall of the shower.

I laughed at her jest. Then realized if she wasn't joking, I'd have to kill Malachite.

My mind spun as I tried to think of a suitable place to make love to a woman for her first time. A bed was preferable, but I didn't have one private enough that I could take her to.

Shit. I was doing this.

"Once I start. I won't stop, Mica. Not this time. If you have any doubt, walk away now and I won't blame you at all. You *should* walk away. Running might be even better," I whispered and felt her shake her head against my back.

I spun around startling her into letting me go and circled my arms around her waist crushing her against me. She was so very slender I thought she would slip through my arms. I wrapped my hand in her long damp hair as I kissed her and used my *calling* to toss all the neatly rolled terry cloth towels on the floor of the first aisle of cubbies.

Mica gaped wide eyed at me as I laid her down and sat back on my heels to take her in. I realized belatedly she'd never seen an aroused man fully nude, so I took her palms and placed them on my chest and ran them down my stomach. My wet hair swung as I returned my gaze to her.

"Don't be nervous or if you are going to be nervous, don't be afraid. Do what you want. I'm here for the taking. I won't push you away again," I promised her, and she nodded, eyes catching at my lap in a way that made me smirk. "Gods be good, Mica. Say it out loud for me one more time so I know I wasn't the dreaming the first few times."

Mica lips pulled into a smile. "I want you to make love to me, Gypsum."

She laid exposed and vulnerable for me on the white terry cloth towels and I stopped fighting it. I unfurled myself over her and she opened herself to me. I didn't tease her or withdraw, I watched her as I held her close. Her breasts smashed against my chest as I guided myself into her.

Mica sucked in sharply and I almost laughed because I was hardly even in yet. I kissed her nose and her cheeks before I pushed a little further. My breaths coming shallow as I began to feel her in a way no other man had. A little deeper and her nails bit into the flesh at my shoulders.

"Balder's brow!" she cursed, gritting her teeth and her whole body went rigid.

I kissed along her jaw ever so gently rocked my hips. "Keep going?" I asked, my nerves getting the best of me.

She nodded blinking up at me and I pressed my lips to hers. "A little more and then we get to the good stuff," I promised, coaxing a little smile from her.

"If it is half as good as earlier, I know it will be worth it," she teased and I felt her muscles relax.

I thrust my hips gently and felt it give inside her as she whimpered and I slid into her to the hilt. I breathed raggedly trying to hold back.

"*Fuck*. Mica," I grit as I tried to think unsexy thoughts.

"What?" she asked, and I let out a self-deprecating laugh.

"You're not using me for this one time, right? I get you at least for tonight?"

She looked at me confusedly. "We will take it one night at a time. I am not going anywhere."

I instantly shuddered and tried to restrict how deep I thrust into her. I rested my forehead on hers as I took fortifying breaths.

"I have wanted to do that for a while now," I said, chuckling as I lifted my head.

She looked shyly at me and I rocked my hips inside her. Her eyes widened pleasingly, and I stood picking her up so our bodies stayed melded together. She weighed nearly nothing.

"I hope you got enough sleep last night, Mica because one very important lesson I learned from my family of ill-repute is nothing is worth doing unless you are doing it extremely well." Mica's eyes widened as I walked her under the shower pressing her back against the tiles. "Here. Back in the combat circle. I am going to take you where we eat lunch every day and I might even take you in the Prime's office since he isn't using it. *Mica.* I am going to take you in every way a man can. I want all your firsts. Give me everything," I demanded in between kisses.

Mica's eyes were as wide as saucers. Maybe she was regretting giving herself to me, but I was drunk on her. I'd never been a girl's true first and Mica had been so adamant about me so I was going to be adamant about this. No stone left unturned. She was going to give it all to me and I was going to give it right back.

I healed her as much as I could, knowing there were some tender parts that would have to heal naturally or else we'd have to go through that whole first bit again. She didn't make any demands of me after I walked her to the first year's wing at dawn when I was done exploring every inch of her body.

I needed more time for a thorough inspection, but the sun was the enemy and I didn't want her reputation spoiled by mine. We'd have to keep whatever we started that night a secret until things settled down.

Still, I kissed her and wished her goodnight. She might've gotten an hour or two of sleep before breakfast.

When the eight of us sat in the spot where I had bent her over not three hours past, her cheeks were permanently reddened and my smile, horribly obnoxious. I pulled Ro aside afterwards and told her things had to change and that she couldn't come to my bed anymore. She pursed her lips as she always did and told me I'd be back because I always came back, but this time it was different because I had Mica.

CHAPTER

SIXTEEN

Brass held me upright or else I might've fainted overcome with emotion.

Brass had purposely withheld my clothes from me though he'd had them all along in his pack with my blades. I wore my white woolen shirt with my corset and thick white pants and fur-lined boots. He had mended my mother's reversible cloak after it had been torn on our way to the Lycans. I had my belt of daggers around my hips, my black wrist blades with their gold lacework molded back on to match the short seax at my left thigh, gold wings and the gold embossed figure of Freya on it. I felt like myself with all my fetishes through my hair and stone pieces at my breasts. Even my fur-lined boots had blades in them.

It took two hours for us to climb down the outside of the rock castle they'd carved, the road wound repeatedly around the tower. It was irritatingly tedious. Brass deftly helped me braid my hair back so the wind wouldn't whip it around my face as we led the Bjorn past the towering rock formations that doubled as a wind tunnel.

Snow and more snow until we reached ice and the base of the Igulbjorn Ice Cliffs. Zlata, Faima, and Asya traded in their dresses for the billowy pants the men wore and tunics that came down to their knees. They carried their babes close to their chests inside their wide shirts. Lyov, Gennadi, and Demyan walked at our opposite end determined to stand at the front but unwilling to walk with us. Klim bounced from our side with the women to the men's side though the train snaking behind us was intermingled.

"Your cousin is a very determined woman," Brass murmured as I leaned against him.

Tawny's wide mouth smiled beamed at me from where she stood at the front line of the Lycans' march. We'd caught sight of their masses pouring over the top of the cliff and waited for them. She was walking beside Amethyst, and whom I assumed was Aoibhe and Blathnat. One Lycan female had black fur like Niall's coat and Kelly green eyes and the other had mottled cinnamon fur that tapered to white near her muzzle and chest. Donncha, in his massive grey mottled bushy fur form, held Siobhan's arm as an Egyptian jackal with Caolan and the burly grey beast that was Tadg on his right and Padraig on his left. His Kelley green eyes glittering even at a distance from within his black tipped white fur.

Tears swarmed my vision as I trotted to them. The Bjorn content to take their lunch for our brief break. They had brought livestock with them since meat was such a critical part of their diet. I had no clue what it took for thousands of people to march. The Wemic and Faunelle had been content to hunt as we walked, but the frozen lands were not generous in their bounty.

My trot turned to a run and Tawny wobbled to me. "How?" I squeaked out before I reached her.

She rubbed her reddening nose, her wide hazel eyes brimming with tears. "I'm the Matriarch Vetr and these are my lands. It is about time I start acting like it. I couldn't sit back while you were captured and Opal is still missing and some cache hole sits in my seat of power."

We caught one another and both laughed for no apparent reason. "How did you convince them to march already?" I asked, swiping at tears.

She licked her lips and looked back towards the Lycans. "I didn't. Niall did."

The black furred Lycan had made his way to the front of the march with Cabhan and Lorcan. A Eurasian brown wolf with warm whiskey-colored eyes and a grey Arctic wolf with serious grey eyes that focused on the Bjorn behind us. Niall smiled wolfishly at Tawny and my eyes bulged.

"You slept with Niall!" I said in a hushed shout.

She leveled her eyes at me. "No. Not yet. I was just thinking about Jett's offer and I know once I get my island back that the lesser families will send over every suitor they have. I already married the first man I made love to. I don't want to only have experienced one more." She glanced away to Amethyst who had walked up behind her and gave me a hug.

"I can tell from your expression Matriarch Vetr informed you that she planned on taking us as her paramours until she decides to marry," Amethyst said and they shared conspiratorial smiles.

"And that she plans to spend the night with Niall," I spluttered.

"My idea, but we're not telling your brother that. He has developed a crush on your cousin," Amethyst said wryly.

I could tell Tawny and Amethyst had taken their friendship to a different level since I'd left them. Brass had reached me and I could feel the Bjorn assembly, edging closer to the Lycan lines.

"Where's Ridge and Quick?" Tawny asked, checking behind us to be sure they weren't somewhere in the brightly colored crowd.

"They went ahead to scout the Natt manor and make sure Styg is ready at Niflheim Arena," Brass said as he watched Donncha, Padraig, and Caolan in her white fluffy arctic form approach.

The assembly of Bjorn had gathered at our back and the strain between the two tribes was enough to make me dull my empath abilities because of how strongly it was suffocating me.

Donncha's deep set midnight eyes peered at Lyov over his canine muzzle. They would not be in their human forms on the other side of the Igulbjorn Ice Cliffs.

"I don't know whether I need to introduce you or not," I said, pivoting my body to work as moderator.

"We know one another well enough," Donncha said, running his eyes over Gennadi's panda like face and settling on Demyan's golden grizzly face whose short muzzle was pulled back in a hint of a snarl.

"Congratulations on your marriage, Donncha. I am glad you found happiness once more." Asya bobbed her head of unruly curls to Siobhan who managed to smile beautifully even as a jackal.

Klim wandered up apparently having been distracted by lunch before noticing that his family had left him and the black bear insinuated himself between Tawny and I. Tawny gaped at him wondering who he could've thought he was placing himself so close to us. His hazel eyes were locked on the Lycans.

"This is Klim. The youngest son of Lyov and Asya," I said, introducing him which I suspected was not the custom.

If Klim could blush, he would have. He realized where he stood and glanced around to find his mother. I placed his age somewhere around my own or younger. I doubted he had seen much outside of the Bjorn lands.

I introduced each of the Lycans before returning to the Bjorn introducing Asya, then Faima whose tawny face was held high as she judged them with her amber eyes, and finally Zlata who seemed content to not have any attention in her direction in the least.

Brass was rubbing his lips together furiously with his head ducked and I fought the urge to tell him to spit it out. We worked out how we would travel together, side by side with the Lycan ruling family camping with the Bjorn assembly.

We marched to war.

I expected our traveling to take a long time with all the children we'd brought with us and the animals, but it was only slightly slower than by trip with Slate and Brass posing as Scarab and Scorpion. Long after night fell, we camped around the rocky hot springs and I was tempted to tell Tawny it was where Ridge had told me she was conceived.

Let her try to enjoy her night after that little tidbit.

"Niall is all over her. He's hardly let her relieve herself alone. I never thought I'd say this, but I wish Jett were here," I grumbled as I settled in next to Brass in our low bleached leather tent.

Not everyone had a tent and many of our traveling companions went to the springs despite the late hour. Many of the men carried the children too young to stay up for the march that had gone on hours after dark. At the springs we were in relative safety. It had been our goal from the start.

"You and Slate took me the *very* long way the first time, didn't you?" I accused as I beckoned Brass to lay on top of me.

Brass let his furs fall at the tent flaps and smirked at me as he took off a few of the blades hidden about his body. "A lot of love will be made tonight. It is what people do in the cold and on the march. All we have to distract ourselves from a battle we may die in is one another. Tawny will not bed Niall alone."

I'd prepared dinner for the assembly and Donncha's family myself with Tawny and Amethyst's help. We made a little fire inside the rocky shelter of the side of the spring where we'd sat shoulder to shoulder as we ate. No glamorous tents like I'd always seen in the movies. We were the poor rebel army.

"What does that mean?" I asked, furrowing my brow as Brass pulled his furs over his waist before he crawled up my legs.

"That means that Tawny is afraid to sleep with someone new. Amethyst is joining them."

I sat up, and he placed his hand between my breasts against my silver chain and the seven stone pieces. "What the fiddlestick! She's going to cheat on my brother? I don't care what he did, two wrongs don't make a right. You and I know that better than most."

Brass pushed down on my chest firmly so he hovered above me and I scowled. "Niall will not touch Amethyst. It is not Niall whom she is interested in, Love."

"I honestly can't deal with anyone else's crazy love life right now. I'm just glad mine is settling."

I unlaced his padded jerkin as he hovered above me and pushed it over his left shoulder as he settled his hips. I ran my thumb over the red Nordic sundial with the flames around it. The sigil of the Red Seconds, he and Slate had tattooed on themselves when they thought I was dead. It had caught on and most of the rebels had the tattoo over their hearts.

I raised my head to press my lips to the mark they'd gotten in my memory. "So you don't want to hear how Padraig is planning to lure the impressionable young Klim to his bed tonight."

I shook my head. "That's what you were rubbing the skin off your lips about? *Nope.* I don't want to know. I'm too busy enjoying your soon to be naked body and worrying why Slate feels like he's going to tear someone's head off right now. Where's Quick?" I asked with a sigh.

Slate wasn't on Elivagar. He was very far away which could mean any of the islands.

"Silver is to the southwest. I believe he's at Niflheim. He's being irked which likely means Styg is annoying him...probably about you," Brass purred as I hooked my finger in the strap at his nape to yank it free.

I loved when his thick hair spilled free. "I wanted Scorpion. He reminded me of you. Go figure. That night in the hot spring when you were threatening me, while I was extremely angry, I wanted you to try to kiss me so I had an excuse for losing control."

Brass's defined lips curled. "We can reenact that scheme with a very different outcome if you're not afraid of Tawny, Amethyst, or Niall coming out of their shelter and seeing us."

I made a contented sound in my throat.

... Have I mentioned how much I love you being a mind reader?...

CHAPTER 17

INDIGO

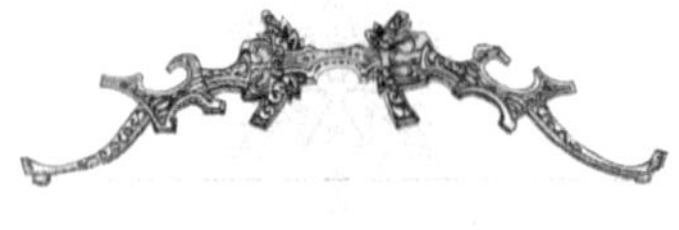

Sterling was right about one thing, I wanted for nothing in my tent. They brought in a full bed on a gilt frame with a blush damask comforter piled high with pillows and a luxurious matching chaise for lounging. I even had beautifully woven carpets to tread upon as I paced my cage.

No matter how beautiful and how well cared for I was with my personal attendant, chef prepared three course meals, dresses of the finest silks, and freesia scented bubble baths, I was a prisoner. The opposite end of my pewter nix torque chain was looped around the bed post at the foot of the bed which I couldn't touch without doubling over in pain.

Scarlett. Jett. Silver.

I thought they were all dead, but now I knew they had to be alive. I thought I caught sight of Jett in the window at Valla U. I had seen Slate and since my pregnancy was beginning to show, I'd kept my eyes away from them. Diamond had shown up and that had been the end of my night.

Dahlia and Willow said they were contemplating letting Sterling take me on as his second wife, but but I knew they were buying time until I gave birth. Then they would give me to Ash. Sterling couldn't accept that his mother wouldn't let him have me. The one thing he had ever asked them for. My poor foolish love.

Silver was far away. For a short time, I could feel him in Elivagar. He was further away, but he had somehow discovered he'd activated his bond and his constant flow of love was enough to break me while I slept with Sterling.

I was a rousen addict. I needed it. I wondered if it did much damage to my son if any. I prayed it didn't. I wondered if Slate told Silver I was with child. What did Jett think if that was him in the window? That had been them in disguise when we left the Beget Oubliette. I was positive.

"Please rest, Indi. Your tossing and turning keeps me awake," Sterling murmured, pulling me tighter against him.

There were nights I wished he would wear Silver's cologne of patchouli, sandalwood, and cedar so I could pretend for just a little while that I was with him.

Deep inside, I wanted to shout at him to go home to his wife and sleep in *their* bed. I never felt guilt for making love to Sterling for years until I found Silver. In a seldom moment of clarity, I pitied Diamond and her inevitable loneliness.

"Sorry, Love," I whispered through my rousen cocktail laced haze.

Sterling had come to accept the sweet concoction as part of my scent. We all allowed ourselves a lie every once in a while.

Indigo Tio, Sterling Haust's khoraz. The Norns mocked me.

ANOTHER NIGHT, another showing of their favorite prisoner. It was the first time I'd seen Sage since he'd beaten me when Thrimilci was overthrown. My half-brother was his mother's son with Jackal's tall wiry build. He offered me his arm, and I looked at him flatly, wondering if he would have the guts to beat me in front of everyone if I let loose what had been building inside me for months.

He looked impeccable in his taupe colored satin sleeveless jerkin in the Ostara fashion, his blonde hair styled in an undercut to complete his polished look. He had big round cornflower blue eyes and pouty pink lips against fair skin like his mother's. Sage also had Delta's rage.

Braziers lit the path between the tents. The army had ruined the university's lawn. If Canis had his way, they would tear down the doors too. No one had known they had built the university with the same materials Scarlett had used to build her arenas and *calling* was useless against it.

"How is your bastard, sweet sister?" Sage asked in a honeyed voice.

"Jealous Ash contemplates bedding me and not you, dear brother?" I retorted.

I never said out loud what was obvious to those who knew Sage best. He married Garnet and she was round with the impending birth of their son. I was never very good at keeping my mouth shut after Scarlett taught me to stand up for myself. It wasn't so much that she sought to teach me, but she was so brave and outspoken... it was contagious. I'd been a meek little mouse when I thought I was the adopted daughter of Alder Var and Delta Natt. I should've known from how my father favored me, that I was really his. At the time, I thought it was because Delta blatantly doted on Sage so my father sought a balance.

Sage forced a laugh in case anyone had heard my words, but his long fingers gripped around my wrist painfully as he led me around the siege machines. They'd torn down the woods to build them.

They never brought me too close to the hybrids of hybrids. I'd heard some Stygians murmur the Abomination Army. No one was taking credit for their creation, and if I was the brainchild behind them, I wouldn't either.

Furry crustaceans, reptile skinned horned beasts, and clawed spiders. It was best not to even glance their way after night fell or you'd never fall asleep knowing they were only a hundred yards away.

Dahlia stood with Canis near their command tent that blended in with the other extravagantly decorated temporary homes. Her pinched face followed my path, and I wondered what excuse she would have for me tonight or if she would even bother. She had been beautiful once. Short strawberry blonde hair that curled under to frame her face and narrow green eyes that scrutinized everything.

Those two had been spending an awful lot of time together and I wondered how Cassiopeia felt about it if the woman could feel at all. Canis was barrel chested and my grandfather's twin. He hadn't aged half as well as Cygnus had. His spiky white hair didn't flatter his round head whose face hinted at jowls. His blue hooded eyes held no warmth whatsoever when I came to stand before him.

"Indigo. How does this evening find you?" Canis had a way of speaking so his upper lip never seemed to move and his sentences all rushed out with a single breath as if he was always short on time.

"The same as usual, great uncle," I said plainly.

Goading Canis would be a major mistake. There was no doubt in my mind that he would kill me the second he didn't need me if I made his life difficult.

"Sterling was held up tonight. I am sure you understand, Indigo," Dahlia said as her upper lip lifted like she'd caught a whiff of a foul smell.

Aside from the unwashed bodies of the Abomination Army, I thought it was actually a very pleasant night. Spring in Valla always reminded me of my father's birth place and on the island of perpetual spring that always carried a floral aroma. It didn't hurt that being blood born to Ostara, Silver carried some of that scent in his skin. The wind blew fresh ocean air over the cliff side the university was built on and was held up by the Yggdrasil.

The enormous Ash tree stretched up from the ocean and was the symbol of Valla University for the Mastery of Guardians. I wore the silver pendant now as all Guardians did who had been proven tried and true as well as my gold and silver torques around my wrists. In addition to my Guardian jewelry, I wore my lapis ring with its silver beveled leaf that looked like a nod to the Var's sigil. Silver gave me when we were engaged and the azurite teardrop pendant Scar got me for my birthday.

"Come into the tent. I would like your honest opinion," Canis said, and gestured with a thick hand to the tent flaps.

Sage led me through keeping his hand on my forearm and his *calling* gripped my nix collar. I wasn't allowed out of my tent unless someone controlled it.

The inside of the tent was hardly a tent at all.

I found the whole decor ridiculous, but utterly Canis with its polished black wood furniture and brushed brass cutlery and dishes that had been left out from supper. Maps, inside and out of Thrimilci and Valla were spread on a long table. Tacked to the walls were sketches of those they deemed outlaws and everyone I cared about who was still alive was in one of those sketches. As well as a breakdown of everyone's talents and their family members.

They were practically portraits and written in penmanship that made everything I'd ever written look like an infant's accidental scribble. I'd seen the writing before. The men who'd written all the public notices and a man who had died the first night of the Purge War, Basil Straumr. Between him and Dahlia, they were the only two to have access to all of Guardian history. I didn't know what the university would do without him there to navigate through the volumes upon volumes of his and the other claviger's written words.

Clavigers were trained for years before the previous one retired. It was all lost. Basil didn't have enough ambition to be a part of the traitors. He just happened to marry the wrong woman. Whomever his replacement would be would have to spend decades going through the entire history to be of any use.

On a pedestal table with recessed lighting sat six stone pieces on the black reflective surface. I'd seen those pieces before though the ones I'd seen were much older and dirtier. These had been newly minted.

Canis moved to stand before the table and reached into his black jerkin to pull out two similar pieces that had an aged look to them. "From the Crathode and the Anguillan. Ash said your sister had six pieces the night before she died. I have had these made to fit the project since they went missing with her body. We wait for the last one to be completed then we take will not need to take the university because we will rewrite history. We will need Dagr blood though."

"They look just like hers, but newer," I answered obediently.

Canis's eyes glittered. Not many knew he was similar to an interrogator like Silver. He had incredible eyesight that could pick up the race of your pulse, the muscle twitch in your cheek, the imperceptible crease in your brow. It was his other talent.

Dahlia had waited outside, facing the sprawling yellow stoned castle that served as the proving grounds for all Guardians since the beginning. I followed her gaze and stifled a whimper.

Copper beads that hung from Gypsum's long sable locks caught the firelight, but I would recognize my youngest cousin anywhere. He watched me every night with his big puppy dog eyes, looking so help-less and sad. Even when he frowned his dimples popped in his olive cheeks. He had grown as tall as Sterling and as chiseled as Ash. When he smiled, girls took notice. It helped that he was easy going and level-headed as his father was.

A red head joined him. Her thin pale arms wound around his waist as she rested her head against his chest.

"Mica Rot. If we get ahold of her father, we could coax the girl to exchange herself for him and then use her against the boy. I have never seen him take an interest in a girl other than my daughter," Dahlia said, and my heart pounded in my chest.

I had to warn Gypsum. I'd known Mica had a crush on Gyps when I saw them sitting at the same table at the induction ceremony. They made an excellent couple, definitely better than Diamond. It was war time though. Everyone you loved could be used against you. Sterling found that out the hard way.

"Or we could use Indigo to persuade the boy to surrender himself," Sage offered, and my blood froze in my veins knowing what kind of torture he would have in mind.

"Indigo is too important to risk damaging at this juncture," Canis said absently.

Jackal watched every night too. He'd made his stance against our family and there was no going back. If they lost the war, they'd kill Crag and probably force Jackal into a marriage or kick him out of Tidings. I had no clue what Jackal would do in the myopic world.

His corn silk hair stood out in the window beside Gypsum's. With so few people filling the windows, it wasn't difficult to spot familiar faces even as high as they were. Crag was deeper in the shadows of Jackal's window. My uncle did always have a soft spot for me, but I did for him too. No one in Tidings took him seriously except for my mother's family.

I sucked in a sharp breath and quickly tried to mask it as Gypsum sent a small circular shadow from his window. It drifted lazily on a breeze towards me and I tried to glance at the others to see if they saw what Gyps was doing.

They had.

Canis plucked it from the air and my heart sunk. He stared at it for a moment before showing me his upturned palm. In it was a single blue morning glory.

"Is this a message?" Canis asked.

"It's meant to remind me of home... of my mother," I said softly.

Pearl had grown the blue morning glory vine in a terracotta pot right in the dining room of the Sumar palace to demonstrate to Scarlett, Gypsum, and Tawny their *calling* abilities for the first time. Scarlett had taken a clipping to the Dagr palace when she moved out and had grown it in the cloister outside her wing.

"That is the only thing it signifies?" Dahlia asked as she sneered disdainfully at the flower.

"It is. Would it be okay... may I please have it?" I asked hopefully trying not to have any expectation at all.

Canis turned fully to me and I felt dwarfed between him and Sage. I could tell he was delving into the flower even though he knew I was being honest. When Canis smiled, it was a quick flash of his teeth.

"Here you are, my dear."

I held the morning glory carefully until I was allowed to go back to my tent and Sage draped the chain from my collar to the bedpost. Sage watched me haughtily as I hand lit the candles around my tent.

"Can I ask you for a favor?" I asked, unable to bring myself to look at him.

I couldn't risk the night in case Ash or Sterling didn't come out. Sage looked amusedly at me as one might a small child that had made a ridiculous inquiry.

"Could you give it roots? That's all," I asked, holding the flower delicately before me.

Sage was unpredictable. He could nourish my single flower or the second I placed it in his hands, he could crush it. It wouldn't make it through the night without his help.

"Why not?" he asked, pursing his pouty lips before I crossed the carpet to the edge of the tent.

Sage made a small hole against the seam of the thick fabric before taking the flower from my palm and I watched as he concentrated. It was no easy feat to grow roots for a plucked flower. Sage was a very powerful Guardian and the only reason he was doing as I asked was to have an opportunity to show his skill.

The tiny bloom twisted in his hand and for a moment I thought he was going to incinerate it, but instead tiny tendrils curled from it as a stem formed and roots pushed forth. He bent in front of the small hole he'd made and slid the flower into it before he packed the dirt around the stem and gave it sunlight and water all with his *calling*. It was what Guardians had been born to do.

He sat back and watched as more tendrils clung to the side of the tent and four more buds joined the first and sucked in a breath.

"Thank you, Sage."

For a few moments, he was the man I knew he could have been. My selective memory of our childhood had only shown me this boy who could grow all sorts of flowers for dyes in the Var gardens until Canis caught him helping our grandmother Ruby collect them to boil the delicate silks Ostara was notorious for. Not another of the Var sons would be poisoned by women. Canis blamed Ruby for allowing Jackal to follow his own path.

"It was only a flower, Indigo," Sage said bitterly before briskly walking from my tent.

I had loved Sage no matter how hateful he was, he was still my brother until his mother cajoled him into harboring such loathing for our father that he had killed him and my mother. Who knew what else he had done. I could never forgive him, but I did feel sorry for him.

"They are attacking the Natt castle. We were nearly taken."

Candles lit in a *whoosh* around my tent and I blinked groggily at the intrusion. Sterling ran his hand across my silk clad stomach as he turned over. Even prisoners wore silk night gowns when they were greater family.

Willow Natt had given her generous genes to Sterling. They shared gorgeous violet eyes and high wide cheekbones. Her raven hair was in loose chin length curls to her heart-shaped face. His sisters paced my tent behind her and my stomach flip-flopped. Quartzite was Ash's wife, waist long honey blonde hair and luminous green eyes on her fair heart-shaped face while her twin was married to Fox Straumr. He had made his stand against them and remained in the university. Nova and Tawny bore a certain resemblance, both with wide hazel eyes and long dark wavy hair. Nova was slimmer and taller, but they all had Natt blood.

Sterling ran his hands over his disheveled hair and dressed as he climbed out of my bed. There was no use in pretending to sleep so I sat up and rested my back against the gilt frame.

"Who was attacking the castle?" Sterling asked in a rasping voice I'd always found titillating.

"The Red Seconds from the arena. They are not supposed to be organized," Nova spat.

Quartz and Nova both carried Ash's children and were very pregnant. They couldn't have been more than a month apart. I could tell from the lack of scathing glances Quartz wasn't aware Ash was spending so much time in my company.

"Why were you in Elivagar? You should stay in Mabon with Diamond," Sterling told them, buttoning his pants.

"Your wife stays in Mabon one night and then the Straumr palace the next. You would know that if you spent less time with your paramour," Quartz said in a calculated tone.

Sterling stopped shrugging into his jerkin to look at her. His violet eyes flashed.

"I am going to make Indigo my second wife. She is my mate. Sister or not, say another foul word against her and you can sit at the Straumr palace and wonder which daughter Ash is spending all his time with now that Crimson and Jade are trapped in Valla U and Scarlett and Jonquil have passed on."

A growl rumbled that was his barghest self-unleashing rattled in his chest and Willow placed her finger tips to Quartz's shoulder where she sat on my chaise. Willow couldn't have been an inch over five foot two. Like most of the Natts, she was petite.

"She meant nothing by it. We are all upset to be rooted out in the middle of the night. We should have waited until morning. There is nothing that can be done now," Willow said pragmatically.

"Any word on if the rest of Elivagar was taken?" Sterling asked buckling his jerkin placated by his mother.

"We had no way to find out and did not dare risk going to the town heart. We never truly held Thrimilci or Elivagar while we did not hold their family castles." Willow crossed to where Sterling tugged on his boots and she placed a kiss on his forehead.

"I will make sure you get to the Straumr palace safely myself. Canis and Cygnus will want to speak, anyway. I am glad you are all right," he said with genuine affection.

Sterling turned to me and gave an apologetic smile. "It will probably be a day or two before I can come back, Indi. I am sorry." He kissed my lips. "I love you."

I gave him the best smile I could muster and watched them all leave my tent. Sterling took the extra time to extinguish the candles so I wouldn't have to do it by hand. I pulled the blankets over my head and cried out for joy.

Jett was back. Silver was sending love and hope through our bond. Scarlett must be alive and fighting with the Red Seconds if they had suddenly pushed back. She was never the type to sit idly by which begged the question... why had they waited so long? Did it have to do with her sons? It was the only logical reasoning I could come up with. The man I suspected was Jett in Elivagar said he had a son. Cherry must have given birth.

Canis wasn't actively fighting a war. He was content to have the Red Seconds shut themselves in their strongholds because none of it would matter once he activated the project. He had been forced to show his hand because Scarlett had begun to collect the pieces and she had let everyone believe her sons were Slate's. She had gotten too close and thwarted Ash's attempts to control her.

Then there was Peak. It was common knowledge now that Peak had taken Scarlett as a paramour. Only a few knew she was an unwilling participant. They wanted Slate's blood, but he was too hard to get ahold of. Gypsum was right under their noses. They would find a way to coax him out once the last piece was completed.

I would worry about that tomorrow, because tonight I would sleep soundly now that the Red Seconds had struck again and if Tawny was alive, she had her island back.

When Scarlett came back from the Merfolk, she said she could smell lust and desire. That pheromones and hormones were as clear as words to her influencing her own body in libidinous ways. I was actively on the rousen cocktails and I knew what she meant. It was a miracle she hadn't bed all the suitors who were constantly throwing themselves at her.

Hypersexual was what Brass had explained. She was prone to sudden bouts of desire that could drive her to irrational anger and frustration. Her drive was more active than the average woman's and now I was just like her.

What I felt was not lust when my blankets were abruptly yanked from my sleeping body. Sterling could be lost in his passions when he was in his barghest form, but he always warned me before shifting. The mattress bowed, and I felt the weight of someone straddling my thighs as I roused, pressing my pregnant belly uncomfortably against the springs.

"Sterling?" I asked in a sleep thick voice and a big hand pinned me down on the center of my back.

My heart beat wildly. Not Sterling. If Ash had talked himself into bedding me, I didn't think he would be the rough sort. Not Ash.

I wriggled, trying to push off the bed and stop my assault. I whimpered as his hands caught my wrists, gripping them so tightly they throbbed so I couldn't throw my elbows back.

Panic. Who had snuck in past Canis and Dahlia's watchful eyes?

"Stop! No!" I squeaked out, my face pressed against the pillow so my muffled voice didn't go far.

My arms were pinned behind my back when his other hand clamped down around my throat. Long fingers flexed and squeezed as I struggled for my life. The rattling of my chain against the frame and my choked breaths was all I could hear over my thundering heart and his heavy breathing. My eyes fluttered. He was killing me.

His fingers grew tired and loosened. Instead of adjusting his grip, he removed his hand entirely as I gasped for breath. It left my throat raw and bruised when he shifted his body. I tried to scream for help, but all that came out was a rasping whimper as his skin rubbed over mine.

I could barely breathe with the sides of the pillow covering my mouth. I was beginning to understand why Scarlett had been so terrified of Peak. He held the life of her unborn in his hands as my assaulter now did with me and the helplessness of it was staggering.

My ears rang and my consciousness seemed to flee as the first strike to the side of my head landed. My mouth opened in a silent cry as my assaulter rolled off my back onto the bed beside me and laughed breathlessly. I squeezed my eyes shut and began to cry.

"No need to cry. You are still breathing… barely." Sage laughed again and a wave of nausea threatened to render me unconscious. "Ash was most displeased when I beat you. I have had to be creative with my punishment. Nowhere that can be seen."

I sobbed harder. Maybe it was a nightmare.

"You can tell Sterling if you wish," Sage said with a wickedly malicious chuckle. "Though, by now you realize he holds no sway over the Knights. Like you, he is a piece to be moved into place when the time is right."

I'd never been more grateful for the dark so he couldn't see my tears. All the times our father kept Sage from being alone with me made more sense. He'd pinch me with his *calling,* smack me with flat air, and give me needle-like pricks along my arms when we were younger. He stopped and I assumed he grew out of torturing me for fun. Now I believed he'd found a different toy to play with.

"You're my brother," I rasped out with my raw throat. "How did you get past Canis?"

There was no way my great uncle would approve of Sage's actions. He may not have held any affection for me, but he wouldn't needlessly abuse me.

"We have all night. Canis took Cassiopeia with Willow and the girls to the Straumr palace. There is only you and I and mother. Feel free to shout for her," he amended, and I croaked out a scream as I sprung up to kill him.

I beat him with my fists, feeling his teeth cut on my knuckles. He laughed as I tried to knee him and caught my hands. I thrashed my head and tried to scream as he rolled me over.

"Oh. Poor sweet stupid Indi. More beauty than brains." He held his mouth open to drip his blood, trickling over his swollen lip onto my face.

I caught his scent and gagged. His normally impeccably coifed hair had fallen free from its place.

"You're disgusting," I spat in his face and he bent his face down to mine to spit his blood on my cheek.

"Perhaps, sweet sister."

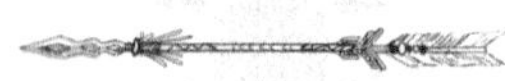

Delta filled the copper tub, her blonde waves brushing her chin as she leaned her statuesque form over the edge to pour in the scented oils. She brushed her fingers over her fair brow and raised her eyes so blue they nearly glowed against her skin. I thought she was the most beautiful woman ever born, but it was only skin deep.

"Get out of her bed, Sage. Come here and let me heal you," she said in her cultured crisp tone.

Sage walked, completely undressed, to tower over his mother so she could heal him. I had put up a fight, I was pleased to see. His lips were swollen, and I had gouged his shoulders with my nails. There was even a bite on his cheek where you could clearly see where my teeth had broken the skin. Then it was gone with one quick *calling*.

My blankets would have to be destroyed. My mattress likely as well from the mess. I had no voice left and my throat was sore to the touch, but it was the rest of my body where there were visible wounds. He'd hit me so hard in the stomach until I vomited. Sage would check on the baby and hit me again. It went on for hours.

Sage kissed her cheek and turned around to walk to the foot of the bed where he'd discarded his clothes. I looked at the morning glory vine unwilling to acknowledge the events of last night.

"Every time they corrupt our land, expect me to exact justice, sweet sister."

I shivered. My head pulsed with the pain he'd wrested from my body. He'd used his hands, his calling, and his teeth. For a few fearful moments at separate times, I thought he'd take it even further and death would be a welcomed respite. Sage relished in my fear of his abuse more so than the actual act. It didn't stop me from wetting myself. I should've known that as insane as Sage had become, crossing Sterling remained in the back of his mind.

"Come into the bath, Indigo. You have ruined your bed," Delta chastened.

I numbly got to my feet and shuffled to the copper tub. Sage swept from the tent without a word or even a backwards glance. He'd accomplished what he'd set out to do.

Once I was in the tub, she placed her hand on the top of my head and I felt the warmth of her healing flood into me. She sauntered to the bed and incinerated the blankets. She would replace them with their exact replicas and no one would be wiser.

"Why?" I whispered, wiping my soapy hands over my face.

She didn't bother looking to me. "You are a khoraz and a Tio, which is redundant in my opinion. What else are you good for? Your sister knew that and now you do too. You are here to please the greater family sons whoever they are and however they see fit. Greater family sons should not visit brothels. If you have a daughter after your son, she will be bred as you have been to please the next generation of greater sons. It is your destiny," she said absently.

I choked back a sob. The full picture was impossibly worse than I thought. The fear that Sage would return to complete his mission, bestowed on him by Delta, created a hysterical fervor in me. "He is my brother," I squeaked.

I didn't dare tell her that Sage failed. The threat of it had hung over me all night and, I had to believe, that was worse than the deed.

"You are a bastard and no sister of his," Delta said, checking over the mattress before crossing the tent to call out to my handmaiden.

The girl brought in new blankets and two black cloaked Guardians brought in a new mattress to exchange it for my old one. It was nothing to her. She'd prepared for it. *I* was nothing to her.

I watched her leave with the men so I was alone with the girl who never spoke other than to ask me how I wanted my hair and which dress I wanted to wear. She began to wash my hair, and I sobbed.

There was no coming back from where my life had taken me.

EIGHTEEN

"I am not asking," Brass growled, sounding eerily like Slate.

"Neither am I," I gritted back through clenched teeth.

Donncha and Padraig chuckled from where they were pressed down on their stomachs beside us. Lyov cracked a hint of a smile at our argument. I would not go back by Tawny and Amethyst. I was not pregnant and there were more than enough women staying back to defend the children should the Crathode find a way around us. They also had Niall who had volunteered for the position which we all knew was so he could be close to Tawny who had undoubtedly made it worth his during lunch.

"They're not all bad. There has to be women and children who are innocent and some men don't *want* to be involved," I pushed.

"She is right," Tadg rumbled in a guttural voice and we all turned to the hulking grey wolf who had probably spoken three sentences in the last year.

"*See.* Even Tadg thinks I should go. I can tell where the women might be being held and I can read their emotions so I'll know if they're doing it because they're forced or because they are evil opportunists."

Brass shut his eyes and shook his head. Occasionally, a Crathode would scuttle across the Illfuss Ice Field before going down the glistening ramps that led below where they lived in caverns along the coast of the Frostfell Mountains. Those mountains encircled the Vetr castle, and we were on the far east end. Quick and Ridge should be leading the arena refugees into Glitra today. We had to rush our unplanned attacked on the Crathode. I couldn't knowingly leave Zlata's sisters and possibly a number of other defenseless women there to be bred. If it was where they were being held.

"If I get in trouble, you'll be able to feel it through the bond," I said softly with my chin on his shoulder.

"Have you thought of whether there may be a Guardian overseer down there?" Brass asked, taking a fortifying breath.

"And that is why we have the bond. I distract them while you all follow my trail to rescue me. It's not a needless risk. Tawny and Amethyst are pregnant and I'm a skilled fighter."

Caolan was quick to point out Amethyst's condition when she exited the rocky shelter after her night with Niall and Tawny. There had been a lot of celebrating for a short time and Niall didn't look the least bit surprised. He also didn't gloat which led me to believe he had nothing to do with its conception. Brass insisted Amethyst didn't bed the Lycan, but I still wasn't speaking to either of them.

Brass opened his eyes and knit his brows. "What if they attack first and ask questions second?"

I tilted my chin up to pucker my lips to his. He didn't kiss me back.

"Then you'll have to come save little old me with all your big strong muscles." He smiled against my lips and sighed.

"You are a very trying woman, Love. You're lucky I plan on having you make this up to me tonight," he purred, and I gave him another peck on his lips before he could argue and hopped to my feet. "Scarlett! Curse the blasted gods!" Brass said in a hushed shout and either Donncha or Padraig yanked him back down behind the snow drift.

I trotted across the ice, the wind whipping at my cloak, making my hood fall back. The Crathode didn't notice me until I was nearly to the foot of the mountain. A pair of patrolling crustacean hybrids spotted me and let out shrieks that made me cringe. I held up my hands as they snapped their claws at me. Beady stemmed eyes looked past me for any other travelers, but the rebels were well hidden.

The only flaw in my plan became glaringly apparent. I had no way to communicate with them. They nudged me with their claws, gashes for mouths emitting clicking noises and sounds as if someone with far too much saliva in their mouth would make. I sucked in sharply when one with a brown stalk eyes and spittle ridden mandibles snapped a nix torque around my throat. It used one set of its two sets to attach a chain to it and turned around on its three sets of human legs. It wore a boiled leather cuirass over its carapace, a scaled tail came down to its knees, I noticed as it turned around.

The second watched me with open skepticism. I recognized this one as a simple crab. Judging from the jagged mottled carapace like piece that extended from its forehead, I believed she was a female. She was cream colored with orange like leopard spots and spikes that formed above her human like brown eyes. Her slitted mouth open to reveal spiky teeth in a vicious smile.

"Bring her to the others," she said in English so I would understand her.

I let the first one who was a male and a shrimp or a prawn hybrid take me down between the mountain where the ground opened up to reveal a winding ramp like the one the Bjorn used to reach inside their stone castle. The Crathode had used the rocks and ice to make a frozen palace of carved ice. The ice was thin enough to see the blue sky from the high ice ceiling. At the visible bottom, a grotto opened up to Crathode doing very well to ignore me and continued their fishing.

I saw them mending nets and taking their hauls into other caverns and had to be jerked into motion. They were regular beings living daily life. I identified the women who were brighter colored with noticeably feminine attributes like trimmer waists or shell necklaces and belts over hide like skirts. Some had young ones on their backs and hurried past with their eyes dropped.

"You are a Red Second rebel, yes?" the female behind me asked.

"Sure," I said in a disinterested tone.

"We are the Red Kings. Did your people think of that before giving you your name?" she asked, her words fitting awkwardly in her mouth.

I chuckled to myself. "No. I don't think they did come to think of it. Red is for Scarlett, the former Second and I think the second part if self-explanatory. What do you have invested in this disaster?" I asked.

If they were going to kill me, they would've done it already. Ice stalactites and stalagmites met to form towering icicle columns that were carved into the intricate patterns the Crathode had decorated their shared home in.

"My father is the king. I am his legacy. We do as he bids." I *felt* the complacency in her emotions. She was living the life she always thought she would. "It was about time the Guardians were brought down a peg or two."

"The Crathode do not have a king. You're a colony with an overlord." I shrugged. "They're not all bad. I've heard Elivagar has had a hard couple decades, but the newest Matriarch would've been better."

"Tell my father he is not king. I would like to be there for your decree. They are all the same. She is a Vetr. No different than the last millennia."

"Your father escaped when the Mint twins took down Karkinos, didn't he?" I probed.

I thought the prison on the back of the giant crab would have been impenetrable unless you killed it, but we had been proven wrong. Slate had been unjustly taken there for a month and had lost his memories because of it. The Mint twins had been running it when we broke in.

"All it took was two of us to bring in a portal so the others could enter. We did not need the Mints, only the portal. We lost a score of Red Kings distracting that creature," she spat.

We had lost one and we almost lost Quick. The thought of Shale made me steel my resolve.

Cages made of icicle bars lined a low prison that lined every inch of the long room. Two Guardians clad in thick midnight blue cloaks with the Natt star inside a circle on it barely visible in the torchlight.

"A woman? She was alone?" the man asked.

"We did not see any others," the female answered.

The guards shared a look and looked me over. I thanked the Gods I had the foresight to slip on my Scat ring so it wasn't turquoise eyes they saw, but beady dark eyes with a long narrow nose and a rosebud mouth.

"Were you alone, girl?" he asked as his scent spiked as it hitched over my curves.

"I was separated from my group. I was hoping to find some Crathode to point me in the direction of Elivagar's town," I told him.

There were glittering eyes within all the cells. My heart raced wondering if Indigo could be somewhere down there.

"Confirm what she says. Kill any males and bring the females. About time we got another human since the last one was the Haust Patriarch's," the first guard said to the other.

My stomach sunk like a boulder in the Ymir River.

"Put her in the human's cell." The second guard took the leash with a gloved hand and I glanced over my shoulder to the female Crathode who followed me with her human eyes.

A single cell with a metal framed bed and a bucket for a chamber pot was all that occupied the room I was thrust into. I turned to the guard and smirked.

He beckoned me with his hand as he tossed the leash inside the cell. "Hand over your blades and I will send in a hot meal and a basin of water."

I chuckled and shook my head as I unclasped my cloak. "Really? Has that ever worked before?"

His brow drew together. "Are you not cold? You will change your tune when your toes lose feeling and start to change color."

I held my finger over the clunky silver ring that distorted my features and smiled as I slid it off. He gasped, and I put it in my pocket.

"Do you know who I am?" I asked in my usual gravelly voice.

He nodded. "I was at your tour in Elivagar. The Khoraz Seductress."

I laughed heartily. "You have two choices. Take this collar off me right now and I will see you get a fair trial *or* I will be your judge, jury and executioner *now*."

He moved to slam the cell door shut, and I pulled two daggers from my belt watching them sail through the air and hit his shoulders so he staggered back. I darted out of the cell before the other guard could hear this shout, but the woman in the cell across from me tore a blade free and slid it across his throat with her peach hand over his mouth.

I ran down the narrow hall to the guard's station and the first man shot to his feet using his *calling* to link to my nix torque. My blades flew true and lodged in his left eye. I watched the blood spurt, and he fell back like a board. I sent a warning through my bond with Brass and his emotions flared with annoyance.

I smiled as I gathered the rings of keys and hurried back to the cell I'd come from. I stopped in front of the cell of the woman who had slit the throat of the guard and scoffed.

"Well, hello again Vanna'ra. Being a traitor hasn't quite worked out the way you thought it would," I said as the inky haired Merfolk woman fixed her brown eyes void of white on me.

"Merfolk khoraz. The sight of me must make your insides pulse. Come here and I will ease your discomfort," Vanna'ra purred.

I sucked in a sharp breath. She had a point. Brass was practically screaming through the bond.

"If I let you out and you touch me, for pleasure or pain, I will kill you without a second thought. You're either with me or against me in this." I sneered.

As deadly female was, she was equally so in her beauty. She had the fervor of a zealot in her hatred for her imprisonment.

"If I could swear you a blood oath, I would. Your sister was here, Indigo, perhaps a week ago before two men came for her. Your Prime gossiped about you with her like tyro girl but another man has fertilized her eggs," she said, and I took the keys off the dead guard and tried them in her cell's latch.

Ash was spending time with her, but not sleeping with her? That didn't make sense. Neither did them both discussing me. I put it aside to ponder later.

"I need your help to free these women. When we finish that, we help them out of this place. Keep the dagger. I can't use my *calling* until someone helps me get this torque off." I stopped as I found the right key. "Vanna'ra, if you do as I say, you have my word I will help you return to your people if you wish it."

We were lucky the Crathode needed keys otherwise I wouldn't have been able to open the cells at all.

I didn't know Merfolk could cry or tear. One single green tinged tear rolled over her high cheek and she nodded her inky hip length curls. I finally noticed she was pregnant, and all she had was the blankets from her bed to cover her. Indigo had been there. Pregnant with these women.

I'd missed her by a week.

I opened the cell pushing the man's body aside with a bloody smear and she took a tentative step and sucked in a deep breath with a flare of the gills at the sides of her jaw. A bridge of peach skin spanned where there should have been a nose. Her ears were sharply pointed and close to her head. She was an octopus underwater. I hadn't seen her since she threw sand dollars as sharp as razor blades at me, Steel, and Slate.

"There is a men's prison somewhere down here where they keep the ones who breed with us."

"Women first," I told her and handed her a ring of keys. "Wait."

I knew Vanna'ra was cold-blooded, but after being used as she had been, clothing was a welcome luxury. I grabbed the cloak from the cell floor and clasped it at her throat. I was standing too close to her and swallowed hard staggering back.

She smiled knowingly. "I would do it willingly, Second."

"Go unlock those cells," I said curtly, and she rushed off.

I moved down the cells opening one after another. Minotaur, Jorogumo, Gorgons, and Anguillan predominantly occupied the cells. My heart broke over and over as I freed the sometimes pregnant, sometimes recently birthed women of all different ages from their prisons. They huddled together in the hall too afraid to leave without a guide. Vanna'ra had given a Jorogumo who was nearly transparent half her keys, and she was making short work of one side of the prison.

I fought tears and grit my teeth as I opened a cell and found one of the Wemic cheetah twins girls in it. She saw my face and recognized me; she immediately began sobbing.

"My sister. She is in the next cell." The young girl that had once seduced Gypsum was very pregnant.

"Wait here, I'll let her out. We'll heal you as soon as a Guardian removes my torque. You're safe now," I told her as I pried my arms free.

I freed her sister, and the two clung to one another as they walked to where the women grouped together after thanking me. At the next cell, I found the first Bjorn.

"You're free, meet the other women at the end of the hall," I told her, but the jade eyed panda woman with long white hair didn't move a muscle.

Most of the women were bare with only their blankets to cover them, but some like the Bjorn had rumpled shifts that had seen better days.

"I have to wait for my sisters," she said numbly, and I nodded.

As I opened the next cell with her hovering at my shoulder, it dawned on me. "You're Zlata's sisters?"

A polar bear woman hugged the other girl fiercely when I opened the cell. At the next cell I saw the third sister who hung her arms out through the icicle bars.

"How do you know Zlata?" she asked in her harsh accent.

"She's here to save you on the surface. Wait with the women. We have to leave together. We may have to fight our way out," I told her, swiping at stupid tears that burned my nose.

When she was free, she embraced me and I had to choke back a sob before she raced to her sisters. I cleared my throat and pushed my way to the front of the softly sobbing women where the crystalline Jorogumo woman was trying to them.

If I had come a week ago, that could have been me too.

I held out my hand. "Scarlett."

"Thre'ik. I knew your sister well. She thinks you are dead. I am glad you are not. I thought I would die in the Beget Oubliette."

The Jorogumo blinked three sets of eyes on its pale white human face and shook my hand with her human one. A fan of pale blonde hair extended from her sharply angled head and an enormous sack of eggs sat nestled on her back.

"You seem like the take charge type, Thre'ik. Can I count on you to push the women to the surface?"

She seemed to rise up proudly on her sets of spider legs so she was higher than I was tall. "I am Empress Thre'ik now that my sister has been slain."

I licked my lips and nodded. "I saw She'ik. I am so sorry for your loss, Empress."

"I am what keeps my people fighting in this war. Once they know I am free, the Jorogumo that are loyal to me will abandon Drik'ir's cause," she said with a snap of her pinchers which were considerably smaller than other Jorogumo I'd seen.

Jorogumo were pushing their way to her to supplicate themselves at her many feet. She urged them up as the women collected themselves.

"Why do I know that name?" I asked her.

"He was my sister's consort who betrayed her and our people. He led the attack against us until I gave myself up. So many died. He will be one of the men leading the army of abominations." Her throat rattled as she spoke that made my hair stand on edge.

"My brother is the Var heir. Jett Var, the son of Alder Var, your former ambassador before he was murdered. If I could swear you a blood oath Thre'ik, I would. We will make this right," I said, gripping her chilled hands.

Her smooth lips parted. "You are every bit the woman Indigo said you were. No wonder they had to silence you."

I sniffed. "I have a very big mouth."

I turned to the women who were clustered together. There had to be nearly a half a hundred from a handful of different tribes. There were Crathode women there who had to be nearing the end of their birthing years.

Vanna'ra pushed her way to my side. "That is all of them."

I nodded and raised my hands. "We have two choices, ladies. We may wait here until the Red Seconds fight their way to us *or* we fight our way to them." I pulled four blades out of my belt and held them up. "I am short on weapons, but you are free to take what I have."

A pink tinged Merfolk woman with hip length red hair forced her way to Vanna'ra's side and she gave the woman a leveled look before she took my blade. Vanna'ra's lips quirked and the other woman placed her slim hand on Vanna'ra's pregnant belly.

"We do not need blades. We have poison and talons. Claws and teeth. We are the tribes of Tidings. Those who seek to stop us, those who sought to breed us, are those whose blood will line these halls until we are free!" Zlata's panda faced sister shouted with her two sisters in tow and a cheer rang up around me.

One of the Cheetah twins gasped and some of the women whimpered and cowered.

I spun around and flexed my pinkies so my wrist blades sprung. A red splashed white crab riddled with deep scratches on his carapace filled the hallway with his massive girth. He snapped black tipped claws and turned pale blue human eyes on a thick head towards me. I saw the mottled crab girl and her prawn cohort behind him.

"Oval told me I had to see the new human. To find we are hosting the Khoraz Seductress herself." His gash of a mouth curled to reveal spiny teeth. "I am Brach, the Red King. Welcome to the Beget Oubliette, Scarlett Tio."

The leader of the Red Kings. The person responsible for the Red King Massacre that shut down Valla U for the better part of two decades. Who had led his rogue tribe to separate Tawny and Sparrow from Ridge so he lost twenty years of his life. Who had murdered my grandfather Flint Sumar, Slate's father, Lark Haust and his family including Brass's mother, and Amethyst's mother, Opal Geol. Who forced my mother, Hawk, and Sparrow to flee Tidings with us so I didn't know about my heritage, my father, my twin sister, my brother, uncle, and grandmothers.

Slate.

It all stemmed from Orion, but Brach had been there doing the killing. I'd already killed Orion at his behest, now Brach needed a reckoning.

Brach was much more accustomed to speaking in English. His mouth moved awkwardly but his guttural voice was crystal clear. When he laughed, his carapace jerked with his shoulders.

"You think my daughter told you the truth? I have been here all along. Ask the women behind you. The Red King gets the first taste." His spiny teeth flashed, and I heard women crying behind me. "Some need more breaking than others." Vanna'ra trembled at my shoulder, and I grit my teeth.

"Men who have tried to take me against my will end up with blades in their throats or their manhood available to them as a charm for a fleshy necklace," I spat.

I wished I didn't have the nix torque around my neck so he could see how I blazed. He snapped his pinchers, and I felt the women move away from me — all but Thre'ik.

"I could not have your sister, but you... your wiles are infamous."

I grunted to stifle the cry of surprise when he scuttled forward with inhuman speed. His foot nearly impaled my leg as I threw myself out of the way. The women screamed as he barreled into them and I raised my blades in time to block Oval's claw. I caught sight of Vanna'ra and the other Merfolk woman and tossed her the two blades in my other hand before spinning away.

We were all clustered together. Cries and screams sounded in my ears with a blur of limbs as I tried to scramble over the ice for a better position.

Oval charged after me but was met by Thre'ik's pinchers blocking her way.

"Scarlett!" one of the Wemic girls shouted, and I rolled to my right on instinct.

Brach's claw snapped where my throat had been an instant before. His sets of feet stomped after me as I tried to straighten. The Merfolk women had joined Thre'ik in her fight against Oval. The prawn hybrid shouted for more reinforcements, I assumed, in warbled clicking speech before leaping over me and into the women who they had abused.

The Bjorn roared.

I took it as a good sign as Brach's forearm collided with my middle as I tried to get to my feet knocking me back into the frozen wall. His claw came flying into my face and I slid to my heels up thrusting so my wrist blade cut the tendons in his arm. He yanked his claw from the ice and backhanded me so I went sprawling like a rag doll.

My head had cracked into the wall of the narrow hall and he scuttled sideways to reach me mowing over Gorgon woman trying to flee. I scrambled to my feet trying to catch my bearings. He'd knocked the taste right out of my mouth. My head swam as his claws snapped out and I parried as fast as I could with my mind still dazed from hitting the wall.

"Why fight so hard? You are not getting out of here alive. You will be my personal khoraz when I am through with you. They no longer care for you since they have your sister," he ground out.

Brach was massive, as big as Padraig in his Lycan form. He could crush me if he fell on my chest or caught me in his claw. If I tried to speak, I didn't think I could keep up my dodging his feet and claws. He rushed me and his carapace cracked the icy wall as I climbed the ramp to get a little leverage. His reach was farther than mine, so I was reversing. I threw the daggers from my belt as I sucked ragged breaths. He deflected with his claws and grinned maliciously at me. I slipped on the ice and Brach charged.

I cried out as his leg crunched my shin. Resisting the urge to grip it, I let gravity roll me as I tucked myself in back down the ramp. Brach gave no quarter. He was on me as I hobbled to my feet and he drove me down as his claw came down on me again.

I imagined him at the induction ceremony exploding from behind the stage and snapping the throats of the weaponless families gathered to watch their children and grandchildren become inductees of Valla U. The fear those people must have felt.

It was similar to how I was feeling. My rage was ebbing and stark terror rose in its place. I couldn't best him without my *calling*. I crawled under a Gorgon and Brach tossed her aside as he followed after me. My leg gave as I tried to get to my feet and I finally cried out as I fell in the hall between the cells. I crawled backwards, my palms slapping against the freezing surface.

Maybe I could trap him in one of the cells.

"The Crathode do not need you to rescue them, Night's Child. They have survived with me to delegate to them for decades. You are useless." His claw clamped on one of the icicle bars and he crushed them, showering the air with shards of the crystal ice.

I pulled my blades from my boots and used the ice bars to pull myself to my feet and hopped backwards, gritting my teeth. "Come on, cache hole. I ate one of your little brothers for dinner last week."

Brach's eyes flared, and he charged. I pushed off the bars and threw both blades. One sparked off his claw, but the other found a home in his thick throat. I could see the bone through my white pants that were coated in blood from my knee down. Brach yanked the blade from his throat and let it clatter over the ice.

I'd slowly been moving backwards and my hand hit the ice that formed the end of the hall. I swallowed hard knowing he had caught me. Normally, I'd rather die than let another man take me against my will. It was different this time, I had two sons waiting at home and two husbands who relied on me. I sent a wild plea to Brass who was still too far away to help and used my wrist blade to slice open my shirt and through the lacings of my corset to my belly button.

If I could put words to Brass's reply, it was to hold on. He was coming.

Brach's charge slowed as I retracted my blades. "When is the last time you had a woman? A *real* woman, Brach?" I asked, gulping air from the stress of our battle. "Not one of these simpering broken souls."

He watched my skin prickle and stepped closer. His sets of legs moved so quickly; my eyes couldn't keep up. I cried out as he caught my throat in his black tipped claw and lifted me off my feet. His spiny teeth slid along my jaw so his fish breath blew into my lungs.

"So much fight in one small body. You are bags of flesh and bone and when I cut you, you spill. That was how Flint died. Trying to hold his innards from spilling over his feet," he said, crushing his carapace to my chest. It forced my air out — which was good, because if he hadn't I would've sobbed. "Lark was chopped to bits and pieces as he howled, overrun by my men. We will do the same to your barghest with you as bait." Strands of saliva clung to his teeth as he spoke an inch away from my face while I blinked at tears.

"You are a monster. You had your own people breeding creatures," I said as I struggled to inflate my lungs.

"Sisters and daughters of men who have tried to overthrow me. Insurance, as they say. It was my idea to take hostages from the tribes. Orion never had a problem with it until his son was caught in the crossfire. I had to kill him once he saw us," Brach said in his guttural voice. "He had Natt blood and his wife, a Dagr. Orion's own insurance that Canis would be forced to include him in his precious project."

Orion, the gods cursed plotter! Sparrow had said Ridge never made his affections known. He likely didn't have any until Orion told him who he was to marry.

I found a reason to smile. "He's alive. You didn't kill him or his wife and child. The new matriarch Vetr is the child you failed to kill. Ridge is back in Elivagar."

"Then I should hurry," he said in a sudden flare of anger.

Blood bubbled from the wound at his throat and my hand held his claw at my own as my feet dangled. He slid his other claw to the waistband of my pants preparing to tear them free from my skin and I sprung my wrist blade. He grunted and stepped back enough for me to slip through the claw lodged in the wall and land sideways on my hip.

I cried out as Brach looked down to me holding his claw to his soft belly where I had jammed my forgotten wrist blade. He staggered towards me shrieking in the high way the Crathode had making me cringe and two furry bodies sprung through the air onto his shoulders. The cheetah sisters sunk their teeth into his soft throat and shook their heads sending black hair flying. Their clawed hands clung to his shell as he tried to ram them off by knocking into ice cells.

Zlata's sisters roared, and he spun around in time to catch two of them crashing into his chest and use their sharp claws to widen the wound I made with my blade. He gurgled and fell back at my feet. Zlata's sisters scrambled off him and helped up the cheetah twins who wiped their muzzles on the sleeves of their shift dresses.

Vanna'ra waited at the end of the hall and ran to my side then pulled my arm over her shoulders. "You're pregnant. You shouldn't be lifting me," I said through gritted teeth.

She spouted out Merfolk, which I vaguely understood as *get your whale behind over here*. The bright red haired Merfolk woman came around the corner and ran to my other shoulder and they helped me hobble past Brach's corpse.

Two Gorgon women and three Anguillan were laid out with blankets they'd taken from their cells over them. Oval and the prawn man were torn to shreds, only their carapaces were left to identify them. Thre'ik stood on the ramp rallying the women back to her.

"Still alive, Scarlett?" she asked with a rattle in her throat.

"Just barely. Can you lead them out? The Red Seconds are inside," I asked.

"Where will you be?"

"The men are victims just much as you are. Someone has to save them. I'll be all right," I told her.

"We shall help," Vanna'ra assured me and I nodded.

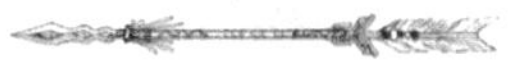

Up the ramp and along an iced bridge over a grotto we found another ramp that led deeper into the caverns. The red head had collected my thrown daggers, and I made short work of the Guardians who had remained to keep the men in their cells with the two women to balance me.

The Crathode Caverns were in an uproar and sounds of fighting echoed throughout.

There were not nearly as many men as I thought there would be. No Crathode males were in the cells, but there were Gorgons, Anguillan, Minotaur, and Jorogumo. Vanna'ra helped open cells as I hobbled along with Red.

A hooded cobra stood at the ready as I reached for the latch. "You wouldn't happen to be Ophio's son, would you?" I asked as I opened the cell.

His mouth fell open, and he nodded. "Did he send you to help me?" he drawled with his tongue, slurring the words.

I nodded. "Zonata misses you and Vernal would have risked just about anything to have you brought back."

Technically, it was all true. I had a feeling Zonata was his mate and the king's advisor had risked betraying his own people to let me know they were going to turn us over to the Stygians no matter what the outcome of the riddling match was.

His slitted nostrils flared, and he made a strangled sound. "I did not want to lay with those women." He looked to the red-haired Merfolk at my shoulder and dropped his eyes. "I am sorry"

"You were not the worst, Gorgon prince," she purred in that alluring way Merfolk had, and he raised his eyes enough to find that she meant it.

"Go. They are fighting their way free," I told him, and he nodded before tying his bed sheet around his waist and leaving the cell with his tail trailing behind him.

None of the men stayed together as the women had. I could hear the fighting coming closer. Vanna'ra waved to us from down the hall to let us know that side had been evacuated and I hurried to the next cell and groaned.

"Was I the worst?"

"I should let you rot in here. What are you even doing here? I just saw you... well I guess it's been awhile."

How easily I forgot about Disir.

Non're smiled at I hated how my loins pulsed. The Merfolk prince was the reason I was a khoraz. His light blue tinged skin was athletically muscled and like the other Merfolk, his sunny blonde hair came down to his trim waist. The things Non're had done to me had changed the way I was wired. His bright green irises ran over my torn shirt and I cursed. I'd completely forgotten about it.

"The Stygians raided the offshore palace that you must remember well enough. My father was trapped into keeping the peace and I fucked goat women and a few snakes. None were as good as you. No one has been." Non're's eyes slid over my chest again, and I clenched my jaw.

"Shut your trap before she chops your cock off again."

Non're placed a hand over his exposed self that had grown during our discussion and *I* had gone through great pains to ignore. I hobbled on one foot to the next cell and gasped.

"Slow down, Scarlett. It is not as bad as it looks."

I sobbed, fumbling with the keys, and Non're moved to place his hands on the bars that split his cell from Sear're's. The Merfolk advisor had long black hair peppered with silver streaks, his heavily skin had a blue tinge and around his large pupils was bright blue. The man hunched on the bed was not that man. He was thin and his hair hung in dirty ropes to his waist. He flashed me rows of shark teeth and I laughed through my tears.

"No, it is, Sear're. I told you to fuck them. It is not all bad. You get used to it." Non're shrugged, and I detected a hint of his depression.

Revenge wasn't as sweet as I thought it would be.

The door opened and crashed into the wall. I pushed away from Red and hopped to Sear're's side. Red took the keys I left in the cell and went to Non're's door. I shook as I ran my hands over Sear're's thin, beaten face. One eye was swollen closed and his teeth were cracked. Wounds that looked old and healed over were scattered over his body. New ones seeped from his dull dry skin.

He tried taking my hands away, but I couldn't help touching him. I wanted to heal his every ache. Sear're had been the one to send a message to Steel letting him know where I was when Non're had me. He was also the one who helped me root out the Merfolk traitors. Two of which were helping me release the prisoners.

Non're was free from his cell and standing with Red at the open gate. "They beat him once a week and starved him. The only reason he is still alive is in case I die; they will have him as a hostage."

"Why would you die?" I asked, cradling Sear're's head.

"Because I have a big mouth." Non're smirked at me and I whipped my head back to Sear're.

"He mocks the guards and the Crathode until they beat him within an inch of his life. He has a death wish," Sear're rumbled.

"I do not like being told *when* and *who* to fuck," Non're said, giving Red a once over. "They broke his legs. He cannot walk. That is why it smells like a chamber pot in his cell."

"We'll be okay. You can go. If you see a Guardian, send them down here." My tears were finally starting to slow and Sear're rubbed his thumbs over my damp cheeks.

"I will," Red promised, and she took Non're's arm leading him away.

Sear're winced as I pulled him into my lap. The big Merfolk man stared up at me with his one good eye as I stroked his hair.

"Feeling maternal, Guardian?"

"I think you know that I manage to be aroused while still caring for you. I am a Merfolk khoraz after all and you are my favorite," I said, mustering a smile.

"By the Mother, you are so warm. This blasted place is freezing."

I sniffled. "I am going to take you home myself, Sear're."

"You are not going to cry again are you, Scarlett?" His hand cupped my face, and I nuzzled it.

"No. Why didn't you just sleep with them? I doubt they would hold it against you," I whispered.

"I thought of you and how you changed the way we take our gifts. One woman to stand up against an entire tribe. It was against your will, like those women. What kind of man would I be if I gave in and raped those women as multiple men had already done?"

"I am going to cry again," I whispered.

"All the same. You are just as beautiful when you cry."

"I'm going to kiss you, Sear're. Not because I'm a Merfolk khoraz, but because you're a brave and honorable man and this shouldn't have happened to you."

"I do not want your pity kiss."

I laughed. "Then take pity on me. I can't stop crying until I can properly thank you."

Sear're's eye scanned my face and his long fingers curled in my hair, pulling my face down to his. I pressed my lips over his broken mouth and tasted the copper of his blood. I kissed his upper lip and then his lower letting my tongue run along the cracks as he inhaled wheezing breaths. His fingers curled tighter in my hair, lips parting as his tongue probed forth and I met it with my own letting it brush his rows of sharp shark teeth.

I had kissed Sear're before when I was pretending to be his gift to root out the traitors, but they had been chaste and without any passion. Brass had taught me what it meant to feel passion and to lose yourself to it. Slate had expanded that knowledge and given it a skill set. I wanted to kiss Sear're so it would make his months of torture worthwhile. For him to know just how grateful I was for his sacrifice.

Sear're's free hand shifted, and I felt him wince as he slid it within the slice of my shirt and over the skin at my waist. His hand at my nape held me in place as he kissed me deeper. I was no longer the one initiating it but was subject to it.

"Married less than a week and already she's got her tongue down another man's throat. I thought I said not Sear're?"

Brass wasted no time pulling us apart because he knew from the bond, I couldn't make myself stop touching Sear're. Gennadi and Demyan waited outside the cell and watched as Brass had to physically push my head away from Sear're.

"I'm sorry," I breathed, and felt Brass jerk my shirt shut.

"I am not," Sear're said in better spirits, and Brass chuckled.

"You're lucky you're half dead or I would've beaten you half to death myself for trying to sleep with the mother of my sons. My wife, Sear're.

But beating you to death doesn't hold the same appeal as it once might have since you cannot fight back."

Brass peeled open one of my squeezed shut eyes and sighed. I knew my pupils were as big as saucers. He took off the nix torque and tossed it on the ground before he held my face and the warmth of his healing flooded through me. As he worked, I delved into Sear're and stifled another sob. If we hadn't come, Sear're wouldn't have survived another month. I healed his eye and lips, mended his legs, and fixed broken ribs. They'd broken his fingers and toes which I righted, but nothing could be done for his malnourishment.

Brass helped Sear're into a seated position beside me and crouched in front of us. He pulled the lace from his undershirt and handed it to me so I could close my corset and it held my shirt shut.

"Are you okay to walk?" Brass asked him, and Sear're shook his head.

"Give me a blanket, Guardian. Your wife should not see me this way," Sear're joked, and Brass smirked, pulling the sheet up around his lap.

"Gennadi. Carry my wife to the surface. She is going to try to fight you, but she'll pass out soon enough. It has been a long time since she used so much energy and needed extensive healing."

I scowled at Brass as Gennadi approached. Brass signaled to Demyan to help him lift Sear're and the grizzly Bjorn reluctantly helped him. I was getting ready to give them all a piece of my mind when Gennadi helped me stand and my head swam.

"Maybe I could use a little help."

CHAPTER 19
JETT

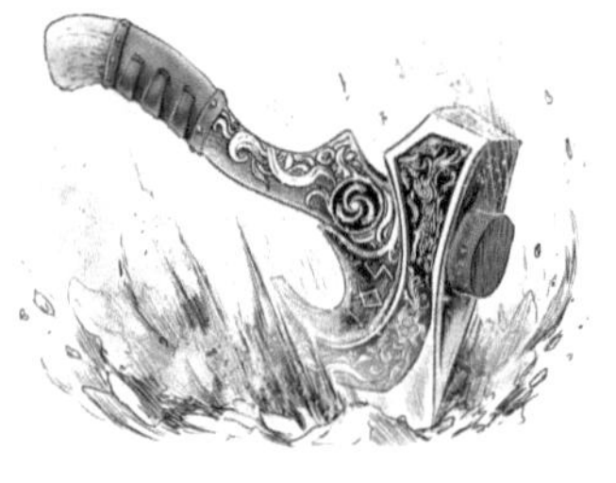

Mirage was tall for a woman, maybe two inches shy of six feet with a toned pair of stems that matched the rest of her taut muscled body. Her straight hair fell around her sun kissed toned shoulders framing a round face a pair of big bright blue eyes. Too blonde and bitchy for Jett's taste, but Quick and Slate never had any complaints until she projected Scarlett.

"Maybe I should get you a pair of blinders so you won't catch her in your periphery," Jett offered.

Her husband, Rikke, the black panther hybrid, was a Wemic scout. He was painted in white swirls where his loincloth didn't cover and didn't appear to feel cold in the land of perpetual fall. Rikke had had a brief affair with Indi that gave the tribesmen a taste for human women.

He boosted her onto Safanad, Scarlett's white Arabian mare Slate had given to her as a wedding present.

"As long as that woman does not look my way or address me, we can work together," Slate rumbled, and Jett ran his hand over his face.

Cherry had forgiven him, many times. She was excited about the possibility of Tawny becoming their paramour and had been delighted

Amethyst partook in the Matriarch's wiles. She was safe with Junior in Folkvangr. He couldn't have her distracting Viper. He was a no nonsense kind of man who spoke in quick clipped sentences. He grew his greying hair long and kept it tied back in a leather throng away from his craggy face. The normally stoic Centaur ambassador had shook with happiness when he met his grandson and saw Cherry for the first time in months. That was when he brought up Lewt's plan.

The Centaur had joined their clans over the summer when they first found Minotaur in Mabon. There were trolls and fairies in Mabon as well. The Risar were there, but no one had been in touch with them since they'd given Scarlett their piece. Jett gaped at Slate wondering how he didn't know Scarlett had treated with the Risar, but Lewt told them it was when she had been in Mabon for her tour with Ash. That explained everything.

Like every tribe she visited, Lewt had a big fat crush on Jett's baby sister. The palomino pony boy couldn't stop riling Slate up about it, which wasn't difficult because Slate had never gone five months without a woman and he was ready to kill someone — several *someones*.

It was hard not to think of Peak in Mabon and the night he hurt Scar. The smell of fall, the crinkling of the golden and scarlet leaves that grew that way all year round, moss covered bridges and the stony knolls. All of it. He used to love Mabon. It was the only island that didn't have a difficult tribe to deal with. Everywhere was safe to travel.

Only Scarlett could find a barghest on the safest island in Tidings to make her his life mate.

Lewt stood beside Mirage with his closest confidants. Jett remembered them from the trip they took as tyros to the fairy and troll village. Hute, the black-haired stallion that Indigo had rode galloped on. Fert, the only female Centaur they'd had with them that day with long brown hair and a tiny scrap of fabric covering her very human chest. The pony boy Tawny rode was there. Goep had a thick Clydesdale body and flowing chocolate mane. Jett knew she wouldn't have done anything with him while being married to Steel, but he did still wonder.

The afternoon sun shone through the Haust castle parapets along the flat roof slit for archers. The grey stoned medieval castle looked as foreboding as ever with its drawbridge up so there was no way to cross the moat. The entire Haust family would be hiding in that castle.

The stony village was made of the same ancient looking stone and moss covered since it was constantly raining in Mabon and streams and rivers cut through every few feet of land. They could just make out horned Minotaur patrolling the brick roads ahead from where they hid in the forest.

"Right. That makes perfect sense," Jett said facetiously.

Slate gave him a sidelong glance. "Amethyst?"

"She's done doing whatever she was doing," he grumbled, thinking it had better been with Tawny.

"Scarlett did not activate her bond with me, but she did with Brass. She is married to him now and they have two sons together. He was her first and he will be her last. A man must wonder where he belongs in that picture. *If* he belongs," Slate rumbled.

Finally, Jett thought. Something had been irking Slate since they went to Thrimilci and Jett thought it was Mirage, but it was Scarlett and her complete life with Brass. Where *did* Slate fit in?

"Don't talk crazy now that you have her back."

"Am I? If I had not chased her, they would have married long ago. Brass only did as I asked him. It was my fault he kept away, why they were apart when he would have made her happy. I do not have much longer left. Weeks," Slate said, keeping his gunmetal eyes straight ahead.

"She loves you. It's always been you. If you hadn't been such a bastard, maybe she'd never have given Brass a second look. She only would have been with you. You said yourself, just days after she arrived, when you two went to check out the bauk, she was ready to give herself to you. That meant something to her. You can't play that game though. You have her now. She is happy *now*. You are happy too, aren't you? She wants to be with you and everything that comes with your damaged self."

Slate's jaw clenched, making his features look even harder. "As long as she loves me, I am happy. I am only thinking out loud. I should have punched Quick in the throat."

"What?" Jett glanced around as he guffawed and silently apologized as the Centaur tribes men gave him death stares.

"For interrupting me with your sister. I should have punched him in the throat and shut him down so we could finish," Slate said with a smirk.

"Gods, you're an asshole. I didn't need to know that."

"You are bedding my cousin." Slate shrugged.

"Not the same," Jett grumbled.

The shrubs parted and a white tuft of hair bobbed about with a glowing green florescent light floating above it coming from the eyes of the fairy that helped guide the little troll around the Minotaur. Fairies were only about a foot high and made from bits of nature, like, twigs and blades of grass. This fairy had fern wings, and a pony tails made of reeds.

Baboo burst from the shrubs with a big smile on her wide wrinkly face. She was all knees and elbows with a short torso and pouchy belly at only three feet high.

"Scarlett's brother!" She called too loudly in a voice that managed to croak and be falsetto at the same time.

Jett moved from behind the towering red wood and beckoned the little troll Scarlett befriended. "Morning, Baboo. What's the good word?"

"Nothing good at all. The Natt castle was taken last night and the Haust are not in their castle. The Minotaur patrols have been doubled." She nodded, shaking the cottony tuft on her head.

Jett and Slate shared a rare excited look as Lewt and Viper met them. "The land is undefended except for the Minotaur. They probably thought the townsfolk were too content to rebel," Jett informed them.

Most of them were. The Haust were well liked and even though Jett wished he could personally raise Peak from the dead only to kill him again, he had been just. Only fifty Guardians were in the arena. People who were loyal to Viper, who in turn had been loyal to Scarlett.

"The trolls and fairies are ready when you are," Baboo said with a nod as she ran long wrinkly fingers over her moss shift dress.

Lewt offered her a hand, and she scrambled onto his back to wrap her arms around his abs. Slate was already disrobing and a few of the female Centaur were taking a keen notice. Scarlett wouldn't like that. He wasn't even sure if Slate went full barghest without her there if he could control his...appetites.

"Then there is nothing left to wait for. Only engage the villagers if they seek to stop us. Aim to disable, not kill," Viper said in a rush.

The four clans of Centaur had divided in two. Half with the fairies and trolls who would not be left out of the battle and the other with the few Guardians from Folkvangr. Jett slid his long seaxes from their black Damascus scabbards that Scarlett had bought him.

Slate was no longer Slate. He was through with speaking. A barb tipped tail swished and Jett made a face. A double row of off-white horns curved along his spine on a ten foot long frame. The two pairs of horns on his head were of the same color. Tusks jutted from his jaw; another set curved back from behind his ears while the third poked up from behind its pointed ears. His muzzle was like a wolf's but his teeth much longer, his body was bulkily muscled, thick across his chest and arms. He turned his silver eyes on Jett who unwittingly took a step back.

"Please. *Please,* by the Mother, tell me she has not let you bed her in this form," Jett whispered.

Slate's muzzle pulled back and he made a coughing noise Jett took for a laugh. Lewt laughed with him.

"I find human women are often intimidated by my hybrid form."

His joke elicited a laugh from his cohorts. At least, Jett hoped it was a joke.

"Slate will take the Guardians and get into the castle. The Centaur will drive the Minotaur into the portal with the trolls and fairies," Viper said with a completely serious face.

"I'll... go with the trolls," Jett said, looking to the tiny frail creature on Lewt's back.

If he got Baboo killed, Scarlett would be distraught. The little troll had been the one to help carve Balas and Spinel's cribs. Viper nodded.

"I will as well."

Viper turned his green eyes to him as if it was a bonding experience for them and Jett sucked in a breath. Not having a father figure had worked out just fine until Alder had been determined to make him his heir and take an active role in his life. He'd even come to his wedding. The fact that Viper and Moon had been withdrawn and quiet types had suited Jett fine. Having a grandson was changing Viper. Jett might actually have to get to know him.

Lewt had a horn on a cord wrapped around his shoulder and the

Centaur gathered spread out along the tree line. There had to be a thousand horse humans there. Jett hadn't even known that many existed, and that was only half. The Minotaur were complacent. There had been no rebellion as there had been in Thrimilci and Elivagar. They would never see them coming.

Lewt blew the horn that looked like a ram horn in a loud *BAROO*.

Guardian men and women quickly fell behind the hooves of the Centaur. Dirt and the lush grass was kicked up into Jett's face as he raced over the knolls and hillocks leaping over boulders on his way into the village.

Slate made short work of the draw bridge. He leapt into the air, claws lodging in the wood as Guardians formed a vortex of wind around him to keep the arrows from penetrating his sleek charcoal back. The thick chains snapped, and it came down hard enough to make the ground quake.

Villagers screamed in fear. Jett resented the fact they had accepted their new regime without any of the pain and fear his island's people had suffered. Guardians wearing the gold trimmed brown cloaks of the Haust with their jumis symbol on their backs raced to the village's edge with blades and staffs, some shooting arrows into the Centaurs ranks and Jett threw up a solid wall of air that stretched his *calling* to its limits. He would never be able to hold it. Scarlett's powers would be very handy.

Red Second Guardians wore red bands around their jerkin sleeves. Jett shouted. Scarlett would say men were such idiots. They were so intent on surprising them; he'd forgotten how adamant she had been about letting the people and the tribes know they were there to free them, not bring a new type of dictator.

"GUARDIANS OF MABON! We are the Red Seconds. Your Prime has lied and manipulated the Hausts. Minotaurs police your roads and —"

Jett cut short. The people couldn't hear him over the thundering hooves and the sound of their own screams. It was a disaster of epic proportions. He could see in his mind's eye the fatal results of their precipitous acts. Hundreds would die. Innocents would die.

The ground shook, and it wasn't from Slate.

Jett turned his furrowed brow looking for the source of the thunder.

Risar wore fur vests over burly chests and thick belted skirts that fell to their knees. Thick furred boots were wrapped with leather straps to cinch them all the way up. Their eyes were beady and dark in wide craggy faces, but they looked human if an earthy brown shade and very large and bulky. They marched down from the trees, walking right through the rivers and streams.

The Centaur had stopped their charge. Slate and the Guardians were already in the castle. Minotaur began running for a clay arch beside the portal gate that hung between two trees with carved giants to either side. The massive doors were whimsical scenes of fairies, centaurs, and trolls. Hybrids couldn't use the official portals, but they could use the makeshift portable ones Orion had commissioned. It was almost comical to see the horned hybrids running in fear of the Risar, who were head and shoulders taller than Jett.

People began to peek out of their homesteads as the roads quickly emptied and Jett ran the rest of the way into the village.

"We mean you no harm. We support a restoration to how things were before Prime Ash Straumr took over. No more Minotaurs in the roads."

Jett was losing his voice trying to placate the frightened people. Viper was a recognizable face, and he had taken up Jett's quick speech, walking amongst the people in their taffeta bustled dresses and long sleeve jerkins of Mabon fashion. The Haust Guardians didn't know what to make of our speech and some put up a fight which the Centaur quickly put down with the help of the nix torques we brought from Valla.

Slate reappeared fully dressed. His dark face tight as he looked to the Risar who had reached the edge of the village and waited patiently to treat with whomever approached first. Lewt was already making his way there with Baboo on his back and Jett moved his feet once Slate started forward.

The two male Risars' voices were deep and guttural as they spoke with Lewt. One's wide head was completely bald while the other had a white strip of hair from ear to ear around his head. A woman just as thick in girth as the male's but a head shorter had white hair topped by a crown of vines and leaves. She stood between them in a fur-lined dress made of rough woven wool.

Her deep-set eyes that were practically devoid of color focused on

Slate as they stopped before the three. "I am Edda, the Risar seidkona. These are my sons Brusi and Anundr." She gestured to the bald one and then the white-haired whose foreheads looked chipped from the rocky canyons of Thrimilci.

The seidkona had come herself. She was a sorceress and led the Risar though it could be argued that no one led them, but they valued her opinion.

Brusi pursed lips that matched his russet colored skin as he leaned his face forward. He flashed flat teeth, each inches wide in a mouth that split his round face.

"Where is the sunbeam with the plump lips and perky breasts? I miss her smart mouth."

Slate growled and moved so quickly, Jett didn't have time to grip him before he was in Brusi's face, *er* chest. The Risar were half again as wide as Slate was which was really something. Anundr laughed.

"You must be the Grar Dyr. The husband she had not bedded. Who soiled her pure heart and conscious?" Anundr bellowed out a laugh, gripping his robust belly, but Slate was taken aback.

"She said that?" he asked.

Brusi leaned back, raising to his full height and Anundr ran dark beady eyes over Slate. Their skin had a dry quality that reminded Jett of porous rocks in the Thrimilci desert.

"She did. She did not say she did not like it." Anundr smiled, splitting his face.

"Have you secured a son?" Edda asked, interrupting their tête-à-tête.

Slate stepped back and looked to her. "Not as yet."

Brusi shook his considerable bald head. "I told her she had months to seduce you. Has she had her sons?"

"She has. How long did you guys speak?" Jett asked, bewildered at the intimacy of their conversation.

"Not long. Some Risar have the manners of beasts." Baboo chuckled.

"She was quick to point it out," Lewt said with a flick of his golden mane.

Cursed Scarlett enticing men of all different kinds.

"When Baboo told us what the Centaur planned. We decided our presence was required. We like our lands quiet. No needless deaths and we plan to keep it that way." Edda made no question as to what she would do to accomplish that. "Send your mate to us when she has completed her tasks. Your wife must be a considerable beauty with a cleverness in equal value for making my sons promise to work with her as our ambassadors. I would like to meet her for myself."

Brusi and Anundr glanced at one another wryly before bursting into laughter and turning to leave. They didn't amble, but moved smoothly and evenly back over the hillocks and rolling hills to where the other Risar stood waiting and they all turned as one when Edda reached them and disappeared into the trees line.

"There are times that I am grateful that it is not only I who have become ensnared in her net. At other times, I want to blind every man and creature near her so she can never find another she wants more than us," Slate said, letting out a gusty exhale.

"Blinding would do little. You have heard her speak. Freya herself is enticed by her alluring rasp." Lewt said with a smile in his tone.

Jett groaned.

"Do you have the ointment?" Slate asked with a smirk.

Lewt and Slate got along which was ground breaking because he didn't get along with anyone who didn't defer to him. Baboo tossed a small jar that Slate plucked from the air and opened. A lemony scent reached Jett's nostrils, and he gave Slate an inquisitive look.

"To make his wife more amorous." Lewt tossed him a tiny burlap bag. "Sprinkle it in her food. For fertility."

Slate arched a brow at Jett who stared at the three unlikely comrades. "Stacking the odds, brother."

"Stop calling me brother. You can't call me brother while openly plotting to seduce my baby sister into having your children in litters," Jett growled.

"It worked last time, though he was not the one to plant the seeds." Lewt chuckled.

Slate was no longer smirking. "There were Stygian Knights in the Mabon castle. They escaped through the portal which we locked."

Viper's eyes hinted at a smile that didn't touch his lips as he patted Jett's back. "Town portal is locked as is the portable portal. The Risar are combing the woods for any Minotaur that may have retreated, and the castle is secured. It is time to bring Cerise and Junior here so we may celebrate today's victory."

Jett looked to Slate. "Another day will be okay."

"I will escort the few who fought to Valla U to the cells there," Slate informed them.

Jett smiled. "I'm going to get Cherry and my son."

CHAPTER 20
GYPSUM

"Come for me, Prime Sumar," Mica breathed in my ear.

My backside stuck to the crescent carved seat of the Straumr patriarch. The gold and silver trimmed black sleeveless robe I'd found in Ash's office had slid up as I moved Mica's hips in my lap.

"*Fuck.*"

I stood sliding her legs from the armrests and laid her back on the horseshoe table the council sat at. Each greater family had a chair with their sigil carved on the back that faced the rows of pews for hearings. It was a private room we didn't have to worry about anyone walking in on.

We weren't being smart. It was lunch and we would both be missing from our table, but I couldn't get enough of Mica and she gave herself so completely it consumed me. I woke up, went to bed, showered, trained all thinking of her. It couldn't be healthy. It'd only been a few days since I gave in to her, but it was as if we had always been together.

I held her creamy slender thighs against my chest in the spot that the Prime had sat during his hearings for generations. Her red hair fanned out around her to slide over the edge of the long table. Her bright pink lips parted to release her little moans. She was obsessed with learning what excited me most. She was highly competitive and strived to be the best. *My best.*

I didn't have the heart to tell her there had only been eight girls before her. Two of which were cheetah hybrids from the Wemic tribe. Shale and Ama who had been killed last year, Diamond, Ro, and two girls from Chicago I'd never see again. Mica was something I'd never experienced before. She gave me all of her. She didn't have to hold back; I didn't have to share her. She was mine. I wasn't just her prop or an addition to her love life — I was *it.*

Most Guardians my age, especially the guys, had twice as many partners as I did unless they were betrothed. I didn't see the appeal in bed hopping when one, or sometimes two, women could meet my needs for extended periods of time. I liked having a connection. I never understood how Slate could see a woman once and never speak to her again.

I ran my hands up her flat stomach up to her freckled chest and felt her thighs flexing before she gripped me. I cursed in Merfolk, a stream of expletives Steel had uttered once when he received a letter from Sear're about Scar, as I spilled inside her. Also not smart.

She wrapped her legs around my waist and I lowered myself to kiss her. "Mica," I breathed, brushing her bangs from her face.

She giggled tightening her muscles around me. "You like my name."

"It's the woman the name belongs to, bunny," I told her, unable to stop the smile that brought dimples to my cheeks.

"Bunny? Like, we go at it like rabbits?" She giggled.

I laughed and lifted her to the edge of the table. "I was thinking more like the Energizer Bunny. The battery?"

"I know what a battery is. As long as you do not call me Coppertop," she said, smiling against my lips.

I chuckled. "Mica. My little bunny."

She hummed wrapping her arms around my neck and I caught sight of a man standing in the left-hand corner past where the transcriber would sit. I slowly removed the Prime's robe from my shoulders and wrapped it around Mica's slender frame.

"My turn to be Prime?" She laughed as I pulled the front closed and helped her to her feet off the dais.

"No. I have a guest."

Mica spun around and she gasped when she saw Slate standing by the door that led to the cells. She ducked behind the desk and began to collect her clothes.

"How long has he been standing there?" she asked, embarrassed.

"Only a moment. Some nonsense about batteries," Slate rumbled with a mocking lip curl for me.

Slate pronounced each "T" in the word as if he was unaccustomed to it. It was easy to forget how much they did or didn't know about outside of Tidings.

I *called* my pants and stepped into them. "Two unexpected visits in one month."

"We took Mabon. We do not have anywhere to put the Guardians until we give them a trial. They need meals, and fresh water to clean themselves. Two tyros per shift should be enough. Not many resisted. Good afternoon, Mica."

Mica popped up in her caftan, her skin a shade that matched her hair. "Afternoon, Patriarch Dagr." She turned to me, straightening her bangs. "I will see you in the great hall?"

She moved to walk away, and I grabbed her waist pulling her to me. Her big brown eyes went wide as I kissed her unabashedly as I would've if he wasn't there.

"Later, bunny," I told her, letting her withdraw, and she rounded the long desk.

Her foot slipped off the dais and she blushed furiously as she hurried down the aisle between the pews. The doors shut behind her and I braced my hand on the desk to hop over it. Slate leaned in the doorway.

"A Rot. The girls are going to shriek with excitement. Your mother will not be able to control herself. Careful. You are going to need this." Slate opened the pack over his shoulder with his calling and floated out a small tin to me as I walked to him.

"You carry *this* tea around with you?" I asked, dropping my tone.

It was the tea the women used to avoid pregnancies in Tidings. If

Slate had it, he was dousing women he slept with. I opened to find loose leaves instead of bags and shut it again.

"I brought it for you. I may be late. She is in season, but I suspect she has not begun to keep track of such things," Slate said, quirking his scarred brow at me with that mocking smile.

Nausea hit me twice. Once, when I thought of becoming a father in nine months and again when I thought I could have conceived a child while having their mother call me Prime Sumar.

Slate chuckled as if he could read my mind. "You deflowered that spring rose. *Again.* Be careful. I caught her scent before. She cares for you."

I laughed facetiously. "Giving relationship advice now that you got your wife back?"

Slate's smile deepened, creasing his chiseled face. It was good to see him smile again.

"I have earned it. Do not put yourself out. I came to deliver the captives and take a last look at Indigo if she is out of her tent so I may report it to Scarlett. Mabon is in celebration today and Jett wants to visit the wight Alder and Wren became so I must take them when I return."

"Let me put my clothes on and I'll go with you."

Indigo wasn't out of her tent, but there was commotion in the camp. The hybrids of hybrids were silent, but the command tents had Guardians in all different color cloaks coming in and out then leaving on horses. Valla was in Stygian hands as were the Tio and Straumr palaces.

"They must have heard they lost Mabon," Slate rumbled with a smirk as he leaned against the yellow stone.

His wavy hair was longer than mine with silver beads with Celtic etching, he wore Indigo's tree of life fetish, the ivory Sumar sunburst, Dagr solar cross, and Haust jumis, all threaded through narrow braids. The front of his hair was plaited back to keep it from his face.

Horse hooves clopped over the grass and Sage rode into view leaping off the back of a black Akhal-Teke stallion. He was leaping off the horse before it came to a complete stop. His normally well-groomed hair in disarray as he stormed to Indigo's tent marked by the pink tassels that blew over its peak.

Slate shifted in the window so we were both squeezing into the narrow frame. A low growl began to reverberate from his chest.

"Is she...?"

I thought I could hear her screaming. Before I could finish asking, Sage dragged Indigo out by her sunny blonde hair and threw her face first onto the Valla U lawn that had turned to dirt on her hands and knees. She let her head hang as she rose, wearing a gold caftan suitable for an Ausa Vatni in its finery.

I jumped when Sage snarled and but a boot to her backside, shoving her back down again so her palms slid over the dirt in the patchy lawn. Canis and Cygnus exited the command tent and looked for the source of the disturbance.

I could see them shout in Sage's direction as Dahlia and Cassiopeia exited the tent after them. Sage's lips were moving, but he wasn't stopping.

"What is he —?"

I gasped as Sage began to reach for his belt.

A roar ripped through the bright spring afternoon and Slate's fingers curled around the frame as he shook. His skin rippled as dark fur tried to force its way from his pores. Slate threw back his head a howled, and I staggered back, covering my ears.

A silver monster with goring tusks and two sets of horns spouting from its head came into sight from the back of the camp. It ran on all fours but it was in hybrid form not a full barghest. The hybrids of hybrids darted away from the bounding beast, unsure of what to make of their bloodthirsty new guest. A short canine snout with long fanged teeth snarled as he tore through the camp to where Sage spun around and darted to the command tent. Slate's fingers curled the stone so tightly dust fell from the wall.

Indigo's hair shook, hiding her face, but we knew she was crying when Sterling reached her in his hybrid form and scooped her into his arms without breaking his run. She looked like a child in his arms as he made off with her. Her nix torque chain trailed behind them until they disappeared from sight.

The tips of Slate's fingers elongated into claws and back as his muscles flexed. He let out a long howl. His neck cording, fangs pushing from his gums until it was answered in the distance by Sterling's own howl.

"You're not going to jump out of the window and run free are you?" I asked, taking a wary step away from him as things began to settle back down in the camp.

"She is his mate. I did not think barghests were pack animals, but the draw... I wanted to help. To run at his side. He felt it too." Slate took a deep shuddering breath. "He will kill whoever tries to hurt her."

"Was Sage —"

Slate spun around with eyes so silver I could see my own reflection in them. "Keep it to yourself, Chief."

I ran through my entire vocabulary to try to find the words. "What did he say to her, Slate?"

"Next time they invade, I invade you," Slate said in an inflectionless tone.

My body shook as I balled my fists. I wished I had something to turn into like Slate or that I could start on fire like Scarlett. I felt like a little boy and helpless.

"Do you think he has...?"

I let my question trail off. We'd both seen Indigo's reaction. Resignation. The question died in my throat; beat her with the belt or worse? I swallowed, turning away from Slate as I tried to swallow the lump in my throat.

"We will take Elivagar and then all that will be left is Valla and Ostara. We will have to hope Sterling wises up to what Sage has done and takes matters into his own hands." Slate glanced back out the window, but none of the greater families were visible. "I have to go back. I have Tawny's auseklis and I have to make it back to Scarlett before she gets in season. We have a prophecy to fulfill."

I nodded unwilling to try my voice, and he placed his hand on my shoulder before he walked away. I wondered what else he heard and what his nose had picked up from their scents.

My heart was heavy when I sat in the window sill to wait for Indigo's return.

Mica walked with River and Beryl for their watch and I told them about the prisoners Slate brought. River went to make arrangements for them to be watched and Beryl got the hint to take his vigilance a little further down the hall.

"You are not looking so good. You did not go to any of your classes. Did you even eat?" Her delicate brows drew together, and I smiled at her concern.

"Indigo is out, I just want to make sure she returns okay. You can sit with me if you like," I told her absently as I glanced back out the window.

The camp had been in an uproar. When Sage left, Cygnus had followed him out all the way back to his horse obviously chastising him. Cygnus had rode out shortly after and when he returned at twilight, Ruby was with him and he began shouting orders at Guardians. A slew of things were brought into Indigo's tent.

I had never seen Cygnus be anything other than smug and demeaning. I knew the change had significant meaning but couldn't figure out what. Ruby hadn't said a single word to Cygnus the entire time. She stood with a queenly demeanor that reminded me of Amethyst as she waited. Cygnus said more to her, but she gave no response in return.

"There." Mica pointed out the window, and I pulled her back so the firelight from the camp wouldn't reveal her face. "Her and Sterling are walking through camp. Goodness, they are both filthy. He does not even have a shirt on... or boots," she said incredulous that a greater family son would walk around in public in such a state.

My muscles relaxed at seeing Indigo in one piece and suddenly I was ravenous and exhausted. I pulled Mica to me and kissed her full on the mouth even with Beryl at my back.

She giggled nervously.

"If you procure blanket and pillows, I will meet you in the greenhouse under the cherry blossom tree by the lotus pond. I will steal us some wine and food. We will make love until dawn and I want you to sleep in my arms tonight, Mica Rot. My little bunny," I purred, running my nose along her ear.

She was already blushing as she shook her bangs from her eyes. "I do not know what prompted this change in you, but I will take it. Say half an hour?"

"Done," I told her and pulled her in for another kiss before letting her go.

I watched her svelte figure glide through the hall and disappear around the corner before looking down to Indigo who was being embraced by Ruby. They both went into the tent together and I thought I understood. Greater families were extremely screwed up, but in his own way, Cygnus cared for Indigo.

I would never raise my children in the greater family way.

That thought prompted me to slap my hand to my pocket where I stuck the tin. I would have to have an awkward conversation with Mica tonight and give her the tea.

I would have to remember to thank Slate again.

CHAPTER 21

INDIGO

Sterling's tears of frustration rolled over the swell of my breast as I cradled his face. It felt good to comfort him and took away a little of the frailty I felt. It also bought me time before I had to return to my tent where Sage would eventually find me. He was going to take me right in front of everyone. My shame and mortification laid bare.

"My family's island. Our castle. Indi, I was going to kill Sage. He has always been too hard on you."

Sterling was human again. He hadn't carried me far into the woods knowing Canis would undoubtedly send a force after us and we had nowhere to go unless he ran us to the Vanaheim Arena.

Despite how much self-loathing consumed me, I had enough joy left in me to be happy for the women who would be freed, if they weren't already, from the Crathode breeding prison.

"They said nothing bad about the Haust. They said we had been lied to. I do not understand. That was Slate at Valla U. He answered my howls with his own, but my people said he was in Mabon. Do you think Orion made some kind of key to open locked portals simply by holding it or a way to communicate over the islands?" Sterling lifted his gleaming violet eyes to me and I shrugged.

"I know less than you," I whispered.

Sterling balanced his weight on his elbows as he brushed my hair from my face and kissed me. "He did not hurt you, did he? I scented his anger before he left the palace. He came through the portal from Ostara and said Minotaur were coming through the portal they set up with the Anguillan. From the portable portals because they cannot go through the main portals unassisted. Sage said he tried the portals to Elivagar and none of them work. The ones to Mabon are all closed. I cannot go home," he choked out.

He felt like he'd failed. He had. I wanted him to take me away, but he would never leave his mother and sisters. Loyal to his family to a fault.

"Let it play out, Sterling. Stay out of it. Keep your sisters out of it. Let the Red Seconds reclaim the land. You know I'll speak out for you. I won't let them take your castle away. I promise, Sterling."

Blades of grass stuck to his palms as he raised them once more to cup my face. "I have never had much interest in Slate, but when he answered my call — I felt kinship. What if they give him my land? He is a Haust."

His thick brows drew together, and I tried not to laugh. "Slate has absolutely no ambition to be a patriarch. He didn't even want to be the Dagr patriarch. Slate is more the *free to do as he pleases* type. He wouldn't want to be stuck governing a land like Mabon."

"Will you stay with me if they succeed? I do not deserve you after marrying Diamond, but I have never been more happy than the days we spent together in the Valla cottage. I want to take care of you, Indi," Sterling whispered.

Silver's bond pulsed like a second heart. I hoped I didn't live long enough to see the end of the war. I would've ended my own life, but I couldn't since it meant ending the life of my unborn son. Even if the Red Seconds ended the Purge War and Silver rescued me, I could never be with him again. I was a khoraz.

No. I had hoped Sage had come into my tent intent on strangling me. The next time he did, I would fight him and hope he lost control. I would welcome it.

"I want you to be happy," I whispered, and his lips kissed lower.

"I want to take off your nix torque. We could run away. Like Scarlett did. Canis sent Guardians after us they are all around us even now, just out of sight. They made me swear a blood oath the first time I saw you after we returned from the cottages. I can never remove your nix torque, Indi. I am so sorry."

I blinked away tears. Two years ago to hear Sterling say that he wanted to run away with me, would've made me the happiest woman alive. I knew he would have had to sworn something along those lines before they would let him see me or he would've freed me long ago. Even if it was just for while we were together.

I stared up at the puffs of clouds peeking through the trees wondering how much longer I would have to live before they would let me die.

Sterling was emotionally wrung out, and I let him nap on top of me in the woods until dusk. The Guardians sent after us didn't appear until I was dressed and we were trying to manufacture clothing for Sterling to cover up his lower half. A Guardian in Straumr purple and white with the lit crescent portion of the moon on his back, approached with pants and jerkin in hand.

What took fifteen minutes to run as a barghest, took an hour as two humans, one shoeless, to walk. When we reached camp, it was nightfall and word that they had lost Mabon and Elivagar in one day was all anyone was talking about. We wound through the camp until we reached the command tents.

A woman who was as skinny as a rail, one of the few who wore her hair up and always in a tight bun. My father's mother turned as we neared and smiled brightly with her wide Geol mouth.

"Indigo, dear. How I have missed you."

She wore a black caftan of silk that gave her dark hair and ivory skin more contrast. She wide dark eyes gleamed below her thick winged brows as she ran them over me toe to head and back again.

"I plan to spend a few nights with you. With all the ruckus going on, I am finding myself lonely in Ostara," she said in her cultured tone, native to Ostara.

Sterling gave my hand a squeeze and kissed my cheek before saying goodnight to Ruby and entering the command tent barefooted. I followed him with my eyes and caught sight of Cygnus watching us at the entrance. He glanced away when my eyes reached him and ducked into the tent.

He knew.

Sage's little scene had drawn attention to what he'd done and intended to do again and worse. I knew Canis and Cygnus didn't approve it. Cygnus must have arranged for Ruby to come see me. I knew my grandmother and there was no way she wanted any part of the war. She wanted to sit in her beautiful glass like castle away from all the fighting and pretend as though none of it was happening.

When Ruby ushered me into the tent, I found a trolley full of covered dishes and a table set for two already waiting. I dared not hope things would get better. The damage had already been done, and a cage was still a cage.

CHAPTER 22
JETT

Slate fished for trout in the shallow brook for our lunch with Spinel and Balas strapped to his chest looking very paternal. It would have been one of those moments you take a mental picture of for later memories, but there was the wight.

They were making good use of Tawny's portal key and had decided to wrangle up Sparrow, Hawk, and the twins to visit the wight now that Mabon was freed.

It was cool in the morning in Mabon and the sky was still crimson with the slow ascent of the sun. The constant rustle of leaves had lulled them all to sleep and continued to generate a calming sensation. They'd ended the night with smiles and an overall contentment and the feeling had lasted until Slate had heard the brook babbling in the distance and tried to prepare them for what they would see.

At the oak tree's massive base was one mossy stump that bent and curved to form two trees in the shape of a joint female and male body. The limbs of the tree formed appendages. Moss and knobs in the bark made their features, they faced one another and could shift enough to look about. They appeared human, but obviously not, as thick waves of leaves formed Wren's hair and the form of Alder's chest was etched in the bark.

Slate had strode forth to the base of the tree and it had turned in greeting. Two souls in one tree intertwined. It was the greatest gift the Mother could bestow upon her most faithful Guardians. It didn't feel that way when Alder's deep guttural voice gave Slate the warning that the Mother was dying and he was the key.

Slate had trudged through and began introducing Balas and Spinel as Scarlett's sons and Wren's warm voice came from the bark shaped into her wide mouth, telling him they did not know who Scarlett was, Jett thought they had made a mistake.

Slate was undeterred. He lifted the boys to the branches that made their limbs and Wren's tree branch arms held her grandsons, Jett understood. It wasn't for the wight that had lost its memories, but for them. Scarlett would have her mother hold her sons in one form or another.

Freya's burly boar, becoming a father had made him soft. Jett had tears dampening his cheeks long before he and Cherry leaned against the stump and introduced Junior. Sparrow had thrown herself at the trunk and cried fiercely into it telling her all that had happened. Ridge's return, Pearl's death, Steel's death, and Jett thought maybe it was cathartic for his aunt to be able to speak to her best friend since they were girls.

Hawk, pragmatic and level-headed, leaned his dancer's form against the stump with his dark intelligent eyes closed listening to the sound of Wren's voice as she talked about love. His silver hair matted where it brushed the bark and his nostrils flared above his sable goatee that was starting to go as grey as his hair.

"Love transcends death," Wren told them and Jett thought he could smell her rose and jasmine soap.

"Love and balance. Remember."

Sparrow's tears had dried and she joined Hawk at the base. They shut their eyes shoulder to shoulder and laced their hands together. Jett sat beside Sparrow and Cherry opposite him with Junior in her lap.

"I wish we could transplant the tree, but it was put here for a reason," Hawk noted.

Jett swallowed hard against the thick knot in his throat and nodded though their eyes were closed.

Jett heard the crackle of the cook fire Slate made to sear the fish and roused from his nap. The wight was just an oak tree. Hawk was sprinkling pecans and grated cheese over the small pan as Jett took a cooing Junior out of Cherry's lap to help the other men.

Hawk passed him the collapsible bowl and the cauliflower and Jett smiled as he took it and began to fill it with water to boil.

"Do you think Scarlett will become a wight when she dies? A little shrub at the base of this tree?" Jett asked, trying to make light of several morbid things at once.

"Wherever Slate and Brass are is where she will be," Hawk said, offering them a tight smile.

"You will soon find out where I will be. Once we take Elivagar, we are headed to Valla to find the project. I have two weeks at most. The Mother will probably make me a stone at the ocean's floor as her own joke while Brass and Scarlett will be the waves and the headland."

Jett stopped heating the bowl. Nostrils flaring and tears burned at his eyes all over again. The urge to chuck the boiling cauliflower was oppressive.

"Scarlett would find that stone. Dive into every ocean, scour every inch until she nestled you in her waters."

Hawk sat back on his ankle bent beneath him. "That she would. Then she would convince the Mother to create her own private pool. Brass's headland to encircle it, her waters to fill it, and Slate's stone at its heart. I had never seen Scarlett so flustered about a boy until we came to Tidings and you walked into the room. She could take meeting Jett and finding out she had a brother, but thinking she was related to you was too much for her. I remember how you cradled her when she fainted. I told Sparrow then that there was hope for Scarlett yet. She never could let herself feel. Not anyone outside the family, anyway." Hawk sighed. "Wren blamed herself for not trying to meet a man when she left Alder and Lark." He swallowed hard. "And for letting Scarlett see how much she missed them. It wasn't just her father she missed, but we couldn't tell Scar that."

Slate stared at them both, one arm banded around his step sons in their hide carriers and the other on the cast iron pan. Sparrow's boots crunched over fallen leaves and jerked them out of their memories.

"Smells delicious," she said and walked around the trio delivering kisses to the tops of their heads.

Slate had always been withdrawn with Pearl's attempts at affection, and it was the same with Sparrow. She didn't care. She was always touching him, trying to stand next to him, and embracing him. He was her sister's son. Nothing he did could stop her from loving him.

Cherry woke and Slate brought her over the twins. She managed to produce enough to nurse the three boys with Katydid's help. When Sparrow asked if Scarlett planned on nursing the boys when she returned, Slate cryptically told them that she had gone through great lengths to ensure a healthy supply.

Jett did not want to know what that meant.

TWENTY-THREE

Two extra days until we were finally camped in the Frostfell Mountains with the captive men and women from the Crathode caverns. Zlata had taken her sisters back to the Bjorn lands, and I'd asked Niall, Cabhan, Aoibhe, Gennadi, and Faima with a contingent of two hundred Lycans and Bjorn together to oversee the Crathode's rebuilding while they figured out who would lead them. I thought there was a nice balance to the partnership.

None of the captives had wanted to stay behind. They were all coming with us and traveling went slower in their weaker states, having been malnourished for months and some of the women were pregnant. We'd found rooms of babies and others with children; all the hybrids of hybrids none of the women had wanted to claim. None except Thre'ik.

Her people had almost been wiped out, and she said people already feared the Jorogumo who were not picky breeders, so what was a few more to be feared? She also confided that her eggs were set to hatch soon and if she was to keep them, she did not want them being outcasts.

She was taking the hybrids of hybrids to Ostara whenever we could safely take her.

Her Jorogumo supplicants tended to the children and slowly the Anguillan had made their way over when they noticed it was too much for the Jorogumo alone. The eel hybrids and the Jorogumo were the dominant hybrids of the children and infants. We had given up most of our tents to keep the children warm. Most of which were not made for cold weather and had no clothes or shoes.

We'd also found another room heavily guarded, and it was a make shift portal room. I had often wondered where the portable portals the Jorogumo and Minotaur had entered and exited and we had found one. A Crathode confessed that the Anguillan had another, but that was it. Vanna'ra came forth and told me her traitors had moved six portals altogether and I had destroyed three. Which left three more including the Anguillan's. I had a pretty good idea of where they would be, Thrimilci, Karkinos, and Valla. Those were only the ones we knew about.

"Freya's burly boar, Love." Brass grappled with me in the tent as I tore at his clothes. "Maybe stay away from the Merfolk until I can recover some."

He was half joking, but ever since I tended to Sear're myself, my khoraz tendencies were at an all-time high even without the rousen.

"Just lay there," I gritted out as I tried to free my wrist from his hold to get to his pants. "You know I don't mind doing the work. It's hardly work at all."

I ate every meal with Sear're until he was stuffed and then helped him do whatever he needed. Seeing him so weak was unacceptable, having others see him in a weakened state was unfathomable. Non're was always hovering nearby with Vanna'ra and Red whose name really didn't matter because Red was so much easier to remember with all the new people I was dealing with every day.

Brass chuckled with an edge of exasperation and dropped his hands. "Scarlett, Love." He dropped his voice knowing how well the Lycans and Bjorn could hear us. "I am only a man. It has been five times already. It is only noon. You do not think they know why you demanded we erect this tent in the middle of the day?"

I freed him from his pants and ducked down to pull him into my mouth. "I don't care. You shouldn't have married a khoraz if you didn't want to have sex frequently."

Brass let out a growl like a groan and caught my shoulders and spun himself around so I landed flat on my belly. His big hand gripped the waistband of my pants as he yanked them down and straddled my hips. I sucked in sharply as he slid between my legs.

"*Oh, Brass.*" I moaned, curling my fingers against the leather floor.

"*Shh.* Do not speak unless you wish half the camp to hear you," Brass said in a low seductive whisper as he bent his chest over my back.

It was an ongoing joke how badly I needed Brass and how I was a Merfolk khoraz. The fact that I had been with Non're had led him to become very popular around the cook fires come dinner time once he made clear he was regretful for how it came about. Brass and Sear're didn't like it, but there was nothing they could do other than threaten the prince and that only made him more popular.

Padraig and Klim's relationship was the other topic of conversation. The two men disappeared all night and returned each morning within minutes of one another. It was the most poorly hidden secret in camp next to the fact that Tawny and Niall had an affair the night before we rescued the captives. Worse yet, that I purposely asked him to oversee the Crathode because of it.

I did, and I didn't care who knew. Donncha didn't disagree with me and that was what mattered.

"I would not go in there if I were you." Padraig laughed as his deep voice called out.

"Nonsense." I heard Quick's voice, and it didn't register until the cold air from outside rushed over my legs. "Frigga's sweet grass! It is in the middle of the day! We are at war!"

"Close the gods cursed flap, Quick!" I shouted as I gripped the back of Brass's legs so he couldn't leap off me.

The flaps dropped, but laughter could still be heard all around as well as Quick's curses. So much for the privacy of the tent.

Brass let out a gusty breath and shifted so I rolled over. "You are wanton, wife."

He helped me take off my boots before removing his own so we could make love. "I know. You're such a good husband taking care of me," I cooed, and he gave me a wry look as he ran his stubble anvil jaw over my chin.

"I never thought I would be glad Slate returned to help *take care* of you, Love."

I ran my hands down his sculpted back and over his taut backside. "You're doing an excellent job all by yourself. I don't have a single complaint other than it takes so long for you to remove all this clothing when I need you."

"Are you using me for my body?" Brass purred.

I made a contented sound in my throat. "*Mmm*, trying to." I blinked. "Brass, what is Quick doing here? He's supposed to be with Ridge and the people from the arena on the other side of town."

Locks of his thick hair had pulled free from the knot at his nape. "You want to stop and find out?" I licked my lips and his dreamy amber eyes twinkled as he came down for a kiss. "I thought not."

Quick and Ridge sat with Donncha, Padraig, Caolan, and Tadg. The remaining members of the Bjorn assembly joined them at the small cook fire they had started to heat their meet for lunch.

"Better, Night's Child?" Caolan asked, raising a bushy brow.

I would never get used to seeing her as a wolf after being accustomed to her human form. It surprised me every time her voice came from that throat.

Brass came from the low tent behind me clasping his cloak back around his throat and stepped back to let a herd of urchins run past giggling.

"Careful, part of the mountain is stone and will cut the bottoms of your feet!" I shouted after them.

"Okay, Mrs. Scarlett!" they called back in a fit of giggles.

Brass rubbed my shoulders and kissed my neck as he moved past me to sit with the others at the cook fire.

"Mrs. Scarlett?" Quick asked, arching a dark brow at me.

I smiled fondly after the children. Lycan purebreds ran with carapace backed eels and clawed furry spiders whom all had an element of humanity to them. The younger children had adapted better than I could have hoped. The older children had not. They were reclusive and petulant. Their language skills were extremely limited and I tried not to put much thought into it because my heart was not healed and I wasn't sure how much more sorrow it could take before I locked myself in a closet.

The hybrids of hybrids that were beginning training to join the army had been left under Gennadi and Faima's care. They would try to help them break old habits so they weren't so combative. Surrogate parents, or so I hoped.

Thre'ik saw me exit the tent and crawled on her sets of legs to me with two hybrids of hybrids in her arms. She wore a quilt on her back to keep her eggs warm and another over her shoulders to hide her human torso. I sat down at the cook fire and began unlacing my corset before Thre'ik handed me a bear-faced snake and a furry baby with nubby horns and eyes void of white like the Merfolk and no nose.

Brass closed my cloak around my shoulder and I gave him a grateful smile as they latched. Thre'ik had developed human mannerisms from her short time with Indigo and she stroked my head before she went to distribute the other nursing babies.

"I... there are no words," Quick said, gaping at me.

I level my eyes at him as the bitter wind picked up through the pass to yank at my hair. "They have a need and I have a way to fulfill it. So many of the women are physically unable because of how poorly they were fed. What are you doing here, Quick?" I took a calming breath. "It's good to see you're all right, but what are you doing here?"

"Mrs. Scarlett?" Ridge asked again since I'd been too distracted to answer Quick.

"She did not appreciate when they began calling her Queen Scarlett," Brass said, ladling the meaty stew into a bowl for me.

Asya leaned close and peeked under my cloak to the bear-faced babe. "Zlata's sisters did not want their cubs?"

"No. I don't agree with it, but I understand it," I said in a hushed tone.

"You are a day late. We were waiting on the other side of Elivagar, as we agreed, but then the people took a vote. They wanted their town back. We had to fight our way into the Natt castle and the people were feeling confident, so we kept marching after we locked the Natt portal. *Oh*, and we had to pass Glitra so we figured we should try to root out the Stygians there too."

I gaped at Quick who flashed me a panty dropping smile.

"As we came from the Niflheim, we ran into the Stygian Knights on patrol. We followed them to Glitra and shut down their base, but there are the creatures they released in the mining town and rogue Stygians who were not at the base when we reached it. The Natt castle was the next logical goal. Elivagar was abandoned. We did not have to fight," Ridge amended Quick's rendition.

I had known Elivagar was abandoned because the usurper in the Vetr castle had evacuated the entire town to Niflheim Arena before shutting down the castle.

"But what about the smoke I saw from chimneys on our way through?" I asked dumbfounded.

"We took Elivagar today. The people returned to their homes and the few we found with smoke rising from the stacks were older folk who did not wish to leave their homes," Ridge said, smiling.

"Scarlett. We have Elivagar back. The Shadow Breakers who had been overseeing the arena have all left to Vanaheim preparing for the next revolt except for Styg who is from Elivagar. He decided to stay with his cousins, Pewter and Siren, until we do not need the arena portal. Ridge wanted to wait until we reached Tawny before he used the auseklis to go to the castle, but... the war is over here," Quick said with glittering eyes.

"I want a contingent sent to the Minotaur in case they have any hostages and for another troop to stay in Elivagar with the Ostara captives until we can return them home. There should be a third group in Glitra to root out the creatures —"

"And the rest can go *home*," Brass said, placing his hand on my shoulder.

I knit my brows. "It feels too easy. Nothing is ever easy for me."

"Klim and I will lead a split group to the Minotaur to scout their actions and report back," Padraig rumbled.

"Tadg and I will go to Glitra," Caolan offered without glancing up from her meal.

"Asya and I will remain in Elivagar until Klim returns to help with the captives." Asya gave Lyov a wide-eyed look, surprised at her husband's willingness to stay and help the children no doubt.

Donncha looked to Siobhan who was with Thre'ik and cradling one of the younger girls. "Lorcan and his wife can stay, Lyov. I am going to return to my lands with the children and women with child. If you stay, I could take your young with us."

"I will stay with Lorcan and wait for Klim." Demyan stood with his bowl and moved to eat with the nearest group of Bjorn gathered at another cook fire.

Lyov grunted. "I will travel with you and the women and children then, Donncha."

Donncha's midnight gaze swept to me and my lips quirked. The Stygians had tried to divide them, but their plan had backfired. The tribes were more united than ever.

Tawny held her belly and trotted through the army to Ridge who stood to embrace her when she reached him. "You're back so soon? Is everything okay?"

Amethyst was right behind her and neither girl realized how disheveled they both looked before exiting the tent they shared. Quick hid a knowing smirk behind his gloved hand, letting his eyes meet Brass's who had his head ducked so no one would see his expression.

Tawny was beautifully flushed with the buttons up the front of her woolen dress askew so the bottom of her petticoats shown more on one side than the other. She wore the puce bell shaped dress in Elivagar style with a modest neckline under her off white cape.

Ridge ignored what was apparent to us all and held her. "I am glad you are all right. Your island is intact Matriarch Vetr. Are you ready to go home?" he asked softly, and Tawny blinked at tears.

"I'm so ready."

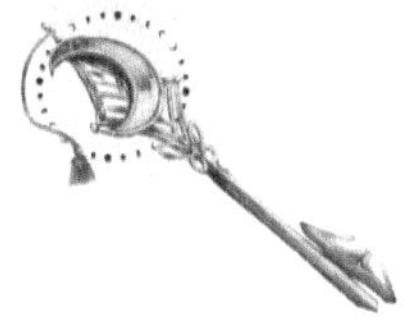

"Are you mad at me?"

I curled Tawny's long wavy locks with my *calling* in the tent I shared with Brass. If Ash wasn't such a complete jerk, he would've been a great Prime one day. I'd taken a lot of his lessons to heart, and one of those I kept with me was to always look the part.

I'd scrounged up a candy apple red gown with alabaster lace trim and ruby buttons. It was a little long on Tawny, but she'd have to deal with it. I carefully lined her eyes with kohl and took out my emergency cosmetics that included gloss, mascara, and a shimmering lotion and applied it to her heart-shaped face as I had been doing for years.

"I'm not mad at you for sleeping with Niall. I'm... my brother cares about you. Do I think he's fallen in love with you, not yet, but I think he could. I'm biased and I think when he finds out you spent the night and then lunch with Niall. I know how it sounds because he's married with two wives, but I really think it'll hurt his feelings. I'm not judging. I have absolutely no room to judge," I explained, taking the two pearls from my hair and braiding one to each side of her head like pins.

"You sound a little *judgey*."

"I know how I sound," I snapped and sighed. "How was it?"

I knew what she wanted. She could never talk about Steel with me because he was my uncle and I would never *ever* want to know about Jett and Cherry or Amethyst, but I could hear about Niall.

Her eyes glittered as I sat back cross-legged in front of her. "Are you really asking or are you trying to be nice?"

"Both," I told her honestly, and she smiled.

"We did it at night with Amethyst, but he didn't touch her at all. Only me. At first he was a Lycan, and it was so strange. I'm not very big to begin with and he was three times my size at least in that form. Amethyst fell asleep after a little while and Niall and I crept into the second bed." Her eyes lit as she squirmed. "I know why you love Brass and Slate's long hair. Niall was so passionate, so animalistic. It was completely different from making love to a man. A human man, I mean." She inhaled, remembering her hedonistic night. "I won't do it again. Be with a man from the tribes. It felt too dangerous. One day, yeah, sure, fun. But..."

"You felt like he could kill you at any second. That the animal within would explode out of him and he'd tear your throat out which scared you but also excited you." I finished for her.

Her eyes widened, and she pointed to me. "Yes, *exactly*. Is that what Slate is like?"

"At first. Then I guess I got used to it. I like that he loses control with me. I know he wouldn't really hurt me on purpose." I gave her a smile as I packed my things away.

"Are you all *judgey* because I've been sleeping with Amethyst?" she whispered as if someone had their ear pressed to the tent.

I shot her a look. "Tawny, you know I slept with a Merfolk woman when they had me, don't you? The princess Larn'ra herself. My first woman was Slate's first woman in a sick twist of fate. I consider myself an equal opportunity love haver. Before I was married, I would have been open to love from man, woman, or tribes. No, I prefer you with Amethyst over Niall. With Niall I felt like you were a bragging right, that you hadn't thought it through. That's why I was upset, not because you did it. But, Jett will be sore about it. You mark my words."

"Jett." Tawny ran her fingers through her curls. "He was not made for one woman" I wrinkled my nose at her and she laughed in a throaty mature way. "He is *hot*. Brad Pitt in Troy hot — I don't care if people don't like that movie, what is undeniable is he was hot in it and Jett... Jett is even hotter."

I gave her a dry look. "Is that out of your system now?"

She snapped her teeth together and smirked. "Yes."

"Good. Let's never discuss it again and *I* am going to pretend I never heard it."

Tawny reached for me and I gave her a squeeze as her chin came to rest on my shoulder. "Thank you."

"It's just make up, Tawns," I teased.

"I know how hard this has been for you. All of it," she said in a hushed tone.

I withdrew and wiped the end of my nose. "Come on. Let's go toss this yahoo out on his fanny pack."

At the edge of the bustling town people in their woolen bell shaped dresses and men in their thick jerkins reestablished their town that would have been at place on the face of a Christmas card. Split granite cottages with quoin architecture and chimneys on each gable puffed a constant stream of smoke into the cold air.

Brass folded up the tent with his calling as we walked behind Tawny in her bright red gown with Ridge on her arm. The people flocked to her with cheery smiles and tears, thanking her for bringing them home again. She shook hands and introduced Ridge causing a near frenzy as her slippered Bjorn boots crunched over the snow encrusted roads.

I was astonished to find the beige robed Valkyries already doing their good work. Their shaven heads could be seen scattered throughout the masses and had offered to take in the children of all ages with help from the captive Ostara tribes' women. The nun like sect were a gods' send. We could send food to the chapel like home the Elivagar Valkyrie lived in until we could send the women and children home.

I kept searching the crowd for Slate and Jett as we walked to the other side of town near the mountain the Ragnarök was held on. Amethyst and Quick were right behind us walking arm in arm before the two tribes we had brought into town. Most of which had never seen more than three people at once.

Elivagar's portal gate was a free standing iron gate with square pillars on either side. From there, we could see the Vetr castle nestled in the rocky snowcapped mountains at the heart of the Frostfell. The picturesque Middle Age castle was compromised of white limestone and a black roof, the only color being the brick red gatehouse that allowed outside entry to the castle. Crow-stepped gables and cornices ringed in pinnacles crowning the expansive castle tops.

"We are early. They will be here tomorrow," Brass promised, pressing his lips to my ear as we crossed through the portal.

My hands reached for the nearest furred claw. The tribes couldn't get through the main portals without our help. We didn't know if we'd need force to take the castle so we were bringing as many tribal members as we could all at once.

The bright white light faded. An older man sitting in a white upholstered arm's chair with the black garb of the Vetr's staff jerked to his feet, startling the other man across from him in white Vetr's garb. Tawny strode forward in her thick gown and their eyes widened in recognition. Then they swung to Ridge on her arm and the first older man fainted. They knew who we were.

Brass caught the older gentleman with his *calling* and returned him to his seat. Tawny gave the other door guard an imperious look and laced her hands in front of her.

"I demand to speak to the man who stole my lands and my castle *immediately*. Take me to him."

The man's bushy white brows drew together, but he nodded emphatically before starting down the room to guide us to the usurper.

The only pop of color was the scarlet red of the Vetr sigil in the black and white pristine rooms we marched past. Carefully carved stark ceilings in delicate lace-like patterns swept through every room, white pillars, wide-open windows, and marble floors in the high contrast colors decorated every inch.

In the dining hall, lattice work wrapped around the plaster sculpted walls and ceiling. Black glass plates sat on a white marble table threaded with silver with matching chairs. A view of the snowy rugged hills spanned the wide windows let in a brilliant light so the black polished chandelier was not needed to illuminate the long room.

Tawny was the first to enter the thrown back double doors and her blood-curdling scream made my pulse race just before Ridge caught her under her arms as she fainted. With her down, I could see what made her shriek.

Tan with wide shoulders and a trim waist like an Olympic swimmer with a smile that put any magazine model to shame, Steel's turquoise almond eyes brimmed with tears. He lifted a chubby mocha skinned baby with powder blue eyes and thick raven hair from a wooden high chair that looked completely out of place. Opal's plump full lips turned down as she began to cry from Tawny's screech.

Amethyst's shriek finally brought me back, and I realized I had been standing and staring for a good ten seconds before I shook myself out of it and darted past Amethyst to cling to Steel.

A sob tore from my throat as I began to bawl. His dirty blonde hair was always tousled, but it was in an unusual amount of disarray. Steel's slate grey padded jerkin was open at the short stiff collar and sleeves pushed back to reveal thinner forearms than I remembered. Stubble scraped my cheek as he laughed through tears and held me trying to pass Opal to Amethyst at my back.

"Ash sent a fireball. All that was left was the crater." I wondered if he understood a single word I said through my tears.

"I took the nix torque from you, remember? I put it on my own wrist. The roof collapsed on me and a beam hit my back. I saw what Ash intended and while the fire raged around me, I crawled into the Ymir River. You sent that wave crashing, and it dragged me five miles before I could get out. I reached the portal door at Vanaheim before anyone else." Steel's strong chin moved against my ear as he spoke. "I went to Thrimilci to warn mother, but she was gone and Opal was there with the staff. I couldn't leave her alone, so I took her with me. I came here and knew the Stygians would try to ambush us so I emptied the castle of the staff and forced them in the streets knocking on doors in the middle of the night and physically dragged them into the portal. I should have done it in Thrimilci, but by the time I tried to go back...the portals were locked. I have the key, but I knew it must have been bad and with Tawny gone... I was the next logical choice to try and save it. Frigga's sweet grass. They told everyone you were dead."

"We thought *you* were dead. This whole time. I'm so sorry, Steel."

I stepped back and tried to collect myself as Brass greeted Steel and then moved to hold me. Amethyst and Steel hugged for a long time before Quick got his chance. While we were all crying and embracing, the staff had escorted the Bjorn and Lycans we had with us to the great hall to wait. Ridge stood cradling Tawny as Steel approached.

"Correct me if I'm wrong, but your portrait hangs in Orion's study.

You're Ridge Vetr, aren't you? That shouldn't be impossible," Steel said, eyes flitting between his unconscious wife and Ridge's face.

The two men were eye to eye with similar builds and easy going attitudes. Tawny and Sparrow both had the similar type, I thought idly.

"I am. Where Tawny and the others had... escaped to. I was stuck. My memories vanished until Scarlett refused to leave me alone and I remembered. You must be Steel. Tawny thought you had passed on. Congratulations. You are having a daughter," Ridge said with a wide grin, and Steel cautiously placed a hand on Tawny's swollen belly.

"Thank the Gods. If this is a dream, never ever let me wake," Steel mumbled.

"It is real," Ridge assured him. "The place... it made you forget the more painful your memories. Tawny forgot much. Months of her life passed by with no clue as to what she had suffered. Leshy magic prevents us from going into detail," Ridge said as Steel led him to a chair so he could sit.

It was an excellent idea. We all took our seats as Amethyst wept, rocking Opal who cried with her for different reasons. It would be awhile before I could pry my niece away from her.

Brass pulled me into his lap so he wouldn't have to let me go and I nestled against his chest in a fit of hiccups. Ridge sat with Tawny cradled in his arm with Steel sitting so close their knees brushed as he leaned to stroke her face or hold her hand. He delved as Ridge tried to describe the mysterious island with the seven gates of indulgences. Ridge detailed how I gave birth to the twins the moment we left; weeks earlier than I was supposed to because my body couldn't take the change. He explained how time went differently for us and for Ridge so he lost twenty years when he stepped outside the island portal.

Steel had been shut up in the Vetr castle afraid to leave Opal and risk the Stygians sending a man in to take Elivagar's seat of power. He had no idea what had gone on since he essentially barricaded himself and the staff nearly five months ago.

We had to tell Steel about Pearl and Reed's executions. How Spinel was taken to the Vanaheim Arena and would have done the same with him to Cordillera, but he'd escaped and found his way to us. He was alive, but not where we could reach him. Brass told him how he and Slate went from island to island trying to evacuate as many people as possible and that they had secured Valla U with Gypsum's help. That we had taken Thrimilci back and now Elivagar. Brass told him how he and Slate had gone to the Lycans to get the piece but they refused to give it to anyone else but me.

"Where is Slate?" Steel asked stoically after struggling through word of Pearl's death.

"He and Jett did a round of deliveries before we move on to Valla," Quick said, clearing his throat.

Steel turned in the chair to look a Quick. "What about Indigo? You guys haven't mentioned her." Steel released his gaze on Tawny long enough to look at each of us and his eyes fell. "I was supposed to protect her," he whispered.

"No one blames you. That night was a disaster," I told him, sliding off Brass's lap to go to Quick.

I sat on the armrest and picked Quick's hand off his lap. His fingers curled around mine the instant our skin met. Quick was simple. He liked attention. He needed it and preferred it from women. I could give him that affection he craved until Indigo was back.

Quick told him how he saw her in Ostara. How it was the only island we had no force on, and that Coyote Regn had his three small children were there alone in hopes some people would brave escaping. Brass went on to tell him about the Beget Oubliette and how Thre'ik said Indigo had been there a week ago. We had passed her on our way to the Lycans. Quick hadn't known that fact and got to his feet.

"I just need a minute," he said roughly.

"Do you want company?" I asked, gripping his hand.

He sliced his head once to the left and a jagged edge of the black Celtic tattoos that covered his left side peeked from his jerkin. "I am going to get a room and take a hot bath. Unless you want to join me?" Quick's attempt at debauchery gave me a small thread of hope to cling to.

"Don't hold your breath, Regn," I said with a small smile.

He kissed my head before one of the black clad servants hurried to ready his room. Amethyst rose from her seat and moved to Steel's side and kissed his cheek.

"I cannot thank you enough for taking care of Opal. We need to talk though, Steel. Perhaps somewhere private?"

There was an undertone in her voice that made me cock my head before glancing to Brass. He had ducked his head, and I got a crick in my neck whipping my head back to Amethyst. I could see Steel's profile; his thick brows were drawn together as he looked at her.

"Amethyst?" Steel said in an admonishing tone.

Ridge shifted. "I can carry Tawny to her rooms unless you wish to do it. Quick's idea of a hot bath sounds very promising."

Brass grabbed my wrist and began to lead me from the room. Tawny's eyes fluttered as she blinked at Steel and burst into tears. Ridge placed her on the chair as he got to his feet and took Steel's hand.

"I look forward to getting to know my son-in-law better. I can take her for you."

"Can we have some privacy?" Tawny said in a weak voice.

Steel's apprehension fell over me like a wet blanket.

"I am here. No need to do it alone," Amethyst said in a sympathetic tone.

Tawny took Steel's hand from her cheek and held it in her lap as they faced one another in the black polished chairs. "I need everyone to leave the room."

Brass swept past them, dragging me along. Ridge and Amethyst were right behind us and I dug my heels in as the double doors swung shut.

"She's going to need me. I'm not going anywhere," I said firmly.

Brass gave me a wry look. "You're going to eavesdrop."

Amethyst was already leaning her ear to the door. Ridge was the only one who had continued down the hall.

"It is not easy finding out the woman you love and married moved on when she thought you passed on, no matter how much time has gone by."

I sighed and mimicked Amethyst's action. At least Steel would have Ridge with in-depth knowledge on his situation.

"I thought you were dead," Steel began.

"Me too," Tawny said softly.

"This is not going how I expected our reunion to go. A daughter? We're going to have a daughter? You have your heir, Tawns. And your father. I can't believe you found him. Hawk must be... Tawny, out with it. What is going on? I thought you wanted everyone to leave so we could be *alone*."

Steel was visiting my island of denial. He knew something was very wrong, but wanted to overlook it in favor of everything going back to the way it was. I was the overlord of that island. I didn't want anyone else on it.

"I... Steel, I was mourning you. I didn't know who had stolen my castle or my island. I was with other men... people. Four others," Tawny told him in a wavering voice.

There was a protracted silence and I could hear the scoot of Steel's chair over the marble floor. "Do you still love me? Did you fall in love with one of these four others? Gods, Tawny it has only been five months, and you slept with *four* people?" Steel's emotions flailed wildly between anger and hurt but found a home in betrayal.

"No! I have only ever loved you. I'm only telling you because you deserve to know what kind of woman you married. I don't want you to leave me. I should have only been with *you*," Tawny said in a cry, and Steel exhaled gustily.

"Was it Quick? You two have always flirted, but I knew you'd never cheat on me," he said in a voice thick with emotion. "Who else? They all know, don't they? That's why Amethyst came on to me. Did you sleep with Amethyst? You said *people*. Does that mean men and women or tribes? What *does* that mean?"

My limbs felt heavy. Some desperate part of me prayed Steel wouldn't ask and that he'd forgive her without needing to know details.

"A male Lycan named Niall —"

"The one that was trying to steal Scarlett from Slate! I met him in Thrimilci on Quick's stag night, Tawny!"

I could hear his pain laced through his raised voice.

"Amethyst —"

"I knew it. She would never cheat on Jett unless she thought she was —" Steel had cut off, and the silence was deafening. "Four. Not Quick, then." Tawny must have shaken her head. "When you kissed him, he said it was because he showed you his talent, Divine Beauty. Is that true or did you do it because you wanted to? Was kissing all you did or did you start sleeping with Jett then?" Steel gritted out.

Tawny sobbed but powered through. "No! I never would have. It was like Ridge said, I forgot everything that as too painful to remember. You think Jett and I would purposely have an affair behind your back? He loves you just as much as I do. When we were free of that place, I felt unbelievable guilt and wouldn't touch him. Then he had to tell Cherry we had an affair and she… *Gods*, Steel, I am so sorry. I only ever wanted you. To be your wife, have your children. I never felt like I missed anything having only made love to you." Tawny sounded like she was groveling. Groveling was a good place to start.

"Jett," Steel breathed. "You know when Wren left, I used to pretend like he and Slate were my little brothers. They *were* my little brothers until Slate turned fourteen and Larn'ra took him. I lost Slate for an entire day until Sear're helped me find him. He was in barghest form, his first shift, when Larn'ra gave him his first mating. She had gotten more than she bargained for that day. Jett was with me. By then we were all the same size even though I was eighteen. I had to bind Slate with nix torques and have Jett help me carry our brother back to my mother as he fought us tooth and nail. I stopped trying to be their big brother then. I knew I had failed them, exposing them to a darker side of sex. That month, Cordillera weaned Slate off rousen with the help of that khoraz, Lynx. You know the one he sees in the brothel? Lera took Jett's virginity so Slate wouldn't think they were more than they were. Neither were the same afterwards. They bedded women twice their age, and neither had a girlfriend like other boys. Not until Jett met Cherry and Amethyst and not until Slate met Scar. They were lucky to find a friend in Quick who didn't mind their competitive bedding." Steel was silent for a time and no noise came from the room except for Tawny's sniffles.

"To think that he had you too… while you are pregnant with my daughter. I thought we had a line. He had tried to steal my girlfriends before but you're my wife. That line shouldn't have been crossed. I take the blame for his ways but this…"

Steel's boots came closer, and we stepped back from the door.

"It wasn't like that. Steel, please! Stay!" she called after him.

Steel's eyes were red rimmed and puffy when he looked at Amethyst who spoke, but his glare cut her short. He looked to me.

"Did you sleep with Quick? You were on this island of no consequences and temptation with them," he asked me in a brusque tone.

I tried to work saliva into my mouth. "I'm married to Brass and Slate. I gave birth to Brass's sons. I had already made more than enough mistakes," I whispered.

"So, *no*. Quick didn't cheat on Indigo either?" he asked, and I shook my head.

"We weren't in as much pain as Jett and Tawny. That place... they weren't lying. Maybe if I wasn't pregnant —"

"Tawny was — *is* — pregnant and still laid with Jett while I was here securing her land taking care of *his* daughter. Alone. I was always alone."

Brass moved past me to Steel's side and gave me a look. "We're going to Thrimilci to return the Merfolk and Wemic." He kissed my lips, and I stood with Amethyst as the two men walked away without a word to one another.

We hurried to Tawny who cried into her hands. "When everyone told you Slate was dead, you held onto hope. You didn't go around fiddlesticking Brass until a month after trying time and again with your bond. By the Mother, you concocted those arenas just to find him! I did nothing but lose myself in others' wiles."

I wrapped my arms around her and let her cry. Amethyst's cheeks dampened with tears and she walked away, carrying Opal tightly to her chest.

"Slate forgave me for getting pregnant with Brass's sons. He needs time. Even if it takes another four months until your daughter is born, he will forgive you. Or maybe he just needs to scream at Jett. I don't know, but I know Steel and he loves you, Tawny. We all know you wouldn't have done it if we thought for even a second that he was alive."

"I should have had a little faith. I don't deserve him."

Tawny got to her feet, her boots sounding over the marble as I led her to their wing. Brass wouldn't let Steel do anything stupid. Steel was the ambassador to the Merfolk and had been with many of their women. Vanna'ra herself had slept with Steel. I hoped Brass would be able to elucidate why bedding one of them again would be a profoundly bad idea.

CHAPTER 24
SLATE

The small mining town of Glitra was an unsavory sort with a mix of miners and blackguards to disreputable to live in the town heart. That night, they blended as they danced in the cobbled streets. Elivagar had been freed and their Stygian guards had been bound and sent to the Vetr castle under Bjorn and Lycan control.

Scarlett and the others had struck without them. The arena had been all but deserted.

The women were back and debauchery ran as freely as the ale all over Glitra. The Dark Dancer was a Shadow Breaker hang out before Elivagar had been free since it was not likely you would find a Stygian Warden in the ale stinking establishment.

The mines had been shut down for the day. Tawny had declared it a holiday and the men and women had been drunk for hours. The permanent black beneath the nails of some identified the mine workers as the heavy makeup was worn by the low born khorazes.

Sweat and booze assailed my heightened senses as Jett and I took a booth instead of our usual stools or one of the rickety tables scattered before the fireplace. In the booth beside ours, a drunken couple were not wasting coin on a room above the bar more than happy to please one another in full view of the other patrons.

The buxom blonde came around her spit shined counter to bring two mugs and sent them sloshing over the table. Her corset was partially unlaced as she moved to the cauldron and ladled stew into our bowls before bringing them back to the table.

She leaned on the back of Jett's booth as her brown eyes twinkled. "Where is Scorpion? Not that I mind your new companion."

"Aardwolf, this is Jawfish," I said in an unusually high voice.

The distortion ring had worked efficiently before I broke my vow of silence to speak with Scarlett as Scat. Aardwolf's painted brows rose, she had never heard me speak before.

"I always did have a thing for blondes. You let me know if you would like some company, Love. Let my new girl know if you would like a room. Had to hire help today. It has been busy since the Matriarch came back."

She nodded to a girl who had her long light golden brown hair plaited around her head in the Elivagar fashion. The girl was dodging a man's groping hand whom she deftly knocked in the nose with her tray as she spun around. Her wide blue eyes swept over Jett and then me before she made her way over.

Aardwolf slapped her dirty rag over her shoulder. "Scandium, year of the alloys. I do not usually hire them when they are still fertile, but it is only for a few days. The men like her enough." Aardwolf cackled as she gave one of Scandium's perky melon breasts a squeeze.

Scandium's thin lips pinched and then pulled into a smile. "Is there anything else I can get you, Loves?"

Her dialect was that of the northern parts of Elivagar. Aardwolf was right about her fertility. She must have recently birthed. I could smell mother's milk under the smell of ale and food... something else like spices and citrus that was masked by the spilled booze. Her fertility was waxing and my nostrils flared at her impending season. Her smile was genuine, and she did not belong in this place or something unsavory would happen to her. Other than her food stained apron, she was clean. Too clean for The Dark Dancer.

"Bread? Fresh, if you have it," Jett asked hopefully, and I scoffed.

She surprised me with a brighter grin. "I just baked some that should be done right about now. It is your lucky day."

She sauntered off with a roll to her hips. She wore a plain navy woolen dress with layers of petticoats rapidly absorbing the booze from the wood floors. A corset cinched her slim waist that accentuated her hour-glass figure beneath her apron. Even without seeing beneath the dress, I could tell her backside would be shapely.

"Stare any harder and her dress will catch fire," Jett said into his mug in a scratchy voice and horsey face.

"Her body reminds me of your sister's," I told him, knowing his face would darken and he would debate punching me.

"I never thought I would be grateful you slept with her. Your blatant innuendos have to be worse than the deed itself," Jett grumbled.

Scandium carried a basket out with a napkin keeping the warmth beneath it and the scent of fresh baked bread was unmistakable. Other patrons shouted for bread and she took note of all those who called to her. Her cheery smile returned as she placed the bread in front of us then she took two shot glasses from behind her back and poured a dark liquid into both. She tucked the container back into her apron when she was done.

"On the house in celebration of the Red Seconds and Matriarch Vetr."

Jett took up the glass and clinked my small glass. "I'll drink to that. Cheers."

I sniffed the drink and caught a sweet aroma before tossing it back. When I handed my glass back to the girl her pupils dilated before she could duck her head and go back to the kitchens for more bread.

"She is strange. She does not belong in this place, but she is a khoraz. I think she drugged me. That shot made her aroused," I whispered to Jett who guffawed.

"Since you cannot see your face, I will tell you. She is pretty and you are hideous. There is no chance she would drug you before at least trying to hit on you. Which she hasn't done. You are paranoid."

I sopped up the tomato stew with her bread and hoped Jett was right.

"It's too late to walk back. Scarlett will forgive you when she finds out we took Mabon. We'll walk back to the arena and use the portal key to go to the castle." Jett's eyes were glassy as he gulped more ale.

Scandium had not hinted at any unscrupulous intentions since she gave us the shot. Jett was right, I was paranoid. She did not flirt with the patrons as the other girls did and she did not tolerate their gropes. More than a handful of men would need their broken noses healed from her whacking them in the face with her tray or elbows.

"I have got to piss," I announced as I slid from the booth.

"Careful, that pretty girl might try to force herself on you," he teased, and I gave him a flat look before going to the bathroom.

I relieved myself and took deep breaths before exiting. The ale must have been stronger. My face felt hot and my skin burned and ached. Jett had better of been right. If the girl drugged me, it would force me to shift. Rousen made all hybrids shift, and I was a danger to those around me when rousen made me deaf and dumb with only my pleasure driving me.

The door shut behind me as the bawdy ballad of a khoraz sang over the raucous laughter in the inn. Scandium stood with her back against the opposite wall before a door and her lips curled.

"You are looking out of sorts, Scarab," she said in a singsong voice.

Had I given my name or had Aardwolf said it?

"It is warm in here with all the bodies," I grunted.

"*Aye*. I am feeling a bit warm myself," she said and her pupils *did* dilate.

With strength I had not thought her capable, she grabbed the ends of my jerkin and twisted me around so we fell into the door that had been behind her. It was a closet of cleaning supplies which I doubted were often used.

"This jerkin must be terribly hot," she said, her nimble fingers slid to unbuckle the plain nickel clasps.

I grabbed her hands and felt as if I had been shocked. Her eyes grew wider as she shot me a steamy smile. This was not the same girl who brought us bread. This was a side of her she strove to hide and had done a damn good job until ten seconds past.

"Stop," I ground out and felt the heat churn inside me.

Rousen. The foolish girl had given me rousen. My skin ached to be touched and relive the burn that slowly intensified. I had to get away from her while I could still stop myself.

"*Shh.* I promise your wife won't mind," she said, running her palms greedily over my stomach to yank the linen undershirt from my pants.

My head swam as I braced my arms on the shelves. "I am married," I said, feeling my eyes slide shut.

Her lips seared the skin below my navel and I felt my fangs push through my gums. Too long. I should have bedded Scarlett once to take the edge off, but I knew I couldn't stop at once. She had left Brass on their wedding night to be with me when the Bjorn had nabbed her. She would have given herself to me then.

Her tongue slid over the hard ridges of my stomach and higher as my belt jiggled. I groaned.

"Please, girl," I struggled out around my fangs.

She would regret forcing me. The beast lurked; muscles bunched ready to take over when I lost control.

"Just enjoy it," she said, pushing my pants over my hips and she moaned as I sprung free.

She had a greedy mouth and soft lips that formed a vacuum over me. It was mere seconds before I spilled deep in the back of her throat.

My claws extended my fingers and shoved her back before she could do anything else. Her *calling* had been working while her mouth had slid over me. I panted as I pried my eyes open, trying to desperately control my impending shift as she pulled her dress over her head to reveal her supple nude body I could make out in the dark closet.

"Take me, Scarab. Any way you want me," she breathed.

I could scent the sweetness of her slick sex. Memories struggled to surface in my rousen addled mind, but I could not grasp them. Her scent alone would have been a great temptation, but the rousen left no room for haggling.

I growled as I lunged at her and slammed her front against the shelves as she chuckled, knowingly arching her shapely backside to me. I pulled her arms high, my claws bit into the skin at her wrists and drove into her forcing a throaty gasp from her mouth.

Her silky hair rubbed against my jaw intoxicating me with her familiar scent. She felt familiar. The way she submitted with no reserve with as if she trusted me implicitly. No woman except one had ever done that.

"Curse the gods. I've missed this," she groaned as I left no room for her to move.

She was up on her toes. Skin slapping rapidly on skin as she wriggled stretched taut by her arms while I took her.

My mind was lost in the murky depths of rousen.

Light flooded the closet.

"Get out!" Scandium shouted over my shoulder with her long lean legs wrapped around my waist.

Her hands were braced on the shelves behind her for leverage as our frenzy continued. I lost track of all time and did not stop to see who invaded our sanctum.

I heard a sharp intake of breath. "You bastard!" Jett shouted.

"I gave him rousen. It's not what it looks like!" Scandium said, her dialect changing.

"He's married!" Jett shouted from behind me.

Married. My brain flailed. Scarlett. By the Mother, Scarlett!

I shoved away from Scandium letting her plop down to the floor and she grabbed her wool dress to her chest with a placating gesture. "Slate. It's me. Don't freak out."

"Who's *me*?" Jett asked as she shifted onto her knees.

I could not process the events unfolding.

I dropped coins on the floor, not looking at what they were and pushed out through the door. She called after me. My body trembled with the change taking place. I had to get to the nix torques in the room.

Faces were a blur of teeth and scents. Too much lust in the inn. I had to get out.

"Slate!" Jett shouted as he and Scandium chased me up the stairs.

I had fucked that woman and it had felt fantastic. I had only made love to Scarlett. I never thought much of seeking pleasure from faceless women until I found I could have much more with Scarlett. Pleasure with a woman was not exclusive to the bedroom. I found pleasure in making her laugh and smile. In imagining a life with her.

Scarlett would have felt all of it. She would be broken beyond repair.

I slammed the door and launched myself at the pack carrying the nix cuffs. The single room was lit by the blue moon. Rarely rented for the night, but frequently for the hour, I could hear the coupling of several couples in the surrounding rooms. I focused on breathing but they came raggedly as I gnashed my teeth and tried to ebb the intolerable sensations myself.

The door opened behind me and Scandium entered, hands raised and partially dressed. "I shouldn't have drugged you. I'm an idiot. But seriously, that was amazing. Like, transporting through time when you were weening me off rousen. I thought since I had the boys, you might be gentler with me. I have gentle and passionate with Brass. I wanted my Slate. Rough and wild. Animalistic."

I shook with the nix cuffs in my claws unable to use words.

She turned around and slowly sunk down to her knees watching me over her shoulder. I could feel the fur pushing through my follicles. My fangs biting into my man's mouth.

"Claim me, mate," she whispered, lifting her skirts over her arched back.

The beast dropped the nix torques and lunged.

TWENTY-FIVE

From the first time I saw Slate deep in the shadows at Valla U, I knew there was something dark and dangerous in him. My subconscious told me to stay far away and stay there, but I was always drawn back to him.

He had hurt me before emotionally, but I could always trust him not to hurt me physically. I knew now there was never a moment he hadn't been holding back with me careful not to crush me. Slate on rousen did not have the same concerns.

I thought it would be a night of steamy, dirty lovemaking with my savage husband. So I put a little rousen in his complimentary shot. Big deal. I was there rooting out the few Stygian Wardens that had escaped Caolan's net since Brass was gone until Steel was ready to come back.

Tawny was so busy getting updated on the island that she didn't have time for me and when she did, she wanted to be alone so she could beat herself up about Jett. Slate had come into the Dark Dancer with Jett and I saw an opportunity to have a well-deserved night alone with him as Scarab and with Amethyst's tweaked distorter ring, I was Scandium.

What I got was the Grar Dyr, but not my Grar Dyr. He was a brain-less animal with only one need for me. Even when I managed to wriggle my distorter ring off, I saw no recognition in his eyes. Those silver orbs had been swallowed entirely by black pupils which had terrified me more than anything else.

I was afraid he might tear out my throat. I had done it to myself. When I was on rousen, I had simultaneously used my *calling* to please my rescuers with a warm suckling wind. Something that was completely unfathomable to me in my right mind. Why did I think the barghest hybrid would have a hard time getting lost in me after five months without intimacy?

Hindsight was twenty/twenty.

Slate's black eyes revealed a sliver of silver. His big hands that had run all over my body squeezed my throat startling me awake when I could no longer breathe. His gloriously nude naked body was between my legs and at first I thought he was trying out something incredibly kinky. Then I'd slapped his hands gently to release and his hands loos-ened, but only to find a better grip.

I couldn't scream. My wrists were chained to the bed by nix torques which hadn't seemed like a bad idea at the time, but now Slate was killing me. Choking the life from my body after hours of the night I'd planned for — wild and totally untamed.

Unfortunately, he was angry. I could tell he was starting to come down and had no idea that I was me. He still thought I was Scandium. For making him cheat on me, he was going to strangle the life from my body.

Now that was quite the pickle.

His jaw clenched as he leveraged his weight on my throat and I knew I had moments if not seconds before I was dead.

If I survived, we'd have a laugh about what an idiot I was.

Jett had already begun that speech last night when I revealed my true identity to him after catching us in our throes inside the closet.

Tears squeezed from the corners of my eyes. My vision swam with spots of darkness sweeping in. He would never ever forgive himself for this once he sobered. Instead of gripping his wrists, I strained my arms against the chains to cup his face. His eyes narrowed and his grip faltered.

"*I am a man,*" he rasped, obviously struggling with the beast inside him.

He threw his body off mine and hunched on the floor where I could barely see his back. The door creaked open with a yawn of the wood and Slate whipped up as I looked at Brass's face appearing in the sliver of open door.

"It's Scarlett, not Scandium," Brass said cautiously. "You did nothing wrong. She's your wife." He tried to reason with the rousen enraged beast.

I sucked in a gasp of air so raw it burned and I choked. Slate had sprained or twisted something essential in my throat and sharp pain radiated through me with every gasp and I couldn't stop them. My lungs demanded air.

I spotted Steel behind him and looked away. Slate wouldn't have tried to kill some young woman for seducing him, would he?

"Scarlett," Slate rasped out.

Brass nodded. "That is Scarlett. *Think.* Try to think. You couldn't have taken her as a barghest unless it was her."

Steel appeared to be keeping watch in the hall as Brass made his way over to me with slow cautious steps. Slate looked down at me in the golden light of the dawn. His eyes flitted to where my inguz tattoo was inked on my hip

He sucked in air sharply and his narrow silver eyes went wider than I would've thought possible.

... Brass, get these off me...

I'd tried my voice and it didn't work. I could see the flicker of recognition in Slate's eyes and I needed to make it better before he could begin his self-flagellation. Only figuratively, I hoped.

Brass was at the side of the spring bed and reaching for my wrists when Slate began growling deep in his chest. Brass froze and Slate moved past him to grab my left hand ripping the distorter ring from my finger. He made a sound like a low wail.

... Now. Please! ...

Brass grabbed my wrists and unclasped the cuffs as Slate reversed to the opposite wall. Brass helped me up healing me in the process.

"*Oh,* Love," Brass said softly as he placed his cloak around my shoulders.

"Shut up, Brass. You're not helping," I snapped, swallowing.

Slate got to his feet, his chest heaving as he looked down at himself. Brass whipped around to Slate.

"Don't do it," he said in a soothing tone.

His hands shook as his mouth pulled into a snarl. "Stay away," Slate said thickly.

His clothing flew into his hands as he ran. I didn't even have a chance to shout before he leapt through the window.

Steel charged to the window with Brass. "Slate!" Steel yelled, heedless of the shards of glass.

The night had been great. A little rougher than I'd bargained for, but I wanted old possessive Slate in his prime. I just hadn't counted on him hating Scandium for tricking him into bedding her, *er*, me. I was strangely reassured and terrified by it.

Steel's boots crunched over the bits of glass that had sprayed the inside of the room as he tossed me my dresses. "My thanks," I said weakly.

"Are you all right?" Steel asked.

"Fine. It was great until about five minutes ago. I think he was stopping himself. He wasn't really going to kill me." I shook my head in disbelief as I pulled my clothes on. "Did my bond accidentally activate?" I asked Brass.

He was still looking out the window. "Yes. He said goodbye, Scarlett."

"Goodbye?" I asked, rising to my feet and *calling* over my boots.

"*It is over. You have married Brass now and have your sons. All I am capable of is pain and hurt. If not you, then I would have bedded another woman. I cannot help my nature,*" Brass said before turning away from the window sill.

My mouth hung open. "He left me?"

Brass moved about the room collecting Slate's things and nodded. I slumped back down to the bed feeling sticky, crusty, and all around gross. I ran my fingers over my hair and realized I had blood crusted over my wrists that had run down my fingers where the cuffs had dug in and again where Slate's claws had scratched.

Brass sat down on the bed next to me and I rested my head on his shoulder. "I messed up big time," I whispered.

"*Nah*, Love. If I had known what you had planned, I would have told you. Slate can never have rousen again. Give him time. Let's get you back to the castle."

I nodded and rubbed the tip of my nose as he helped me to my feet. "Slate?"

My brother poked his head in the room and blinked groggily at me then cocked his head as he took in first Brass then Steel. His full lips parted and the color left his face.

"Steel?" Jett said, forcing his name from his throat.

"Not a good time, Jett," Brass said, stepping towards both the men.

Jett's face twitched uncontrollably as he moved in embrace Steel. He was oblivious to the rage Steel felt. His tan cheeks darkened and his canted his chin as he cocked his fist back and floored Jett with a punch. Brass grabbed Steel around his chest as Jett stared in astonished bewilderment at Steel.

There was a moment where Jett had no idea why Steel would hit him and then realization dawned and Jett's face fell. I rushed to Jett's side and helped him up as I healed him. My healing wouldn't fix what needed fixing.

"Steel, we thought you had died. I —"

"Fuck you, Jett. You fucked my pregnant wife! You brought her into your sick world and invited her to sleep with your wives. I was the only person in the world she had been with. She was mine and mine alone. You couldn't just let me have *one* thing. You couldn't stand that she never gave you a second look once she saw me. You were Wren's son, Slate was Lark's son, and I was the son that was left behind. I never minded even though Pearl felt like she always had to make it up to you two. When you would hit on girls I brought around, I never cared. Not once. Not until Tawny. You slept with my beautiful, pure wife who is carrying my daughter, Jett." Steel grit his teeth and blinked rapidly at his gleaming eyes. "I don't want anything to do with you. You're not my brother. Brothers don't do shit like this to one another. Where's the line? I want to know what line you wouldn't cross." Steel stabbed a finger in Jett's direction and his eyes widened even further. "She gave you her auseklis?"

Jett touched the Vetr symbol around his neck and I helped his fumbling fingers unclasp it. "She gave it to me so Slate and I could get back to Scarlett faster," Jett said in a faraway voice.

Steel used his *calling* to take it from my palm. "This is for spouses and children. Not for home wrecking bastards. Next time you see my wife tell her I'm not coming back."

Steel stepped past us on the floor and his heavy footfalls could be heard down the steps.

"Steel, don't!" I called after him, and Jett looked to me dazed.

"He's right. I could've justified it if you and Quick had forgotten too, but I forgot two wives and a daughter. I am a fucking asshole. I don't deserve any of them. I shouldn't have let Cherry suck her in." Jett sighed and his eyes focused. "Where did Slate go?"

I gestured to the open window. "He freaked," I said as we helped one another to our feet.

"Frigga's sweet grass, he must have... Are you... okay?"

I shrugged in my grimy tavern wench dress. "Slate left us. Have a nice life. *Adios.*"

"He'll be back, baby sis. Don't sweat it."

"No. He's gone. I'm done chasing after him. He walked out on me. *Us.* Whatever. He can do whatever he wants." I sighed as I collected the glass in a little pile and sent it out the window.

"Scarlett?" Brass's fingers rested on my shoulders, and I turned to face him.

"I'm sorry you saw that. I'm okay." I leaned on my tip toes and gave him a kiss on the cheek. "Really. I want to go home and see my sons."

Brass's concern melted from his face and he pulled me into an embrace. "I love you, Scarlett."

I dug out my mental lockbox, blew off the dust, and shoved all the emotions Slate had brought out in me and buried them deep.

I had a gorgeous husband and two baby boys. I would have to help repair the relationship between my brother and my uncle and between Tawny and Steel, but it was hard to not feel like I was on the right track.

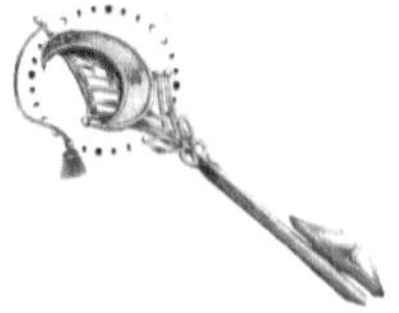

Word of what Steel said to Jett went over like a lead balloon. Tawny refused to meet with Jett and buried herself in Elivagar's day to day with Ridge. We caught two Wardens on our way out of Glitra and brought them back with Tadg, Caolan, and their forces.

Padraig and Klim hadn't returned yet when we said our goodbyes to Donncha, Siobhan, Asya, and Lyov who went with a small contingent of men and all the women who were pregnant and the children. A larger number than I suspected would want to stayed behind to hunt down the creatures who had been released in the town heart and others wanted to be a part of the next step of our plan.

I said my farewells to Thre'ik and the other captive women from Ostara before leaving Elivagar with Brass, Quick, Jett, Amethyst and Opal. When Jett had walked into the dining hall when we arrived at dinner time the following day, I had completely forgotten about Opal. Jett had cried like I'd never seen him do before and while being elated his daughter was returned to him, fell deeper into despair over the split with Steel.

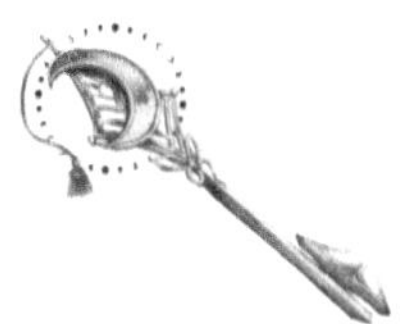

Brass slipped back under the white down comforter that was the most modern item in our Dagr palace wing. He lifted the white sheet to join me in my makeshift tent and gazed at me with heavy lidded amber eyes.

"I will never tire of seeing their tiny sleeping faces. It's a shame they will eventually grow up to be men," Brass said in a hushed tone as his plump lips made for kissing curled.

I felt my cheeks round as I smiled back. "They'll have to grow trimmed stubbly beards too. Since they'll be just as pretty as their father," I told him as I reached out to graze his anvil jaw.

"You *do* think I'm too pretty, don't you?" he asked in faux consternation, drawing his thick dark brows together.

Brass wasn't just pretty, he was gorgeous.

"Pretty doesn't quite cover it. *Breathtaking*," I purred with an impish grin I knew would make my eyes twinkle.

Breathtaking was what he called me the night he first made love to me...or was it that following morning?

The blankets sunk in around us and I laughed as Tree-gold began to purr obnoxiously. The enormous cat was more than fluff, she was meat too. No cat should get that big, skogkatt or not. Brass pulled the blankets down and stroked her snowy coat.

The bedroom was dominated by the enormous white bed. Flowing sheer white panels swathed around the bed in a canopy with piles of pillows along the white upholstered headboard. The walls were a pale green where a long distressed dresser was pushed and had my mother's pictures in glass frames as well as intimate pictures of Slate and I kissing. I hadn't added any of Brass and I yet, but I had a few favorites at my apartment in Chicago I planned to retrieve. Blue morning glories overflowed in vases to either side of the bed at the nightstands instead of my usual pink peonies.

Across the room, our bathroom was decorated in aquamarine and coral with a porcelain double sink and clawed bath tub large enough for two. Low tiled walls divided the room which hid a huge shower. Water sprayed from every direction, there was even a waterfall of sorts at the entrance that fell across the low wall so no one could see you if you were showering past it. I was obsessed with that shower.

"I suppose it is time to get up," I said, stretching.

We had hid in the Dagr palace for the last two nights after our return from Elivagar. The Sumar palace had been a hot mess. Steel had retreated there and left as soon as Jett came with the girls. That was how we ended up back at the Dagr palace with Steel and Quick in tow.

Brass watched me cross the room to the walk-in closet and grab my champagne satin half robe before I strode through the wing. The first thing I did every morning before I readied.

I peeked in on our sleeping boys that now had full bellies. Their bedroom was one of two in the hall adjoining our bedroom, the other was a bathroom. The first thing you noticed when you opened their nursery were the paintings. Above the Balas's troll made crib was one of the paintings my mother had sold right before we moved. Sparrow had tracked it down. It was the tree of life with deep curling roots, a blazing golden sun shone down on a cat and a deer dancing next to a pond a mermaid leaned from. A second painting was above Spinel's troll made crib. It was a whimsical painting of a merman sitting astride a Centaur with the solar cross of the Dagr sigil in the sky and a lion hybrid with a charcoal barghest.

Their room had sea foam green walls and a dresser complete with changing table. An off-white plush chair sat in the corner piled with stuffed animals next to a short bookcase filled with bright colored titles. A wood carved rocking horse sat to the side, a picture of my mother and I was framed of us picnicking at the lake. Slate had designed the lay of the room himself before we lost our child.

Brass walked in behind me and leaned over Balas's crib. He took the back of the frame off and took out a rumpled letter splattered with blood. *ALDER* was scrawled across the front written in my mother's handwriting.

I turned away. I couldn't deal with whatever secret she revealed to my father.

I moved through the dining room double doors that had enough space for a circular table that sat six. It matched the coffee table, and the chairs were upholstered in the same dusky blue as the living room with a white hutch. One of our mother's paintings hung on the wall across from the collection Moroccan lanterns that hung in whites and blues above the round pedestal table.

White marbled tiles spanned the floor of the light dusky blue front room where there was a soft beige couch and oversized chair. Throw pillows in varying shades of creams scattered across them. Sheer curtains framed the arched doors that led to the covered walkway before the cloister.

With my *calling*, I opened the slatted doors along the gallery. Lombard bands lined the grey stone monolithic columns that wrapped around the covered walkway that looked out into the manicured cloister. At the bend, a wrought-iron table for six waited for us in the shade where I used to eat breakfast with Hawk and Sparrow every morning.

A morning glory vine grew on an iron lattice from a clipping I'd taken from the Sumar palace beyond the cloister shrubs, not visible from where I stood. In my absence, one of the staff was kind enough to keep it up so it wouldn't die.

Brass made a contented sound in his throat as he wrapped his arms around my waist and settled his chin on my shoulder. "You're brooding, Love."

He must have set the letter down since it wasn't in his hands. He probably rad in my mind that one more thing might break me.

I shut my eyes and sighed. "My oath to Ash has been fulfilled. I'm ecstatic. Can't you tell?"

Because I'd lain with Slate before and after midnight, it counted as two of my ovulation days. I made love to Brass once the following day and not since. It had been less than my best performance. Merely a means to an end, which Brass understood.

"Is he still on Thrimilci?" he asked, running his nose along my earlobe.

I nodded resting my hands on his forearm.

I would not take out my anger with Slate on Brass. Slate had been doing Gods only knew what with the Gods only knew who. What I *did* know was that he was on Thrimilci and having a drunken party. He'd been viciously nauseous last night and gotten into a fist fight. I'd curled in the shower until it stopped sometime early that morning and slept about an hour until the boys woke up for a feeding.

"We need to find him and tell him —"

"He doesn't need to know, Brass," I murmured.

The image of Quick's lovelorn face again at breakfast when I'd tell him I wasn't going to look for Slate would break my heart. I wasn't ready to share my news. Indigo hadn't activated her bond with Quick and he was convinced it was because she didn't want him anymore. I told him that wasn't possible.

"Fine. I'll lead you to him, but Jett comes with us."

Brass exhaled gustily blowing my long hair over my ear. "I thought you might say that. I will borrow Steel's auseklis and round him up. You have one hour to prepare, Love."

I nodded and hugged myself when he moved away from me. Anxiety did a jig in my mind stirring up all kinds of unwanted thoughts. I spun back to Brass who had reached the dining room double doors.

"Brass."

He stopped to give me a questioning look. His long hair falling more heavily to the left brushing his dark honey clavicle since he'd trimmed it.

"You won't run for the hills now that I have Slate's child growing inside me?" I asked, twisting the sash of my robe between my fingers.

Brass walked back to me with the deadly grace of a man who knew his way around his weapons, not to mention the bedroom. He tilted my chin up to look into my eyes.

"You don't appear to be on any drugs."

I slapped his hand away with a reluctant smile as he chuckled and he scooped me up into his arms. "Come. I have waited enough days. I don't care that he'll feel it. I want to make love to my wife, in our bed. Under the roof where our children sleep. Frigga's sweet grass, Love. I love you," Brass said as he brought me back to the bedroom.

Groin vaulted ceilings with Corinthian grey stone columns and marbled tiles spanned the Romanesque halls of the Dagr palace. We marched in silence to the portal room. Brass, Steel, and I walking abreast before Quick and Jett. It was one of the most uncomfortable silences of my young life. The stone walls were lit by recessed lighting, making it look like a cathedral as it lit the sculptures of the Dagr matriarchs along the walls like saintly beauties. They'd have to chisel horns on Slate's and not because he was a barghest.

Brass had brought the twins to Cherry and Amethyst for safe keeping while we went out on our adventure. He laced his fingers through mine as Steel used the auseklis to open the Dagr door and the white light enveloped us.

CHAPTER 26
JETT

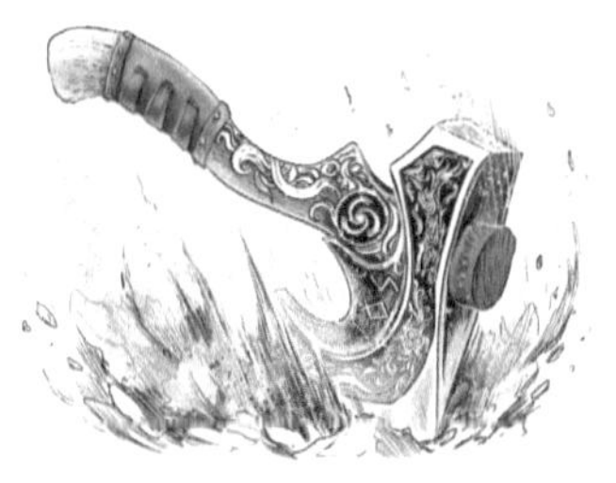

The hot air of the island of perpetual summer was most welcomed. Their eyes took a moment to adjust from the scorching morning sun reflecting off the tightly compacted shimmering white stone road. The iron patch work door was framed by a fifteen foot high white and blue mosaic arch. A spiraling iron work formed a blazing sun, the Sumar sigil, just beneath it.

Past the portal gate, the shimmering road zig zagged up the sloping cliff side. White stucco adobes lined the roads with royal blue shutters and roofs. At the top of the cliff was the white Sumar palace with several pointed domes and turrets in metallic blue and golds glittering in the sunlight. Its arched hundreds of windowless windows were sculpted into the face of the palace. The rivers Mani and Sol rivers flowed behind the palace to a water fall a huge semicircle balcony hung over.

Jett had married the girls there. Steel had proposed to Tawny there.

Jett's chest felt as though a Jotnar sat on it. He'd been so ecstatic Steel was alive, he'd forgotten all about having slept with Tawny. It wasn't once or twice, or even brief. They had been in Disir for months.

Jett and Tawny had been sleeping together for nearly five months. Jett had brought her into their world. Deep into it. Amethyst had told him about her steamy night with Niall and Jett was loath to admit he was jealous. More than a little bit. He was hurt on top of which and there was no one to drown his sorrows with since Quick and Brass were living with Steel at the Dagr palace and Slate was M.I.A..

Scarlett walked between Steel and Brass down the market street lined with shops. White plaster buildings with gold embossed signs and blue mosaic patterns that stretched along both sides started to come to life again since being freed.

Scarlett gestured down another compressed white road and they followed her direction. It was a train wreck, and they were the passengers. Scarlett shouldn't be with them. Brass had warned him it could get ugly. That Slate was out drinking and fighting if Scarlett's spontaneous vomiting was any indication.

The glass store fronts had been replaced along the roads. The Stygians had ordered destruction when Hawk wouldn't open the palace gates. Foot traffic wouldn't pick up until after breakfast. Jett's rumbling stomach reminded him of how empty it was. Wrangling errant husbands should be done on a full stomach.

"In there," she said in a dry tone.

One road in Thrimilci was of the unsavory sort. Across from the two story building with a gold painted sign that read *Call of the Wild* was a dilapidated building that was once the khoraz brothel. The bar the khoraz had picked up their cliental was burned to cinders next to it.

Scarlett knew where they were. She'd caught them across the road for Quick's stag night.

Brass rubbed his lips together, pulling them into his mouth. "Is he —"

"Asleep... for now," she answered curtly.

Scar had placed them in charge of one another's actions. That had gone out the window when Slate had essentially tried to murder her while on rousen. Only the men with them and possibly Cordillera knew that rousen made you crave pleasure and *sometimes* killing gave Slate pleasure.

Brass slid his hand along her jaw to tilt her face up to his. "Stay here, Love. Your job is done."

She wrestled with wanting to say something biting and swallowed it back.

Brass moved into the building, one of the few who didn't have a glass store front or the pillars that lined that front of most of the others. They wore the lightweight v-necks of Thrimilci. Quick was the only one to wear a pack which Jett assumed had nix torques in from the way the bag clinked. There weren't many places to hide their blades with the sleeveless shirts and fitted pants tucked into calf-high boots. Hopefully, they wouldn't need blades to get Slate to come with them.

Jett took up the rear with Quick between him and Steel. It was best that they kept their distance or Steel might sucker punch him again.

All those places seemed to be decorated by the same sleazy interior designer. Brightly colored gauzy fabrics were draped throughout the first floor. They moved past the girl at the front counter and walked up the granite steps pushing colored glass beads that caught the light out of their way. A sultry woman's voice was crooning through the halls where scantily clad tribes women sauntered.

Quick and Jett shared a look. For all Slate's womanizing, he kept it to the human variety. Brass walked close to each closed door trying to pick up the thoughts from inside. It would be a near impossible feat if they were asleep.

"Ahead on the right." Scarlett's gravelly voice startled them, and Quick cursed.

"I do not like you in here," Quick said, voicing Jett's concerns.

"I've been to worse," she said, effectively making them all shuffle their feet and avoid her eyes.

They were the rescue team who had saved her from Non're's pleasure palace. The brothel was a lot easier to stomach.

Brass's nostrils flared when Jett turned back to face him. Steel met his eyes for the briefest moment and Jett's stomach twisted when he saw disgust there.

Brass stood in front of the door Scarlett had indicated and pointed to her and then the floor outside the door. The universal signal for *stay here*. She made no move to accept or deny his demand. Brass had no choice, but to go inside and hope she listened to him for her own good.

"Why is she so dressed up?" Quick asked me as we waited for Brass to open the door.

A crystal sun dangled at the edge of her hairline from a silver chain. She'd taken extra care with her wavy hair, making it into loose golden curls. Her almond eyes seemed to pop against her tan skin with the dark shadow she'd used to shade them. All her visible skin shimmered, making her look ethereal. Three strands of crystals hung off her shoulders of the empire waist dress, that led to a heavily beaded center that connected just under her chest where the beaded belt started out narrow and grew wider the closer it came to her sides. The fabric didn't start till just above her breasts in an inverted U-shape.

"Don't you recognize that dress? I've seen her wear it twice like armor. Once was on her wedding day to Slate; the second time was at the funeral Sparrow held for him. She doesn't plan on being on the sidelines today. He's going to see that dress."

Quick furrowed his brow but was distracted as Brass disappeared into the room followed by Steel. Quick hurried in after them so Jett had no choice other than leaving Scarlett in the hall.

Brass stepped over broken booze bottles. Antique gold curtains hung in the windows and matched the Chantilly sofa. The golden sheets on a king size bed were intertwined about his lower legs. Steel put his hand on Brass's shoulder and a silent communication passed between them.

A number of creative ways to wake him came to Jett's mind as he waded through the evidence of Slate's nights. *I'm going to kill you*, was followed closely by, *You're going to die bastard.*

Her voice was what startled him awake. *"My heart and appendages belong to you, Torch."*

Her gravelly tone was flat but it might as well have been a scream for what it did to Slate in his barghest form. He sprang up, jostling, clutching the blanket over himself. Scarlett held up the end of her dress as she stepped over a broken glass bottle and continued towards the bed. Slate looked at each of us as if it was our fault.

"Without you, I would be lost. My light in the darkness, my hope," she continued.

Slate slid down the bed to climb over the foot and *called* his pants over to him then began to step into them in his barghest form.

"You should not be here," he rasped, turning his silver eyes on Scarlett.

"I will never be with another woman as long as I live," she said, stopping in front of him.

"Get her out of here," Slate growled as his eyes flashed.

Jett and Slate were the same size in human form, but when Slate was a barghest, he was a half foot taller and his muscles bunched and heavy. Jett learned long ago not to get in Slate's way when he was a barghest. It was if two different people were in one body.

"You look alive to me so you must understand my confusion," Scarlett said flatly as she tapped a clear bottle with the toe of her silver heel.

"Stop that!" Slate roared, and she lifted her eyes up to him.

Quick made a face in Jett's periphery. There was no evidence he had actually been with one of the Minotaur or Gorgon women who sashayed down the halls, but why else would he be at a khoraz brothel. Those women had bargained their bodies for transport from their home islands. Most decided to stay after their debts were paid because they were well cared for and everyone needed friends.

A woman with long black crimped hair and horns that extended from just above her hanging ears stopped in the hall and stepped into the room. A thin layer of dark fur formed to her curved shape that gauzy fabrics scarcely covered.

Steel and Jett whipped to Scarlett, expecting her to burn the whole place down, but she calmly kept her eyes on Slate.

"How much does a khoraz get for two nights?" Scarlett addressed the yak woman.

The yak woman brushed bangs away from her bovine snout and appraised Scarlett.

"Do not speak to them," Slate growled, blocking Scarlett from the near nude woman.

"Two nights with such a rare breed? Around three thousand gold daymarks," the yak woman replied.

Scarlett beckoned Quick who ducked his head from his brother and the rest of us as she opened the pack he wore and pulled out five sacks of coins. She tossed them onto the bed as the coins shifted and clinked.

"One more, Quick. For his troubles. Four thousand. Then again, I have always over valued you."

She turned away from Slate and took Quick's arm, forcing him to walk as her escort. Slate's clawed hand reached out to her back, his red hot anger chilled, but let it fall.

"I know you." The bovine's heavy breasts swayed as she pointed to Scarlett. "You are the Khoraz Seductress."

Scarlett stopped mid step and Quick held fast to her arm. "Come on, Mrs. Scarlett. You do not want to stay any longer."

Quick pulled her tightly to him and tilted up her face so everyone else was out of her eyesight. She searched his eyes and let out a heavy breath.

"I am the mind reader, not my brother," Brass said dryly, and Scar took a step back from Quick and let him walk her out.

She stopped just outside the room and looked at a stunned Slate by the bed. "Congratulations. Your cock gets to save Tidings," she said coolly before she turned down the hall.

"Get out," Slate mumbled. The Minotaur woman hesitated. "*GET OUT!*" he roared, and Jett ducked his head covering his ears.

Steel was slowly making his way beside Brass and Jett was trying to angle himself so if Slate lost it, he could catch him from behind.

"How could you let her come here?" Slate rasped.

"Fuck you." Jett was surprised it came from his own mouth.

Slate turned his tusked jaw to Jett. "You want to unleash me on your sister again? I am an animal. I should not be with human women. I do nothing but hurt them."

"Our wife, not just any woman. I don't want to be anywhere near you, but not because you could've hurt her. Do you feel nothing? Months of mourning her, wishing we could do things differently, and look at you. She didn't care about the other night. She still loved you and wanted you," Brass argued.

"She does not need me. She has you. Go, be happy. I am bowing out." Slate began to shrink and return to his man form.

He sat on the bed and leaned forward to pull on his boots, his hair hid his face.

"You're not an animal. You're a man. You lost control. The worst scenario happened, and she understood. She stuck by you, fought for you when you lost your memories. When everyone told her you were dead, she held tight to your memory. What are you doing?" Steel asked him, shaking his head.

"Are we done?" Slate rumbled before getting to his feet.

Brass wasn't as fast as Quick, but he pivoted his body and Slate fell back on the bed, blood streaming from his nostrils. He smirked at Brass.

"Feel better?" he rumbled.

The muscles in Brass's jaw flexed. "She's pregnant."

He spun on his heel to storm from the room. Jett was left with Steel.

"Her scent... Tell me again. Not that I believe Brass would lie."

Steel helped Slate to his feet and Slate looked between him and Jett. "They told us on our march here." Jett sighed.

As much as he wanted to be happy for them, it was the beginning of the end — prophecy nearly fulfilled. Slate's death hung over their stretched necks like a guillotine.

"My... wife left me. She began seeing one of my good friends and became pregnant with his sons. I welcomed death," Slate said as he pulled his shirt over his head.

"You and Brass had a bargain. I made no such bargain with him," Steel snapped, stabbing a finger in Jett's general direction.

"I didn't use her. I know you think all I wanted to do was —"

Jett cut short when Steel whipped to him. No one had ever looked at him with so much hurt and anger.

"I asked her to marry me."

He meant for it to reassure Steel he wasn't using his wife, but Steel's face contorted. "Are you in love with Tawny?"

Jett struggled for an explanation. "I — She — We thought you were dead! She was lost and miserable... I wanted to help in any way I could. I would've married her, and yeah, I probably could have fallen for her. I would've raised your daughter as my own. I would've been whatever she needed me to be." He was shouting by the end of his speech and Steel hadn't moved to punch him again.

"What did she say when you asked?" Steel asked, his tan cheeks reddening in patches.

"She said *probably not* and then she slept with Niall as soon as I was gone. I think the message was clear. She didn't love me. I reminded her of you and home. The girls were good to her. I'm sorry, Steel. I wouldn't have shamed your wife and daughter. I swear it. I would've done right by her." Jett came very close to groveling at his feet, but with all the broken glass he decided against it.

Steel's brows drew together. "Fucking Lycan," he murmured. "What if she enjoyed herself so much she doesn't want me alone any longer? I can't stop thinking of your gross dick in my wife."

"It could be worse. It could've been Slate's dick. You could be Brass and have to share your wife after he probably fucked a goat."

Slate didn't so much as crack a smile, but Steel's lips twitched.

"Opal misses you," Jett said in a low tone. "What can I do to fix this, Steel?"

Steel pressed his lips into a hard line. "You can't." He left and took Jett's spirits with him.

"He didn't punch you and he met your eyes without snarling," Slate said fully dressed. "That is something."

"Where are you going?" Jett asked.

"I have things to do. Her bond is active. She should not have seen me... *here.*"

"Why are you running away from her?" Jett asked following him down the hall of the brothel. "She's carrying your child, Slate. Don't abandon her," he said in a whisper as the bright sun made him squint when they exited the brothel.

Slate stopped and looked at him. "What if I hurt her again? What if I cannot control my urges? I could cheat again."

Jett shut his eyes not wanting to hear any more excuses. He saw red from the bright morning sun and took a steadying breath. By the time he opened them, Slate was gone.

At the end of the road Brass waited with Steel, Scarlett and Quick. Jett jogged over to them and Scarlett scanned his face.

"He's made up his mind," she said in a tight voice. "I should've expected it. He ran the first time too."

"Baby sis —"

She held up her hand, stilling his tongue and slid over to Quick. Scarlett sought comfort in his presence and leaned into him when he put his arm around her shoulders. He led her down the road so she could be left alone with her thoughts.

"Does that bother you?"

Steel nodded to where Quick had inappropriately slipped his hand within the back of her dress and was rubbing her skin with his thumb. Scarlett was still leaning into him and had hooked her thumb in his belt.

Jett could see Quick speak to her every so often and his lips would brush the top of her head.

Brass let out a long breath. "Since they came back from the mystery island, they have been... connected. Quick seeks comfort in her because she reminds him of Indigo and because he knows she won't sleep with him. It doesn't stop them from being intimate in other ways. Case in point."

He gestured to where Quick stopped to buy a quiche and held it up to her mouth to take a bite. She did without a second thought before lacing her hand with Quick's free hand. They had always done that in Disir. It seemed at home there. Here it seemed strange that they were so close, but not sleeping together.

"I don't think they could feel loneliness where they were, but somehow managed to draw close together to offer one another comfort. I'm slowly trying to reprogram her, but it's hard because Quick has no one. No one that can give him what she can."

Steel made an effort not to look at Jett the walk back to the portal, but at least he hadn't punched him. It *was* progress.

TWENTY-SEVEN

Brass and I wheeled the cribs through the halls of the Dagr palace. They were going to stay at the Sumar palace until the war was over and we had to go to Valla. I was going to start crying again.

"I feel like you're leaving me and taking my sons away," I said in a wavering voice.

"I suppose I am, just not in the way you mean."

Brass turned to me once we were in the portal room and embraced me. The love and warmth I needed to stay strong flowed into me.

"I love you," I whispered, burying myself in his chest.

He tilted my chin up to meet my lips and brushed his against mine. "I'll never get sick of hearing you say that."

Brass's kisses were phenomenal. From our first one, that I gave him within minutes of speaking to him, to the current one that reminded me of why I grew sullen whenever I saw him with a woman before we were ever a couple. I positively melted for him. I was a cartoon version of myself, lips puckered as my pupils shaped into hearts and my ears flapped like wings, making me float into the air.

"I forgot what I was saying," I murmured against his lips.

"That was the point. You're over thinking it, Love. He's your husband. You know him. He loves you. You *assume* he was with those women. Granted the evidence is against him, but you would've felt it through the bond."

"You're enough for me. I don't need him. I need you," I whispered as I fell back on my heels.

We were back to the original subject. Slate. I had no desire to acknowledge my twice errant husband.

Spinel began to squeak and grunt in his crib. It was time for them to leave.

"I'll be back later."

Brass placed a chaste kiss on my lips before he used Steel's access key to open the portal and gave me one of his warm inviting smiles before pulling our sons' cribs with them inside, through the portal.

"What a bastard. Just going to leave you high and dry?"

I turned to find Quick leaning at the end of the hall with one of his panty dropping smiles, I returned those smiles now as I sauntered over.

Quick held his arm out for me and slid under it, looping my arm loosely around his trim waist. He kissed the top of my head.

"We all appreciate you taking one for the team and bedding that bastard. Myself especially, Mrs. Scarlett," he told me, leading me back to the rooms.

"He can go back to whatever existence is left to him. Which is none, because he was miserable before I came along and he will be miserable again."

"Come. I have not been held in some time. My brother has been stealing all of your time along with those urchins for nephews. You are not wearing any underwear beneath that robe are you?" He felt my shoulder for a bra strap and chuckled. "I am glad some things have not changed."

I was barred from bathing with Quick. The normal respectable part of my brain that was pre-Disir knew it wasn't appropriate and if Brass was in the tub with Indi, my feelings would be hurt. I pulled a chair outside the tub and washed his hair and back for him, knowing it was wrong, but wanting to give Quick the affection he craved.

His thick dark hair normally so carefully coifed had dried into a short nest that stuck up all over the top of his head. Quick had wrapped himself around me in my bed so I slowly began disentangling our limbs. He groaned and pulled me tighter.

"*Mmm*, Dove," Quick purred in a sleep thick voice.

My heart may have imploded with the love and affection I felt coming from Quick. Then he rocked his hips and my eyes bulged. He was aiming those lush lips of his in a less friendly way.

"Quick!" I said in a tight squeak and his eyes shot open.

I wanted to let him keep dreaming, for him to imagine he held Indigo for a little while longer, but he would hate himself if he groped and kissed me. He blinked at me with his brows drawn together so a little crease folded his skin.

Reality hit him like a truck and I saw his hope fail. I kissed his cheeks, trying to pull him out of the suffocating melancholy.

"A few more days and we'll go to Valla. I promise. Quick?" I promised fervently as he scooted to the edge of the bed and ran his hands over his hair.

I gently rested my hand on his tattooed shoulder and got an idea. I sliced my hand with a blade of air and scooted beside him, slinging my leg off the side of the bed to face him. I took his hand and did the same to him as he gave me a mildly interested look through his despondency.

"I swear on my life, in one week I will have done everything in my power to reunite you and Indigo," I vowed, clutching his hand to mine and wrapping him in ropes of air so he couldn't get away.

Quick struggled against me trying to free his hand from mine. I knew what the vow meant. I'd be dead in one week if we didn't have Indi back. He was trying to pry our hands apart, but my *calling* was stronger.

"My name is not my own, it is borrowed from my ancestors. I must return it unstained. My honor is not my own, it is on loan from my descendants, I must give it to them unbroken. Our blood is not our own, it is a gift to generations yet unborn, we should carry it with responsibility."

My skin tightened as my blood vow sunk in it. Quick had clamped his hand over my mouth before I finished, but even mumbling them against his fingers was enough.

Quick searched my eyes. "That was astoundingly stupid. Brass is going to strangle you." He licked his lips. "I do not know how to thank a woman without sleeping with her."

I pulled his hand from my mouth. "I think you just say thank you."

I smiled as I sat on my cushion at my friends and family Brass and I convinced to come for a miniature party before the hardest part of our fight began. A pajama party, as it would happen so we were relaxed and comfortable. Some a little more comfortable than others. Brass had lent Quick a shirt to match with the low hung pajama pants the other men had worn with sleeveless linen shirts.

As an added bonus, Gypsum was secretly smuggled from Valla U to the Dagr palace. As an extra added bonus, he had brought Mica. I could catch the scents of attraction and hers for him had been intense from the first time they met. I was trying hard not to ask prying questions.

The new couple took the edge off an otherwise tense party with Steel and Tawny under the same roof since he left her. She looked lovely in a burgundy baby doll nightie with a pleated skirt and a bow just above her swollen belly and below her breasts.

Cherry had chosen fire engine red teddy and Amethyst wore deep purple satin negligee that came down to her ankles. Mica and I had not gotten the memo on the sexy pajamas. She wore green linen shorts with white polka dots and a matching white tank top while I wore my hair in a sloppy bun on top of my head with an oversized Chicago Bears t-shirt and grey cut-off sweats.

We all sat in the cloister with squat candles I collected around us on a blanket stacked with assorted cushions. Covered trays full of finger foods were at the center of the blanket ringed with pitchers of dark troll ale Baboo had sent over to Slate for helping to free Mabon. Since Slate wasn't there to collect, I'd called dibs.

I swallowed a sip of water from my crystal goblet and gave Brass my most salacious grin when he glanced my way. He knew exactly what I was thinking — him... me... naked. I no longer cared that my bond with Slate was active.

Tawny sat between Brass, on my right, and Gypsum with Steel and Quick after Mica. Jett was on my left so Cherry closed the circle, sitting next to Quick. Indigo was missing — a gaping hole in our family.

"Let's play a game. We need to celebrate the cumulative birthdays of Tawny, Brass, and Quick," I said, finally getting sick of the awkward silence aside from the Bluetooth speaker playing songs.

"And your pregnancy," Brass announced, and the girls squealed in delight.

I was bombarded with hugs and congratulations and fought hard not to let my mood sink down to the dirt. "We just found out two nights ago, so fingers crossed everything goes well."

"Slate's?" Gyps asked, and I nodded, feeling the uncomfortable questions readying to tumble forth.

"We can't play quarters because there's no hard surface," Jett said drinking deep from his goblet and cutting off all further pregnancy or Slate questions.

"And there's no way we're playing Flip, Sip, or Strip," Gypsum interjected, making Mica blush.

"I never," Quick said with a twinkle in his eye.

Tawny snorted. "Scarlett loses."

"Hey!" Gods, how long had it been since I blushed so hotly? "I'll start, smarty pants. I never…" I paused to think about it and more than one person, including my husband, burst into laughter. "You guys are cache holes. I never did anything with someone's sister."

Jett lifted his goblet and pointed to Quick and Brass. "You bastards better drink deep."

"I have never been pregnant," Brass said, smirking at all the girls who drank except Mica.

"I have never been to Paris," Tawny said, and Quick booed her choice.

"I have never been with a man," Gypsum said, smirking as he gave Mica a kiss on her cheek that made her blush down to her kneecaps as she drank.

"I have never been with a woman," Mica said in a high soft voice.

Cherry giggled, and I made a face. "I feel like that question needs clarification. Human woman, right?"

"If they had a hole instead of a pole it counts," Quick eloquently elucidated, and I drank.

Tawny drank her water as well with her eyes on the dish of buttered lemon shrimp. Steel watched her out of the corner of his eye.

"I have never slept with two people in the same family," Steel spat, and Quick laughed as I drank with Tawny and the girls.

Quick and Jett also drank since we included cousins.

"What kind of women do we consort with?" Quick teased, and I threw a pita wedge at him. "I have never slept with someone more than thirty years my senior then named my sons after him. Anyone?"

Luckily, Brass was no longer sore about that.

"That seems awfully specific," I grumbled as I drank and watched Mica's eyes widen.

"I have never bedded one of the governing Guardians of Tidings. No heirs," Brass said with heavy-lidded eyes.

"Okay. I see your game now," I joked playfully, but remembered Tawny and cringed when Jett and the girls drank with Brass and me.

After all, I had been Second.

Several rounds of unfair *I nevers* and I had taken to the dance floor and by dance floor, I meant the patch of grass before my blue morning glory vine. Quick got up with me so we were the only two dancing until Gypsum pulled Mica to her feet and danced barefoot beside us.

Cherry stole Quick away when Jett and Amethyst got up to dance and I plopped back down by Brass. I gave him a kiss and smoothed my fly aways back into my disheveled bun.

"Have I ever mentioned that you have a very graceful neck, wife?" Brass whispered, and my skin prickled.

"You have, husband."

I understood why Brass had decided to remain seated. Steel and Tawny were sitting in their original spots like strangers. I got up and Brass whacked my backside before I sat between Steel and Tawny, taking my goblet of water with me.

"I never forgave my husband for his *considerable* transgressions." I gave Steel a wry grin and drank deep. "I never slept with someone thinking my husband was dead." I looked to Brass who gave me a rueful smile when I drank. "I never grew attached to someone I was in —" The Leshy power that bound Disir prevented me from saying the name. "On a hidden island with." I drank again. "I never made a choice that hurt someone I loved very much."

I drank deeply dumping the last dregs on my throat and got back up to sit by my husband. I laid my head in Brass's lap and refilled my water goblet.

"Fighting again?" Tawny asked.

"Aren't we always?" I asked in a stilted tone.

Jett and the girls left when Gypsum carried a drunken Mica back through the portal. Tawny had come with to use her auseklis to allow access to both destinations. Jett and Tawny still weren't speaking, but she was talking to the girls who each hugged her before they left.

I didn't have to ask Gypsum if things were serious between him and Mica. They were in love. I could *feel* it coming from them all night. I gave my chief a kiss on his dimpled cheek before he carried her through the bright white light. Tawny came back a second time, and I sighed as Brass wound his muscled arms around my waist and led me through the hall.

When we got back to the wing, I hurried through my nightly routine and crawled into bed. Brass hadn't made it back from the bathroom before I was sleeping.

Brass's gusty sigh ruffled my hair, and I pulled his arm tighter around my waist. "What's with the heavy sigh?"

"Tawny returned. Steel had passed out in the cloister. They are arguing," Brass said in a delicious whisper against my hair.

The situation was sigh inducing. My guess was before she returned, he would've done anything to have her back. The fact that she had been with Jett and his wives or Niall shouldn't have had any bearing on what they had together.

"I'll be back. It's crazy that they're still fighting about this. Life is too short."

The argument I expected where Brass told me to butt out didn't come as I left the bed. I knew why and was bravely trying to ignore just how short life was in Slate's case. I hadn't come up with a way to save him even if I hated him. Time was the enemy and it was going way too fast.

I opened the slats on one of the arched doors and frowned. Tawny was still in her baby doll nightie and trying to keep Steel from walking away.

"Do you think for one second I would've been with someone else if I knew you were okay? I'm in love with you, Steel. I have been since our first night together. I knew you were special. I had been with other guys before, but I'd never been *with* them. Not until you," Tawny said, holding onto his wrist as he tried to pull away.

"Go! I can't even look at you without imagining Jett being with you," Steel said, sounding frustrated.

"You can't keep avoiding me. Frigga's sweet grass, Steel. I am having our daughter. I need you with me. I don't want anyone else," she told him.

They grappled, him trying to free his wrist and her freakish strength still holding like a vise.

"How do I fix it? Name it. I'll do it. You didn't... stray. Get lonely?" she asked tentatively.

Steel's face was shadowed in the dark, but I could feel his anger. "No, Tawns. Unlike you, I couldn't think of much else other than the fact that I'd lost my wife and unborn child," he spat.

Tawny stepped up closer. "You must have been very lonely," she said in a low voice.

Steel glanced down to the grass hidden by the ring of shrubs that encircled the cloister. "Not lonely. I hurt too much to feel anything else. Opal, and having to care for her was the only thing to keep me going every day. I miss her."

"*Oh*, Steel," Tawny said sympathetically and took a step towards him.

He looked at her through his lashes. He looked sick to death of fighting her and was only doing so to prove a point. Tawny shrugged her sleeves of her nightie to her shoulders and Steel's chest filled.

"I've missed you so much. I thought I'd never feel whole again. No one else could ever make me feel the way I feel about you. When I thought Ash had killed you, I had never felt so defeated, so shattered. Without you, I'm not sure I could ever really be happy again," Tawny murmured.

Steel swallowed visibly as he watched her pull her nightie over her head and it dropped from her finger tips. Her skin was luminescent in the star light. She was lovely, pregnancy looked good on her.

"You don't know how often I prayed for the Mother to return you to me. I love you, Tawny. I have only ever loved you," Steel whispered.

If they weren't standing across the covered walkway, I wouldn't have heard them. Tawny launched herself at Steel, who caught her tiny frame around her ribs and lifted her so her legs wrapped around his waist. Steel groaned when she sucked his bottom lip into her mouth.

I felt Brass's presence before he had come up behind me and gave the sash of my robe a tug so it fell open. His big capable hand cupped my breast and tugged on my hardening peak.

"You're insatiable." I turned, and he held me still as his other hand slid between my legs.

"You have never been a voyeur except when you could not stop watching Slate," Brass whispered in my ear.

"Starting with my uncle and best friend isn't going to do the trick, babe," I told him dryly.

"So sure?"

He pushed my face with his to look through the slats. Steel had carried her to the little wrought-iron table and laid her back. Tawny laid back so her hair spilled over the side and Steel kissed down her body to pull her thighs over his shoulders.

Brass's smooth skin met my backside, and I grabbed his hand. I leaned on my tiptoes as he slowly pushed into me. He made a contented sound in my ear and I shifted my hands to brace the door's frame. It was totally unlike him. I loved my love making sweet Brass, but I also loved when he acted out of character.

Just a little naughty.

Tawny was already crying out and Steel looked ready to explode when he frantically shoved down his pants and stepped between her bent legs. She began crying out again, a high pitched moaning I thought she must be faking because who on earth climaxes that easily? Brass guessed my internal question and chuckled as he drove into me in slow fluid motions.

Steel picked her up off the table and fell back into a chair with her in his lap. She began to move as Steel buried his face in her chest.

"By the Mother. I thought I would never bury myself in your beautiful breasts again," Steel said roughly, and Tawny laughed throatily.

Her rich laugh had the effect that Slate's voice had on me. Steel's fingers left red imprints as he clutched her to him breathing harshly. She pressed open-mouthed kisses to his face as he caught his breath.

"Again?" she asked hopefully, and Steel chuckled.

"Gods, Tawns. I missed you."

"Yes, then?" she asked.

"Till first light, if you can take it. I've had months to prepare for tonight," Steel said, gripping her nape to kiss her.

"At home. I want you in our bed," Tawny breathed.

Steel bent his head down as she arched her back and suckled at her chest. "One more here," he said in a muffled voice, and turned her around in his lap.

Brass picked up his speed as Steel took Tawny. Their skin smacking matched ours until my toes curled on the cool marble floor. Brass moaned in my ear as Steel groaned out on the walkway. Tawny must have reached her point of ecstasy twice more from the way she screamed. It couldn't possibly be normal.

Brass barely pulled me away from the door in time for Steel and Tawny to pass. I panted on my back beside him and he shifted his shoulders to kiss me.

"Do you feel like a proper pervert now, Love?"

I reached for his face and trailed my fingers over his stubble. "Yes. If we play *I never* again and you reference this night, I'll deny it with my dying breath."

Brass chuckled, and I had the privilege of watching his sculpted dark honey muscles flex.

Tawny's flushed face hovered over mine and I jerked in the bed and ran right into Brass who had tucked the sheet up under my arms. For an instant, I thought she was going to berate me for watching her and Steel have sex, but quickly dismissed it because she'd been looking for an *in* to discuss sleeping with my uncle since they began.

"Demyan," she squeaked out.

I rubbed my eyes and sat up to find Jett, Quick, and Steel with her. Brass tucked the sheet around my bare backside as I tried to gather my wits.

"I know I don't have much for modesty with this group, but maybe my uncle, my brother, and brother-in-law could wait in the dining room?" I said, blinking at the haze that clouded my eyes.

Brass brought over my robe which he must have *called* in from the living room floor and I slid my arms into it gratefully. "No time for modesty, Love. Demyan took a woman hostage last night and forced his way through the portal in Elivagar."

I gave Brass a quick kiss as I tied my sash. "Was anyone else hurt?" I asked, running my hands through my tangled hair as I stood.

"Klim," Quick said stiffly.

I froze. When I left Elivagar, Klim and Padraig had gone public with their affair, which was more serious than any of us had suspected since the two were planning on staying in town with no end in sight.

"Is he okay?" I asked, already knowing the answer.

"Ridge came as soon as he heard," Tawny said. "He couldn't save him."

Steel wrapped his arms around Tawny and she buried her face in Steel's chest. Jett watched the reconciled couple with a mix of emotions that looked like relief and regret. He was going to have to lock that down.

"What about Padraig?" I asked in the tone I used for conducting business as Second.

I needed the information first and in private I could mourn.

"He was badly injured. Ridge believed the two men stumbled upon Demyan doing something he shouldn't and when confronted he attacked Padraig first, knowing the Lycan could over power him, and his brother would hesitate," Quick reported, sitting down on the bed to lean against the headboard.

"Did anyone else leave? How are the tensions between the Bjorn and Lycans? Who is the woman? Does she have a family? Children? Husband? If he killed his own brother, no one is safe. I gather he went over to the Stygians which means they will know we're alive and that I have two vulnerable souls in Thrimilci and Tawny is half way through her own pregnancy." I paced. "They'll also know that Quick is alive and he'll be after Indigo."

"We will have someone toss the room Demyan was staying in and see if we can find anything that links him to the Stygians," Quick said, dropping his tone. "We can move Cherry with the children to the arena in Ostara with my brother since it will be the last island they would look."

"Demyan was Willow Natt's liaison when she was the Bjorn ambassador," I breathed. "Why am I just hearing about this now?"

Tawny's thick arched brows knit. "I spent the night. Scar, I didn't want to worry you...maybe it's coincidence, but the woman he took was about your height and build with dark blonde hair."

"Looks like we're going to take this show on the road." I sighed. "Amethyst wants to come with, I take it?"

"She says where I go, she goes. Cherry is trying to convince her to stay," Jett said with a wry smile.

"We'll meet you guys at the Sumar palace in thirty. Pack for a trip."

I gave Tawny a broad smile to calm her nerves and to let her know I was happy for her and Steel. She returned it lacing her fingers through Steel's and he tucked her close to his chest as they skirted Jett to leave the room.

Jett watched them go out of the corner of his eye and Quick moved to clamp his hand to Jett's shoulder. "Give it time. He just forgave her and I doubt you can do for him what she can."

Jett's cheeks inexplicably reddened, and he left the bedroom with Quick.

CHAPTER 28

GYPSUM

"My hand is covering my eyes." Scar's voice cut through my dreamless sleep. "Brass thought I might find you in here. It's just me," she continued. "We've had to move our plan up. Are you up? I'm afraid to look."

Mica and I hid blankets under the Prime's chair in the hearing room. Spending the night with her was addictive. I didn't want to spend another night without her. She gently shook me and I opened my eyes to find her blushing.

Scarlett was a legend to some of the tyros. They idolized her and loved her. Mica had been a nervous wreck last night casually drinking with the youngest female Second in history. She had felt out of place with the other girls in their slinky night gowns until Scar showed up in a Chicago Bears shirt.

A lot of things had changed, but not everything.

"The Second is here. Wake up," Mica whispered fiercely, yanking her tank top over her head.

304

I caught her around the middle while her arms were in the air and she stifled a yelp when I nuzzled her chest. I took the hem and pulled it over her face, making it catch on her lower lip so it smacked back together. She gave me a dry look, trying to hide her smile.

"I'm here. Give us a second." I turned to Mica. "Get it? Second give us a second?"

Mica laughed facetiously as she pulled her shorts over her hips and stood. She gave an awkward wave towards the double doors at the end of the room.

"Good morning, Mica. Did you have fun last night?" Scar obviously meant at the palace, but Mica always thought everyone knew what we were up to so she blushed a tomato red.

"It was fun."

I lifted my hips, chuckling as I pulled up my pants. "Is everyone with you?" I asked her as I got to my feet with my shirt in my hands.

Scarlett wore a cotton long sleeve shirt and snug brown pants tucked into her supple leather boots. All her blades were strapped to her thigh, hips, wrists, and tucked into her boots. Her caramel waves fell to her waist which softened the look.

"They are, except Cherry... and Slate. Your parents are back in Thrimilci, Ridge is in Elivagar and Viper is watching things in Mabon. Mirage is with us too." Scarlett's tone went flat. "Rikke is keeping her company."

I finished dressing and took Mica's hand as we descended the dais. "Okay, let me change then we can get started."

Adrenaline raced through my body. It was happening today. Only the provosts and I knew the extent of the plan. I hadn't even told Mica.

"Meet us in the dining hall." Scarlett gave a stunning smile before leaving us alone again. Her hips rolled below her slim waist as she shut the double doors.

"Gods, it is easy to see why men like Slate and Brass would condone sharing her. She is so beautiful," Mica said in awe.

"They've been with beautiful women before. They're everywhere in Tidings. It takes more to keep a man ensnared. Men who have any sense," I said.

Mica's big brown eyes glittered with amusement. "What do I have that keeps you ensnared, Patriarch Sumar?"

"Who says I have any sense, bunny?" I teased before nudging her to the door.

I pulled her back again and kissed her until she sighed against my chest. We always left separately. I wasn't prepared for people to start rumors about Mica. My family would always be part of the rumor mill.

"I do not care what anyone else thinks," Mica whispered.

Of course she didn't. She wouldn't be with me if she did. I had to care for both of us.

"Hop along. I'll see you in the great hall, bunny." She slid her palms down my linen sleep shirt, and I gave her backside a squeeze as she left.

I sat in the wood pew and tried to steel my nerves. When it came down to it, the nerves would fade as they always did, but up to that point I'd be on edge. Mica wouldn't want to be around me then.

Scar and Brass were happy, and Slate would come back. He could never leave her for long. Odin's eye! They were having a baby! Steel was alive and with Tawns. Jett and the girls got their daughter back and had a little future womanizer which left Quick. I was an expert at wanting something out of my reach... less so as of late.

My entire family plus the Regn ate at the very front of the hall at the benches the tyros sat at. I marched past my usual seat where Mica sat between Malachite and Celestine across from Jade, Ro, Zircon, and Beryl. Crimson usually showered after the tyros were at breakfast so she wouldn't be down until later. I acknowledged them with a smile before continuing down the long aisle.

Tawny gave me a wide mouthed smirk as I sat beside Quick. I was preparing myself for the teasing I would receive for Mica. Not because they didn't like her, but because they liked her very much.

"I love her. After we imprison all the Stygians, I vote we send out an engagement notice." Scarlett raised her hand.

Tawny giggled and elbowed Steel in the ribs who gave me a rueful grin. Scar took Brass's arm and raised it before shooting a glare at Jett. Jett chuckled and raised his hand with Amethyst.

"Someone needs to support him," Quick said folding his arms over his chest. "He will marry when he is ready. If there is hope for Slate and me, there is hope for him."

"I'm not sure how I feel about being lumped in with you and Slate," I said wryly and Quick gave a feigned look of hurt.

The others laughed and let their hands fall.

"I do not have to tolerate this kind of treatment." Quick left his empty plate and got up from the bench before starting down the stretch of hall.

Scarlett shot to her feet and looked down to Brass. "You don't need me for this. He shouldn't be alone."

I expected her to walk after him, not jog. Half the men's eyes caught on the lovely Seductress's chest in her scoop neck top until she looped her arm into Quick's and slowed. Brass pinched the bridge of his nose as he did when images coming from other's minds were especially bad.

"How many husbands do you suppose she needs before men stop acting like she is up for grabs?" Jett cursed.

"She's only getting two," Brass said, his eyes following them out until they turned into the hall. "So, the plan is simple. We take half the forces on each of the three islands, bring them in through the university and distract them with an attack while Scarlett takes Jett, Amethyst, Tawny, and Steel where Storm-pale leads them. Slate, Quick, and I will lead the Shadow Breakers at the Vanaheim Arena into Valla's town heart."

"What about the tyros? They'll want to fight too," I said, scooping out a spinach and mushroom omelet from the platter.

"We need you here. The provosts and you are charged with pulling Indigo out of the fray. Scarlett made us swear blood oaths to stay together. If they try to take her to the portal in Valla, we need to be there to stop them. They won't kill her — she is too valuable," Brass said.

Jett ran his palms over his head. "I can't fucking stand this."

"Jett," Amethyst called after him, but Jett was prowling the way Scar and Quick had gone.

"She rarely comes out this early," I explained.

"Quick's bond is active. Thank the gods Scarlett's vow prevented her from activating hers," Brass joked.

"I've got to see her with my own eyes," Steel said, getting to his feet.

Jett stopped at the end of the hall once he heard footsteps coming after him. Steel's pace slowed and Tawny held her breath. Steel kept walking and when he reached Jett, his arm lifted and he placed it on Jett's shoulder as they entered the hall together.

Tawny took in a shuddering inhale, and saw Brass slip her a kerchief.

"By the Mother," Amethyst murmured.

I'd never heard the old Prime's refined daughter curse before. I spluttered.

"Amethyst!"

"All that silence and awkwardness was tiresome, was it not?"

"Yes," Tawny exhaled.

Brass groaned and heads turned so quickly you'd have thought they had whiplash. Mirage was parading around in Scarlett's skin with her black jaguar panther husband at her side.

I liked Rikke. The Wemic scout was a good man, *er* cat-man. He looked strange in a loose pair of black pants and a sleeveless linen shirt like we wore in Thrimilci as opposed to his usual roughhewn loincloth. His black fur was streaked with swirls in red because he was a warrior all the way up to his white furred jaw. Fetishes adorned his long, black mane while his lime eyes with their vertical pupils searched us out.

Rikke's smile was feline when Brass got to his feet to greet him. Faux Scarlett spotted Rosasite and knew to sit rather than interact with our family especially while projecting Scarlett. We all got up and greeted the big cat man, he held our napes as he pressed his forehead to each of us in turn. His smile never faltered.

"We passed Scarlett in the hall. She said it was okay Mirage projected her ahead of schedule," Rikke said.

"Demyan has likely told them she is alive. It does not matter anymore. We only need their focus here and if Ash is with the army outside these walls, he will want her," Brass explained.

I moved to sit down next to Malachite and he gave an impish grin before returning his gaze to Mirage's projected image of Scarlett. Ro and Mirage were friends and Malachite knew Mirage from Shadow Breaker headquarters. Rosasite's exotic honey eyes glittered at me. I knew she wondered when I would come back to her, but the answer was never.

"This is over, I take it?" Mirage couldn't mimic Scar's gravelly tone, so her smug slow way of speaking maintained.

She gestured to Ro and me, and I nodded absently not wanting to offend Ro.

"Locked up here in the university, little else to do in your free time than bed sport."

"Where is Hopper?" Malachite asked, cutting off her interrogation.

She shrugged her shoulders and in the plunging Ostara caftan, her faux breasts jiggled. "Since Slate is not going to kill me until the war is over, he is trying to reestablish ties to the Breakers. He figures I am safe with Rikke."

Grasshopper ran the blades shop in Thrimilci and was one of five captains along with Brass and Slate under Grand Mistress Cordillera of the Shadow Breakers.

Tawny rested her thin hand on my shoulder. "We're all going to try to see Indigo if you want to come."

Zircon straightened as he stared fixedly at my sister. Tawny looked up with an expression of having felt someone's eyes on her and her eyes slightly widened before she briskly caught up to Amethyst.

"Matriarch Vetr is nearly five months pregnant," Malachite said, shocking the hell out of me. "And married to a Sumar son."

"Looking is not offensive. She is a lovely woman. I appreciate her fine form," Zircon said in a deep voice.

I clenched my jaw and tried to ignore his polite appreciation for my sister.

Jade laughed. "What he means is, any more bosom on her tiny frame and she is going to tip over."

"Gypsum." Rikke's sleek furred hand rested on my shoulder. "Would you show me the way? I have changed my mind. I think I will see Indigo as well. You will be safe here, Anthias. Yes?"

Her lips tightened, but she forced a smile and nodded. "I know them."

Rikke and I strode out of the great hall and Rikke scratched his cheek. "I believe she is angry with me now. She knows I mated with Indigo and she is why I had a taste for humans. Is it true she would project other women while mating?"

I practically stumbled over my own two feet. "*Um.* Yeah. She's slept with guys back at headquarters as Scarlett... I've heard. Their Grand Mistress too, but it's all rumors. Doesn't she do that with you?"

"Never. I have only seen her project Scarlett and only for noble purposes."

I wanted to scoff but held it back. He was being earnest. He believed his wife was a good woman and I wouldn't ruin that image any more than I already had.

CHAPTER 29

INDIGO

If Sterling was with me, I wouldn't be able to hide it. I could barely choke down my breakfast as I sat across from Ruby listening to her ramble on about the new fabric she brought to have another dress made for my ever-expanding shape.

I hadn't had any nightly visitors since I began sharing a tent with my grandmother. It made the deepest part of my marawacian/rousen stupors more difficult, but Ruby was usually conveniently away so I could lay helplessly in my bed until it passed.

Silver was here in Valla, not a hundred yards away. My heart was thundering in my ears with the whoosh of my blood, I couldn't focus on a thing.

"Would you like to go for a stroll? I could really use some fresh air," I said, rudely interrupting my grandmother, so she stared at me like an owl for a moment before she agreed.

"Why, yes, dear. That sounds lovely."

Ruby swept from her chair as I ran to the mirror. I smiled at myself like a loon. I'd worn my favorite prison dress, the powder blue that matched my eyes that had a sheer layer underneath the heavy silk so when I walked you caught a glimpse of my tan legs. The wide belt was stark white and silver with metallic sky blue threads in a jacquard pattern that also lined the hem. Ruby looked at me quizzically when I put on lip gloss and finger combed my hair to fall over my right side to my waist.

"I do not think you are due any visitors for some time yet, dear. Not since Sterling ran off with you." Ruby creased her forehead, not sure what to make of this development.

"I know. I want to look my best is all," I said cheerfully as I looped my arm through hers.

She wouldn't care if I was looking around, but if any of the others caught me, they'd want to know why. When I stepped out of the tent I staggered. He could see me. His longing and love was palpable, it had a scent — patchouli, sandalwood, and cedar that would stick to my skin even after I showered.

While my eyes adjusted to the sunlight, I tried to get Ruby to walk me along the castle walls to the ocean. We'd done it once or twice before so we wouldn't have to look at the army. Once more wouldn't rouse suspicion. I didn't see Canis or the others when my vision cleared and I let Ruby continue her dress talk, leading me towards the castle when I looked up.

I slapped my hand over my mouth for fear of screaming out his name. He was just what I remembered. The face I dreamed about at night. If he leaned any further out of the window, he would fall over the side. He was devilishly handsome. Tall, with perfectly coifed thick dark hair. His anvil jaw looked stubbled from the ground. He never let it grow, it shocked me into staring harder. My Silver groomed more than any man I'd ever *heard* of. He looked as miserable as he felt in my mind.

I took a chance. I prayed he would forgive me if Sterling or, may the Gods forbid, Sage visited anytime soon. I took off my earring while Ruby wasn't paying attention and stabbed my finger as hard as I could. Blood welled over the pin prick and I rubbed it under the lapis stone where our bond tattoo was.

Remarkably, my feet were still shuffling along. Ruby was distracted by the cut of lace she fretted she may have paid too much for.

Dear gods, how he loved me.

I didn't deserve such love. I was a khoraz. I didn't even know who the father of my child was. I gave up hope he might be alive within seconds of feeling his bond snap. He deserved a woman to match his love.

I was missing him so bad it hurt. It hadn't been this bad since the first few days in the cottage with Sterling when I couldn't speak I was so deep in my depression.

I couldn't tear my eyes off him. He looked like he was shouting down something, but he was too far away for me to hear. Light golden brown hair swayed in the window, trying to pull Silver back.

Scarlett. No one else could touch Silver like that and not have him bop them on the head.

"*I LOVE YOU, REGN!*" I shouted like a total lunatic, making my poor grandmother cry out.

"Indigo. My dear gods. What was that about?" Ruby chastened.

I had to glance away from him. "I thought it looked like rain. The grass is so dry. We could really use it."

Ruby looked where our feet were walking and nodded. "We could nourish it ourselves. We really do not want rain with that army around. Their stench would be insufferable."

"*I LOVE YOU, DOVE!*"

His voice. His sexy smug voice. My heart felt as if it might explode.

"You look a bit peckish. Perhaps we should go back." Ruby turned us around so I could face his window again.

Silver was gone, but Jett and Steel stood in their place. Steel was alive!

Not even Sage could ruin my day.

CHAPTER 30

JETT

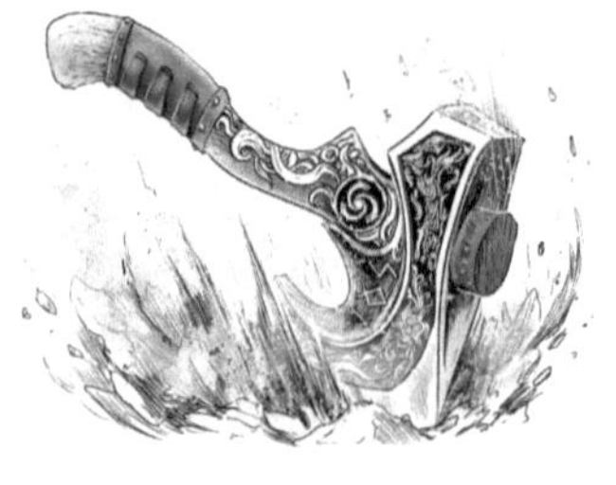

As mad as Jett wanted to be that Quick had nearly fallen out of the fourth-story window with Scarlett hanging on to him, he couldn't blame the guy. Scarlett cradled Quick to her chest as he tried to collect himself with Steel and Jett graciously ignoring their friend's breakdown.

He wasn't crying. Not really. Hot tears of frustration. Jett was feeling them himself. It was temporarily keeping him from basking in Steel's reluctant forgiveness.

"Stay strong," Scarlett cooed. "Just a few more days. I swore to you, you'll have her back."

Quick had fallen to his knees when they pulled him inside. His fingers were curled in her pale green cotton shirt where his arms could practically wind around her twice. She wiped his tears gently as he rested his head on her chest.

Indigo was so close, but so far. It was the cruelest kind of torture.

"If you that jar I gave you, we can —"

Quick abruptly pushed Scarlett back so hard she staggered. His face was a mask of anger as he stood and she gaped at him scanning his face for a reason for his violent behavior.

"Stay away from me, Scarlett," he said brusquely.

"Okay," she said in a small voice. "I was just trying —"

"I know what you were trying!" he shouted at her, making her flinch. "With your soft lips always kissing me, rubbing your perky tits in my face — you are married to my brother!"

"I was only —"

"*I know!*" Quick shook his fists at her, and she retreated a step as Brass came down the hall with Tawny and Amethyst. "I have had enough of it. Do not touch me. Do not come near me. I do not need you holding me whenever it strikes your fancy."

"But —"

"If it wasn't for her adamantly telling you no in..." Jett couldn't say Disir. "While we were *there,* you'd have to explain to Brass why you slept with the mother of his children." Jett had had enough of Quick's unfair diatribe. "She's only tried to help."

"It would not be the first time," Quick said scathingly.

Scarlett blinked as if he struck her and Quick's heated expression fell. He took a step forward, obviously regretting his rash unkind words. She stepped back again.

"You're right. The Khoraz Seductress, right? I slept with your brother, then moved onto Slate. I dangled myself in front of Non're so he would take me and make me a khoraz. I was practically begging for it when Peak invited me to his castle. We all know I don't regret Spinel, and if I had done a better job with Ash, maybe he wouldn't have tried to kill us. What kind of compassion could a whoring khoraz have that didn't involve trying to get someone into bed?"

"Scarlett. Fuck," Quick said visibly deflating.

He needed to lash out, and she was the closest one to him. We all understood that. Quick needed to vent, but he was taking it out on the wrong person. Jett moved to lead her away, and she shrugged him off. Her almond eyes gleamed.

"Whatever," she said, spinning around and saw their audience.

Rikke and Gypsum had come up behind the others. Brass glared at his brother, while she skirted them and left the room in a storm.

Tawny's doll-like face had progressively gotten redder with anger and her head nearly popped when Scarlett shrugged her off too. Tawny fixed her best glare on Quick and marched over to him.

"'Quick' Silver Regn, you great big buffoon! You owe her thanks a million times over! Brass may have forgiven you both in time if she had let you do to her all those sweet things you whispered to her those nights..." She couldn't say it either. "But don't you think for half a heartbeat Indigo would have if you fiddlesticked her twin sister. You should be kissing the ground she walks on for saving you from a situation like the one Jett and I got ourselves into. She was the only one out of the lot of us, including Ridge, who didn't forget that she was in love or that her sister loved you. I would slap you, but I don't think you meant to take it out on her. Do it again though, and I won't care about your grand heartache or how miserable you look moping about. I *will* slap the taste out of your mouth."

Old Tawny was back. Jett wasn't sure if he was allowed to smile at her yet so he dropped his eyes and covered his mouth with a hand.

"By the Mother," Quick said miserably. "That was a new level of bastard even for me."

Steel shifted on my right and a little squeak came from Tawny. Jett lifted his eyes long enough to see Steel opening the nearest door with Tawny's toes dangling nearly a foot off the floor. Her squeal could be heard through the door as soon as he closed it.

Gypsum groaned as he moved past Brass with Rikke to the window. "Is Indigo out?"

I grunted and turned to the window with them while Brass had a one sided conversation with his brother. The monster army milled about just outside the camp of tents. They had very little order. Some could be seen rutting right out in the open.

Amethyst slipped under Jett's arm and he kissed her cheek as they stared down at Indigo's quiet tent. "She was. She activated her bond with Quick. He lost his mind when she shouted that she loved him then he got mad and laid into Scar."

"He just feels helpless. He didn't mean it," Gypsum said pragmatically.

"Yeah, Chief. We know," Jett told him, breathing in the fresh spring air coming off the ocean.

Rikke narrowed his eyes as he looked out the window. "Reski will not believe his eyes. I am not sure I believe them."

"I've got to find Storm-pale so he can lead you guys tonight."

Gypsum grimaced listening to his sister's giggles coming from behind the closed door. Brass and Quick had disappeared so Rikke was left with him and Amethyst.

Gypsum was trudging down the hall went Jett called after him. "Hey, Chief!" He turned around, raising his thick raven brows. "Careful. Red heads steal your soul," he joked, and Amethyst slapped his chest.

Gyps smiled, making his dimples pop. "She can steal whatever she wants. I'm all hers."

"He is in love," Amethyst said wistfully as the youngest of their group continued down the hall.

"He's a goner," Jett agreed.

The sconces along the yellow stone hall were dimly lit, but it was enough to make out Quick's profile where he sat in the long window. Steel and Tawny were the only ones to join them for a rushed dinner. Tyros milled about everywhere with provosts organizing them.

Scarlett had to activate the works, or project depending on who you asked. Ash told her it had the ability to control time. She was counting on a grand epiphany to show her what to do once she activated it. The war wouldn't be won with the activation of the project. They would have to force the army back so when Slate's forces came up behind them, they'd have no other choice but to surrender or fight. They'd be crazy to fight, but Canis and Sage had nothing to lose.

They knew Slate would join in the battle. No matter how bad things were between him and Scarlett. He wouldn't sit this one out. Brass had been waiting for Tawny and Steel to leave their room, Jett suspected to borrow an auseklis so he could retrieve Slate from where ever he was.

Quick turned away from the outside long enough to identify Jett and his chest fell with a sigh. "Has Scarlett resurfaced? I feel like an asshole."

"You *were* an asshole. I haven't seen her since your blow out. She hates leaving her sons. Makes her feel like a bad mom. She'll come out of hiding before we leave."

Jett rested his head on the cool stone and gave Jackal and Crag a nod who stood two windows down. There were tyros stationed at every corner of the castle to watch for unusual action overnight. Gypsum told them Jackal and Crag always took the shift after dinner.

Jett looked out the window where Indigo was being led around by Cygnus. The parade Asp Sandr had called it.

Whenever Cygnus looked away, she looked directly at them. Jett awkwardly held out his hand in a wave and her lips quirked, raising the beauty mark on her right cheek. She looked as beautiful as ever. Quick blew her a kiss and he sucked in sharply, most likely because of whatever he felt through the bond. Jett had thought about activating his, but he wouldn't want to know what those two were sending one another.

"You'll be alright for a while?"

Quick gave him a wry smile. "Did not think you would have to be in this position, did you? I feel better and yet worse. I have probed her with my *calling* and it evaporates before it reaches her."

"By the end of next week, she'll be back," Jett promised.

Quick glanced away, his face drawn. "Sooner than that, I hope."

"Everyone's doing the best they can," he said in a hushed tone.

"Scarlett swore on her life... a blood vow. She has five days left after today."

"Are you fucking kidding me, Quick? How could you let her do that? Curse the gods! She's terrible at blood vows."

Quick didn't look away from Indigo as she was led back to her tent where Ruby waited outside. "Short of knocking her unconscious, I could not stop her."

Jett wished he could breathe fire to best show how furious he was. "No one *lets* Scar do anything," he said before stalking off.

Jett thought he knew where Scarlett had taken refuge. He'd never been in her office during her short term as Second, but he had been to the previous Second's so he knew where to look.

He turned the filigree knob to her office and stopped in the door way.

Scarlett loosed a Wemic curse. Slate must have taught her that one. Jackal would be so proud. As it turned out, she could speak one of the tribal languages. The literal translation of what she purred was *"Your hard touch makes me insane"*. What it meant in Wemic was much dirtier and shocked Jett that his baby sis would say it.

Thankfully, her rose marble desk blocked their lower halves and one of his hands blocked her chest. She sat in a high-backed, rose velvet, tufted chair in front of a painted portrait of their entire family that an artist must have rendered from other portraits. Oddly, Brass and Quick were in the portrait too which must have been commissioned back in December when Scarlett and he were on the serious outs.

Technically, Brass sat on the chair.

Her hand curled in Brass's hair from behind as she rested her head on his shoulder. Another Wemic curse tore from her throat. The literal translation was, *"My insides are outside"*.

Jett knew the etiquette for interrupting a buddy while he was with a woman, but what about if that woman was your sister? They were married so did they get some kind of *get out of jail free* card?

He *called* air around his head when Brass started to say her name and squeezed his eyes shut. Jett wasn't going to have any luck erasing that image from his mind.

Brass lifted his gaze; half his hair had fallen free from the leather strap at his nape and clung to his stubble and sweating neck. Scarlett whipped her head up and yelped, slapping her hands to her chest. Her hair was in a tangle from where it's been rubbing against Brass. Beads of sweat ran between her hands and collected on her brow. Jett couldn't fathom how long they must have been together if one was worse than the next.

Jett shut his eyes again and shut the door behind him.

"Usually, you would step out of the room before you shut the door," Slate said in an amused tone.

Jett's eyes opened and found Slate leaning against the wall in the corner where the shadows were deepest, arms folded across his chest as he watched Scarlett and Brass. Slate gave him a mocking lip curl as the couple shuffled about, dressing. Slate nodded to them and Jett glanced out of the corner of his eye before turning his head completely back to the desk.

Scarlett's tan cheeks flushed as Brass took a seat on the edge of her desk while she sat in the high-backed chair. She probably thought she was glaring, but it was a feisty little pout.

"Go on. Whatever you've got to say, get it out. I'm not ashamed." She was still breathless.

Jett wasn't sure if she was speaking to him or Slate. Slate made no move so Jett powered through.

"I can't believe you swore a blood oath to free Indigo in four days! What were you thinking? As if you aren't under enough pressure. Do you need more stress? Do you have a death wish? Who will raise your sons if something goes wrong, Scar?" Jett chastened, his voice steadily rising.

Her mouth fell open. Not what she was expecting.

"It was rash. I wanted to make Quick feel better," she said softly. "All the good it did me."

"You did what!" Brass leapt from her desk edge and gave a glower that Slate would approve of.

She dropped her gaze. Jett gave himself a mental kick. Then she leapt into action opening her drawers and pulling out vellum and a pen.

She licked her lips and lifted her gaze. "Just in case."

Slate crossed the room and tore the paper out from under her pen. "No. No *just in case.* Faith and hard work. You have two sons to care for... and my bairn —"

Scarlett's eyes flared like hot coals. "You don't get a voice. You ran out on me. On *us.* Me and Brass and our sons." Her hands swirled in the air to encompass the three of them. "I am sorry. I didn't know. You should have let me apologize —"

"I cannot forgive myself!" Slate roared.

Jett took a step back.

"I don't care! You just have to be there! Here! Where ever I am!" Scarlett shouted back. "You selfish cache hole! We're facing the end of our world and you ran out on me again!"

She beat her fist against her desk top as her chest heaved. Slate glared down at her eyes glinting in the dim light coming from the sconces.

"Looks like we both could meet the gods by next week's end."

"Looks like," she huffed back.

"There is no other place I would rather be than here with you," Slate told her, and her brows quirked with the shot of hope he gave her.

Brass pointed to a shelf lined with thick volumes of books to the left of her chair. She had quite the collection.

"Love?" Brass asked, and she tore her scowl from Slate to look where he pointed and she whipped back to me cringing.

"Hmm?" she asked in feigned ignorance.

Slate knit his brow and moved to look at the volumes. Whatever they were, it caused Scarlett to temporarily forget her anger with Slate.

"These Shakespeare's volumes from the turn of the twentieth century... they are not my grandfather's prized collection, are they?" Brass asked smoothly.

"*Oh*, those? A gift for when I became Second." Scarlett pulled her lips into her mouth and waited for his reply.

Brass ran a hand over his stubbled jaw so it rasped. "My grandfather was a collector of rare things. Anything, really. Books, flowers, but his favorite was women. I was not allowed to touch these volumes, and he *gave* them to you."

Scarlett turned in her seat to look at Brass. "He probably felt guilty for omitting the truth. Why do you sound so angry?"

Brass cautiously pulled one of the volumes from the shelf and opened it in his hands. "He took you to a Shakespeare play on your birthday?" he asked, delicately turning a page.

"Yes. Please don't take your anger out on the books. I really like them," she said, curling her fingers around her armrests to stop herself from taking the volume from his hands.

"Was Spinel in love with you?"

Slate looked like he was trying to communicate to Brass and he was ignoring him. Jett wanted to fade into one of the portraits.

"You're the mind reader. I know he was fond of me. He never used the word," she said, sounding exasperated.

"He was at HQ the last night you competed. Did you not see him?"

"I did, but you and Slate were there. So was Peak and Ash. I avoided him," she said, watching him turn another page.

"That didn't clue you in to who he was?" Brass asked without looking to her.

"We didn't so much as kiss once I found out who he really was... except in... where we were. When he said goodbye. He didn't show to my tour through Ostara. I didn't remember him from Copper's Ausa Vatni. When I sent him a message, I asked the messenger if he knew a Balas in Ostara. You had never invited me to your home before. I didn't know it was yours. Besides, his carriage picked me up from the portal when we met. I thought he was a wealthy silk mogul or something."

Scarlett had gotten to her feet and rested her hip on the desk a few feet away from Slate and Brass.

"He never mentioned me?"

Brass slid his eyes to Scar, and she dropped her hands from her chest. Brass was upset and hurt; Jett recognized that look from the way Steel had been looking at him.

"He did. Twice. We ran into Peak and Willow our first date and Peak said something scathing about the Regn. I grew hot tempered and said a few things I shouldn't have. Then the last... night, he asked me if I was considering you as a suitor. It wasn't out of place because —" she cut off and she shot me a look, pleading for help.

"Because what? You instigated your second meeting, yes? Did he even try to tell you of our relationship?"

Brass felt betrayed by Spinel and Scarlett. Jett wanted to remind him of their two baby boys. He doubted it was the first time they'd argued about Spinel.

"I instigated it. It was after I asked Ash to remove the block on Slate's mind and Slate had completely cut me off. I asked Spinel to be my public escort to help me maneuver through Tidings's politics. He never told me his name. I didn't care to know it. He tried to tell me that night, but I thought he was rejecting me. After what happened with Slate, I was feeling fragile. I started crying —"

Brass sucked in sharply and snapped the book shut. "Crying." He scoffed. "That explains much."

Quick was renowned for cheering up vulnerable women. He couldn't think clearly while women cried, he only wanted to make it stop with pleasure. From what Scarlett had said, every time she was upset, Brass had been there to fix things in any way he could. It was a family trait.

Brass slid the valuable book back in its place and started to leave the room. Scarlett growled and hurried to the door blowing past Jett and threw herself over it holding the doorknob.

"I know you feel betrayed. I know you're still upset with Spinel, but I'm the only one here to vent at. Fine. Be mad at me *next* week. This week, I need you. Both of you. If something happens and we're fighting, it will break my heart one too many times. I cannot apologize *enough* for not knowing he was related to you, but please don't punish me now. Haven't we punished each other enough to last the rest of our lives?"

She knit her brow and stepped away from the door, letting Brass leave if he chose too. He searched her face and sighed.

"You're right, Love."

Scarlett's pupils dilated as she tilted her face up to Brass so they nearly swallowed the turquoise of her eye. Brass's hand whipped out to her nape, and she gasped, wetting her lips.

Freya's burly boar!

Jett skirted them and hurried through the door.

They seemed to be making up for months of separation. Jett had done that himself with Tawny's aid. Steel would be burying his face in those pillowy breasts right about now.

He was going to have to not think about her in that context anymore. Steel and Tawny belonged together. She didn't belong with him. He had no chance of keeping her in the long run.

"Jett." Scarlett was breathless as she pulled away from Brass and stepped past him to stand in front of Jett. "I shouldn't be telling you this, but I can see that you're having a difficult time with... things." Her hairline was still damp as she glanced over her shoulder to where Slate was sitting in her chair and watching her with his head canted down towards the desk. "Tawny slept with Niall because she didn't want to have only slept with one more man before she settled down. She told me she wouldn't do it again. She was going to stay with you, Amethyst, and Cherry. I thought you should know."

Jett searched her face. He smiled and kissed the top of her head before leaving.

THIRTY-ONE

In addition to the blindfold, Slate *called* shadow and wind around my head. He tucked me tight to his body as he led me to his surprise destination.

"Was this planned or —"

"Spontaneous. I have never been one for planning unless it came to how you were cared for," Slate rumbled.

He ran his thumb over the top of my hand where he held it. All my other senses seemed heightened. His hard body against mine, the beat of his heart and steady breaths, the spicy cloves and sunburnt leaves scent of his skin mingled with a manly musk singular to him.

Brass had borrowed Steel's auseklis and gone back to the khoraz brothel to bring Slate to Valla while I was busy with the provosts and getting Storm-pale's report from Gypsum. Slate wore the portal key around his neck so I knew we weren't staying in the university.

"I know. You're like a baby sometimes. Everything you want, you want it *now*. When you don't get it, you throw a fit. Everything is in the moment and it's always the end of the world."

"Are you finished, Torch?" Slate asked in a dry tone.

I pursed my lips, biting back retorts.

Slate stopped us and gripped my shoulders. "I did not bed anyone. I was not intimate in any way. Lynx owns the brothel, and I wanted a place to stay. She knows I would never touch her. I have not since your last competition. I swear it."

Jealousy flared inside me, making me ball my fists and my nails bit into my palms. I knew he hadn't been with anyone. His bond was active. I was so distracted by Brass, and Quick's harsh words, I wasn't paying attention to where he was.

"Why are you here now? Have you changed your mind? Do you want to be with me?" I asked softly, afraid of his response.

"I almost killed you."

"I don't care —"

"I care —"

"Don't leave me and your unborn child, Slate," I interrupted.

He sighed. "I am here," he said roughly. "I love you, Scarlett."

My breath hitched. My hands flew to the blindfold, and I yanked it off since he'd stopped *calling* shadow. His midnight brows were drawn together on his bronze chiseled face as he searched my eyes.

I slapped him jerkily and his eyes widened. I shoved him as hard as I could at his cinderblock like pecs.

"You cache hole! You're saying goodbye!" I cursed at him and shoved him again.

He chuckled incredulously. "Torch —"

I looked around. Moonlight shimmered over the Mani River where we picnicked with Quick and Indigo. The distant roar of the falls behind the Sumar palace was a stone's throw away.

"I can't believe you have the nerve to lecture me on having faith when you've resigned yourself to dying! Fight! Fight for *me*." My speech dwindled down to a squeak as my shoulders slumped.

Slowly, I let my eyes shut. Dear gods, had I ever felt so defeated? What we were trying to do felt impossible and trying to boost everyone else's moral forbade me from confiding that I had no fiddlesticking idea what I was doing. I had ideas. I had dreams, but a lot of things had to go my way for them to go right.

Slate lifted my chin with his knuckle as he stepped in close. "Normally, when a man tells a woman he loves her, she expresses herself in turn."

His voice was smooth and hands were sure, but his emotions spun.

"Never, *ever* tell me you love me again. You call me Torch. That's all I want unless for some strange reason, you feeling *extra* loving. Then, show me. I love you, Slate. Forever and always. Yours, mine, the world's, for all time. No more goodbyes. Promise?"

"No more," he agreed.

He held up his other hand and in it was his open pack. A tan plush throw, a grey jersey cotton fabric, and a bottle of pink champagne with no glasses.

"I thought you said you didn't plan?" I asked, knitting my brows at the contents of the pack.

Slate pulled the grey fabric out of the pack and held it up. "You wore this dress your first time in Thrimilci. Do you remember? It was the day I bought you your short seax."

I would never forget the way Slate had pushed up the hem of my dress and strapped it on touching me so intimately after having just met him. From the beginning, our chemistry had crackled in the air like lightning.

Slate's full lips tugged into a mocking smile when he saw recognition in my eyes. "I always wanted to tear this dress off you with my teeth. I want to see it in scraps by my boots."

My insides pulled traitorously at his vivid imagination.

It was early evening. I had a long night ahead of me, and not just with my bronze god. Time had always been my enemy.

I grabbed the hem of my shirt and lifted it over my head and felt his callouses scratch across my stomach. Warmth unfurled in my belly in two very separate ways.

Slate exhaled heavily, so it nearly shuddered out. "You carrying my bairn..." He needed a moment to collect himself. "I almost killed you."

"It was an accident. But next time, if you're drugged, and some woman seduces you, let me kill her. Don't strangle her in bed. I thought we were trying out a new kinky alternative."

Slate chuckled in spite of himself and lifted my dress over my head as I stepped out of my pants. The jersey fabric molded to my skin, it was a lot tighter on top than it used to be and looser around my hips and ribs. I had just a little more weight to gain back.

"It is a deal."

Slate's tone had dropped, and I looked up at him through my lashes careful not to make any sudden moves. Silver orbs reflected the moonlight and his stance was loose, pack on the ground. The plush throw floated like a magic carpet to spread out behind me.

"Now let me take it off."

When he smiled, it should have given me nightmares. His mouth was full of the finger long fangs of the barghest, but instead I wriggled, standing up and a low growl in his chest began.

"Going to chase your rabbit?" I purred, taking a step away.

"Down whatever hole she leads me."

Trying not to blush was futile, but then again, so was running. I got three steps over the sandy bank before he grabbed me around the waist. He moved so swiftly, then I was on my back, fangs sliding gently between my skin and the material as he tore it away.

"I *need* you, Torch."

"I love you, too."

"Your presence is required, madam."

Brass found us at the palace tucking the boys in for the night. We couldn't spend as much time as we wanted to at the river. Duty called. Luckily, duty had kissable lips and a great fanny pack.

We decided to move the boys and Cherry to the Bilskirnir Arena in Ostara since it would be the last island the Stygians would look. Opal and Junior went with and so did a larger portion of my vulnerable heart.

I sighed running the back of my fingers down the plump cheeks of Balas and Spinel who held one another as they slept.

"Our little family has never been in the same room together," I said wistfully.

"We should all go see your parents' wight. I took them —"

"You took them? Yourself?" I asked in amazement.

Slate regaled me with his Mabon trip where my mother, in her oak tree form, held my newborn sons.

I sniffled, clutching Slate on my tiptoes. "If we weren't so pressed for time I'd make love to you all over again."

I kissed him lightly before dropping back on my heels and sliding my hand into Brass's. "You're giving me ideas, Love," he murmured, his lips rubbing against my ear.

I schooled my thoughts and said what could be my last goodbyes to my sons before we left. Only a few more hours.

CHAPTER 32
JETT

Tiered chandeliers hung from the high ceiling of the grand ballroom. Tiny mirrored pieces were nestled into the stone walls reflecting the light from the chandeliers like starlight. Bjorn, Wemic, Faunelle, and Lycans with red arm bands signifying their Red Second affiliation, mingled for the first time, to Jett's knowledge, between glittering pillars that lined the enormous room. Platters of food were being passed around from each tribes homeland. At the center of the grand ballroom a meeting of the tribal heads had begun to take place.

The ballroom was the largest space nearest the Valla University portal room. Once the tribes filled this room, they would have to begin to fill the halls of this floor and then work their way higher. They didn't want to use the dining hall so there was a place for tyros to eat and maintain some semblance of normalcy.

There was a constant flow of tribal folk from Thrimilci and Elivagar. Provosts pointed out the way to the ballroom and then they found their sect within the room to set up their roll for the night. The Mabon tribes would be with Slate and Brass in Valla's town heart and the Shadow

Breakers, but somehow Lewt had managed to enter the university, probably with Viper's help.

Reski, the Wemic Chief had stayed back in Thrimilci with his wife and Keen's wife. Keen's golden eyes spotted Jett and gave him a practiced feline smile. Gold fur covered his body that grew lighter under his chin and down his chest and stomach, all painted n red swirls for war. His weighted loincloth bespoke his desert life.

When Jett reached him he clasped his nape and tugged his forehead to his own, his mane of hair threaded with feather fetishes and wooden beads brushed Jett's shoulder. Jett gave a quick nod to the golden skinned palomino horse that was attempting to make himself smaller but wouldn't shift into a man in front of the crowd.

"It is good to see you, Jett. I have not found your sister yet."

Not a man or beast, or even a man beast, could resist his baby sis. A boisterous laugh swelled from behind Jett and he turned in time to meet Tikee's greeting. The lynx man had ears long and high on his head with reddish brown and spotted fur sticking straight out. He was a burly hybrid man who laughed loudly and, often, too close to ears.

"We are all here to save these cursed lands," Tikee bellowed though it was his normal speaking voice to his own fur stuffed ears. "I am thinking about making my own abomination army." Tikee elbowed Jett roughly in the ribs as he cast a roving eye on the other tribe's women.

"Greetings. How does the day find you?"

Jett smiled at Adal. He was the only tribal head who had come to Valla U aside from Lewt. Padraig was leading the Lycans with Caolan and Tadg. Lorcan and Blathnat were to stay in Elivagar to manage the tensions between the few remaining Bjorn.

The Faunelle chieftain was half elk with fetishes that hung from his tall antlers. His tawny face matched his and short fur coat with a black deer like nose, but no muzzle. He wore roughhewn pants and a strap crossed over his chest that held a quiver as he leaned on a white staff that was topped with an oblong cage. A sheathed blade was strapped to his hip, his unstrung bow was resting against his pack.

"Excellent. How does the day find you?" Jett returned.

He grinned with flat teeth. "I became a father this morning. Raud gave birth to a female fawn."

"Congratulations. Not that I don't appreciate your leadership, but shouldn't you be with her?"

The serene elk man smiled as if he knew all the secrets of the world. "What kind of father would I be if I did not fight for the best world available for her on the day of her birth?"

"Raud said it was okay," Keen said with a wink.

The other men chuckled; all save the Lycans who looked out for blood in their werewolf forms. Jett cut through makeshift beds to greet the Lycan trio who were apart but not away from the other tribal heads.

Caolan managed to look prim even as a wolf. The other two were enormous to either side of her.

"How are you Padraig?"

"I will be better once I have my teeth sunk into that traitor's throat." His ears turned back and he gnashed his teeth.

"Who's leading the Bjorn?" Jett asked.

Now that Klim was dead and Demyan had turned coat, Gennadi was with Niall and Cabhan at the Crathode caverns keeping the peace and Asya and Lyov had gone home with the women and children, that left no one to wrangle the Bjorn.

"I am. These are Klim's men. They trust me. Lorcan and Blathnat will have their hands full with Demyan's men and your interrogators. Ridge allowed for their use in rooting out any more traitors," Padraig said in a thick burr.

"Tadg and I are responsible for our lot. Do not worry. Padraig is not exaggerating about Klim's men trusting him. They had all gone to the Minotaur lands and set them straight before returning to town. They got to know one another well," Caolan said in her lilting tone.

Suddenly, a cheer rang out in the room and Jett looked for the source of the commotion. Rikke walked in with Quick and they made a bee line for Keen. A thousand tribesmen in as single room even as big as the ball-room was still cramped. They had whittled down the army into a quarter of what they had on the islands, leaving the pregnant women and children in town or back at their lands. They couldn't leave anywhere else unguarded so they were spread very thin.

Scarlett had entered the room, dressed as she was earlier with Brass and Slate flanking her in all black Shadow Breaker gear like death embodied if such a thing was possible. The look had the desired effect even if Scar's features were far too bright to be commanding. A hush fell over the room as she stepped into it, the flow from the portal room coming to a standstill.

"Thank you all for coming. What we do tomorrow has never been done in Guardian history. That you are here with us today when it matters most, will not be forgotten. Those of you who know me well, know I do not make vows lightly, but I vow I will make sure you are treated with fairness from here on out. Once we win the day, of course," she said with a wry smile that beamed across the room, ricocheting into every man and woman's heart and out again.

There were chuckles all around and then she *called* in baskets. "We have the Faunelle and the Wemic to thank for our Red Second identifying bands, which I recommend you wear at all times. We have these thanks to the Bjorn who brought us their nix materials, Centaur, troll, and fairies who melted them down, and the Risar for reforming them. They are made from the cuffs and torques they used to steal your men and women. They will protect you from *calling*. They are yours to keep," she told them, and the tribal heads walked to the entrance way where she stood. Each grabbed a basket with help because they looked to be heavy.

Jett made his way towards them and caught up with Lewt when Tadg passed with a basket of nix torques, but the smaller kind that fit around your wrist. Only the ones that went around your neck caused pain and couldn't be removed.

"I guarantee you none of their people have these. They don't care about the tribes at all," Jett muttered to Lewt.

"No, but she does. I am learning that your family does not play by the Guardian standards." Lewt gave him a smug look that made him sniff.

"No one has ever accused us of fitting in."

They reached Scarlett and she smiled broadly at Lewt. "Not looking for a date tonight?"

Jett knit his brow wondering what that meant, but Lewt laughed heartily.

"Only human women fear my equestrian anatomy. The tribal folk know better," Lewt said suggestively, and Scarlett giggled obscenely.

Jett expected Slate to roar and tear out Lewt's throat, but the two were unlikely friends. He laughed while Brass had his lips curled beside him. All bets were off when Keen pushed through the fray and swept Scarlett off her literal feet. He nuzzled her neck, but for the second time since they met, he didn't kiss her.

Her face was flushed beautifully when he set her down. "I don't think that did anything to help my reputation," she joked.

Keen laughed. "You are among beasts. We catch your scent, Scarlett. You are with child and Slate has imprinted on you. Anyone thinking they can come too close will be rightfully challenged and lose. I catch two scents. Your other mate's?"

Scarlett blushed to her scoop neckline. "They both are. I'm carrying Slate's baby," she whispered the last word as if she couldn't quite believe it herself and it was much too fragile to send out into the world.

"Scarlett!"

Quick pushed between Lewt and Keen as if he had to fight his way there. Jett looked behind him and noticed a line of sorts had formed to meet her. Maybe he did have to fight.

"I am a proper bastard. I do not know what I would have done without you the last... *gods,* it has been nearly half a year. If you had not introduced me to Indigo, I would not have her to lose her. At every turn, you have been there for me. Saving my life, encouraging Indigo to commit to me, making me a man worthy of her... keeping me faithful when I had lost faith. I know everything you sacrifice is for those you love and the easy route would have been to sleep with me and apologize later, but you did not do it. You are a stronger woman than I am a man and I do not deserve your forgiveness."

Scarlett's brow had knit tighter with every sentence. "I love you, Silver. There's nothing to forgive. Families fight." She gave a little shrug and Quick collided with her pinning her arms to her sides as he lifted her off the floor in his embrace.

"Truth. Your sister's emotions are playing with my mind. I feel as though I will burst into tears at any minute," Quick said, muffled against her hair.

"Then we'll hide and you can unburden yourself on me," she whispered.

"I love you too, Mrs. Scarlett. I would kiss you, but I believe I know where your mouth has been."

Brass ducked his head hiding a laugh, but the truth glittered in Slate's eyes and Scar's full body blush. "You'd better not. We need at least two boundaries, Regn."

Scarlett withdrew from Quick and began to greet her fans. Her bright smile was enough to boost the spirits and calm the nerves of tomorrow's impending battle. She was the face of the Red Seconds and had gone to these tribes personally to win them over.

Brass turned away from his position as escort to turn a broad smile to the doors. Jett glanced over his shoulder to find the new Patriarch Regn. The eldest Regn brother had all of Brass's intensity and none of his family's known womanizing. Brass pulled his arm around Scarlett and began to lead her to where Coyote stood. She looked as if she was trying and failing to dig her heels in.

There was no denying Coyote was a Regn. Dark hair to his shoulders with the front pulled back and dark intense eyes with olive skin like Quick's — Regn to the core. Brass managed to drag her to him and she smiled tightly as she offered her hand. Coyote pulled her in for an embrace and she began to blush a shade of red Jett had not seen her color to in ages.

"You will have to marry in Ostara so I may attend. Your sons are doing well, Butterfly is with them so I may speak to you," he said smoothly.

His eyes latched onto you, trapping you in place. Jett wasn't sure he blinked.

"I thought Butterfly was here?" Scarlett asked, fidgeting with her hair.

"She was with Magnolia guiding the tribes. There has been an unexpected development," Coyote told her.

She looked up to Brass who furrowed his brow. "That is?"

"Gorgons have arrived outside the Bilskirnir Arena," Coyote began.

Scarlett gasped clutching her hand to her throat. "We'll go there at once. How many do you suppose are there? You should have brought the children with you."

She went from nervous sister-in-law, to Second, to scolding mother all in a single breath. Coyote smiled fondly at her and her cheeks reddened again.

"You misunderstand. They want to join us. The Gorgon prince,

Chatus, approached with his wife Zonata. Am I mistaken? They claimed to know you."

Jett scoffed. Chatus must have been the hostage the Stygians held over the Gorgons and why they had attacked when Jett and the others had gone to get one of Scarlett's stone pieces. Scarlett rubbed her temple as she contemplated her next move.

"I'll meet with Vernal. He's the king's advisor, bright green with orange eyes, he doesn't have legs. I'm not sure how else to describe him. Chatus... I didn't know his name when we rescued him. He'd be all right too." She sighed. "If I was Zonata, I wouldn't let my husband out of my sight. It would make more sense if I went with you." She lifted her gaze to Brass.

"They want to come back into your good graces after attacking you? Send the Gorgon King and his advisor. He can bring two more of his choosing. We shall wait here," Brass said, checking over his shoulder for Slate.

Coyote's lips quirked. "I shall return in a few minutes." His intense gaze swept back over Scarlett and Brass, and his smile deepened before he left.

"Is it pointless to ask if he knows about Spinel?" she asked, grimacing.

Brass was like a different man than the one who looked ready to ignite her prized book collection. He slid his hand into her hair as he cupped her face in a very public display of affection. She got all moon eyed as she looked to him and her legs seemed to turn to rubber.

"All of Tidings knows, Love. He doesn't care. He knows how I've felt about you from the beginning. I had to tell someone the most beautiful woman in Tidings begged me to be her first lover."

Her eyes widened slightly before he kissed her chuckling as he did it, then her body curved to his and he was the only thing keeping her upright. She looked dreamily at him with a lazy smile when Slate walked up.

"The Gorgons have sided with us?"

"So they would have us believe," Jett muttered, remembering all too well the venom they spit in Cory's open wound.

Scarlett had dipped her toes in that dating pool and came away scalded when the too nice, young Shadow Breaker nearly died on their mission. He wound up dying for her anyway when an attempt was made on her life. One of many attempts.

"I am disappointed the Aves have not made contact," Slate rumbled.

Scarlett pulled away from Brass until he couldn't hang on to her with his fingertips. "We could always send Brass into Ostara so one of his girlfriends will spot him and come to his aid."

"I doubt that. They were displeased I chose to spend the night with you rather than them the last time we stayed," Brass said with a smirk.

"Was that Coyote?" Quick asked. "Are Balas and Spinel okay?"

If Scarlett hadn't already forgiven him, his genuine concern for his nephews would have clinched it. "Yeah. The Gorgons showed up at the Ostara arena. They want to join us."

Quick's upper lip lifted as he sniffed derisively.

Coyote led in four Gorgons. Ophio, king of the Gorgons walked with Coyote. His black skin shifted over his muscles as he moved in an undulating motion even though he had legs. Beads formed a collar around his neck and crossed his chest. His hood was flared with yellow bands when he turned his black eyes on Scarlett. Beside him was a Gorgon Jett had not seen before whom must have been Chatus. He had a powerful build like his father. His scales were black with two beige bands across his throat. Black glittering eyes found Scarlett right away and his lipless mouth lifted.

Behind the pair, were Zonata and Vernal. The mountain king snake hybrid had orange and white stripes over her black body and a head full of writhing tails that coiled to her waist. Vernal was small compared to his brethren and the only one to wear fabric over his shoulders like a robe. The others had strategically placed scales and beads as coverings.

Forked tongues slithered in and out, tasting the air. They each wore layers of brightly colored beads around their necks, they crossed them over their chests with fabric wraps around their waists or around their heads. The snake hybrid men were six feet tall with small rounded eyes in flat scaled heads. Some had legs with a tail that extended from the base of their spines and others had no legs at all but a thick undulating tail. Only Vernal didn't carry a spear in his scaled hand.

Ophio spoke in a slurred hiss with hard "K"s and "T"s. Coyote responded because Scarlett couldn't speak a lick and Ophio's gaze dropped to her belly.

"I underestimated you... and your will. You did not have to free our people. The problem would have solved itself if you left them there to die. Is what Chatus says true? You rescued snakelets and hatchlings from the prison?"

"That does not sound like an apology to me," Slate growled.

Scarlett rested her hand to his chest. "Thre'ik, the newly stationed Empress of the Jorogumo offered to take all the unwanted," she explained.

"I want mine," Chatus spoke English with his thick accent. "I recall each I was used for. If another could tell me which birthed our... the spawn. I would take them. Zonata agreed." He looked back to Zonata who had been scrutinizing Scarlett all the while.

"He says you fed them from your own teat," Zonata said over his shoulder.

Scar tugged on her cotton neckline. "My sons are less than a month old. While I am away, my sister-in-law feeds them. Why I wouldn't do it for newborn babes while their mother is away when there is a shortage of... supply, doesn't make any sense. Of course I nursed those babies. As often as I could. You do realize, Chatus, that the hybrids between tribes are infertile? The older children, too young for war, cannot reproduce."

"A Guardian. Second to only the Prime. A greater family daughter fed unwanted tribal bastards?" Ophio asked in disbelief.

Scarlett narrowed her eyes and stepped closer to the Gorgon king. "I've been proven tried and true, but not because I've passed concocted perilous challenges. Somewhere along the way, the true meaning of what it meant to become a Guardian has been misinterpreted. I am a Guardian in the truest sense. I guard those who cannot guard themselves. I nurture what needs nurturing and I strive for balance. It's not about greater families or my position. I'm a woman able to nurture and strike a balance after an egregious wrongdoing, so I do."

Jett could hear a pin drop. He looked to the tribes behind them and saw those who had settled into their makeshift beds were standing. The entire room was watching Scarlett. Slate and Brass seemed to feel the quiet and looked to all the faces that had listened with rapt attention.

How long had it been since Guardians looked after the tribes instead of subjugating them? There was no balance. Guardians were trained fighters, not nurturers. How long since someone had given them a voice?

"They were right to fear you," Ophio said with a flicker of his tongue. "My people are yours, if you will have us."

Scarlett licked her lower lip. "My sons are in Ostara. We need people here, but Ostara needs someone to fight for her. Would it be much trouble to divide your force in half and leave them at the arena?"

"You are asking?" Vernal finally spoke from behind Chatus.

"Your help was invaluable, Vernal. You have my thanks. Yes, I am only asking because it would be the next step in returning Ostara back to her people." She abruptly turned to Chatus. "How did you get to Ostara? You're supposed to be with the tribes in Elivagar."

Chatus's smile returned. "I brought the Gorgons and Anguillan to Ridge. He gave us escort home. Thre'ik and the Jorogumo remained. The Anguillan you rescued feel as I do. We want to join you."

"We'll believe it when we see it," Jett said, taking the wind from the prince's sails.

"It is as you say... I do not know what to call you," Ophio said.

"Scarlett," she told him and offered him her hand.

It wasn't a Tidings greeting, but Ophio lifted his hand anyway and she clasped it with her own and gave it one stiff shake.

"I'll see your babies returned to you, Chatus. I'd appreciate it if you started calling them Mélange instead of the other horrible names they've been branded with. Spread that around. Coyote, would it be too much to escort the Gorgons through?"

Scarlett began dictating orders with minor changes from Brass and Slate. The other tribal heads moved in to introduce themselves to the Gorgon royals. Scarlett was oblivious to the effect her words had on the other tribes. They respected her if not loved her.

CHAPTER 33

GYPSUM

The waves of the pond lapped against the edge from our motion. The provosts had been very lax with their reprimands concerning tyros and their extracurriculars. It would come to an end as soon as Scar figured out how to beat the pants off the Stygian Knights.

Mica rested her head on my shoulder with her arms wound around my neck as I floated in the lily pad pond. The cherry blossoms shook from the tree sprinkling us with pink petals and Mica turned her face up to the stained glass ceiling of the greenhouse. Her slender hand pushed her damp bangs over her face lit by the moonlight before she returned to the crook of my neck.

"Our whole world will change tomorrow," she murmured.

"It'll be better," I said lazily as I floated over to the stone edge of the pond.

It wasn't so much a greenhouse as it was a whole other world of flowers, plants, tress, and all kinds of greenery. Every greater family had their own greenhouse or conservatory, but Valla University's was the grandest.

"You act as if Scarlett will still be leading us. It will most likely be Crag or Sky who will be voted Prime."

"Both good choices," I told her, lifting her from the pond and onto the manicured grass. "I think Scar plans on retiring after all this is through. She'll keep Vigrid but retreat from the limelight if they let her."

She hurried to grab the robes we set out and handed me the white terry cloth when I got to my feet. I wrapped my arms around her back as she started to dry her bangs and kissed along her narrow jaw. Under the pink blossomed tree were our pillows and blankets. I frog marched her to the base of the tree. Her fiery hair matted against the grey pillowcase as she laid back.

I folded back the robe at her creamy slender thighs and ran my thumbs from her knees and lower. "I'm so glad you didn't give up on me, Bunny."

She reached for me and I lowered myself against her. A warmth spread through my bones making me drowsy that had nothing to do with *calling*.

"What is *that* face?" she asked, poking her finger tips where my cheeks dimpled as I smiled at her.

"Nothing. This is very nice."

Nice wasn't the right word, but it was close. I rolled onto my side and she turned to face me. Her lids were heavy, her fresh citrus scent with the floral all around us made me feel as though *she* was all around me.

"It *is* nice," she said in a hushed tone.

The lush grass beneath the blankets made for a soft bed. Like camping, but better. I rested my arm on her hip and let my eyes slide shut. She giggled, and I peeked at her with an eye.

"Just once tonight?"

"I am not leaving you wanting, am I, Bunny?

"Not at all. This is just as good as the other," she said dreamily.

My sentiments exactly.

I let my eyes fall shut, the image of her lashes fanned across her cheekbones imprinted on the insides of my lids. Sleep was imminent.

"What is that sound?"

A quiet conversation had slowly begun to rise from the entrance of the greenhouse. Tyros came in to use it as we did and we always gave one another wide berth for privacy.

"Then stay," Scarlett hissed. "I didn't mean for anyone to see me. Take these. Give them to my husbands."

"You will make better time with me. Leave the scrolls with another. They will search every inch of the university; they will find them if you dropped them on the floor anywhere."

The male voice sounded familiar, but I couldn't place it.

I reached for my pants and began to dress. Mica started to grab her clothes, but I placed a hand over hers.

"Stay here. I'll be right back." I pressed a kiss to her lips before I grabbed my boots and shrugged into my linen shirt, hurrying to catch Scarlett.

A man with golden waves that fell down to his waist and sun tanned skin turned to focus sapphire blue eyes on me. Scarlet wouldn't cheat on Brass and Slate. Especially with someone so unlike her type, but he would be considered a good-looking man. He was familiar, but I had trouble putting a name to the man. Was he a Shadow Breaker?

"Gyps!"

Scarlett moved from behind the man who only wore a pair of black linen pants he must have borrowed from someone taller than him the way they folded at his ankle.

"Where are you going? Without your husbands. In the dark."

It was obvious I was swimming, so she didn't ask, it would also be obvious that I had been with Mica from the love bites I knew she'd left on my throat.

Scarlett rubbed her ultra-full lips together. "I have seven of nine pieces. Canis has the other two. I am the key.

> *Salvation comes from the shamed daughter's babe.*
> *Temptation takes shape, her love lights the flame.*
> *The son of the beast is finally claimed.*
> *In his blood, destiny takes aim."*

She held up a tiny vile of blood. "I got it from Slate. The Stygians don't know of Slate's prophecy. I have to be the one to activate the works… even if that means going to the works alone and risk getting caught."

Shivers ran down my spine. Slate's prophecy made me want to retreat back to Mica's warm welcoming arms.

Storm-pale had nothing but bad news to report. The Mélange army surrounded the university, but just off the coast south of the Straumr palace, was the Crathode and Anguillan being led by Drik'ir. The deceased Jorogumo Empress's consort had a small contingent of the spider hybrids roaming the borders and organizing the most loyal troops. They had built a bridge out to the cocoon like formation. At the center of the cocoon was a gaping hole which revealed a circular surface several stories down.

That was as much as Storm-pale had seen. The Northern Goshawk had a limited human understanding of what he saw. Scarlett had been silent when I explained it. She had thanked me and went in search of Brass with her trolley of food in tow. That was an hour before dinner. She'd been plotting since.

"I can't risk Slate coming to the Natt project. He's going to die there. I don't think they can force me to change history, so once I activate it… I'm going to stop Natt from building it by whatever means necessary," she said, knitting her brows.

"How will you get back if it doesn't exist?" I asked her in a thick voice.

She pulled her bottom lip into her mouth and shrugged. "I don't know. I don't even know if I'll be born. If any of us will… but it's the only thing I know will stop the war without deaths."

"I am going to take her."

"Lewt…" She gave him an exasperated look, in her hand she held two scrolls

Lewt! The Centaur clan leader could shift into a human. I wasn't used to being able to meet his eyes level with my own.

"I'll go, too." I pulled my socks out of my boots and started to pull them on.

"Absolutely not. Gyps, if I get caught chances are some nasty things will be done to me but at least I'll be alive. They'll kill you, Chief," she said as she searched my eyes.

"I'm guessing you're pressed for time and that you did something to

Brass and Slate so they wouldn't notice you were gone. I wouldn't waste time arguing if I were you." I lifted my head to check her expression and stamped my foot into my boot. "I'm coming or I'm going to run up into the ballroom and announce that you're sneaking out. I don't disagree with what you're doing, but I won't let you do it alone."

I'd heard a rumor that Slate was in the castle. It was good those two made up, and from the sounds of it, things were back on the right course.

"Then I am coming too." I looked up to the heavens and wondered why I hadn't whispered.

"Mica. I can't let you do that," I told her, turning around and saw she was already dressed with my scabbard in her hands.

She pursed her bright pink lips. "Then I shall go upstairs —"

"You can come. Do you have a weapon?"

"Scar!" I whipped from Mica to her and back.

Mica's big brown eyes grew bright with excitement as she nodded. "In the prep room."

She turned to run and get her whip when two sharp bursts of air whistled past me. Mica turned around touching her backside and then toppled into the grass. Scar ran over to her.

"What did you do to her?" I shouted, and she squatted holding up two thin bone darts.

"Bjorn darts. I stuck three in each of my husbands. I was thinking about sticking you, but I could use the company when Lewt leaves me. If we get into trouble though, both of you run. Deal?"

Scar tucked the two scrolls she carried into Mica's pocket.

"Come here."

She looked up to me and she looked like the girl I knew in Chicago. I squatted beside her and rolled Mica onto her back, straightening her hair. She didn't so much as flutter an eyelid.

I picked her up and carried her over to the bed we'd made. I brushed her bangs before I set about taking off her boots so she'd be more comfortable.

"I always thought that leaving Slate was the worst thing I'd ever done. If I never did, I never would have let myself love Brass. They're so similar and yet different. I'm amazed every day that I awake and find that they still love me."

Mica's freckled chest rose and fell with steady breaths. "What's your biggest mistake?" I asked, pulling the blanket up to Mica's chin.

"Fighting how I felt about them. The first week I arrived in Tidings, I knew I was different for Slate and he was different for me. The moment I met Brass, he took my breath away. I never should have entertained Ash as a suitor. Do you love her?" Scar asked, sliding her fingers into my hair.

"I think so," I forced out roughly as Scar handed me two copper beads from the narrow braids I wore.

Scarlett wore Slate's silver beads. It was as close to staking a claim as I would get to do and let her know I was thinking about her. Maybe she'd even forgive me sooner.

"You'd don't have to leave her. You can stay."

With one fiery braid between my fingers I pinched on the two copper beads that blended with her hair and stood. "I'm coming."

Scarlett handed me the scabbard Mica dropped when she collapsed and I buckled on my long and short seax with my axe. "Those scrolls. Are they for Brass and Slate?" I asked her as she started out towards the back of the greenhouse.

"No. One is for both of them and the other is for the family. Not you anymore I suppose."

Scarlett seemed distracted as she pushed in between closely grown bushes and greenery at the far wall. Lewt didn't question her. Perhaps he thought if he remained quiet she would forget he was there so he could join them all the way to the site of the project. Scarlett began pressing on panes of glass using a stream of her *calling* with it. A combination of light and wind every time she pushed.

"I filtered through what Ash saw as Prime. Second is a glorified secretary though I did get to be in with the in crowd if you're into that sort of thing. One day, a report of a breeze came across my desk and instead of sending someone to inspect it, I came myself. I did that a lot to get out of the office. I found a hidden... here it is."

She pushed a pane of purple and it unlatched with a click before hissing as it opened. Wheels and mechanisms turned within the ground as it sunk into a crack below.

"It's right upside the cliff. That's why they haven't used it to invade the university. You can't access the greenhouse well enough for an attack. We'll have to be quiet. This leads right into the woods where they have watch guards patrolling."

Scarlett stepped out and offered Lewt her hand as she pressed her body to the wall of the greenhouse. Vertigo assailed me as I looked down at the rocks below. Waves crashed and foamed like rabid beasts waiting for the meal dangling before its face.

Lewt took Scarlett's hand reconsidering his persistence to join them on their fool's errand. I stepped over the pane of glass that stuck up from the soil a few inches and as I flattened myself to the outside of the greenhouse, my boot heel caught on the pane and heat rushed through my body. My balance never really faltered, but the fear of falling was enough to make me dizzy.

"That's how it closes. By pushing it in."

I saw that she was right, the pane was already halfway to meet the other stained glass. Scarlett sidled along, hair whipping at her face from the windy coast breeze and she took a moment to pull up a black light-weight scarf around her head like we wore on desert trips in Thrimilci. The Centaur looked uncomfortable making the dangerous trek in his human form. Golden blonde hair tangled about his face so he squinted in the darkness of midnight as he blindly followed Scar.

I could see the roots of the Yggdrasil tree from where we climbed. The massive ash grew right into the rocks. The way the university was built, but its highest parapets out at the farthest edge of the cliff. There was no way into the university from that side. The closest one was the main entrance they used where the Mélange army had destroyed the lawn.

Our backs finally hit stone, and we had come to the battle grounds. The shelf of the cliff side began to widen and very slowly, my breaths leveled out. I rested my head back against the cool aged stone and took fortifying breaths until my heart was no longer running its own personal marathon.

Scarlett pressed a finger to her lips that she covered with the scarf so only her luminous eyes shone. She knit her brows at Lewt who gleamed like his own star with his golden skin and hair. Lewt smiled rakishly at her and began to take off his linen pants. She kept her eyes around the bend of the battle grounds while Lewt shifted.

It wasn't so much shifting as it was suddenly he expanded. One minute he was standing on two legs then he grew taller, a second pair of legs pushed from the first as human legs and morphed into hooves until the lower half was a horse's.

Scarlett reached up a hand and Lewt swung her up effortlessly and she wrapped her arms around his middle. Lewt offered me his arm, and I gave a little hop before sliding up behind Scarlett. She really did smell like apple pie with a hint of warm vanilla.

When Lewt began to gallop, I lunged forward, squashing Scarlett between us and she fought a smile. He must do that often.

Trees whipped past us and I ducked my head to keep my cheeks from getting windburn. Lewt could gallop faster than any horse I'd ever been on or heard of. He knew where he was going, Scarlett must have told him.

I searched the skies for Storm-pale. It'd been months since I'd been outside with him. His shadow in the star light would signal his arrival in time.

The small woods turned into mountains. We covertly crossed the cobbled road patrolled by Mélange and began to descend past the town heart of Valla. We'd have to make our own way over mountains because the roads were crawling with the Stygian's army. Lewt had turned back into a man and Scarlett handed him his pants. We walked towards the crimson dawn not stopping to eat or drink, remaining in constant motion.

The weather was warm and good for traveling. We allowed ourselves quiet conversations while in the mountains since not another soul would hear us. Scarlett pulled out a plastic device and shrouded her chest in her scarf as it filled with her milk. She placed more fabric inside her shirt and gave me a rueful grin as she pumped.

Storm-pale arrived when we were eating breakfast and said all was well at the university.

"Jett will probably be storming up to our room soon. Brass and Slate will be asleep for a little while more. We were supposed to leave before dawn," Scarlett confided, her scarf down around her neck.

"It'll be a day behind. That's okay," I told her as she nodded absently as she clutched the stones at her chest.

Scarlett didn't carry food in her small pack. Ridge taught her to pollinate her own plants and trees so she only carried seeds in a long tin. Inside were more square tins all labeled with what she kept inside. It was ingenious. She said that was the way it used to be. Valla University for Guardian Mastery hadn't produced a true master in some time. Decades, it would seem.

I wanted to dislike Ridge, but they didn't have a negative word to say about him. He was reserved, kind, and thoughtful. Kind of like my own father and that made it better and worse at the same time. My mother was married to two men. How would Scarlett's children feel about her arrangement?

When the road mountains leveled out, we got back on Lewt and he soared over the Valla landscape. It had been a long time since I'd heard Scarlett laugh and sound carefree. You'd be hard pressed to find someone frowning on the back of a Centaur.

Rolling fields of wild flowers gave way to farms and crops we galloped across in a blur. The Centaur clan leader didn't need much rest and with the countryside devoid of Mélange, we made excellent time.

We skirted the Straumr palace at twilight. Minotaur patrolled the outer grounds, so we steered clear. Lewt crossed the road from Valla to the Straumr's and took us deep into the woods as we aimed towards the coast. He slowed to a trot as he traversed the thick brush and Scarlett was using her little pump again.

"When we reach the encampment, that's as far as we'll need you, Lewt. Go back the way we came and if you feel confident, go to the university. Slate will have found my scent trail there and probably has a guard on the secret entrance so they can let you in. You could always head straight south along the coast to the Ymir River. The Vanaheim is there and if you wear this, they'll let you in."

Scarlett replaced the pump in her pack and shifted in front of me to pull out a red band and tied it around Lewt's wrist like a bracelet. Lewt held up his wrist and gave her a smile over his shoulder.

"Laying claim to me, Scarlett? It is about time," he joked.

Briefly, we stopped for dinner. Scarlett grew, then toasted potatoes in her bare hand while I diced garlic and onions. Lewt was hunting. The appeal of hunting my own food was lost when I could hear the animals' cries in a language I could understand. I craved meat, but I couldn't kill it myself.

Storm-pale didn't understand my logic. He gripped my shoulder as I worked watching with mild interest as Scarlett collected what she could to replenish her stores. He reported that we were very close to the coast where the project was and we'd soon run into troops.

Lewt brought back two hares in his man form and tossed Scarlett back her blade which she caught midair and rammed back into her boot.

She was looking more like her old self. Not as skinny as when she resurfaced from the mystery island, but it could have been because she was at peace for once. Not having to decide between Brass and Slate, one yanking her arm one way, and the other another.

I skinned and gutted the hares, giving Storm-pale his pick of the leavings, before putting them on a spit and roasting them with flames coming directly from Scar's hands. She passed a potato to each of us which she'd split and smothered with the fixings I'd prepared.

"Clever, beautiful, *and* she cooks," Lewt said playfully.

"Everyone contributes. I only throw it together. I never get the chance to cook while I'm at the palaces or castles who have an entire staff to do everything for us. I might have something you can eat that with," she told Lewt and *called* over a fallen branch before using blades of air to whittle it down.

A rough looking three-pronged fork floated over to Lewt. "I will not complain, but *this* is a sad fork," he teased, and Scarlett laughed.

Scar and I *called* bites into our mouths with air when we didn't have access to utensils. Lewt ate with an amused look while we opened our mouths to float in more food. There was no satisfaction of tearing off a bite this way. There was a visceral need to bite and tear which we did once we split the roasted hares.

"Everyone knows we're gone. To say that Slate and Brass are angry would be putting it very mildly. Our bonds are active. They are at the arena south of here." She sighed. "We are going to continue alone. It'll only be another hour before we reach the first patrols. Thank you, for all your help," she said, expression unreadable in the shadows of the forest.

Lewt stared across the short span between them. "Please do not get yourself killed. You and Slate are the first Guardians the Centaur have entertained other than Viper in decades. You are also our first glimpse of hope for the future of your kind."

Scarlett had dropped her hands into her lap putting down the hare. "I like to think that I've given a taste of hope to all the tribes who've heard what the Red Seconds have to offer. Tawny, Jett, my Aunt, Sparrow, Slate, and even Gypsum here, they're all a different brand of Guardian and if something does happen to me, they are the heirs that will run the council."

"Not all of them have the passion for the tribes as you do. You treat us as equals."

"Gypsum has never discriminated against the tribes," she said wryly, and I could hear the smile in her insinuation.

Lewt chuckled, lightening the mood once more as we finished our meals with Lewt questioning me about just how indiscriminate I'd been.

Lewt grabbed Scarlett's nape and pressed a firm kiss to her lips before she could shove away. She laughed when he released her.

"Slate is going to kill you."

Lewt pulled her scarf up around her head and tucked her long hair within it. "I did not want to regret never having tried."

"Thanks for the confidence," she said still smiling and pulled the scarf over her mouth.

She nodded towards the woods and Storm-pale took flight when we started out. Our footsteps were cautious, so we made little noise as we moved between the trees.

Several times we had to fall to our stomachs within the ferns and the brush to hide from a patrol combing the forest edge. We were slowed to a crawl running between trees when the scent of the ocean permeated the air. Patrols were everywhere.

Torches lit walking paths making it difficult to move about, but easier to hide within the flickering shadows. Scarlett ran to the tree I leaned against as two Anguillan strode past. We could hear the waves against the rocks not far to our left.

"There's only the bridge," she whispered.

Through the trees, we could see they had chopped down part of the forest to construct a wooden bridge out into what looked like a huge boulder poking out from the water. It was a dome that led down to the project.

It was so very close.

"Storm-pale couldn't tell how they got down the dome, but it's a far fall to the ground. My guess is stairs or ramps. I can't imagine the Anguillan are very good climbers or —"

Scarlett tugged me to her, squeezing me tight as she sucked in a deep breath. "We'll go straight for the water, swim to the top of the cocoon, and fight our way down. I hope what I'm supposed to do with the pieces is self-explanatory. I love you, chief. If I get caught, run. At any cost, you get the hell out of Dodge. I'm relatively safe, but you aren't. If they have you, they have the only heir to the Sumar and they'll be able to control your parents. Do you understand?"

I wanted to believe that my parents would never give up the island or one of themselves for me, but I'd be wrong. My mom had been through too much to ever let another one of us go. She'd offer herself up in a heartbeat. On the other hand, I could never leave Scar when she needed me.

I nodded, and she withdrew. "I love you too, Scar," I whispered, thinking she wouldn't hear me, but she turned her head and gave me a thumbs up before running at a crouch towards the gentle sound of waves.

It was a trap.

They must have been waiting for one of the Red Seconds to try the very act we were attempting. We darted from the forest to the water's edge and Crathode exploded from the water. Before we had a chance to *call*, fine metal nets we should've been able to tear apart with our hands flew from spring loaded barrels they aimed at us.

Scarlett was one step ahead of me, the top of her head in the water. It was the pewter nix torque material; they'd made it into chain mail like links with weights at the end so when they struck us the heavy balls tangled at our feet. We could only remove nix material if it was opened ended and could slide off. I struggled anyway in the sand until the Crathode scuttled to where we laid helpless.

The last thing I saw was a claw as big as my head crash into my face.

"On your feet, Sumar."

Sterling's stern voice sent me into palpitations. I shifted against the cool grass and blinked against the bright sunlight. When I wrinkled my brow, I could feel the gritty crust of my dried blood. My hands were bound together, and I pushed myself up off my side with an elbow.

Scarlett was gagged and her hands bound by nix torques as mine were. The lead of her torques was tied to a saddle in which Ash sat. She looked furious. Blood matted her caramel hair and had trailed down into her brow. Beside them was Sage and tied to his saddle was Lewt.

Lewt looked to have put up a fight and hadn't been healed. He was in his human form and stood putting his weight on his right leg. His body was coated in bloodied dirt and his black pants were torn. He wasn't gagged, and neither was I which made me furious I missed whatever Scar said to force them to gag her. It was probably awesome.

Sterling pulled me up to my feet with a feigned roughness that was firm but not painful. I tried to play into his exaggerated actions as I straightened. Behind us the Gothic styled Straumr palace loomed. In an upstairs cathedral window, Diamond pressed her palm against the glass. Sterling followed my gaze and gave me a shake before tying my lead to his saddle.

Cursed nix torques. I hated the blasted things.

"When that Bjorn told us you were alive, I urged Canis to torture him so we could be sure it was the truth. I am *ecstatic* the bear was honest. He hates you. We knew you would attempt to reach the project," Sage said in his feigned sweet voice.

It was hard not to sneer when he spoke. They didn't give us notice before their horses moved and mine and Scar's arms were yanked before we could begin to follow.

The three men rode together. The Crathode who had nabbed us were long gone, and I had no memory of the morning's travel to the Straumr palace. Sage, Sterling, and Ash didn't address us as if we were beneath their notice. When I couldn't hold it any longer, I asked to relieve myself. I was surprised to find that they didn't torture us and make me go in my pants.

Scarlett was led deeper into the wood by Ash and came back a few minutes later disheveled, red faced, and wrathful. Ash had a smug smirk when he hopped back into his saddle and held up her silver chain that carried the stone pieces, pulling it over his head. Not knowing what happened was eating at me and I could tell Scarlett wanted to talk.

We took the roads, so it became apparent we were riding back to Valla University. Scarlett swerved to Lewt who limped along and eventually he gave in and wrapped his bound hands over her shoulders so she could help him walk. The three men on horses didn't comment. We weren't fed or given water. Scarlett's shirt was damp with her mother's milk that changed the grey cotton material to nearly black. Aside from making note of it, none of the men said a word. Her pack and blades were strapped to Ash's saddle. My scabbard was tied to Sterling's.

"I did not make it half an hour before I was surrounded," Lewt said in a hushed tone.

"How did we get to the Straumrs?" I asked in a whisper.

"You were carried over the shell of one of the Crathode. Scarlett was walking as she is now. She is only bleeding because she back talked that blonde one and the Crathode bopped her on the head before he gagged her. I tried to get away in my Centaur form and broke my leg running through the forest. I had enough time to pull on the pants before they reached me."

Sterling looked over his shoulder at them. He was a barghest. He would be able to hear everything Lewt just said. I cursed internally for forgetting such an important detail.

CHAPTER 34

INDIGO

"I am sorry, dear. We have to go back to Ostara. I wish I could take you with me."

Ruby packed her own clothes as I placidly sat at the small pedestal table. It was only a matter of time after she left that Sage would come for me. Reports were coming in that Valla's town heart had been taken. It was now occupied by the Shadow Breakers. All portals were being locked. Willow had gone to Ostara already with Cassiopeia. Ruby would meet them there at the Var castle.

Ruby summoned a servant clad in the green and gold of the Var's and the man carried out her bags. She turned to me, clasping her hands.

"One last walk?"

I nodded and got to my feet, leaving my half empty plate, and took her arm as we went out into the night.

Not enough could be said about how beautiful Valla was in the spring. It didn't have the thick humidity Ostara did, or its manicured flower beds. Valla's flowers were wild and for some strange reason, reminded me of Scarlett and our father.

The camp was in a frenzy as they had been every time we lost more ground. The command tents held an air of foreboding you instinctually stirred clear of.

We were standing in front of the siege machines which were complete when riders approached. Only the high command and greater families rode horses so we turned to see who was coming.

I pressed my palm to my rounded stomach when I saw the greater family sons ride into the brazier lights. Bile churned and my belly cramped. Then I saw why they were so happy and gasped. Behind them were three bedraggled people dead on their feet.

Scarlett half carried Lewt. You couldn't mistake the twinkly eyed Centaur. Gypsum was the third. His entire forehead crusted with old blood and dirt. Then the worst realization of all — Ash wore her stone pieces. It really *was* her.

"Bring her to Indigo's tent. The other two will go to Canis. He will likely make an example of the commoner," Ash said, coming down off his horse to three of the black cloaked Guardians who hurried to do the Prime's bidding.

"Yes, Prime." They agreed as Sterling and Sage dismounted and walked towards us.

My feet were rooted to the soil. It had to be a nightmare. No way could we have gone through so much adversity to wind up in Stygian hands.

The horses were led away by one man, while the other two took the leads of their nix torque cuffs. Scarlett struggled as they lifted Lewt's arms over her head and was pulled the opposite direction of Gypsum and Lewt. Her feet dragged as the Gyps and Lewt tried to stay near her. I started forward, but Ruby put her hand on my shoulder.

"We shall meet her in the tent and help her get cleaned up. You do not —"

Ruby abruptly stopped open-mouthed, and I whipped my head to the captives. Scarlett was yanked forcefully forward until she fell flat on her face. Gyps and Lewt fought harder against the single man to help her up. Her guard bent down to help her up, and she twisted.

If I blinked, I would've missed it. As he bent, she pulled the blade from his sheath and didn't have time to call out before she rammed it into his throat. She twisted from where she laid on the ground and threw the blade into the chest of the man who held the leads to the other two men. She rolled to her feet and sprung on the dying man as he gripped the blade in his chest.

With the man's blood pumping freely like black oil into the dirt path, she used his limp hands to pry free the torques from Lewt's hands. She did the same to her own and placed her palm on Lewt's leg. He expanded and his horse half grew from his human legs.

Gypsum reached for her, but she stepped away, fingers yanked down the gag.

"*GO!*" she screamed and her head whipped around until she spotted me. "Get Indi!"

Lewt scooped Gypsum onto his back with a push of air from Scarlett, shouting all the while and took off into the woods.

"You will not get another chance," Ruby's voice jerked me to my senses.

I followed Scar's eyes as she nodded towards the university. She turned to face the two Guardians approaching us and started throwing fire balls indiscriminately. They were put out right away by *calling* water but it caused just enough distraction for us to get lost in the panicking people.

I started running. My arms pumped with my heart. We were getting away. Maybe this was her plan all along.

The smell of ashes and blood filled my nostrils. I could hear Sterling shouting my name from far away. Gypsum held onto Lewt from all he was worth as they galloped through the camp and I saw the point where we would meet with Scarlett covering their escape.

Lewt's eyes swerved to the woods. Ash had joined Canis and Cygnus who had come out of their command tent to find the source of the commotion. Scarlett had left Gypsum's nix torques on for a reason. Their *calling* couldn't touch him. He veered towards me with Scarlett on his heels.

Scarlett collided with me and I clung to her even though I was taller. She was always stronger.

"Tell them that no matter what happens, I will never ever stop loving them. If we all are different people when this is through, I will search the ends of the earth for them through time if I have to," she said with a warbling voice. "Don't let my sons grow up without a mother," she whispered before she withdrew. "Don't look back," Scarlett said, and unsnapped the nix torque around my throat before putting her discarded nix cuff on one of my wrists opened so I could slide it off, but no one's *calling* could touch me.

"Scarlett!" I sobbed.

Scarlett never faltered, protecting me with her own body when we were faced down. The world was a blur of angry faces, fire and smoke. I absorbed Scarlett's power and felt fear and anger that weren't my own.

The pinched face of Dahlia Natt emerged from behind a tent. She opened her mouth raising her hands to *call* and Scarlett didn't hesitate for a heartbeat. Her blade handle stuck out from the gaping mouth of Dahlia as she made a few choking sounds and then collapsed.

She gave me a shove, and I was lifted under my arms between Gypsum and Lewt's bodies. His blonde locks whipped my face as he jerked into motion.

"*RUN!*" Scarlett shrieked.

Scarlett hopped over Dahlia's body as if it was nothing. As if she hadn't just killed a woman who taught her every weekday for two years and was supposed to be her mother-in-law. She turned to face down another set of Stygians coming our way from the woods we were nearing, the red skull and sickle emblazoned on the breast of their cloaks.

Lewt galloped alongside the university, his hair flying into my face as I pressed myself tight to his torso. Gypsum's arms clamped around my waist as he looked behind to Scarlett.

"Look out!" Gyps shouted.

I glanced up to the maple about to topple us off his back and felt his arms release me. The bark scraped my head and tore my dress as Lewt staggered and righted himself. I jerked around dizzily to find Gypsum.

"*DON'T STOP!*" he yelled from where he laid on the grass, blood covering his olive face.

"No!"

My scream was lost in the thundering of Lewt's hooves. I craned my neck to watch as Gypsum glared defiantly at Cygnus and Ash who got him to his feet by his collar. Cygnus placed his hand on Gypsum's back and probably told him something that sounded perfectly reasonable as he was led away, casting me one last glance before the trees grew too thick between us.

In the woods, Lewt's hooves crunched over dead branches and

brushed over the tops of flowers as he leapt over bushes. His body blocked me from branches that would have otherwise knocked me about the face and tugged on my caftan. Guardian traitors were on their way back to camp and either were too preoccupied with the smoke coming from there or didn't care that I was escaping. If they *called*, I didn't feel it.

Lewt's body slowly began to shrink between my legs and I screamed as he stood naked before me. He gave my shoulders a stiff jerk. His golden cheeks were damp, his sapphire eyes gleaming.

"I left her for you. It is what she would have wanted. Hold my hand. We will need to help each other."

My thoughts came sluggishly as I nodded and let him take my hand leading me to the ledge between the stone battle ground wall and the ocean below.

Our feet shuffled, never lifting from the ground, as we slowly rounded the wall. Neither of us spoke, but I could *feel* his deep sorrow. He cared for Scarlett, possibly more than a friend and not just because she was stunning.

Ocean spray misted up to us as the wind whipped my dress. We'd reached the greenhouse. Lewt shouted against the water something about purple and gestured to a pane of stained glass. I nodded and listened to him shout about light and wind. I *called* and the purple pane of glass whirred as it slid down just far enough so a lip of the window would need to be stepped over.

Once Lewt was standing beside me in the thick copse of trees, I pressed the pane again and it slowly rose until it clicked into place. Lewt and I were up against one another, trying to force our way between closely grown trees.

We stumbled out into a clearing to find Tawny and Steel wide eyed. Lewt was moving past me completely nude and my head swam.

Steel and Tawny had run to me. I blinked lazily at them. I wasn't a totally useless worm, as I'd feared. I was due for my rousen cocktail. My brain would start to shut down soon. It was a very small consolation after having done nothing to aid in our escape.

Just then, Silver, Slate, Brass, and Jett came around a copse of blossom trees and ground to a halt when they saw me. Silver's cheeks were damp. Had my devilishly handsome Lothario ever cried a day in his life?

"Dove," he said thickly as he took long strides towards me.

I'd lost Scarlett. I understood that now. She never meant to escape with me, she wouldn't leave Gypsum. I ran and I left her. I left her to them. Whatever she thought she would suffer would be far, *far* worse.

I fell to my knees screaming. I couldn't use words any longer. All I had were my tears.

CHAPTER 35
GYPSUM

Cygnus healed me and brought me into the pink tasseled tent that Indigo stayed in. Ash snapped the nix torque around my neck and set the hoop at the end of the chain on the bed post of the pink jacquard bed.

"Feel free to clean up. Diamond will be in to retrieve you. We will bring Scarlett in shortly," Cygnus promised, sweeping from the tent.

"My sister will be eager to see you." Ash gave me a smug look. "Scarlett has unwittingly handed us the last piece of the puzzle. Dagr blood. Your blood will not be spilled until we are where it is needed."

I wished I could punch the bastard in the face like Slate and Chris had done. Even Indigo had slapped him.

"Did you steal those pieces from her?" I spat.

His brow quirked. "She has many more secrets than she used to. Pieces must be given. You are our incentive. She would do anything to protect you."

He left the tent, and I walked over to the tub filled with cool water from a bath Indigo must have taken earlier in the day. I dunked my head and grabbed a towel to dry my face. I straightened and water spilled down onto the tent floor. The white pedestal table where Indigo's dishes remained from dinner included steak knives. I grabbed them before anyone could enter and shoved them into my boots.

There was no notice before Scarlett was tossed head first into the tent and collided with one of the wrought-iron chairs. I jerked my chain tight to help her up and felt the icy pain like a blade into my spine with her just out of reach.

Her hair hung in bloody ropes around her face and she was filthy. She scrambled to her feet, backing into me, and I pressed a knife into her hand.

"When the Knights arrived at the palace, this morning, and informed us that Valla had been taken. I thought today was going to be a bad day."

My skin crawled at the sound of her half-brother's voice. He let the flap of the tent close and used air to tie it down. Scarlett moved in front of me, blade tightly gripped in her palm.

"I see the Prime doesn't care if one of his closest confidants committed patricide. It's probably because you're his half-brother. He must have a soft spot for you." Scarlett's stance was at the ready, her muscles loose as she antagonized Sage.

Sage's fair skin reddened; his relaxed posture bunched as he balled his big hands. "You are a liar," his honeyed cultured tone dropped as he spat the words at her.

"Your mother and Crag Straumr sired Ash and Diamond because Crag wanted out of their betrothal and Dahlia happened to be barren. Orion had the means and the ambition. Canis had the control over our grandfather to force him to marry your mother once she'd birthed. Do you remember your mother carrying Diamond?" Scarlett paused and I could hear her smile. "Douse that flame just a little? I wondered why you hated me even before you found out we shared a father. It should have been obvious that you were in love with —"

Sage moved fast. He lifted Scarlett off her feet by her throat, her feet kicked in the air as he stepped away from me so they were out of reach.

He sneered. His fingers clenched the soft fleshy skin below her jaw. I lunged out for them and was snapped short by the nix torque.

"You are lying," he said through clenched teeth.

"I am many things, but not a liar," she rasped out.

Sage snarled and tossed her through the air so she slid down the tent wall. I slowly reached down into my boot for my second knife. His smile turned to something worse than sinister as she got to her feet. I strained the chain, gritting my teeth.

"Can't handle a man? You've got to pick on a woman?" I spat at him.

Sage didn't acknowledge my existence other than to begin a freezing pain so intense through the torque that my vision blackened as I was brought to my knees.

"No matter. Ask our sister how I feel about half-siblings," he said, stalking towards her.

Scarlett was up in a crouch, her face pained. "What did you do?" she rasped.

"Only used her for what khorazes are good for. You should know, you are one yourself."

The pain stopped, and I gasped for air on my back, looking at the flickering shadows of the candles on the roof of the tent. My eyes caught on the vine that had begun to grow on the tent wall. The blue morning glory I'd sent to Indigo, she'd managed to give it roots. It reminded me of what I was fighting for.

"How could you? You killed our parents, killed my unborn child, and raped our sister! You're not a man, you're a monster!" She sobbed.

"Perhaps, but what does that make *her*? What will that make of *you*?"

Scarlett struggled, grunting and wailing until I heard flesh strike flesh. Fabric rustled as she cried. I struggled to roll over and get to my knees to help.

"Sterling promised me he would take care of her," she whimpered.

"Do not worry. I took care of our Indigo," Sage said in a honeyed voice. "I shall take care of you too, Scarlett. I have wondered if Ash's boasting had any merit. How good is your mouth, Scarlett? Should we find out, *hmm*?"

"Not in a million years," she spat.

"So sure, are you?"

The nix torque around my neck grew so cold it burned. The pain was like hitting a funny bone in my throat but a hundred times worse. I grit my teeth until I couldn't take anymore and I screamed. I thought he was causing pain before, but this was much worse.

"Okay!" Scarlett shouted. "Stop hurting him."

Sage sniggered. I opened my eyes as he dragged her by her hair to the white wrought iron seat. His belt jiggled after he released her hair and she slid her tearful gaze to me. Bruises marred her tan throat where his fingers had dug.

"Don't," my protest croaked out.

Tears burned my eyes. I'd take the pain ten times over before I'd let her submit to Sage. My brain refused to believe he did as he claimed to Indigo. I couldn't process Scarlett's intentions as Sage took the seat and gripped her head again, dragging her roughly to her knees. I caught the glint of the knife in her palm.

"Use those diamond white teeth of yours and you will be sure to eat pureed foods for the rest of your miserably short existence."

He sat back in the chair, forcing her to shuffle her knees to get closer. Panic consumed me as she let him bring her head to his lap. Sage sucked a deep breath, and I shut my eyes as I struggled to my feet.

Sage screamed. Not that of a man in ecstasy, but in fatal pain. I watched in disbelief as Scarlett chewed, blood running down her narrow chin to splatter over her grimy grey shirt. He was still screaming, holding his middle. Scarlett took the other chair, leaping from her knees into a crouch with a knife in her hand and bashed Sage in the face.

Not his middle but his lap. Scarlett chewed and gagged and chewed some more before swallowing. She was speaking to me, but I couldn't clear my mind of wondering what she could be eating. She couldn't keep her mystery meal down and voided her stomach on the tent floor as she staggered to me.

She grabbed my wrists, her hands coated in dark red blood. Scarlett took Sage's limp hands and curled them around the nix torque at my throat. She pushed her hands over his so the clasp popped open and used one of his fingers to move the latch aside.

My torque was open. I was free.

She was speaking again and holding up her wrists. Sage was alive. Blood was spilling from his ragged severed member as he twitched. Scar growled in frustration and took my hands with her own and placed them over her cuffs.

"Chief! They took my pieces. They have a Dagr and a Natt. We messed up big time." She pointed to us both, and my stomach managed to drop even further.

Sage started to move, but she didn't slow when she grabbed my hand and darted out of the tent. Guardians had heard sounds of our fight and stood a few feet away.

Diamond walked down the dirt path separating tents between Ash and Sterling. Our eyes met, and she shook her head in the torchlight. Smoke and evidence of the destruction Scarlett rained down on their heads was everywhere. She was their own personal harbinger of doom.

Scarlett jerked my hand, forcing me to move, and I staggered as she started to run.

Our running didn't last long.

CHAPTER 36

JETT

Scarlett's letter didn't say goodbye. It was, *see you in another time.*

Brass and Slate had gone temporarily insane when they woke the two slumbering giants and found her missing. They knew something was amiss that they hadn't woken up long before breakfast. They had assumed they were recovering from a vigorous night. Scarlett must have waited until midnight before she left them.

Mica had been aggrieved. Scarlett had been on a drugging spree. She was the one who had to brave Slate and hand him the scrolls, then she faced Tawny who may have been even more fearsome with her brother missing than Slate was about his wife. That was until Mica self-consciously rubbed the copper beads she had threaded through her long fiery hair. Tawny took one look at Mica's gleaming eyes and pulled her into a hug. The thin red head was nearly a half foot taller than Tawny but seemed little more than a girl when she broke into tears in Tawny's arms.

Slate and Brass spent the day speaking to the tribes before going with the original plan as Scarlett dictated. The two men went to Vanaheim to bring the Shadow Breakers and the refugees into the town's heart with Steel's auseklis.

It had been a long, sleepless night. There wasn't much left to do until Slate and Brass returned and they could put an end to the siege. The day passed with aching slowness. Tawny and Steel took Mica to the Bilskirnir to see the twins and get out of the university where the Purge War was inescapable. Tawny wanted to introduce Mica to her parents, so she tagged along to meet officially meet Hawk. Tawny was already calling the poor girl Gypsum's girlfriend.

Jett wandered the halls with Amethyst under his arm slowly making their way to the windows to watch Indigo take her nightly stroll. In a few weeks, they would find out the gender of their newest addition. Everything was riding on Scarlett's hunch being correct. They were just the distraction.

Fox came barreling around the corner of the hall and Jett pulled Amethyst out of his way.

"Hurry!" he said wild eyed before breaking into a run back in the direction he came.

They knew it was bad if Fox had come running. Scarlett bad.

The provosts gave the tyros weekends off from classes as if they would travel home to visit family. Mostly, they let them hold dances in the greenhouse. The zero tolerance ban on partying lifted for the time being.

Down the hall of windows where they always stood watch, the provosts leaned on the window frames. Flames flickered on drawn faces.

"Gypsum! He's here?" Tawny had the skirts of her scarlet caftan in her hands as she darted to the window beside Jett and Amethyst. "His bond —"

Tawny's eyes grew to saucers as she looked into the camp. Steel and Mica were a few feet behind her and elbowed their way to the windows. All the running around and shouts had drawn the attention of some of the tribal folk and tyros who clustered in the windows.

Scarlett. Gods be damned.

Scarlett had killed two men and Gypsum was riding on Lewt's back towards the woods. Scarlett was at their heels. She started throwing fireballs left and right. Tents everywhere ignited. Pandemonium broke out as the human portion of the army doused the catching flames. She slit throats, gutted grown men, and turned the tents closest to the castle into a raging inferno.

Indigo appeared as if out of nowhere and Scar tore the nix torque from her throat, squeezing her tight. She shoved Indigo hard into Lewt's flank and Lewt and Gypsum picked her up off her feet.

Dahlia was in one of those tents with Delta. She thought to stop Scarlett single handedly and was proven wrong. She didn't even blink when her blade flew true into Dahlia. She was dead.

Scarlett screamed. "RUN!"

Jett saw why Indigo wasn't helping and why no one's *calling* seemed to affect her, she wore Scarlett's open cuff around her wrist. Scarlett was facing off with more men. Amethyst gasped, clutching Jett's wrist.

"Did you know she could fight like that?" Amethyst asked, watching Scarlett draw attention away from Indigo fleeing on Lewt's back.

Most of the Stygians wore nix bracelets so her *calling* was ineffectual against them. She'd picked up blades off of one of the men she'd slaughtered. The path was clear so she shifted and broke into a run. Jett shouted out to her.

Tawny cried out. At the tree line, Lewt tried to stop as Ash toppled a tree in his path. Gypsum had the air knocked out of him and laid on the grass facing the night sky, unmoving. He sucked in a deep breath coughing and Jett heard Mica whimper. Gypsum's nose was bleeding freely.

While Scarlett faced off with a handful of Stygians, Sage snuck up behind her and bashed her head with the butt of his axe. She collapsed to the ground but was still moving. Scarlett's boots left gouges in the dirt as Sage dragged her down the path, he treated her little better than a dog.

Gypsum and Ash faced off. Chief's eyes fixed on Ash and it was apparent to all those in the windows he was trying not to look their way. Cygnus swept in with his charismatic smile and friendly manner. Gypsum backed down, still bound by his cuffs and took him into Indigo's tent.

Jett's mouth was ajar as he took in disbelieving breaths.

"We will free them. If they wanted to kill them, they would have," Amethyst said soothingly.

"Unless they plan to execute them as they did Pearl and Reed," Jett said, maddened by her optimism.

"What do we do?" Tawny asked, sounding dumbfounded.

"Thank the gods your mother and her husbands aren't here," Steel said, resting his chin on her forehead. "Indigo and Lewt might have made it through the woods."

Jett nodded. There was that. Gypsum was walked into Indigo's pink tasseled tent by Cygnus and Ash who exited a moment later to rejoin Canis and Sterling outside the command tents. Jett clenched his jaw watching Sage drag Scarlett around by a combination of her hair and her rapidly dirtying shirt.

Sage flung her between the tent flaps head first where Gypsum had been brought and went in after her.

"We are prepared for battle on your word."

Keen came up behind the group to lend his support. The other tribal heads were with him. Jett nodded without leaving the view of the Mélange army. He dry washed his face hoping a different scene would be waiting once he reopened his eyes.

Instead he saw a beautiful woman riding a chestnut mare that matched her thick hair that fell past her shoulders. The young woman knew precisely where she was headed. Gauzy lavender fabric in the Thrimilci style with a sweetheart neckline hugged her down to her shapely hips. Diamond Natt had a sweet soft look that hinted at an innocence she would be losing if it had not already been lost wearing that particular dress.

Jett tried very hard not to glance Mica's way. Gypsum's future laid with Mica, not Diamond. The greater families knew he was her paramour. It was a black stain on the future patriarch's reputation before he knew how to cultivate one...or that he needed one.

"Lewt is probably at the green house entrance," Steel offered. "Mica, would you like to join us?"

Mica's slender arms were wrapped around herself. Her fine-featured face wilted like a plucked rose left out in the sun without water on a hot Thrimilci day.

"No, thank you. I am very tired," she said dejectedly as she started down the hall, the tribes and tyros making room for her retreating form.

"Mica..."

Tawny let the young woman go. Hanging out with Gypsum's family wouldn't bring her any solace even if they all preferred her company to Diamond's when it came to their youngest cousin. No one else knew about Mica and Gypsum's relationship, but the family and his closest friend, Malachite. The hurt she felt at being replaced after such an intense whirlwind was unmistakable. It reminded Jett of Scarlett, but Gypsum was no Slate.

Dahlia's lifeless body was being carted off into another tent to be cared for. Diamond would likely mourn her mother and Cassiopeia would be out for revenge.

"We'll go check to see if Lewt braved the cliff a second time," Tawny said, rubbing her belly bump as Steel twirled the end of her hair at her back in his fingers.

Did a heavy shape slide down the side of Indi's tent, Jett squinted into the darkness and smoke.

Jett wrapped his arm around Amethyst's back to lace his fingers with hers at her hip. "Do you want a chair?" she asked, leaning her ebony locks against his shoulder.

He wouldn't be leaving this spot. Not with his sister there. Lewt had a lot of explaining to do which would probably end with, *no one* lets *Scarlett do anything.*

"No thanks, babe."

Two plain sisters with absolutely no talents whatsoever but pleasant personalities... that would've been a sweet life.

Jackal moved to stand the spot opposite Amethyst. "I would not put anything past what she can accomplish."

"She can't possibly get them into worse trouble. At least Scarlett fulfilled her vow to Quick this way."

"What vow is this?"

Jackal asked and Jett gave him a rueful grin before turning back. "It's moot now."

Camp began to stir. A few Guardians that were also Stygian Knights, stared at Indigo's tent and walked casually towards it. Whatever gave the men pause didn't reach those in the castle. A pair of men stood further down the path with eyes on the pink tasseled tent.

Sterling, Ash, and Diamond broke away from Cygnus where Ruby joined them and were headed towards Indigo's old tent.

Scarlett erupted from the tent flaps covered in blood from her nose to her chest, her hand firmly grasped Gypsum's as she yanked him into a run. Her eyes were hot coals peering out above the gore. Jett said a silent prayer as they all held their breath.

"Look out!" his own voice echoed in his ears as he hung out the window.

Delta had been lying in wait until Scarlett thought she was in the clear. Her whip cracked out and Scarlett's feet flew out from under her. It didn't burn. Scarlett's elemental fire winked out as she gripped her throat where she'd been slammed onto her back.

Jett noticed the end of the whip was silver and when Delta loosed it from Scarlett's neck, it remained. A magnetic nix torque. Gypsum had no defense against the air ropes that bound him without Scarlett's help. Delta hurried to her while she gasped for air and locked the pewter around Scarlett's throat.

Ash snapped a torque around Gypsum's throat and gave the lead to Sterling. Diamond took it from him and appeared to say a few angry words before the three marched away to disappear into one of the greater family tents.

"No!" Jackal's shout was drowned out by an inhuman roar that climbed from the depths of the castle.

Slate was back.

CHAPTER 37
SLATE

The battle for Valla had been bloody.

Valla was the seat of power and their retreat had been harried until they reached the mountains. We did not have the man power to chase them to the Straumr palace or the Tio's which were both under Canis's control.

"Regretting burning down my headquarters?"

Lera's slow smoky way of speaking used to make my cock go flat to my stomach, now it only stirred. I was Lera's khoraz. Torch did not understand that until she was forced into being mine.

Perhaps it was the charred remains that opened to an abyss several stories below street level or it was the burned buildings they had ignited to root out the Stygians like rats, but the world smelled like smoke and death.

I tossed the stone from my hand, listening to it hit every rafter on the way down and rose from my crouch.

"The only regrets I carry are those that kept me from being with my wife."

Cordillera had always looked decades younger than her forty-odd years, but it had been a hard winter on my longtime lover. I dusted my hands as I turned to her. She was almost a foot and a half shorter than I was. Her dark chin length waves had a coating of soot from the fires, her high olive cheek bone was smeared where she had wiped perspiration with the back of her hand.

She arched a thick manicured brow above her narrow dark eyes. "Her reasoning is sound. That must be why you and Brass did not go after her."

Debris settled under my boots with each step. I had been healed, but my clothes were stretched from my shift. I had torn men apart with my clawed hands and fangs. Blood coated my skin, mine and others, hours after the battle had been won. I needed to walk. Brass understood. Torch would not activate her bonds, but she was on the island. To have her so close was maddening.

Lera was head to toe blood red leather on her petite frame and armed to her sly red lips. It was an outfit she preferred in the bedroom. I had not let her wear that outfit with me since I was eighteen and being submissive to anyone was no longer permissible in my world. She understood. I was part beast. If I was bound, it was against my will.

Scarlett changed everything. I would do whatever the cursed woman asked.

"So you say," I agreed, moving past her.

We took them at dawn when they were switching shifts. Only fifty men were killed, but they had holed up in part of the star formation fortress hence the fires to smoke them out. Not many tribes were there. They had assumed no one would take them from the inside. From the outside, Valla's heart was impregnable.

She caught my wrist, and I stopped. Old habits died hard.

"Eat. You are no good to anyone, much less her, if you are weakened."

Muted moonlight twinkled in her deep-set eyes. I could scent Chafer lurking near. Cordillera broke the one vow she ever made in remarrying. It was good to see her in relative happiness, though for now, the part of her that collected young lovers was gone along with her father. She had watched from the Vanaheim's covered balcony as they marched Spinel out and demanded that she give up and turn over Brass and me. It was only a small relief he lived but still so far out of reach.

I grunted in answer. I had filled myself on the blood of men. I wanted for nothing but Torch.

Brass activated his Shadow Breaker tracker long enough for me to know he was looking for me. A strong pull that could make your feet move involuntarily and then it stopped. Torch would've felt it with her bond.

"Come out, Chafer. I am not going to run off now that we have Valla back," Lera teased, and the sharp featured man detached from the shadows at the opening of the dead-end alley.

His two long seaxes crossed over his ripped back. Chafer was built like a blade, high angled brows, angular jaw, all sinew and lean muscle. For some unfathomable reason, he and Torch got on well. There was no love lost between us.

"Best not. I am counting on Scarlett to reclaim her beast so she can domesticate him and lose all appeal to you," Chafer said, lithely walking to us and pressing his lips into a firm line at her hand touching me.

She dropped it and navigated the rubble to the end of the alley with Chafer at her back. I wondered if at their ceremony if he stood just behind her then too.

As in Mabon and Elivagar, the people in Valla danced in the cobbled roads with one another, wine and ale flowing freely. You could tell who had fought by their sooty faces and matted hair that had dried after battle.

The celebration was what I avoided. The blow to the Stygians was to be rejoiced, but I preferred to drink my wine in the obscenely white bed I had chosen for my wife while she straddled me as naked as the day the Mother made her. She would flash her alluring smile with dreamy eyes, her caramel waves slinking over her silky tan skin as she rocked herself.

"Dibs."

"We agreed. No calls on first dibs," I said, feeling Brass come up on my right.

Valla had not been ransacked, and the town had run fairly smooth under the Stygian Knights. Still, Guardians did not like change and they did not like going against tradition. Having the few tribal folk inside the town was a mistake as was shutting the gates inside the star formation town. What Guardians disliked most was having their freedom taken away.

We had locked the portal gate and left the outside gates closed for the time being. It was only a matter of time before Scarlett fulfilled her end and life returned to our new normal.

"With that image in your mind, I am willing to change our rules. Tell me, in this fantasy does she make you a sandwich after you finish your drink?" Brass jested.

"After she is through pleasing me," I told him wryly, and Brass laughed.

At the hexagon heart of town, bonfires were lit before the portal gate. The flames cast deep shadows on the free-standing stone gate with sculptured tree branches twisting into a sculpture of a woman, hands extended to form branches that eerily reminded me of Wren.

Shadow Breakers used pieces of the buildings we burnt as kindling. The smell of roasting Cornish hens and rosemary mixed with the sweat and blood which did nothing to diminish my hunger. Many bairn would be made that night.

The thought settled uneasily in the pit of my stomach. Scarlett carried my bairn. I should've been with her. *We* should be with her. Leaving me with nothing but a note had gotten old after the first time, offering my first taste at true pain, the like of which I had never known.

"At dawn. We need you to begin the march to Valla University. Will they be ready?" I called up to the pair walking ahead.

Lera did not turn. "I am Grand Mistress of the Shadow Breakers. I say they will be ready, so they shall."

Chafer and Lera blended in with the crowd. Hopper had joined them for the battle. Mirage was with child and Rikke was more possessive than ever and Hopper felt good about leaving her to her husband.

Hopper gave us a nod with eyes that matched the darkening sky and brought over two mugs of troll ale for us and clacked our mugs with his before settling to watch the partiers. He folded his heavy tattooed arms across his stocky chest.

"You are not celebrating," Hopper noted. "Worrying about Scarlett?"

"Aren't we always?" Brass said with a wry smile.

"She is strong. I would not worry so much. Time and again, she has proven herself a surprisingly capable woman."

I grunted. Hopper was the first of five captains within the Shadow Breakers. Brass and I made up the third and fourth, the second was dancing with a man a decade younger than herself by the bonfire and our fifth had died in battle. We were all close.

"She is stronger and more fragile than she seems," I added.

Hopper nodded, his dirty blonde hair sliding down his back. "I understand that sentiment."

Brass left us to retrieve us our dinner. Hopper was not the kind of man who needed to fill the air with needless conversation. He was content to share in the silence. Men had died today.

The exhaustion of the day began to sink into my bones with a weariness that was not entirely from the battle. Worrying about our rogue wife was a full-time job. Not for the first time, having a second husband was working to my benefit. Another man who understood.

Brass brought over full hens on spits for each of us and we ate just outside of the merriment. "We could join them. We did win after all."

"I may come back with you to get my sister out of the eye of the storm," Hopper said out of the blue.

I did not blame him. I would not want my sibling at Valla U if I could prevent it.

Pain and anguish nearly as bad as when Peak had abused her stemmed through the bond that shot through my system like a lightning strike. A low wail tore from my throat and my mug seemed to fall in slow motion to the cobbles.

Scarlett.

What would cause such a strange mix of emotions? A terrible burning pain with a bottomless rage and hurt that I could not begin to understand.

"Is it her?" Brass asked, blocking out the bonfires with his face just before he dropped his own mug and grit his teeth.

"Where the fuck is Quick?" I asked through clenched teeth.

"I will get him," Hopper said and was gone before we could tell him to meet us at the portal.

"She is to the north," Brass said somberly as we cut through the smiling crowd that seemed to mock us.

If she was back at Valla University before she had a chance to activate the project, that was the very worst-case scenario.

Quick's brows were at his hairline when he shoved aside a couple latched to one another at the mouth by the gate.

"What is wrong?" he asked, scanning our faces. "She... she is okay, right?"

Scarlett had a way of getting under the skin of the most unexpected men. For once, Quick's love for her was not amorous though he did not understand it. He had never been close to a woman he had not bedded who was not related to him.

"We need to find out. She is back at the university," Brass said as I slid the auseklis into a tiny slot at the base of the portal.

"I will lock it," Hopper said, coming up behind us. "I told Lera you were leaving."

I did not acknowledge that he spoke. Scarlett consumed my mind. She was fighting. Her thrill stemmed through the bond in a way I had felt before, but there was a resignation to it. It was that resignation that worried me most.

The vine carved door like all the others that lined the long portal room of Valla U from tapestry to tapestry shut after Quick. It was too quiet as if everyone in the old castle held its breath. Brass picked up his pace, walking through the yellow stone halls dimly lit by the sconces at such a late hour.

Pain assaulted me so viciously I roared, and Quick fell to his knees covering his ears. Brass staggered and ran. My face twitched while Scarlett's uncontrollable emotions saturated me. I nearly collided with Brass when he slowed to push his way through the spectators that crowded the windows that faced the lawn the Mélange army was camped on.

Jett was blinking rapidly to dry his eyes. "I —" he cut short and whipped his head back to the lawn.

Cords stood out in his throat as he swallowed and I walked in a trance to the window. Her pain through the bond felt like my own. Brass came up beside me as we stood in the window beside Jett's.

Scarlett was dragged by her hair to a tree stump that Delta had called over from the discarded wood by the siege machines. Scarlett coughed, blood coated her mouth and jaw, down to her neckline and was all over her hands.

What had she gotten herself into?

Sage stumbled from the tent they held Indigo hostage in with his hands over his lap. I could hear what he screamed with my heightened senses.

Canis strode from the command tent with Cygnus. Ash waited looking in a stupor at the scene. The men surrounded Sage and then traveled as a pack to where Delta stood like a wrathful goddess over her stepdaughter.

I was dizzy with rage and pain.

"What did he say?" Jett asked, fearing the answer.

"She cut off his manhood and ate parts of it," I responded in an expressionless tone.

Brass could see what was in her mind with her at the edge of camp being held so we would see her. Sage tried to take the whip from Delta, but she held fast.

"Fucking khoraz whore," I repeated before anyone asked what Sage shouted in Torch's face.

She spat weakly at him. Ever defiant, our wife.

Delta passed the whip to Sage and moved to stand where Canis waited. Commotion with Ash and Cygnus drew the eye.

"Scarlett killed Dahlia," Brass whispered.

My Torch.

Sage unfurled the length of black leather and cracked it. Sharp pain lanced through the bond as Scarlett's body jolted where she was hunched over the tree stump. Blood covered the front of Sage's pants, and I tried to get a grasp on our combined anger.

"I cannot leave her there," I said roughly.

The beast was not just rattling his cage, he was gnawing the bars, scratching every inch for weakness. I might be able to get to her before they killed me.

Jett's face reddened in anger as the muscle leapt in his jaw. I flinched as Scarlett's pain was my own when the whip landed across her back.

"You think I don't want to save my sister? That I haven't wanted to save Indigo?"

Brass stepped between us and watched Scarlett jolt as Sage struck her again. Macabre blossoms bloomed on the dirty grey shirt. His face was a mask of hatred as his arm raised again. Sterling shuffled Diamond to a tent they used when staying at the camp where Dahlia's corpse must have been kept.

Brass's breaths came quicker as he gripped the frame of the window. "Tell them, Love. Tell them, please," he whispered to himself.

Canis stepped forward and caught Sage's upswing. Sage's round eyes flared until he saw who stopped him and pulled his axe, letting the whip fall to the floor. Scarlett's back was a zig zagging of open gashes from the repeated whip bites.

"Return my grandniece and we will prevent any more harm from befalling your leader," Canis said, using his amplified voice.

Quick grabbed Jett shirt in his fists, spinning to face him. "Indigo got away? Where is she?" he asked, barely getting the words out in a rasp. His eyes darted back and forth searching his bond out with her.

"She ran free of the woods. She will be at the greenhouse if she wasn't caught," Jett said, unsure of how to feel about the exchange of sisters.

Sage put his booted foot on Scarlett's oozing wounds and she stifled a cry of pain. Sage brandished his axe detailing exactly what would happen if we failed to trade back the twin sisters. Quick rubbed his jaw, his scent pained and reluctant much like all of ours.

Scarlett shifted her head and addressed Canis. "Why bother with the trade? All you need is me," she said with Sage's brown leather boot grinding into her shoulder blade, forcing the wounds to pulse with pain.

"Because you have either lost or given birth to the Dagr heirs. Indigo likely carries a barghest son in her belly," Canis said stiffly.

Scarlett worked saliva into her mouth. "Delve."

Canis looked down at her before gesturing to Sage to let her up. Sage grabbed the hair at her nape and yanked her to her feet. She was raised up on her tip toes as Canis removed her nix torque, giving her a look so she knew Sage's axe at her throat was not an idle threat. Canis placed his palm on her flat belly, the blood from her back dampening the tattered shirt front.

Canis stood head and shoulders over her; she was dwarfed between the Var men. Canis scanned Scarlett's face.

"How do I know it is the Dagr's and not the Regn's?" he asked her, replacing the nix torque.

The physical fight was drained completely from her, Sage's vicious hold on her hair was the only thing holding her upright. Torch could still give an impressive death stare.

"Because Brass is sterile. I've only lain with my husbands and we've actively tried to conceive a son to activate Storm Natt's project. Bring an interrogator if you must, but Ash knows I had to try to conceive during my first ovulation because of a blood vow I swore to him," she said, slumping.

Canis called out to Ash with his amplified voice and the Prime came trotting like a lap dog.

Canis asked Ash if Scarlett spoke the truth and he verified it, removing his nix cuff himself and delving. "She must be punished," Ash said firmly.

Canis straightened and appeared to contemplate the situation as Sage grudgingly set down his axe. He turned towards the university and amplified his voice once more.

"It would appear the exchange is acceptable. Thank you for the remaining pieces and conveniently supplying us with not only the leader of the Red Seconds, but the pregnant wife of Patriarch Dagr," Canis said, inclining his head to the windows. Shadows hid his hooded eyes from the flickering braziers.

He looked back to Ash and Sage. "Mrs. Tio, you understand the predicament I am put in. You disfigured our heir and murdered the Prime's mother."

"You scarred my husband and killed my parents, grandparents, and my husbands' parents. I still owe you a few," she said defiantly.

Cygnus stood with Ruby at the paths that intersected between where Dahlia's body had been taken and where Scarlett stood. He appeared to be trying to placate her. Sterling disappeared with Diamond into another of the greater family tents while Delta strode back to where the siege machines were.

"Be that as it may, these acts require balance," Canis told her.

I relayed their interactions to the others without being asked. Amethyst clutched onto a miserable-looking Jett.

When Delta reappeared, two black cloaked Guardians with the silver interlocking triangle of the Valla Guardians carried a construction between them.

"No!" Brass shouted, jerking forward so Quick had to catch him before he climbed out through the window.

Scarlett did not recognize the boards that fastened together. The two Guardians beat the legs of the stocks into the soil in front of the university and Scarlett's fear surfaced through the bond.

"An eye for an eye, Second," Canis said matter of fact as he nodded to the two men.

Sage pulled a knife from its sheath and sliced the fabric from her body, occasionally cutting into her skin with his negligent wielding. She curled around herself to hide her body.

"Be glad you are already with child so those who use you will not fill your belly with a bastard," Canis said as Sage forced her head and hands into the stocks.

Canis melted a metal plate on the side so there was no need for a lock. "I will heal you should you need it. We would not want someone to get carried away and risk your pregnancy."

He left her with that and strode back to his command tent leaving her with Sage and Ash. Scarlett's panic surged, and I turned away from the scene, pressing myself to the wall, squeezing my eyes shut. They wanted to humiliate her and take away our morale. It was working.

"We'll go free her. She is right there. We could do it together," Brass said with an edge of insanity fueled by the terror Scarlett could not quell.

I gave a curt nod, swallowing hard against the helplessness. Scarlett's legs had given out, and she hung limply as Sage unbuckled his pants, taunting her about Indigo. Ash did not know what Sage had done to Indigo. He looked at Sage with disgust that he masked before Sage could witness it. Brass was too consumed with Scarlett's emotions to confirm or deny Sage's boasts.

"I am always up for a Scarlett rescue," Quick told them.

"Let's go," Jett said in a rush.

The tribal heads around us readied weapons with no intention of being left behind and knowing full well most of us would die getting to her. There was no way they would let Scarlett go. They'd be planning for us to make a half-baked rescue attempt and yet we couldn't stop ourselves.

Ash seemed to be faced with an internal conflict and set his hand on Sage's wrist before he could plunge himself into my mate. Sage gave him a furious look and Ash appeared to be at a loss with himself.

"I... want her," he uttered.

Ruby was marching down the path *calling* a chair in her wake with a book tucked under her arm. She walked directly behind Sage and Ash and unfolded her chair next to the stocks and sat down. She opened her book, *The Three Musketeers,* and began to read aloud.

The gods cursed Straumr boy was still in love with Torch. Relief drained his body of its fight as Sage gave his grandmother an annoyed look. Ruby was spoiling his fun.

The impending torture and beating had sapped Torch completely; with the relief of Ruby putting a stop to her abuse, she promptly passed out. Neither man would force themselves on Torch with Matriarch Geol sitting beside the stocks, facing them down.

They turned from Scarlett's slack form and walked back to the command tent. Ash glanced over his shoulder at us in the window, his eyes flashing with anger and irritation. He knew he had a weakness for her and he had shown us all how deep that frailty went.

Ruby set down her book and gestured for a young woman to come forth. The girl carried a wash basin and rags. Ruby trickled water over Torch's back and dabbed at the jagged gashes that striped her back.

"Go to Indigo. If anything changes, I'll activate my bond," Amethyst promised. "She's out of harm's way for the time being. Take advantage."

Quick was practically hopping from foot to foot. "I can go to her alone."

"We're coming," Brass said with resignation.

"She is here!" Quick shouted to no one in particular as Brass, Jett, and I tried to keep pace.

Torch was pregnant. She was going to have my bairn. The only thing standing between her and abuse was her grandmother who refused to choose a side. Brass jogged at my side; his brow permanently furrowed as we both tried to reconcile what Sage must have already tried with our wife in order for her to have been able to mutilate his manhood.

"He didn't," Brass murmured so only I would hear. "Not with Indigo. Not yet."

But the intention existed.

Jett was a mass of conflicting emotions. We lost Gypsum and Scarlett, but Indigo was freed. Not even Quick could experience the joy he should have felt at getting his betrothed back.

We were a step behind Quick when we reached Steel and Tawny disappearing behind the blossom trees. Lewt was blood covered and completely nude as he came into view. Quick whirled around to the trees with us on his heels.

Indigo, windblown, but otherwise unharmed. There was something off about her as if her mind was not right.

I could smell the salt of Quick's tears. "Dove," he managed.

Indigo's pupils dilated to nearly consume the soft pale blue of her eyes when she focused on Quick. She was a rousen addict. Quick was too distracted by her return to see her state, but Brass murmured so only I would hear.

"We have to get rousen. Her mind is shutting down."

Indigo fell to her knees and started screaming incoherent shrieks. Quick fell down in front of her trying to pull her hands away from her hair to keep her from tearing it out. She poured so much sadness and pain into her screeching a knot formed in my stomach. Jett moved beside her along with Steel and Tawny who hovered above their kneeling forms.

"Indi," Jett said thickly as he delved into her.

Brass sucked in a deep breath before moving to stand beside Quick and whispered in his ear. "She has to weaned off rousen."

Quick looked at him angrily as if Brass lied out of malice. Jett had heard him and got to his feet.

"Ash has some in his office. It's marawacian rousen cocktail he was giving Scarlett. That must be what she was on to keep her subdued," he said stroking Indigo's head one last time before taking off at a run.

Indigo's nails bit so deeply into her palms I could scent her coppery blood. Her eyes fluttered and Quick scooped her up as she collapsed.

"It does not make any sense," Quick said, getting to his feet unconcerned with hiding his tears. "If she thought I had died, the only other man she would have been with would be Sterling. He would not have to drug her."

Tawny and Steel clung to one another and Lewt began to slink away. I grabbed his shoulder, digging my fingers into his skin to be sure he would not move.

"I doubt Sterling used it on her, Quick," I told him cautiously. "I believe he claimed her. They did it to keep her from fighting back. She was likely despondent when you died. They would have started to give it to her so she would not feel your death," I continued.

Quick clutched her tightly to his chest. "Well, that shit is fucking over," he ground out.

"There comes a great deal of responsibility with weaning a woman off of rousen. Are you prepared for the repercussions? People are not always gracious when they become addicted to a person. She would be your khoraz."

Steel cursed. Quick glared at me as if I spoke nonsense.

"I want to take care of her for the rest of her life," Quick snapped.

"And if the child is not yours?" I asked.

Quick looked down at the swell of her belly. "It could be."

"And if it is not," I pressed, not wanting him to be disappointed or worse, should the child be Sterling's.

"You love Brass's sons."

I gave Quick a wry smile. Comfort was not one of my stronger suits.

CHAPTER 38

INDIGO

Silver. What a dangerous man to be addicted to.

He cried for me. He questioned me on rousen when my mind prevented me from being able to tell a few white lies to spare us both and he had cried. Not a single tear or two, but a deluge of hot salty tears that trickled off his five o'clock shadow. He begged for forgiveness for not being there and not protecting me. And I hated him for it.

Before I'd fallen deep within the rousen's grasp, Slate had updated me on Scarlett. Just when I thought I couldn't fall any further, I did. He also informed me that they would be weaning me off the rousen with Slate carefully monitoring the dosage since he himself was a rousen addict as was Scarlett and he had weaned her off.

Silver had then taken me to the men's showers and warned everyone who came near that if they dared enter that he'd personally push their bodies out through the Valla fourth story windows and out onto the lawn.

My rousen addled mind wanted to make love, but Silver had thoroughly washed me reveling in my swollen breasts and belly. He had taken so much care to dry my hair and had a jar of my lotion from home that he used liberally over my skin. Only then did he take me to one of the unused bedrooms in the men's second year wing and threatened even more people about entering without his express permission.

Four beds were nestled in the alcoves of the room, but only one was made up with a ridiculous amount of pillows and a bowl of stew waiting. I didn't want food, I wanted Silver. He was so hard I swore he was beginning to turn purple, but only after I finished my stew did he take me in his arms and kiss me.

Patchouli, sandalwood, and cedar would stick to my skin for days afterwards.

The first time was *so* fast.

Crying and only two minutes until he spilled his seed? Who was the man impersonating my Silver Regn?

He asked if the boy could be his and I told him it could only be his or Sterling's. He asked me how long I'd waited until I slept with Sterling after our bond snapped and I told him it was that same day. He wouldn't speak to me for a time afterwards, but I made it up to him. I had never been the one getting turned down. I wasn't sure Silver *could* turn me down.

He confessed he had not been with another woman since me five months past. I should have felt something... anything... Later, I felt tremendous guilt.

Even on rousen, I traced Silver's jagged black Celtic tattoos with my index finger as our limbs were intertwined. He kept giving me an inexplicable look, as if he blinked I would disappear.

He hated me on rousen. He wanted my biting retorts and sharp tongue. He begged me to move into the Regn manor when we ended the Purge War. I couldn't form words. All that worked was my pleasure center — to give and receive it. I wanted him to take me every way a man could, and he did. The first time was a fluke. He was ready to last the night and did.

When I woke up tucked against his body, I felt sick. The rousen's strongest effects had worn off, and my soul had been laid bare. Maybe I would've told him all I'd been through with time, but his prying had unearthed things I couldn't face about myself much less admit to. The bottom line was that I wasn't ready, and he hadn't thought about how I felt.

"Dove?" he rasped in a sleep thick voice.

"I'm going to shower. I want to see what the status on Scarlett is."

And to see what my freedom had cost my sister all for mine and Silver's happiness. She was a mother of two, she couldn't be risking herself.

I *called* a white knit robe with tiny pink blossoms he'd procured for me and slid it onto my bare shoulders with my back to him. I could catch his scent before he roped his arms around me and kissed my ear.

"I will go with you. By the Mother, how I missed you, Indigo," he whispered.

More guilt.

"I can shower alone. All the men are probably stinking because you put the fear of the gods in them."

I wriggled free of his strong reassuring arms that radiated far more love than I deserved and slipped out of the room leaving him stunned.

I'd been on rousen for months. My self-control when it was low in my system was excellent. I didn't need to be restrained.

The halls were empty so early before breakfast. Before my shower, I decided to check on Scarlett. There was a barrier in my mind preventing me from accepting what had gone on. How could I have been so useless and inept? If I had paused and had her back instead of fleeing like a coward, she could've been with us.

I slowed as I came down the corridor pulling my robe tighter at my chest as I continued to the windows. Keen and Rikke were with Brass and Slate as well as three Lycans, two male Gorgons, Lewt, and Adal. Jett and Steel were huddled in the window beside Slate's.

The men and the single female Lycan swerved their gazes to me as I approached. Rikke was the first to reach me and gave me a very inappropriate full kiss on the mouth, his whiskers tickled my nose and I stifled a ludicrous giggle.

"We were all very worried about you," he said, failing to stop the purr that emanated in his throat.

"I'm as good as can be expected," I said, blushing and keeping the front of my robe closed tight. "I hear a double congratulation is in order."

Rikke's feline grin spread proudly. "A human woman. I would not have predicted that before I met you."

My blush deepened and Keen saved me pulling me in for an embrace. The Wemic man wasn't as jovial as he normally was, the twinkle in his golden eyes gone.

"You make a lovely pregnant woman, Indigo."

"Thank you, Keen. I hear your cub is due any day now."

"Any day," he agreed, nodding.

I gave a tight smile and inclined my head to my brothers-in-law and the other tribal heads I hadn't met before. Lewt gave me a brief hug and offered a solemn apology before I reached Jett and Steel. The two cocooned me with their bodies as I faced out towards the lawn. My bare feet were cool on the polished floor that seemed to turn colder and swarm over me like breaking through thin ice.

She was naked and asleep as was Ruby who sat guard in an uncomfortable wrought-iron chair she must have taken from my tent. Tears pricked my eyes. I was fornicating with Silver and she was half dead.

"Scarlett!" I shouted, sniffling. "I'm so sorry."

Jett sighed. "Don't waste your breath, we tried —"

The top of her head shifted, and she furrowed her brow trying to look up at me. "You made it," she said with a raw voice. "I hope your bond isn't active."

She was pretending to be asleep so the men wouldn't address her. I could understand why she wouldn't want to engage in conversation as helplessly vulnerable as she was, but I couldn't stop myself.

I shook my head stupidly, and the men gathered in the windows. "Not mine. You shouldn't have done that," I said, choking on my words.

In the sunburst light of the sky, her back was ribboned with crusted wounds and bruises, but Ruby had cleansed what she could without healing. I could see her upper lip at this angle and her cheekbones which rounded, so I knew she was smiling before I heard it in her voice. Her hair fell to the sides of her face so I could only see a hint of the black finger imprints Sage undoubtedly left from choking her.

"I couldn't very well leave you there. Quick must be ecstatic," she said shifting her blood-shot eyes to search him. "Still sleeping? Doesn't surprise me," she teased in a raw voice.

She was joking and smiling while she was certainly facing death. Scar was naked and prone in the stocks with a dozen men above watching her and numerous behind her. I was completely baffled by her cavalier attitude.

"He's awake," I said stupidly.

"Did you tell them?" she asked her, sore throat strangling.

I licked my lips. "Not yet." I turned to Slate and Brass, stepping from the window. Both men were already looking to me as well as the tribesmen and women. "She wanted me to tell you that no matter what happens, she will never ever stop loving you... both. If we all are different people when this is through, she will search the ends of the earth for you, through time if she has to." I swallowed, unable to meet their eyes, knowing what my presence to relay that message cost them.

"You promise to take care of my sons?" she asked. "If something goes wrong and I —" she cut short, struggling to keep her voice steady.

She looked towards the window Brass and Slate stood in for the first time, but for only an instant. Scarlett couldn't control her emotions and her deep despair broke through when she looked at the men she loved. I had absorbed her empath abilities while she laid the path for my escape.

"Whenever I try to do right by you, I end up taking things away. Every single time. It's terribly frustrating," she said with a hint of humor. "If they... I won't make it easy on them. If... Brass has two, he can share. He's better at it than you are." I could hear the smile in her voice.

She stopped after her admission, and I swiped at my chin where the tears had congregated before spilling onto my robe. "I promise," I shouted against the lump in my throat, trying to ease her mind.

Her head bobbed. If she sniffled I couldn't hear it from so far away. "Good. Don't let them do anything stupid either. Only one parent is allowed be an idiot. I think we all know who that is."

"Slate?" Jett offered in a voice I barely recognized.

I was astonished to find that I could smile, some of the tribesmen even chuckled. Scarlett's light golden brown hair was shivering, she was sobbing. The impotency of the situation became glaringly clear.

Ruby had awoken sometime during our conversation and folded her hands over a novel she laid in her lap. Her back was to us so she faced the camp. They would've been able to see everything from here. I couldn't believe how far they could see and how clearly.

"Torch," Slate called in a tone I had no idea he was capable of using. It only made her cry harder.

"Love, we know how it ends," Brass said, sounding resigned.

Scarlett's hanging hands clenched. "That's exactly why I had no choice. I can't live in a world where I didn't try everything to save him."

Slate's prophecy. Arms wound around my hips, but instead of leaning into Silver, I pulled away and went to find a shower before breakfast.

"Indigo!"

Silver was wounded, but so was I. Letting him give me comfort when Scarlett was trapped out there made me hate us both all over again.

CHAPTER 39
GYPSUM

Sterling left us alone in another ridiculously elaborate tent. He could come back at any moment, but when Diamond started tearing, I had to comfort her.

"Scarlett is safe for now. Ruby is keeping watch over her," Diamond murmured into my chest as her arms wound around my waist. "My parents..." she choked off. "I have missed you so very much."

I ran my hand down her soft chestnut hair. "I've missed you too. You saved my life. A lot of lives with your little trick. If I hadn't followed you into the portal room, I don't know if my parents would be alive as well as countless others."

She shifted her head against my chest and blinked gleaming lightest green eyes at me. "Make love to me, Chief," she whispered as she pulled my face down to hers.

I kissed her chastely before taking her hands away from my face. She knit her brows together.

"I'm sorry, Diamond. I can't be your lover anymore. I still love you, but you're married and I have to think about —"

"Mica. I have heard she joins you in the windows. Keep her but keep me too." Diamond lifted onto her tiptoes again to kiss me and my stomach flipped as I took a small step away.

"I can't. I owe her my loyalty. I'm in love with her. When this is over, I'm going to ask her to marry me," I confessed.

"It is not over yet and you are here with me," she persisted.

I clasped her hands at my chest. "Diamond. You're not listening. I appreciate the risk you took, but you and I... this affair is through. I can't destroy my family's name any more."

"I am in mourning. I need comfort. Comfort only *you* can provide," she insisted, drawing her brows down.

I nodded and changed my hold on her hands. No one told Diamond no.

"I know. We're all in mourning, but I can't be your paramour any longer. I *can* be your friend," I offered, giving her a small reassuring smile.

Diamond stepped back, snatching her hands away. "Not good enough. I have not lain with my husband since our wedding because he saves himself for *your* cousin."

She took in a deep breath swelling her chest at her low-cut neckline. The dress was for me. It was in the loose flowing fabrics of Thrimilci which she rarely wore.

I softened. "Diamond," I coaxed her back to me, but she stomped out of the tent.

My nix torque was looped around the post of the bed. There was a copper tub, but I couldn't fill it without help. Sterling was careful to make sure there were no weapons I could fashion from things in the tent. I contented myself to sit on the floor and lean back against the bed frame.

I didn't rest for long before Sterling entered the tent with Ash, Canis, and Diamond who hung back by the tent flaps. I clambered to my feet wondering what they had planned for me.

"Diamond has come up with a solution to all our problems. I am astonished one of us had not thought of it sooner, but she is confident she can win you back. For coming up with a reasonable answer to our little conundrum, we are giving her you." Canis stepped back and Ash took his place to stand in front of me.

I ignored them all to look at Diamond. She didn't really want it, she was angry and feeling desperate, but she'd regret it. She wouldn't meet my eyes.

"Diamond?"

"It will not hurt. I doubt you will come to any harm. Your family will follow to save you. They are predictable in that way," Ash said almost soothingly.

"Wait—"

Diamond's words were cut short when Ash removed my nix torque and the combined calling of Canis and Sterling held me in place so Ash's hands clamped down on my head.

"Do not worry. We will put him to sleep and you may stay with him until he awakens," Sterling said flatly. "I only agreed to this so Sage and Delta will be kept away from Scarlett..." Sterling's violet eyes flared as he cast Diamond a look over his shoulder. "It is the least I can do."

"Scarlett is mine," Ash whispered so only I heard it and Sterling would with his heightened hearing.

His piercing gaze intensified, and I held him flipping through my memories like someone thumbing through a book looking for a certain earmark. Suddenly the rapid images stopped, and it felt as if an intense pressure was forcing my head together. It wasn't painful, only uncomfortable until it faded.

My eyes fluttered shut as the most beautiful caramel skinned woman rushed to my side. "I am so sorry." She sniffled as I fell leadenly into a dreamless sleep.

FORTY

The temperature rose with the sun so I stopped shivering and could go back to pretending like I was sleeping so the others wouldn't try to speak to me. I couldn't imagine my situation getting any worse unless they gave me over to Sage, but I had a hard time believing Ash would let that happen.

"Ruby, you need to get ready for the day." Cygnus's voice didn't hold the condescending tone it usually did.

Ruby leaned forward enough so her big dark eyes that reminded me of Amethyst's checked my expression. She swallowed and let her distressed look melt away to coolness.

"I shall be back shortly," she said, rising, and I felt a thin robe placed over my shoulders.

It did little for the surge of panic I felt at being left alone. I tried not to fight in futility against the stock I'd been put in and to keep my whimpering to a minimum.

"We will release you shortly, Scarlett," Cygnus said in a stern tone, but no anger was in it.

Hope was a dangerous thing. My hope had been through Dante's Inferno and now it was back, a glutton for punishment. But to lose hope was to die.

It was more likely that releasing me didn't mean I'd be their pretty prisoner as Indigo had been. I didn't have the rapport with them that Indigo had. I held no loyalties for them nor them for me. I was on my own. *Worse.* I was a slave to their every whim. I wouldn't let them hurt Gypsum and they knew my compassion was my greatest strength and greatest weakness.

I could hear footsteps of men over the scoured grass that had been fried in Indigo and Lewt's escape. Slate and Brass's anger flared through the bond and I could feel Jett's helplessness and frustration. I tried to get my emotions under control, I knew what I felt influenced them and if they tried to rescue me, they'd be killed.

"Stay still," Ash said in a toneless voice. "I do not want to have to threaten you if you should try to run again."

I couldn't *call* a lick. I couldn't sleep while terrified one of the Mélange wouldn't care Ruby was there and force itself on me. I'd seen them rutting in full view when we were brought in. I didn't think I could stand much less fight. I couldn't even scream. Sage had damaged my throat so the hole my head was through rubbed roughly on my tender skin.

"Okay," I managed, and watched Sage out of the corner of my eye as he melted the latch.

The top half of the stock lifted and Ash caught me under my arms. He adjusted the robe as I staggered, trying to use my own legs so the tribal heads wouldn't think I was weak. I couldn't. I needed to be healed. Even the light fabric on my back felt like salt in the wounds from Sage's public whipping.

"Was there ever a time you thought you could love me?"

I whimpered as Ash tried to hold me so he wouldn't irritate any of my lacerations, but it wasn't possible and everywhere his hands grazed felt like his fingers were made of hot pokers.

Everything was on the line. I could be nice if I had to. Gypsum's life may have depended on it.

"Once or twice," I admitted, "when I first met you."

Before I'd laid eyes on Slate or Brass, I could have loved Ash before I'd known his true nature. All before.

My head swam from the blood loss and the knob the Crathode left after mouthing off to Sage pulsed. Ash's eyes were on the windows behind me when he held me up and lifted my crusted chin. I tried to pull away but I could hardly keep my head upright.

"Dagr... your wife has returned. Have you celebrated by whoring?" Ash antagonized Slate, who was likely getting ready to shift into a barghest and leap out the window.

"This isn't you," I croaked. "*Please*. My sons need me." Reminding him of my fertility and hoping to buy myself time was the only card I had left to play.

"Two boys. They were Regns all along," Ash said, dropping his eyes back to mine and then lower to my extremely sore chest. "*Twice* I have given up on you and wound up regretting it. I will not do it a third time."

"Curse the gods!" Brass shouted out the window, and I tried to turn to see him.

Ash held my face. "Never again. This war ends now."

For a split second, I thought he was going to kill me. He spun me around so I faced the windows. The faces of the men in my life gazed down in horrified expressions. Sage had removed the stock and was returning with a snide expression on his face. I'd tried to permanently disfigure him, but only succeeded in making myself vomit all over Indigo's fancy tent. I hoped there was still enough that remained so mutilated that he wouldn't be able to spawn another child to curse Tidings lands.

"She won't be the same person," Brass said with an air of fervor.

"I am counting on it." I could hear the smile in Ash's voice. "Savor these last moments of her love because the next time she sets eyes on you, I will take great care that she despises you."

Realization of what he planned caused me to summon strength I hadn't known I still had. I didn't. As I struggled, dark spots crept into my vision, but he held fast. I reached for my *calling* and came up with vapors.

"I won't stop loving you!" I swore to them.

My eyes flitted between the silver mirrors and the molten amber as I tried to hold on to my memories. Ash knew exactly what he was looking for. An image imprinted in my mind, meeting him at the masquerade before I turned to see Slate in the shadows. Tears streamed down my face. He was going to obliterate Slate and Brass as well as everyone I'd met in Tidings from me.

"Gods be good and let me remember one day," I whispered, feeling his block force its way into me, severing me from over two years of my life.

My sons, all I'd suffered, all I'd survived. So many times I wished to forget the things Slate had done to me, to forget the deaths I'd witnessed, and the mistakes I'd made, but not in exchange for losing all the good. There was love and family I'd made with Slate and Brass, friendships I'd cherished, and the obstacles I'd overcome. I was a sheltered girl when I came to Tidings and, after too many hard won trials, I was a woman with the power to do real good. Ash was taking it all away. I didn't want to be that girl. With the memories being ripped from me, I knew I would do it all over again if I would wind up where I had ended. All of it.

I'd found light in an abyss of darkness when hope was all lost and I believed I was irreparably broken, I'd found happiness. I'd found love. So much love.

Warmth flooded me as if I had been slowly dipped into a hot bath. Smoke and soot assailed my nostrils. I could taste its pungent scent on my tongue. Strong arms held me up, and I knew instinctually that it was all that kept me on my feet. Was I paralyzed? Had I been in a fire?

My eyes fluttered, and I was painfully aware of the intensely sharp pain at my breasts as I gazed out at the cloudless blue morning sky. Slowly, my eyes fell over a sprawling yellow stoned castle that stretched as far as my eyes could see. I felt leaden and exhausted, moving my head required energy I didn't have.

I knew the castle. I'd seen it in my dreams all my life with the woman's voice... and the monsters. My eyes fell over the windows. Men that weren't men, but lions and wolves, snakes, and bears staring at me with horrid expressions I couldn't process. A dark horned beast I had no name for howled and I screamed. *Monsters.*

The strong arms turned me gently to a hard chest. "You are safe, my love."

I couldn't stop screaming, but it tapered off with my sharp breaths to mewling. "Who..." I knew him — Ash. "Where am I? What's happened? Where's my mom?" I asked frantically trying to recognize where I was.

I didn't. My mind reeled.

I only wore a thin robe and nothing more and I could feel how dirty my skin was not to mention my own body's odor. What had happened to me?

Ash cooed, curling those sensual full lips. "I will tell you all. I have you now," he soothed, and he scooped me into his arms so I could bury my face in his chest.

Sleep stole my consciousness despite my fear.

CHAPTER 41
JETT

Brass's breaths came raggedly as Ash carried Scarlett off. Slate was emitting a low growl that threatened to become another howl. It's what had scared her half to death. She wasn't the woman who befriended every tribe she visited. She was the naive girl from Chicago and the barghest Slate became was something out of a horror movie.

"We —" Brass choked off and Quick pulled his arm over his shoulders. "Our sons. She remembers none of it. *Nothing.* He blocked everything from the moment he met her. She only knows him here. I —" he broke off again.

"Tawny," Jett whispered and turned to Steel who stood beside him.

Steel's eyes widened with excitement. "Tawny!" he repeated and broke out into a dead run down the hall with tribesmen jumping out of his way.

If not Tawny, they would get Sparrow and Hawk. There wasn't a chance they hadn't done the same to Gypsum. That was where they'd gone first after Diamond had stormed from the tent looking wrathful. Had the innocent girl betrayed him?

Jett looked to Slate who appeared to be in physical pain. Quick was leading Brass away who had had one too many terrible turns when it concerned Scarlett to be able to stand another.

"I've got to warn Indigo," Jett said, trying not to sound as defeated as he felt.

"We do not care — that much is clear. Not enough of us care anywhere. We are not wise — for that reason, mankind dies. To think is much against the will. Better — and easier — to kill."

Ash had been the one to take and return Slate's memories. They didn't know anyone else who had Ash's skill at mental manipulations to help Scarlett. With everything they were facing, it felt like a dire blow to their cause.

"It is worse," Slate rasped out, slowly returning to his man form. "She could kill us all. If they turn her and teach her to *call*. She has the ability to slaughter everyone. We cannot fight them with her in their camp."

Ophio glanced around the Lycans to address them. "Why had she not used it before to obliterate the traitors?"

Slate gave a wry smile as he watched Ash disappear into his tent with *his* wife in his arms. "Because she sees the best in people. She hoped to bring some of them back to our side. The loss of innocent life was not worth ending the war in so bloody a manner. We have to win her back or none of it matters. She is now their greatest weapon."

"Tawny," Jett reiterated. "She'll trust her, if she trusts anyone now."

Jett moved away from the window to find Indigo. They should have seen it coming. Why Ash hadn't done it before was a fluke. He'd probably thought he could change her mind with his charm and his smiles. He didn't understand her. He still wouldn't and Jett had to hope that Scarlett could still see through his ruthless ambition.

CHAPTER 42
GYPSUM

"You're married."

My protests were feeble as the caramel skinned beauty climbed into my lap at the small cafe table where I was attempting to eat the dinner she'd brought me. She hadn't left when I bathed, or when I dressed, and looked to have no intention of leaving me alone for quite some time.

"We have been lovers for two years, Gypsum Sumar," she said as she pulled my hair back so she could press her pouty lips to mine.

I'd be lying if I said I wasn't interested, but the things she had told me about my family and the war had left me in a less than excited mood. In fact, I felt like crying or punching something. I'd taken a fall and had been in a coma. My aunt, Wren, was dead. Killed by the enemy, as were too many others to even contemplate.

"Make love to me, Chief. It has been too long," she breathed, and I groaned as her hands deftly found my blazing sun belt buckle.

I wore a sleeveless bronze jerkin that went well with the copper beads I had threaded through my hair that fell all the way to my shoulder blades. It was like I'd been sent back into the past. I hardly recognized my body, taller, broader, and more muscled than I thought I'd ever be, I felt like I'd been implanted into another person.

"Chief!"

I heard Scarlett's voice outside the tent before she barreled through with Ash just behind her. Diamond smoothly climbed from my lap a second before they came in and I scooted further under the table to straighten myself out.

Scarlett wore a shimmering champagne dress, with soft curls and enough jewelry for a queen. Tears stained her cheeks as she wrapped her arms around my head pulling me to her chest which I was ashamed to notice had changed too. She looked so much more mature, like a grown woman. Not the girl I knew at all. Her waist was slimmer, cheeks and lips prominent, and yet the same.

I stood, having sorted myself out and held her gently to my chest, surprised to find that I was much taller than her. She was small in my arms, but she was my cousin Scarlett who treated me more like a little brother than a cousin and I didn't have a single memory without her.

"They're all dead," she whispered as her fingers curled in my jerkin.

"I know, Scar. I'm sorry. We'll get those assholes back," I promised.

She nodded and looked up at me smiling and patted my chest. "You're so different." She chuckled between sniffles. "Like a man."

I grinned back feeling my dimples pop in my cheeks. "I was going to say the same, but you know... a woman."

She giggled and Ash handed her a kerchief over her shoulder. She glanced back at him and blushed. Her husband. I'd met him briefly before my bath and he'd filled me in. Scarlett was a *mom*. She was only twenty-one, according to them though she looked in her mid-twenties.

Ash wound his arms around her from behind as Diamond sat in the other chair. "We are planning to eat supper with the family and afterwards, we shall go to the project to finally end this war. We have to leave by the cover of night so the enemy will not see us."

Scarlett's face was a permanent shade of red. She'd never had a boyfriend much less a husband, and she was completely clueless as to what she should do while he held her. *I* was baffled by it.

"Sure thing. However we can help," I agreed.

We ate spring salads and mutton with mint sauce and a spread of fresh vegetables and fruit they'd grown in a small garden inside a nearby tent for the families in command. We ate with Scarlett's grandfather Cygnus and grandmother Ruby who took a keen interest in her. Her half-brother Sage, and stepmother Delta, were there, but weren't the friendliest people I'd met. Diamond and her husband Sterling were quiet unlike Ash who couldn't keep his hands off Scarlett. She was regaled with stories of her birth father, who had sadly perished last year.

Her great uncle, Canis, sat next to Delta, and the two spoke in quiet tones until it was time for us to leave. Scarlett burst into tears at having to leave the grandmother whom she was just getting to know until Ruby assured her she would be around when we returned. There was a sadness to Ruby as Cygnus and Ash each took their wives in hand. Scarlett tugged away from Ash and wrapped her arms around Cygnus's waist. He was a very big man, a half foot taller than I was, but all the blonde men were big.

Ruby lost her composure and sobbed harder. Cygnus blinked down at Scarlett as she murmured. "I may not have my father, but at least I'll have your memories of him. Thank you."

Cygnus pulled her away and knit his brows down at her. "You have a second chance. We will make sure you are taken care of, Scarlett."

Ruby hugged herself and Cygnus moved to take her away. Ash did the same to Scarlett, and she offered me a tight smile before letting him guide her. Delta took her son's arm, leaving me with Canis once Sterling and Diamond left.

"Get ready, son. The world is riding on our shoulders."

I nodded and plopped into one of the chairs when he left. Scarlett had been abused. Her memories had gaps since they'd pushed her out of a window. During my coma, my parents had to defend their native lands and left me to be tended by Scarlett's extended family. My memory was even further gone than Scarlett's.

The hardest news they'd given us of the day was that Tawny had been brainwashed. She was behind enemy lines and had no idea of the kind of trouble she was in.

I leaned forward letting my face fall into my hands as I worried about my big sister. We had to get her free.

CHAPTER 43
INDIGO

Chairs lined the windows along the side of the hall. We were supposed to be attacking in the morning, but now it was postponed until we could figure out what to do with Scarlett and Gypsum in the Stygian camp.

They'd erased her memories. She didn't know I existed much less Jett, her husbands, or Steel — not a single one of the tribes. All her hard work, all her strife — gone. I knew it was a bad thing to forget so much, but I was having a hard time seeing the negative points. I would willingly forget the past two years.

Still, I didn't have two kids and two loving, if flawed, husbands.

Brass's hair hung free as he rested his elbows on the window sill staring despondently down at the tents. Silver had filled me in on everything during our midday rendezvous. Scarlett was completely unaware of the emotions she was transmitting to them through the bond. Ash was taking full advantage of her loss of memories. Slate had to be taken away from the windows by a few of the men when he lost control.

That would be a definite downside of the loss of memories. I'd want to know who my enemies were.

"It took nine months for her to let me into her bed. What could he

"

have said to make her give herself up so willingly?" Brass asked no one in particular.

I popped the cork on the vial of purple fluid and drank in all in one gulp. "That he is her husband. That they have a family. That he loves her," I answered with a sigh.

"She's old Scarlett. Afraid to take risks, afraid of her emotions...all about marriage and family even if that means sacrificing being in love," Jett said from two windows down where Amethyst sat in his lap.

Tawny sniffled. "I can't believe this is happening."

Steel held her closer in the chair beside Jett's. We all lifted our heads when heavy boots fell signifying Slate's return. He didn't look any more in control than he had earlier. Silver's gaze swept over me and my nostrils flared taking in their scents before I returned to the windows. They'd been sparring so Slate could burn off some steam.

We'd seen Scarlett briefly when Ash walked her to and from a tent. All of us had been glued to the scene since.

"Have you taken your dose —"

"Like clockwork. I never forget," I snapped, cutting Silver short.

He blew out a heavy breath, and I watched him swagger over to Brass's chair out of the corner of my eye. Slate and Silver were both shirtless and a sheen of sweat glistened over all those rippling muscles.

How dare he walk around like that while I was on rousen. What if I had a sudden bout of desire I couldn't control? I had better let him know he shouldn't have been tempting me where I couldn't have him.

I got up from my seat to give Silver a piece of my mind when Slate spoke. "I do not think I can win her back a third time. She screamed when she set eyes on me," he rumbled.

He was speaking under his breath to Brass and Silver, but I could easily hear him as I stood on Brass's right.

"We will. We have to. She wouldn't have given up on us. She didn't give up on you," Brass told him, but there was no spirit in his words.

The fight in Brass was gone. We needed to bring his sons back for a visit so he could remember what he fought for.

"Easy for you to say. She shoved her tongue down your throat minutes after you met her. It was not so simple for me."

I knit my brows as I stopped before Slate. He arched a straight brow so long lashes nearly brushed as he looked down at me from his unscarred side.

"She's always fought how she felt about you because it was strong from the start, not because she didn't. You're so... dangerous and... intimidating... beautiful."

His brows lifted which would have been a cry of surprise from another man just before I lunged. It was hard to climb him while he was not bending down to me and his slick skin gave me no traction, so I gripped his hair, making him growl as I molded my mouth over his.

Heat rolled me under. Slate had a simmering lust that all khorazes had inside them. I was blinded by it, completely consumed as hands tried to pry me off him.

CHAPTER 44
JETT

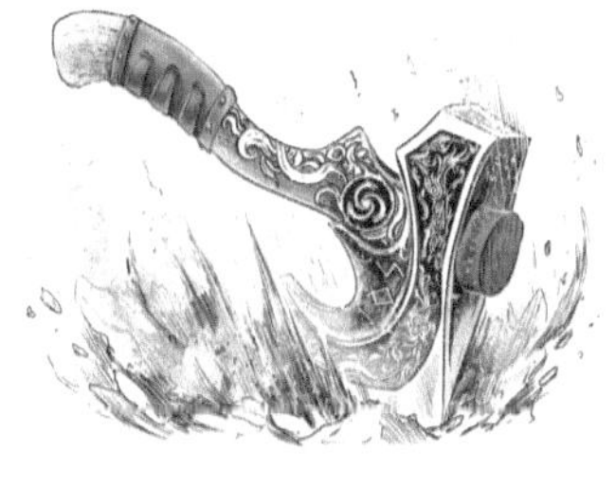

Quick looked ready to cry as Indigo tangled her fingers into Slate's long hair, refusing to stop kissing him as Jett and Brass tried to unwind his hair from her curled fingers. Quick had his arms around her waist and succeeded in jerking Slate's head sideways with her feet off the floor still trying to get to him.

"I fucking hate you," Quick ground out.

"She is your khoraz. Give her a command. She does not want me, she only wants —"

"Shut your mouth! It's bad enough you sullied my baby sister you will not —"

Jett fell back. Light poured forth from Indigo and Slate's open eyes and mouths, from their fingertips and nostrils. Slowly, they levitated into the air as if gravity no longer affected the two of them.

Jett heard the girls gasp. He and Steel were the only two to see this before. They were nine years old and thankfully Steel had kept his head being a little older. Nothing had been the same afterwards. Slate had foreseen his death. How could any little kid live the rest of his life with that knowledge?

Jett had decided that Divine Beauty wasn't so bad. Being a prophet was the worst. Who wanted to know the future when you couldn't change it? Slate was a glorified time capsule. He stored all the prophecies of his ancestors and then he had his own.

"I can't see their minds," Brass whispered as he held Quick back.

Indigo had absorbed Slate's prophet abilities. Jett was willing to bet she'd regret it.

Their voices joined as one and sounded far away.

"The wheels turn, those who have frozen watch those spurned.
She was given the key to end their world. Sacrifice. Watch her burn.
Fate was sealed from the start. Only one can save her bleeding hearts.
Balance struck with a foe thought friend. Fire always comes to a woeful end."

"Grab her!" Jett shouted at Quick.

Steel and Jett caught Slate as he fell like a ton of bricks to the polished floor. They grunted with the effort of keeping him upright. Indigo was cradled in Silver's arms and she came to quickly. Her eyes settled on Slate who was lifting his head and seemed to be having several facial tics at once.

"You were *wrong*!" Indigo shrieked. "It was never you!"

Her brief moment of clarity cost her the bit of control she had left. Rousen pulled her under and her powder blue eyes were swallowed by her black pupils so rapidly Jett and Steel stumbled back, causing the three of them to fall. Jett knew he wasn't the only one covering up his lap.

Indigo's nostrils flared as she purred and her sight set on Quick. He did his best to keep her from tearing his clothes off before he got her into the room across the hall.

Slate sat on the floor staring blankly at the wall. "We cannot let her access the project. We will lose Scarlett."

Brass whirled around to the windows. "He's taking her away."

Jett pushed off his back and got to his feet scrambling to get to the windows. Scarlett rode in front of Ash with Gypsum beside them on his own stallion. Canis, Sage, Diamond, and Sterling were all on horses and a pack horse carried supplies.

"They thought to sneak off," Jett cursed.

"We swore Scarlett a vow. Slate has to lead Lera's forces." Brass balled his hands into fists.

"By the time you gather supplies, Quick will be able to maintain things with Indigo on the road then. I will catch you up."

CHAPTER

FORTY-FIVE

The only thing that was missing was my mother.

I had a gorgeous husband who seemed to be infatuated with me, two sons with my aunt and uncle while I was in enemy hands, but they saved me.

Ash drew me a bubble bath and climbed in with me. To my knowledge, it was the first time I'd seen a man undressed. He filled me in on everything while he washed my body, letting me lean back against his chest.

Men with names straight out of a comic book had forced themselves on me and branded me so we were eternally bound. I could feel their emotions every second of the day and I hated them. I couldn't enjoy my stolen moments with Ash in the bubble bath, they felt such sorrow and grief it felt like my own. *Still*. Ash had used his magic fingers on me as he suckled and I had known pleasure like I'd never known before... not in my memories.

The emotions had grown so strong from the men who'd branded

me, that I'd burst into tears. I wanted to make love to my husband, but I couldn't. Their pain felt like mine and I couldn't tell the difference.

Ash couldn't keep his hands off me as he told me about our relationship while we rode. We took the long way around through the mountains in the middle of the night so the Red Seconds wouldn't follow our path.

I could feel one of the men in my mind somewhere south of where I was as opposed to two other men who were back where we came from. The further they were, the more muted their emotions.

"Rest, my love. We shall have to ride all night. *Sleep.* I have you," Ash promised, and I bent my head back lazily to give his peach scented lips a kiss.

"The Red Seconds are coming up the road from Valla," Sage reported after he returned from scouting ahead.

Canis glanced back at me and Ash gave my thigh a reassuring squeeze. "The barghest and the Shadow Breakers."

"We have to go back," Sterling protested.

I'd woken up around dawn to find Gypsum slumped over his horse but hanging on. He roused at our standstill.

"We keep moving. None of it matters if we can turn back time," Canis said, urging his horse forward.

"What about Scarlett's grandparents?" Gypsum asked. "They still die."

"Try not to be such a myopic. There is a grander scheme at play," Sage bit off in his hoity-toity, uppity tone.

Sterling glanced at me with sympathy in his unique eyes before following after Canis. Gypsum scoffed and shook his head before heeling his horse forward.

"It will all work out, my love," Ash promised in my ear.

We camped in the woods after a long day of riding and Ash told me we were close to his family's ancestral home, our home and where our children would grow up. I wished I had seen it, but he promised we could on the way back.

We only had four tents. Sterling and Diamond retired after we ate around a small cook fire and took one of the tents. Gypsum offered Sage his tent since Canis took the second and Ash set up the third for us. The sounds of Sterling and Diamond being intimate made Gypsum drop his head, but I saw the look of confusion in his eyes. Diamond had been trying to get close to Gypsum the entire day. She said they were friends, but I wondered if maybe they'd been more than that. Sage turned Gypsum down and laid back against his roll while Gypsum erected his tent.

I wanted to get to know my half-brother better, but whenever I caught him looking at me, it was with a sneer. Since I was younger than he was, it became clear that my mom had an affair with our father. I couldn't blame him for not liking me. I'd never get answers from my mother and Ash had simply said the flesh was weak.

He didn't know my mom. She wouldn't have broken up a family.

"We have a long day ahead," Ash said and took my hands, leading me into the small tent nothing like the miniature mansions back at the camp.

Ash liked me in purples and whites. The dresses he'd packed for me were all light flowing fabrics in a variety of those shades. He helped me out of my dress and carefully placed it within my case.

"Are you going to teach me how to *call* tonight?" I asked as he slowly removed my last articles of clothing.

I wished I wasn't so shy, that I could remember our times together. He was so confident and knew my body well, but I felt like a bumbling idiot. Any pleasure I'd give would be purely by accident.

Ash began to disrobe and my anxiety skyrocketed. The men's emotions in my head went the opposite direction and tried to drag me down with them. Ash had a chiseled physique, the like of which I'd never seen outside of a fitness magazine. It seemed all the people took excellent care of themselves.

"I am going to make love to my wife. There is always time for *calling* later," he purred as he prowled up the length of me.

The crickets and churring of insects kept me awake, but at least I wasn't alone with my embarrassment. I wasn't as virtuous as I'd been the day before, but I couldn't bring myself to make love to my adoring husband.

What was wrong with me?

Horse hooves woke me and my eyes burned like I'd gotten too close to the fire last night. Ash wasn't in the tent and I could hear voices outside as I readied. Women, two of them had arrived from the Straumr palace.

When I exited the tent A short blonde with big green eyes in a fair heart-shaped face glared at me. Her and her brunette cohort were both very pregnant. The other girl had a slimmer shape with olive skin and hazel eyes, but the two had to be sisters. Their mannerisms were identical as was their immediate distaste for me.

"Scarlett, this is Nova and Quartz Natt," Ash explained, gesturing to the brunette and then the honey blonde.

"Pleased to meet you... again," I added since surely such hatred must be warranted.

Nova spoke over me. "Mother said we should not come."

"I am starting to think she was correct." Quartz sniffed.

"No need to be petulant. We are history in the making. Be ready to ride in fifteen," Canis lectured. He used his magic, which they called *calling* the elements, to break down his tent.

Gypsum meandered towards me with a set of apples and buttered bread in his hands. "Your stepbrother is a jerk and your great uncle is taciturn at best."

"Blood is the only thing we share, I guess." I dropped my voice, "I can't believe he's letting my grandfather risk death. I hope we can stop the war in time."

Gypsum shook his head. "I can't believe you said that with a straight face. If you weren't here, I'd say my imagination is getting damn good. I'm not totally convinced this isn't a dream."

He didn't appear to be joking.

"I feel the same way, except..." I blushed, thinking about my time with my husband.

"The imagination doesn't have enough banked for certain things," he teased.

I shifted closer to Gypsum, so I had the comfort of his body heat. "It doesn't. *I* don't. I think those girls like him. I wonder where their husbands are."

Gypsum and I watched Quartz and Ash dismantle our tent while she snapped quiet questions at him. Judging from his smug, unruffled demeanor, it wasn't uncommon for them to interact in such a way.

"I'm glad you're here, Chief."

CHAPTER 46

INDIGO

Without a tent, my nightly dose as well as the other few times I took it a day, was nearly impossible to hide. Silver did the best he could to keep the noises I made to a minimum.

"Do not shut me out, Dove," he whispered.

Silver was not made for whispering. The others were likely pretending to be sleeping to offer some semblance of privacy. I didn't care. The rousen ran my life.

"I love you, Indigo," he breathed, and my body flexed beneath his.

Silver's head rested on my shoulder as he caught his breath. I could hear my own heavy breaths as I gazed up at the stars. There was a fresh breeze coming off the ocean coast and if it was before the Purge War, I would have been blissfully happy. Instead, I couldn't so much as tell Silver to keep his voice down because the others could hear every word.

Silver's skin stuck to mine as he kissed my cheek, his breaths tickling my hair. "I hate rousen. I would give anything to hear one of your smart mouth retorts." He sighed, and I shut my eyes as he pulled the thin blanket up around us.

"They are using tents so she won't be able to see the stars tonight," Brass murmured.

I opened my eyes as a large shadow passed between our sleeping forms. Slate sat down beside Brass and rested his arms on his knees.

"You enjoyed showing her the stars," Slate said dryly.

Brass chuckled and gestured to the sky. "It's the Milky Way. Below Deneb, is the swan, Cygnus. Beneath to the right is the constellation Aquila the eagle." Brass's arm shifted. "That star is Antares in Scorpius, the one that looks like a teapot is the archer, Sagittarius, and in the far right, the scales of Libra."

Slate had grown up on the islands so he must have had an idea of the constellations visible to our islands. He listened patiently as Brass finished before updating us on the war.

Jett and Steel had joined them and Silver leaned back searching my eyes before rolling off me but tucking me to him. He was loath to ever let me more than an arm's length away. I wouldn't have minded it if I didn't feel like he did it out of pity.

Poor Indigo, the abused orphan who didn't even know whose child she carried.

"They are at the university. Canis must have passed us on the way and continued. He has no plans to save his brother. He did not so much as send in reinforcements from Ostara," Slate explained.

"He could have. We passed the Tio palace," Steel noted.

"He plans to activate the project and change everything. I do not think he even cares about his own life. He is a radical. I asked Lera to wait. I know Indigo is close to Ruby and would hate to have her be collateral damage." Slate grunted.

Brass inhaled slowly, and I heard him slap Slate's back. "Did not think you could change so much."

"I doubt he did either. It's a good change. You value life," Steel reassured him.

I turned in Silver's arms to face him and nudged his nose with my own. "I value *you*," I whispered, and he squeezed his eyes shut.

"I am sorry for questioning you on rousen, Dove. I do not want any secrets between us. I am glad to know everything. You hate it, I know. We will get through it together." Silver promised.

I sighed as he slanted his mouth over mine. My brain was too foggy to come up with anything spiteful and Silver took it as a good sign.

It was my fault our morning got a late start, why every morning started late. I had to take a heavy dose first thing to maintain my level of brain activity. Taking the rousen was much worse in the daylight where Silver and I couldn't pretend we were alone. Instead, the others walked a little ways away while Silver tended to my needs. He liked to joke as if it was lightening the mood, or what had happened to me. He called it, preventative care. What he did prevented me from attacking one of my sister's husbands or worse, one of my family members.

We walked through the woods following the coastline in complete silence until we reached the unlit torches that lined a path that had been made within the last year. I stayed near Amethyst and Tawny. It was common practice for me to leave Silver's side as soon as I was physically able. It was bad enough I had no choice over being with him for hours on end.

Silver walked with Slate, Brass, and Jett. Steel floated between the two groups, not wanting to be far from Tawny and frequently wrapped his arm around her to place his palm on her small belly.

I glanced back to Silver, where he was trying to studiously ignore me. A twinge of guilt turned my stomach as I slowed so he would catch up. His eyes widened as I pulled my hair over my right shoulder and held my hand out for him. At the very least, he was helping me overcome my addiction. I *should* be kind. I could keep my distance without being mean.

I slid my arm around his waist and he scanned my expression as I urged him to walk again. I didn't want to talk. I only wanted to keep one another company. His body relaxed as I inhaled his scent, not his desire, but his natural manly odor that would forever remind me of our many nights in my bed. I could even tolerate his palm on my belly, delving into my son. I could even tolerate his sigh and the kiss he placed on the top of my head.

Slate stopped and lifted his nose to the air as it flared while he sniffed. "Jorogumo."

Silver pushed me behind him and Tawny and Amethyst were shoved into me with the men pulling their blades around us. My every breath took an eternity. Birds flew overhead in the warm spring afternoon. A breeze tugged on my dress, leaves rustled showing their paler undersides and my whole body tensed. The weather was rapidly changing.

"A storm is coming," Brass whispered.

The thick shrubs and surrounding trees exploded with multi-legged bodies and pinchers. Amethyst screamed. Her hands outstretched for her calling to try to keep the rogues at bay while the men moved with fluid strikes dismembering the tribesmen that came close. Tawny and I had fought against the Jorogumo before and were prepared for how terrifying they could be.

Gore splattered us as the men moved outside the circle. Slate shifted into a seven foot tall barghest hybrid and roared. The Jorogumo nearest him flinched back which seemed by accident until two Anguillan crept up in their spots with machines that looked like cannons. They each hit a spring, and I tried to use my *calling* to deflect the net that launched, but my *calling* evaporated.

Slate was hit by both nets and the momentum knocked him into us in the center. Tawny cried out as Slate tried to shift back, howling in pain. Steel turned to try to free Slate from the net and get Tawny out of the way when arms roughly grabbed me from where I laid on my side.

Silver checked me over before turning back. I realized why the sounds of fighting had stopped. Jett and Brass were tied in ropes of air and a massive furry spider with cobalt blue marking on a dark body and a mohawk of black hair stood between Cassiopeia and Delta.

We knew that it would happen, yet it was disheartening all the same. The thick legged spider man with a bulkily muscled human torso and face, other than his three sets of pitch black eyes, tossed down nix cuffs.

"Drik'ir," I spat.

"Indigo Var. My condolences on your worthless father."

Jett grunted as he struggled against his invisible ropes. I sneered at the deceased empress's consort.

"I met Thre'ik. If you think —"

"Quite enough, Indigo. None of that matters."

Cassiopeia strode forward in her navy caftan. Her blonde curls rested on her shoulders as she gave us all superior looks form her frosty blue eyes.

"Not even Dahlia's death?" I asked haughtily.

Cassiopeia's eyes tightened, but it was Delta's who used her air to slap me hard across the cheek. I squeezed my eyes shut against the sting and felt the others around me struggling against their bonds. The other Jorogumo had more cuffs and were threading a long chain between them so we were bound to one another, by our wrists and again by our ankles.

"How does it feel to have raised a murdering rapist?" Silver ground out helping to push my hair from my face.

"She is a greater son khoraz. Her sole purpose in life is to be used," Delta said matter of fact.

If the others didn't know about Sage, they did now.

"Gag them. Canis will have reached the project by now," Cassiopeia said as she oversaw our binding and gags.

"You went much slower than we anticipated. Alas, the khoraz has her needs." Delta lifted her celestial nose into the air as she sauntered away.

I used the gag that cut my lips as it was forced into my mouth as my reason to cry. I had wanted to be like that woman. She may not have raised me as her daughter, but she was the foremost female influence in my life and she despised me. Silver was bound and gagged next to me and offered his arm for his reassuring support.

Dread closed in on us like nooses around our necks. Clouds churned above to steal the sun's rays from our faces.

Scarlett regaining her memories was the only thing that could save us. She had to rewind time. She *had* to.

We walked, arms and legs heavy with chains one after the other to the project.

FORTY-SEVEN

I shivered involuntarily as the enormous spider man drew close. The ground was hard packed dirt cleared of all its tree, but in my mind I could hear his feet skittering. I pressed close to Ash when he stopped before us.

It was definitely a he.

"We cleared the area, as you asked," the spider man said with a rattling in his throat.

"Thank you, Drik'ir. My wife is unaccustomed to the tribes." Ash patted my shoulder, and I turned my face away from the pincher framed mouth of the bright blue spider.

His three sets of eyes like gaping light sucking holes in his grey face were hard to turn away from. He pinned me in place as he spoke.

"I have heard of you. We have never had the pleasure," he said in a very clear deep voice — the only part of his tone that signified that he was inhuman was the rattle in his throat, or maybe it was his chest.

I couldn't find my own voice, human, or even an animal's grunt.

Ash chuckled and led me away. I felt the others behind me as the dirt gave way to sand and we were at the ocean coast. A long wooden bridge spanned across the water to a topless dome that looked to be made of sandstone.

My low heels clacked across with Ash's scuffing boots. Canis crossed ahead of us with Gypsum at my back. He gave me a smile he meant to be comforting, but it was tight and the feeling of fear tasted metallic in my mouth.

I knit my brows and watched as Canis stood at the lip of the dome. The waves crashed against the outside walls, spraying us lightly as we met Canis. Vertigo made me stagger when I looked deep into the dome that was lined with a ramp.

"What is that?" Gypsum asked as Canis started down.

"A sundial," Ash told him.

Four lines intersected at a center circle, each with symbols on each of the eight triangular piece portions. More script encircled the sundial in runes I couldn't decipher. I wondered if I could before the enemy pushed me from the castle windows.

Slate and Brass. I *would* get my revenge.

"What does it mean? Those... glyphs..." I asked as we tromped down the planked ramp.

"*Power at all costs, costs everything. For the sake of their souls. May their ancestors never forged,*" Sage said from the back of our parade.

"Storm and Wind were married. Wind feared her husband's power, and they each found followers to go against one another. It was the only civil wore the Guardians have ever had until this one. Hardly a war. Wind saw no alternative other than to kill herself. She did it on this floor and Storm was distraught. He killed himself immediately after and the project was never activated," Sterling explained.

"Storm said he saw the project in his dreams. He created it using a power the like of which the world had never seen. They say it could wind back time. We need a Tio descendant to control it. That is where you come in, my love. You are the key. The key to access the power to change the world."

We'd reached the bottom of the dome stories below the water. A light dusting a gritty sand covered the slightly raised circle that formed the sundial light from the high sun seemed to spotlight. The sky was rapidly turning grey, and the spotlight went out as a cloud crossed over the top of the dome.

Quartz and Nova glowered at me and Ash so I released my clutch of his jerkin and shifted to stand nearer to Gypsum. He bent his knees to whisper into my ear.

"My heart is in my butt. Am I the only one who feels like death is in shrouds with his sickle tapping on their shoulder?" he asked.

The red skull and sickle on Canis's black jerkin wasn't helping matters. It was such an ominous symbol. It was hard not to think of death looking at it.

I nodded. Ever since we came within sight of the dome, something that felt very wrong had slowly inched up my spine. Every instinct in my body was warning me to run very far away. Whatever was there, it was dangerous and possibly bad. *Very* bad.

I swallowed rubbing my palms together as the others spoke. Canis pulled a necklace from within his jerkin and parted from the others to give me the nickel sized charms. I held out my hand as he held them out. They were stone and all in different shapes. I held them in my palm and felt Canis's eyes on me.

"You go back. You go as far as you can and you take us all with you. Do you understand?" he asked in a rapid voice.

"I do," I said quietly.

"There is no room for error. If you cannot go all the way, go to the beginning of this project. If you cannot bring us, do what is necessary to get Storm to activate the project. Stop Wind." Hooded eyes scanned my face, and I gulped.

"Okay. How?"

My mind reeled with the responsibility he was lying on my shoulders. The only thing I could think of that I was ever responsible for was myself, and I never did anything wrong. School, part time work, and home. That was me. We never even had a pet.

"However you can."

My eyes dried as I stared at him. Kill someone?

"Our guests should be arriving soon."

Sage looked happier than I had seen him in the few days since we'd known one another. He wasn't the kind of man you enjoyed seeing smile. If he was smiling, there was no good news to be had.

Shuffling began to scrape the wood planks, and I craned my neck back to see the source of the noise. A glamorous older woman accompanied by a statuesque blonde led eight prisoners.

Gypsum wrapped his arm around my shoulders as the prisoners reached the ground level. If Gypsum's heart was in his fanny pack, mine was beating against the dangling thing in my throat. I could hardly breathe. These men had abused me, forced themselves on me, killed my parents, and brainwashed Tawny.

A woman with a regal bearing focused in on Ash. She somewhat resembled Diamond, with long dark hair and creamy mocha skin. Two of the men had similar colorings, tan with turquoise almond eyes shockingly similar to my own. The one with a crew cut was as tall as a man with long midnight hair and a silver scar over silver eyes. I couldn't look directly into those eyes, they seemed to be reading my soul.

Beside him was a man that wasn't a giant like the other two, but just as powerfully built. His golden eyes were so sad and hopeful I knew immediately which one he was in my mind. They weren't the eyes of a man who would abuse me. His emotions were totally unfiltered. If I didn't *feel* them coming from him, his face was an open book. To his left was a man the same size with short stylish hair and tattoos that crept from his collar. He was leaning into a beautiful blonde whose powder blue eyes were focused on Gypsum and me.

Then there was Tawny. They were all gagged. Tears streamed down her face into the fabric around her mouth. They had fought before they were captured.

"She's pregnant?" I gasped.

"I want to talk to my sister," Gypsum demanded and was moving past me in his finery.

I wound my hands in my shimmering silver dress as I hesitantly followed.

"She is married to her uncle. It is an incestuous child in her womb," Sage practically purred.

Sterling was moving in my periphery to the blonde as Gypsum pulled the gag from Tawny's mouth. I wrapped my hand around the stones and hugged myself as I came to stand beside Gyps.

Tawny sobbed. "They've brainwashed you both! *We* are your family! This is Jett, your brother. Indigo is your sister, Amethyst is your sister-in-law, Quick is basically your brother-in-law. Those other two, the big scary one, Slate, is your husband. You're pregnant with his child right now and the pretty one whose always making moon eyes at you, that's Brass. You and he have the most beautiful identical sons —"

I knit my brows unable to believe a single word she said. She sounded insane.

"And this is your uncle... Steel?" Gypsum asked eye to eye to the tousled haired man.

"Yes, but he's not really our uncle. Hawk isn't my father," Tawny stammered.

She jerked her manacles forcing the chains on Steel's hands to shift they were so closely bound. Probably so they couldn't fight, they could hardly scratch their noses.

"Hawk isn't our father!" Gyps shouted.

She shook her head. "No. Not my father. My father is Ridge Vetr. Cassiopeia is my grandmother and an evil bitch along with her bitch of a daughter and —" Sage pushed between Gypsum and I and yanked up her gag.

I stared at Tawny. "We'll get you help, Tawns. I'll fix it," I promised her as Ash came and pulled me away.

Sterling had pulled away the blonde's gag and was beginning to take off her cuffs. The tattooed man was struggling against his gag as Ash led me before the men I feared more than anything else I had ever known.

Brass and Slate.

Ash pulled his long blades out, he called them seaxes, and picked up my wrist placing one in my hand and curling his fingers around it. He shifted to stand behind me and lifted the blade so it rested over the heart of the silver-eyed man.

"Sterling, releasing her may be precipitous. Only a moment longer," Canis told him off to my right.

Sage came to my side and opened my clasped palm, removing one of the pieces. "Sumar."

He beckoned Gypsum who backed away from Tawny without taking his eyes off her. Sage took Gypsum's palm and sliced it with his magic. Gypsum winced as Sage slid the stone piece indelicately through the wound and gestured to the center of the sundial.

"At the center is a circle. Put the piece in place and stand on the Sumar sigil, the blazing sun." Sage said without inflection.

Gypsum gave Sage an equally cool look as he moved across the sundial. I watched as he pushed the piece into place. That sense of doom was screaming in my ears.

"Chief!" I shouted as he found the triangular section with the blazing sun.

He glanced back and gave me a genuine dimpled smile. "Let's just get this over with. Time to save the world, right?" He joked as he stepped onto the sigil.

I yelped as his body went rigid. Blue light illuminated the symbol beneath him and seemed to freeze him in place and shine until it lit his entire body in the eerie blue light.

"No!" Indigo screamed and her head fell when Gypsum's head fell back, eyes rolled back until only the whites shown.

"You said he would not be hurt!" Diamond cried.

"We have to activate the entire project now. If we do not, *then* he will die." Delta moved to be closer to her mother.

Ash was speaking to me, the seax still in my hand. I jerked back and my eyes met Slate's. My mouth fell open as I fumbled for thoughts.

"Get your revenge, my love," Ash whispered in my ear. "It is the only way you shall ever overcome."

"I... I don't —"

"You will never be able to move forward. You must."

I knit my brows. Love the like of which I had only read about in books was streaming through me from the silver-eyed man as if his heart flowed directly into mine.

Too much was happening at once. I thought I knew what I wanted, but I needed more time to think. I did know one thing. I wasn't a murderer.

"This won't bring my mother back," I whispered and let my eyes fall.

I opened my hand to let the blade drop, but Ash tightened his grip and thrust forward. I cried out as I felt the man's skin give and Ash plunged the blade into his heart that beat with his love for me.

"No, no..." I murmured. "This isn't what I wanted." The man fell to his knees as Ash drew out his blade.

I watched in slow motion as Indigo ran past Sterling, her hair flying behind her. She did a peculiar thing then; she reached her hand out so her fingers grazed Ash's bare arm then lunged for me. She gripped me so tightly I stared at her as we toppled over. Her pregnant belly smashed between us.

Commotion broke out with the captives. The golden eyed man bent down to Slate, pulling his head in his lap when Ash drew his blade back a second time. Slate's image passed through my mind and I cried out, holding my jaw where pain lanced through me.

Quick had worked his gag free. "He almost killed her! You swore to Scarlett you would take care of her, but Sage stripped her and *beat* her within an inch of her life!"

"No!" Tawny's gag wasn't completely covering her mouth and her wail tore through the dome.

Indigo's face was a mask of consternation as my eyes sought the source of Tawny's scream. Ash lunged and when he drew back. Brass had fallen behind Slate on his side, the seax hilt had fallen as still as the man it stuck out from.

Memories rushed into me and I gasped painfully, choking on my saliva.

"Do not listen to the boy. He is a Regn, a liar," Cassiopeia said.

"*Fuck*, Brass." Quick sobbed. "I am not a liar. Ask her what he did the night we took Elivagar. Heal my fucking brother! He is dying!"

Brass... Slate... What had I done?

Indigo's tears splattered on my face. I was lightheaded. It couldn't be real. We helped one another up to our feet.

Sterling was looking at Indigo. "Did he —" he couldn't finish the question.

"I'm back," I said simply.

Indigo dropped her eyes and Sterling had his answer.

Everything happened at once.

Sterling shifted, his clothes tearing from his body in an instant until a great silver barghest launched itself at Sage. Indigo darted to Quick, and I ran past Ash diving to the spot Brass and Slate laid.

Blood pooled beneath Slate and I knew the instant I saw his snowstorm grey eyes that the life had left him. I grabbed Brass, ignoring the pandemonium and the screaming. Quick was free and while he deflected Ash's long seax, Indigo was trying to keep Nova and Quartz at bay with her *calling* while trying to release Jett from his nix cuffs.

I should've helped, but if there was the slightest chance I could save Brass... He wasn't supposed to die. Not Brass. Slate had always assumed it would be him, but it was them both. My emotions couldn't begin to process their deaths.

I slipped into numbness as I held my palm over Brass's bleeding heart. Brass's image in my lap flashed in my mind's eye and unspeakable pain shot through my hand numbing it to my elbow.

An arm tugged on my elbow and I blinked at Jett who had tears in his eyes. "He's gone, baby sis. We need your help."

Blood soaked my dress as I looked down at the amber eyes that held more love and faith than any one person had a right to. I began to remove the nix bindings on him and Slate, and Jett moved away. Amethyst and Tawny used their *calling* against Nova and Quartz while Cassiopeia was firing fireballs at Steel.

Canis and Jett were locked in a duel while Quick tried to defend against Ash, but his arm hung limply at his side. Quick was losing. Indigo used a short seax, plunging it over and over into a body beneath the ramp as Sterling roared.

I could hear footsteps on the wooden ramp when I was yanked to my feet. Delta grabbed me. Her face was a mask of horror as her *calling* viciously ripped into me.

Indigo had returned my memories after absorbing Ash's talent, but Delta was working much faster, erasing much more. I forgot Pearl, then college. Memories of Chris and prom, my entire high school experience vanished.

"Did you wonder where Ash got his talent? I will enjoy killing you first hand rather than assigning the task to my second-born son," Delta spat in my ear.

Hawk, Sparrow, my mother... I couldn't remember my own name.

"Delta!" A man with wide hazel eyes and dark close cropped hair hopped off the ramp. "Let her go."

"*Ridge*," she spat. "Mother always knew you were a traitor. I heard you joined the Red Seconds against the family."

"Tawny is my family. You always had too much ambition Delta. You could have had everything if you —" Ridge's eyes were soft when he looked at his sister, but his spear was at the ready.

Bodies sprawled around the circle at the center while two men fought with blades. One man taller than the other, both looking determined, neither waning, blades flashes and sparks clashing in a constant clanging in my ears.

Delta shifted, using my body as a shield.

"Her brain is fried. She is of no use to anyone. Take her. Death is too good for her after what she has done." Delta shoved me so I fell face first into Ridge's chest.

He caught me and I spun around in time to watch a crystal clear figure come up behind her and send a dozen spikes through Delta's body. Blood and gore sprayed over me and Ridge as we both flinched. The crystal figure became a blood soaked blonde woman who heaved as she fell to the floor voiding her stomach.

"It is alright. Indigo, right?" Ridge asked softly as he laid me down.

I shifted my head against the grit ridden floor and watched a man with tattoos stagger over sideways. Another leaner blonde man leaned over two limp pregnant women and then placed his hands on two other girls. There was blood everywhere. More bodies laid before me that two dueling men hopped over to continue their battle.

"Scarlett, help me!" said a man with piercing green eyes.

His words meant nothing to me.

He knit his brows as he looked down at me. The other man knocked away his blade and thrust. The sword entered his body soundlessly. Green eyes widened, but never left my face. He stumbled onto his knees and cupped my face as hot blood pumped from the gaping wound in his chest.

"As much as I loved you, it was never enough. You *never* loved me." He creased his brow as he fell down beside me, our faces inches apart.

I blinked slowly as his hand went slack on my jaw. I should've felt something. I should've had a reaction, but everything that made me *me* had been erased.

The man he was fighting lifted me up under my arms and carried me to the center of the circle. Rain drizzled down on my face from the dark churning storm clouds above.

I felt nothing. I understood nothing. I just *was*.

My hand was peeled open and more faces appeared above. "Indigo, can you try to get her mind back?"

"I can try, Jett, but..." Her hands held my head and she shook her head. "She's like an infant."

Jett brought me to my feet as Ridge carried a body on his shoulders while he ran up the ramps. I limply leaned against Jett.

"Canis and Sage are dead, but Nova, Quartz, and Cassiopeia are alive. Unconscious, but alive."

"Thank you, Steel. We have to activate the project or Gypsum will die."

"No!"

"*Shh*. Tawny, we won't let him die," Steel promised.

"If we activate the project, we lose Scarlett," Indigo cried.

"Dove..." His words were filled with meaning I couldn't process.

"We don't have a choice." Jett sighed. "Everyone take a piece. Diamond, could you fill in for Straumr?"

"Yes," came a weak voice.

They all sounded far away. I couldn't recognize faces or names. I stared blankly at the floor with barely enough energy to stand as one by one the people around me pushed pieces into a circle and blue light flooded the space.

Large hands lifted my jaw as a kiss was pressed to my forehead and my eyes slid to the ground. "Quick's got you. Ridge and Steel will be down in a moment. We've all done our part. Turns out some things can't be done on your own, baby sis. I love you. We'll help you through. Don't you worry."

I was shifted to another set of arms slick with rain as he bit a blade into my palm. I felt a cold hard piece pressed to the gash and quickly taken away as another blue light went on.

"Mrs. Scarlett, you have to focus. I cannot stand here with you when you activate it. You have to stay still until the light can catch you like the others. Go back. Bring back Slate and my brother. Freya's burly boar, bring back my mother, yours, Slate's. Fix this gods' cursed mess. I know you can." He pressed a kiss to my cheek and positioned my hand over the center of the circle. "Just push," he said and sped off.

I staggered into the circle forcing the piece into place and felt the heat rise in me. It wasn't a blue light. I was engulfed in pure blue flame.

My dress rippled; my hair beat around my face as lightning struck somewhere above. The pieces each person stood on trembled with a hiss of air as the thick lines that divided them receded. Slowly, the lines began to spin beneath the protruding slabs with a rapid *thud thud thud* every time a line passed under a triangular piece. The wind picked up and tore at their clothes. I felt as though I was being torn apart from the inside.

I gasped. White surrounded me. It didn't make any sense; I was trying to rewind time... had I gone too far? Maybe I'd died.

The white world shifted though I didn't see a single thing move.

I was a snow leopard named Kikka mated to Glinski. We were so deeply in love with one another and lived a simple life in the Wemic canyons with a dozen cubs of our own.

The scene swirled and took on a new shape.

In the ocean waters, I was the tiger shark hybrid, Char'ra. After a long courtship, Sear're and I became exclusive where we reigned over the Merfolk court deftly managing the king and his children. We made a powerful pair.

The waters disappeared, and I was high above the earth. Pavo had convinced me, as Nella the meadowlark, to let him share my nest. Our hatchlings were the most beautiful Aves and one of our sons mated with a Guardian for life. We were terribly proud parents.

I live more lives, each one as a tribal member. A Bjorn, a Crathode, a Jorogumo, each life has its complications, but I'm happy. None of my choices lead me to where my human life brings me. I was a Minotaur, an Anguillan, and a Faunelle. I managed to have a full life as any person, sometimes with children, sometimes without. I had power, and then I didn't.

Lewt and Pert, the golden Akhal-Teke, race the wind along the Mabon ocean coast. I was the clan leader's wife. He built me a special hut close to the water outside of our village so I can birth our many children. We make love on the shore as humans but run the forests as Centaur spending our free time with our foals teaching them the troll and fairy customs to whom we were close.

Vernal barters for a game of chess because he knew I'd cherish it. Dae, the boa constrictor, chose not to have a mate while she advises the king and his queen. The Gorgons are highly competitive within their tribe. Vernal and I had our work cut out for us, but my closest companion and I eventually get the Gorgons to quit their bickering and work together for the betterment of the tribe as a whole. The tribe had never been more prosperous.

The scene swims again and I slapped Niall's face. None of the Lycans could believe Niall married. As Aisling, the maned wolf, I had my work cut out for me. I fell in love with the man he could be rather than the man he was, but he was a work in progress. We fight fiercely but love fiercely if our half dozen pups were any indication.

"Enough!" I shouted into the whiteness and my voice didn't sound like it was coming from my body. It didn't sound like I had a body at all. "None of that was real."

"You lived each one of those lives on different planes of existence," came a woman's voice I knew all too well.

My chin wobbled with tears burning in my eyes. Suddenly, I was standing within the bright whiteness in a white dress, but as Scarlett the elemental.

"Don't get all existential on me. I know what life is mine. Come out from where ever you're hiding. I need to rewind time; I have to fix the royal mess I've made of my life and save my family," I shouted angrily into the white.

A woman formed out of thin air. Long dark waves fell to her elbows, her dark almond eyes shown with warmth as did her wide smile and slightly squared jaw. The urge to cry assailed me again as I looked at the form of my mother.

"My mom is a wight in Mabon. You're an impostor. Just tell me how to work this thing," I snapped, sniffling.

"I am the Mother. I am whomever you perceived to be *your* mother."

She beckoned me to her, and I blinked when she appeared before me, or maybe it was me before her. In any case, I granted myself a slight reprieve. I hugged the woman. She smelled like jasmine and roses, just like my mother had.

"Saving your family will not save the world," she said in an inflectionless tone.

"I don't care. Just save them," I said petulantly and drew away from her.

"You are night, my child. The key to end the world. Come," she told me.

I opened my mouth to give her a piece of my mind, but the next instant I was standing in front of Valla University. I barely recognized the sprawling castle. My hand clutched at my chest as I took in the scene.

I'd seen it hundreds if not thousands of times. Carnage. The Stygian Camp beneath the walls of Valla U was on fire. The Mélange army was scattered and the ones who tried to fight were untrained. Fodder for the Red Seconds. Death and destruction reigned supreme.

It was frozen in time and I was thankful because the scent of bodies roasting must have been oppressive. I walked through the still bodies on the front lawns of where tyros were supposed to be learning to balance the world. Lera and Chafer had led the Shadow Breakers to come up behind the Mélange. Hopper was with them as well as the team I'd helped Brass recruit who weren't in the university. I picked up my skirts as I stepped deeper into the battle.

I slapped my hand over my mouth to stifle my cry as I came upon the crushed command tent. Canis had let Cygnus stay behind knowing they couldn't possibly defend against the Shadow Breakers and the tribes alone. Ruby had stayed behind and looked to have been on a horse behind Cygnus when they were both struck down. They held one another in death. Despite myself, my nose burned with unshed tears before I moved on.

Deeper into the battle towered a white barghest as big as Slate but with blood-red eyes. An albino barghest. He looked unhinged — bodies strewn about him. I wondered if he was merely a hybrid of some kind of Minotaur and made a mental note to investigate the grisly beast further.

A few feet away from the albino barghest was Asp. She looked to have run out without a weapon in her hands in hopes of being defeated. She never recovered after Shale's death. I couldn't imagine how depthless her loss was. Her dark up tilted eyes stared blankly at the black churning clouds above. I glanced past her to find Boa fighting in the vanguard to reach her body.

Wemic, Lycans, and Bjorn formed a wall of fur clad bodies along the outer walls of the castle. They clashed against the Mélange who hadn't run in fangs and claws. I saw Keen and Tikee, Tadg, Caolan, and Padraig all fighting in the front lines. Adal and his Faunelle were in the second wave along with Ophio and his Gorgons. Behind them were the front doors to the university.

I pushed fur and blood that hung in the air with a hand to make way between the fighting bodies to look further into the university. It floated until I dropped my hand to look to the entrance steps. Fox, Crag, and River crowded the steps, hands outstretched with their calling faces scrunched in the effort. Behind them were Sky and Ford at the doors trying to keep the tyros inside who wanted to join the fight. Malachite and Beryl were pressed against their arms. I could make out stretchers with injured tribesmen where Fern, Mica, Magnolia, and Wisteria were tending to the wounded. Tyros crowded the windows intermingling with the other tribes, their faces all frozen in anger or fear. So many people. So much hate.

I spun taking in the horrific scene feeling overwhelmed.

"You can fix this," the Mother told me.

I squeezed my eyes shut and looked up at the black clouds lit from within by lighting. "No one can fix this. There's no trust. These people will never forgive much less forget what has happened. The islands will be more divided than ever before. I thought the war would end with Canis, Ash, and Sage's deaths or convictions, but the people of Thrimilci and Elivagar will never forget that Ostara and Mabon didn't fight back. There are monsters, real *evil* creatures, that hide in the stretching shadows for victims that the Stygians unleashed." I turned to her. "Tell me how to rewind time. I'll go back as far as I need to save Wind or Storm, or whatever you need, but I'm going back and I'm stopping Orion from unleashing the Red Kings. I'm saving Robin and Opal Geol, Lark and Flint. My parents can be a family. Hawk and Sparrow belong together, Gypsum *will* be born. Just tell me how."

The scene shifted again and the feeling of vertigo made me widen my stance so I wouldn't fall standing still. The Mother wearing the guise of my mom grew luminescent. We were underground in a huge cavern. My breathing hitched as my eyes caught on the snout of a golden serpent.

"Is that what I think it is?" I asked in a hushed tone.

"Leshy magic is not powerful enough to create such a project. It required the last dragon, and *you* activated it, thus awakening him. The project was a trick. It does not do what you were told."

I gaped at the dragon whose maw I could walk into standing perfectly straight. Its massive scaled body caught the glow of the Mother's luminescence.

"Who imprisoned it?" I asked, hoping I could email that person and figure out how to do it again.

"No one. Dragons cannot be controlled. He went to sleep, that sleep lasted centuries until today."

I turned my head back to her. "How do I make it right?"

"Try."

The scene shifted, and I fell to the rapidly dampening gritty ground. The lines were shifting back into place as my family slumped to their triangular portions, a heavy rain soaked us through. I pushed myself up on my palms and came face to face with the pool of blood from my nightmares.

I had my memories.

"Scarlett! What happened?" Quick ran to me, helping me up as the ground quaked even though the lines were in place.

"It doesn't work," I told him, and I watched his devilishly handsome face fall as I staggered over to Slate and Brass.

A sound like splintering wood rang through the dome and the hiss of water sprayed as the wall cracked. Quick ran to where Indigo laid and licked his lips as he looked at the others. While Steel ran ahead with Gypsum over his shoulders, Ridge had hoisted Tawny up. He'd already taken up Nova, Quartz, and Cassiopeia. Quick cursed and lifted Amethyst onto his shoulder.

I bent down kissing Brass's cooling lips after I removed the gag and then Slate's.

"Get up, Scarlett. We need your *calling*," Quick shouted.

Sterling, Diamond, and Jett laid within the circle alive, but unconscious.

We wouldn't make it. Steel was knocked back by a sudden split in the wall that a deluge of water poured from, destroying the ramps. Quick shouted and ran to him where he'd fallen back. Steel wasn't moving. I breathed deep and pulled the oak leaf fetish from my hair. I had no other alternative. Maybe Quick, Ridge, and I could each save a person — *if* we could save ourselves.

I stabbed the ground where Slate's blood met the sand and called sunshine and water coaxing the little wooden leaf to grow.

"Get up! We will all die without your help!" Quick cursed.

I watched as the leaf spread, forcing a bark beneath it. The bark widened and circled back to itself growing higher. Branches clawed into the tumultuous sky and with a *whoosh* leaves crested the top. Roots lifted the earth and the walls of the dome crumbled further.

Two patches of moss parted for a bearded mouth as he wriggled his roots for feet and branches for hands. Two knolls blinked down at me above his long bark nose as the Leshy took me in.

"John. Thanks for leaving me for dead in the bowels of the Vetr castle," I said, coolly ignoring the water that had begun to pool around my folded legs.

"Ah, daughter of spring and summer, yet here you are," John said in a grandfatherly way.

"Save them and help us out of here. That's what I need."

Nothing else mattered.

"A life for a life. I had, but one yet you ask me to save many more than that. Pick one and I shall save him." John gestured down to Brass and Slate beside me and I narrowed my eyes.

Thunder rolled in the distance. "Am I to sacrifice everything for nothing? Choose one love over another and live with that decision? I can't make this choice."

My stomach sunk when I found the solution. From John's expression he knew what I was thinking. I blinked at tears and got to my feet.

"Are you certain that is your choice?" he asked, his voice not sounding half as friendly as he had been a moment ago.

I glanced down at Slate and Brass and the others. "Help me save them," I whispered against the rushing waters. "Take me instead."

"Scarlett, what are you promising, you rash girl!" Ridge shouted at me as he cradled Tawny.

"It is done," John said simply, and he opened his twiggy palms, letting two specs of light drift down.

One sunk into Brass while the other found a home in Slate. I'd done it. I'd promised myself I wouldn't let them die, and they wouldn't. The rest was up to them.

"The Mother always did favor her Guardians." John leaned back with a sneer of his mossy lips and winked out of existence.

I screamed as my legs stiffened in pain. Roots burst from the shoes on my feet and I felt my legs fusing together. I expected to die. This was worse. My body widened as I grew taller, my skin darkened and grew rough as my arms elongated. My dress tore, and I watched as my hair fell out around my roots.

"Quick! Ridge!" I shouted. "Bring them to me!"

Ridge and Quick stood beneath me as I kept growing so I scooped up Brass and Slate and put them into my highest branches. Quick passed me Amethyst and Indigo and ran to grab Jett while Ridge handed me Gypsum, then Tawny. It was getting harder to bend and my memories were being stolen once again. Steel was in my branches as Ridge climbed up with Diamond.

"Sterling! Quick, don't leave him!" My voice was changing to have an echoing quality like my mother and father's wight had.

Quick growled and pulled Sterling over his shoulders. I bent down in time to pull him off the floor which collapsed beneath him. The walls were crumbling down, and I hurried to lift them all free of the falling debris and swirling waters.

The waters came up to my bark chest as I straightened at over twenty feet tall and growing. I pulled the remnants of the wooden bridge over ignoring the way my skin had turned into bark and elongated and Quick hopped on so Ridge could pass him the unconscious bodies. The beating rain began to ebb as they used the bridge like a boat and laid each person out. We'd saved them all.

On the shore, Lycans and Bjorn stood with damp matted fur watching the scene with three bodies lying on the relatively dry sands.

Indigo was the last body down with Ridge who hopped free of my branches. Quick's gold-flecked eyes gleamed and he blinked against the rain.

"I really wanted to spend my life growing old with them and our children. Help them forgive me one day," I said as Quick nodded and let loose a sob.

"You cursed, beautiful fool. They will never get over you. None of us will."

The waters churned and bubbled. I put a branched hand on the bridge and gave it a gentle shove to glide over the water to safety. Maybe I was going to be pulled under. Maybe I was going to truly die after all.

Water exploded all around me and I twisted as air ruffled my strands of leaves. I stared after the golden dragon that lit from a crack of lightning as it flew into the dispersing black clouds.

Maybe it was good I didn't have to fight a dragon.

My fight was over.

CHAPTER 48
BRASS

All my life I wanted the voices, the constant murmurings, all the awful inner thoughts of every person I had ever been near to stop.

They had.

I chased her in a sunny field of wild flowers. Her caramel hair flew behind her, her cheeks rounded with her bright beautiful smile that could bring any man to his knees in supplication. Balas was in her arms and Spinel was on my shoulders. As angry and hurt as I was at her for having been with my grandfather, her choice in names had brought me incredible joy.

"Despite what Guardians think, I am not all powerful."

The air rushed from my lungs when the field vanished and I stood in a room of white with a dark-haired woman I recognized standing across from me. Her plump lips always seemed purse and her dreamy green eyes twinkled.

My mother.

"Slate was supposed to die, they both were. They are too dangerous together to live. It was their destiny to die," she told me.

It was not my mother, but someone wearing her face. It was cruel.

"She was not supposed to find you and fall in love. Your sons were never meant to be hers. Because you and she fell in love and had your sons, your brother and the other elemental will have children. They were not meant to be. The elementals should have died with them. The project was not supposed to be activated."

"The Mother. I don't know what you expect from me. Slate and I are dead, leave me to my peace," I told her, and focused on trying to conjure up Scarlett and our sons.

"You taught her sacrifice and how to make the hard choices. While Wren and Sparrow unwittingly made her fear, more than anything, living while those she loved died. The pain they felt at having left Lark and Ridge behind to save themselves and their children left echoes in her." Robin sighed. "You are not dead. She made a bargain for your life. Yours and Slate's. I am with him now."

"No. I refuse," I told her as I began to tremble. "I *can't* live without her," I whispered.

My mother's plump lips quirked. "When I chose the Regn, I knew you would be irresistible. It is in your blood. You will find happiness again, Brass. I promise it."

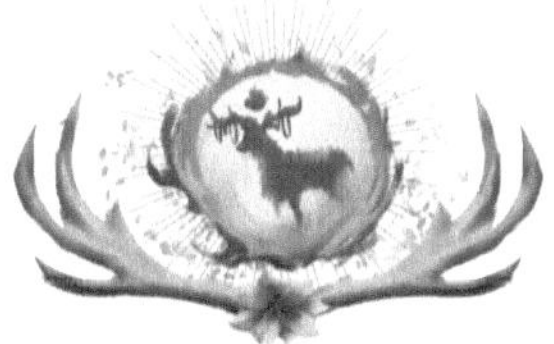

I gasped in sand and rain as Slate roared. A storm broke overhead and dark churning clouds gave way to the bright sun. My limbs felt leaden as I clambered to my feet, but my body wouldn't work as I wanted.

I was alive.

I remembered my death. We had all been bound and gagged when Ash first ran Slate through and then he plunged his long seax into my heart. Scarlett didn't know us and had been appalled. It gave some solace that she hadn't done it herself. She wouldn't have to live with our deaths on her hands if her memories returned.

Who had paid the price for our lives?

I fell forward on my knees at the shore and braced my fingertips on the wet sand as a drizzle fell over me. Slate swam out to the giant willow tree that grew from the waters. The wight had a face made from its bark and it was unmistakably Scarlett even from where I kneeled.

Slate reached her and shouted unintelligibly as I hung my head. Another generation of Regn men without a mother. I could hear the soothing coos coming from the wight that bore the soul of my beloved and it was almost too much to bear. Being a wight was supposed to be the greatest gift the Mother could give. It felt like an act of cruelty. She was there but not. She had no thoughts of her own.

"How could you!" Slate roared at her.

He shifted and shifted back until he exhausted himself and swam back to shore to toss himself on the sands next to me on his back.

"I was the one to die. Never her. Never you. I do not care what that bitch said."

The Mother had told him the same. I had no comfort left to give.

CHAPTER 49

INDIGO

Silver and I leaned into one another with our bare feet buried in the sand. My tears had dried up, but Tawny's still flowed on our other side between Gypsum and Steel. Jett's body heat from where his hip met mine was what we both needed to feel connected as he held Amethyst. Slate and Brass sat closer to the shore and hadn't uttered a word since Slate's temper tantrum had finished an hour earlier. Wight Scarlett's sweet words and welcoming branch arms were more than their sanity could bear.

Ridge had come to Valla U and found the battle had started and we were all missing. He'd rounded up the Bjorn and Lycans in Elivagar and came through the Vanaheim Arena. Drik'ir was dead, and the rogues captured or killed. Nova, Quartz, and Cassiopeia wore nix cuffs and were being escorted back to Valla U.

"We are leaving. We have horses should anyone else wish to come," Ridge offered.

"We'll join you." Steel said, helping Tawny to her feet with Gypsum's help.

Gypsum's guilt was palpable no matter how Steel tried to comfort him. I'd try to return his memories when my strength returned, for now, I couldn't light a candle.

Sterling shifted to lean forward past Amethyst and Jett to where I sat. "I will go. Indigo…" I turned to meet his sorrow filled eyes. "I… am sorry. I do not deserve your forgiveness, I know. You will tell me if the boy is mine?"

"If he comes home a barghest, I will send him to you *after* I'm through shouting at him… if that's okay by Diamond."

The others were listening, it was hard not to, but we no longer had secrets to hide.

"I would never keep a child from its father," she said simply. "I am very sorry about Scarlett. I liked her… very much."

Words caught below the lump in my throat. "I'm sorry too. About all of it," I told her, barely choking out the words. "I know Basil will always be your father, but Crag is a good man. He'd be willing to be more."

"More?" she asked.

"Since he and Delta were your birth parents?" I knit my brows when I caught her startled expression.

"I did not know that, that makes us first cousins," she said, looking to Sterling.

He stood with a sigh and gazed down at Diamond. "I would be your family, care for you, if you let me."

I felt Silver's head shift to watch her slip her hand into Sterling's as he helped her to her feet. Sterling tucked her to his body and looked to all of us.

"My sisters are very pregnant…"

"They will not have to raise their children in Karkinos. I swear it. I promised you I wouldn't let you lose your lands, and I meant it." Silver's anger at my promises simmered.

Ridge smiled. "I happen to know the Matriarchs' Vetr and Dagr very well as well as the Patriarchs' Sumar, you are Patriarch Haust so one more vote for the majority."

Jett and Amethyst spoke at the same time. "We are the heirs, we'll support you," Jett said listlessly. "I can't guarantee leniency for your grandmother though."

"My thanks," Sterling said before returning his gaze to mine. "I hope you can forgive me one day."

"One day," I told him, glancing back out to Scarlett the wight.

SILVER KISSED the top of my head when he came back from hunting. Dusk was beginning to fall, and the sky was a brilliant yellow and pink hue that reminded me of the wedding ring Brass had gotten Scarlett.

"We only have one dose of rousen left, Dove," Silver said softly.

"I know," I murmured.

"If we get enough Guardians, we can transplant the... it. Maybe in Ostara? We could get a boat?" Jett had been trying to figure out the impossible for the last two hours.

"We shall ask when we return," Amethyst placated him.

"Here is food for dinner and enough to last you through breakfast," Silver said, placing the food in Brass's pack.

He gave his brother's shoulder a squeeze and walked over the sand back to me. Ridge had cleared the beach, so the bodies were on a pyre behind us made of the bridge remnants. Other than the giant willow tree growing out of the ocean, there was no other evidence of there ever being anything amiss.

"Come on. We have to round some people up to help us," Jett said, dusting off his backside.

I didn't have the heart to tell him it wouldn't work, so I nodded and let him help me to my feet.

Valla University for Guardian Mastery was a graveyard. The Red Seconds had won the Purge War, but it was hard to see it that way when so many had died. Cygnus and Ruby had been some of the firsts to perish when a white barghest had burst into the enemy camp and started a panic within the Mélange.

Asp's death followed shortly after when she snuck out into the thick of the fighting. Padraig was the only other person I knew who had been killed in the day's pointless battle.

Cassiopeia, Nova, and Quartz were kept in the cells inside Valla U along with Willow. Their cells could hardly be called such, more like tiny apartments with the ability to speak to one another through the thick glass panes.

Coyote was waiting for us when we arrived and Silver gave him and the other provosts a briefing before he took me back to the Sumar palace. Coyote had news of his own. The Gorgons had joined the Anguillan that had come from Elivagar to march on Ostara's town heart. They defeated their own rogues and chased the Stygians out with the help of the Aves who had taken the Var castle from the air. Ostara was won and plans to install Jett as Patriarch were already in motion.

So much death and all for nothing. We were no further or better than we were before. There was a festering ulcer where the love for my father and sister had once been and I wasn't sure if it would ever heal.

CHAPTER 50

GYPSUM

My stomach rumbled. I hadn't eaten since breakfast when Patriarch Jett Var and Matriarch Amethyst Geol had left with Cherry to go back to the Geol castle they were remodeling.

Ostara had been under new management for the last month and a half, and I was closer every day to retrieving a slew of lost memories. Thre'ik had taken the Mélange infants and younger children under her figurative wing with the near nonexistent Jorogumo tribe. The older Mélange were offered a stretch of land in Ostara, not far from Jorogumo lands in case the children decided to join the older Mélange tribe once they could care for themselves.

Ridge was living in Elivagar and was not acting like my mom's husband — thank the gods. He was crucial to Tawny's management since my parents had their hands full. Both islands had dangerous creatures stalking the streets that the Stygians had unleashed. My father was forced into being the Sumar patriarch since they weren't coming clean on my whereabouts. Not until my memories returned.

Valla U wasn't in session until the tyros could be temporarily reunited with their surviving family members and the lawns could be restored. There had been a solid week of funerals, so I'd heard, and every island had been in mourning. The Guardians were just starting to rebuild in more ways than one.

I grunted as Tree-gold pounced on my stomach to join her blue-eyed sister on the couch next to me. No cat should ever be as big as a dog, much less two of them. Bee-gold purred contentedly as I scratched her snowy fur.

Their fur stuck to my skin from all the humidity in Ostara. I'd taken to wearing the loose drawstring pants the Aves provided and nothing else in the quaint cottage. I rested my head back on the armrest in the front room preparing for my siesta.

"Gods' cursed Natt," Quick grumbled just before he slammed the door upstairs.

There were only two bedrooms in the cottage that Alder used to keep stocked when he was ambassador to the Jorogumo. There was a large garden out back and we had a pond for fishing and a chicken coop so we wanted for very little. I was content to sleep on the couch.

Quick stomped down the steps and shot me an exasperated look. He wore midnight blue pants in the same style as mine. He flung himself over the back of the sofa chair and wiped his hands down his face.

"She only wants me when she needs me. She is going to leave me," he said muffled by his hands before he let his head fall back.

Indigo had procured books upon books about nursing and when my parents visited they gave her as much information about hospitals as they could. She was leaving him. She was addicted to him and to Sterling and she had another two weeks left of being addicted to the sweet purple fluid she drank twice a day.

I knew for a fact Indigo wanted Quick much more than twice a day. The walls in the cottage could've been better insulated. Not to mention it was impossible not to walk in on them because they were everywhere. I'd taken to walking into rooms with my eyes closed.

"Can you blame her?" I asked him. "She loves you. She just needs time and space. She doesn't have a choice anymore on how she feels about you. You'd run too."

Quick narrowed his eyes at me. "Who asked you anyway?" he grumbled.

Three rapid knocks sounded on the door and we frowned at one another. We weren't expecting any visitors. We'd been placed far out of the way just to avoid them. Of course, they'd made sure we had a portal for easy access, but it was hidden in the trees and only our immediate family knew where it was.

Footsteps on the stairs drew our attention away from the door. Indigo was wrapped in a sarong the color of her namesake with a cherry red halter made of twisted fabrics that exposed her swell of tan belly. Quick stopped at the bottom of the stairs in front of the door as she slowly descended.

"Are you going to get the door?" she asked softly.

She wasn't trying to hurt him. She'd been through a lot and needed space.

His face hardened as he turned to the door and swung it open. Two men crowded the plank door. One with a red beard and shoulder length fiery hair, his sapphire eyes swiveled to find me and he smiled. His name came to me like information suddenly shoved into my brain from my ear. Luckily nothing else fell out the other side. Sky Tio wore the silver trimmed gold robe of the Tio Patriarch with a silver starburst on the back. The other man bore a stern expression on his ebony face, the only hair on his head, the straight brows over dark narrow eyes. Words forced their way into my mind. Crag Straumr wore a sleeveless deep purple robe with white trim, the outline of the moon emblazoned the back with the crescent filled in.

"Please, come in," Quick said dryly to the new patriarchs.

"We did not mean to intrude," Sky said, glancing at me and back to Quick. "Your family told us where we could find you."

"What can we do for you?" Indigo asked as Quick moved to sit in his original spot.

"My niece has hoped you were well. I am glad to see it is so," Sky said, looking at me.

I pulled my lips into my mouth and shook my head sitting up.

"Sorry. I'm having difficulties with my memories. What was her name again?"

"Mica Rot." Sky's eyes dropped, and I shrugged.

"It's not ringing any bells. Sorry. Let her know I'm alright, please? Some things come to my head as soon as I see it, or them, but other times it takes more than a nudge."

"She thought it might be something along those lines. I will let her know."

"Thanks," I said awkwardly as Bee and Tree chased one another up the stairs.

The back door slammed and Slate's heavy steps came in from the kitchen. He wore specially dyed black drawstring pants and his long hair was threaded with fetishes and silver beads all braided into one thick braid at his nape. A bright red handprint marred his cheek as he stormed in followed by Brass's chuckling.

Indigo moved to sit beside Quick and she tucked her feet up beside her as she leaned into him. I watched him sigh as he wound his arm around her. Neither of them could help themselves.

"Do not wake the boys," Indigo gently chastised.

"If you take her the first time again..." Slate growled.

Slate clenched his jaw when he set eyes on Sky and Crag.

Brass entered the room with his hair neatly combed into a knot at his nape and his beard kept trimmed close to his jaw. He pulled a pear out of the pocket of his red pants and tossed it to Indigo who craved them during her pregnancy.

"I'll take what is offered. She has not been offering, but I have to stand a better chance than you. After all, she has not slapped me...and she gave herself to me first before." He chuckled. "No," Brass said out of the blue.

"*No* what?" Slate rumbled.

"We have given all we are willing to give to the Guardians. We are retired," Brass told them.

I groaned. I thought I knew what they were talking about. A bigger secret than even my hiding place.

"I have a mouth. I can give them my answer."

She placed her basket of freshly picked produce on the rectangular table in the adjoined dining area and put her fist on her cocked hip. She wore a green sarong tied just below her fist and a top like Indigo's in yellow. Her caramel hair was piled on top of her head with a twisted headband of the same green and yellow.

Scarlett's pursed her lips, meeting Slate's glare with her own glower. She was deeply tanned from the hours she spent outside in the garden, and it made her eyes pop. A sheen of sweat covered her toned belly all the way up to her high cheek bones and brow. She looked fantastic.

Sky and Crag stared at her in disbelief.

"You wouldn't be here if you didn't already know I was alive," she said in her gravelly voice.

Our Scarlett, alive and very well.

CHAPTER

FIFTY-ONE

It wasn't the heaven I'd envisioned. Heaven shouldn't be white.

I wanted for nothing. I was at total peace. I was connected to all the other wights through the Mother and could receive her messages and feel what they felt. My mother and father could communicate to me with a single thought. I was never alone.

... The Mother is dying...

... The Yggdrasil is dying...

... Nidhogg is free...

The Mother was a bit melodramatic.

The world was *always* dying. Not my section — it was right as rain, though I was new to the job.

My mind floated in the white free of responsibility and need. It reminded me of what I always liked about floating in water. I was weightless.

"Not as bad as you thought?" my mother's voice cut through my dreamless state.

"It's not," I answered, and she appeared.

450

My mother in her loose white dress was before me. I looked down at myself and saw I had a form again. I wore a shimmering white dress that hugged me in all the right places.

"John has been the most difficult of my Leshy to bring to heel. He has always resented my Guardians. Years in Orion's dungeon did not help matters. He overstepped." She looped her arm through mine and we began to walk, although I wasn't sure if we actually moved or not. "An egregious error on his part has caused a great imbalance. He needed two lives. When he took you, he bargained for one. You are four."

She shifted her hand before me to show four tiny specs of light. One penetrated my heart while the other three flew into my belly.

"Triplets?" I squeaked.

"Two boys and a girl. So you see —"

"I won't pick my children to die instead," I said in a rush covering my belly.

She nodded. "Nor would I expect *you* to. I have a happy medium. You made a bargain with your husbands? They are accountable for one another; they share you and the life they have built with you. Now they share a life. One life, a life you saved when you rescued John, for two souls. Nothing shall change, they will not live shorter, only when one eventually perishes, so will the other."

"I'll take it." I spun to her, sticking out my hand, and she smirked at it but didn't take it.

"As I knew you would. I am afraid you will have to start from scratch. As for your memories, I promise... you will remember with time. I will even offer you a gift."

I dropped my hand and held myself higher. "I don't want any of your gifts."

The sly smile on my mother's face was so foreign she looked like a different woman altogether. "I have more to balance so you will take my gifts and not complain. Your Slate will not complain, to be sure. I will also restore Gypsum's memories. I will need him in the days to come. Did you know he was the only zoolinguist in Tidings? I need him and I need him to focus on *my* needs."

"What does that mean?" I asked, searching her face for any expression I recognized.

"Reunite the people. That is all you need concern yourself with, my child. The war is not yet over."

My bare feet partially submerged in dark water. The green light faded rapidly behind me and I glanced out at the horizon. There was nothing as far as I could see. The night was clear so I could see every star. I had no idea the night sky held so many. I turned to face the other way and saw a cook fire illuminating the shore and two men beside it.

At my pink polished toes, there was nothing for me to walk on. I was standing on water. I swirled my toe in the cool water and shrugged. I could swim if it didn't work.

I hopped and landed firmly on the top of the water. I giggled. I could literally walk on water.

It may be the best dream ever.

I hopped from foot to foot across the water until my feet hit the sand. I pushed my long wavy hair away from my face as I glanced up to the two men. I threw my head back and laughed throatily.

Yes. Best dream ever.

I waggled my pink polished fingers at the two gorgeous men sitting open-mouthed at the fire. I kneeled as I sat and gave them my best smile.

"Are you seeing this?" one with a trimmed stubbly beard asked the one with a scar that went from his hairline to his left cheek over his narrow silver eye.

"I am afraid to move," his voice came from his belly in a deep rumble I felt in my toes.

"I must have been particularly good in a past life. Seeing as I do not have experience with men, much less men like the two of you... I don't know who I want first." I shook my head as I took my time looking them both over. "May I?" I leaned forward and plucked the stick the one with amber eyes had in his hand and took a bite of the meat he had roasted on it. "This is delicious. I don't think I've ever been hungry in a dream before."

They were barely breathing. I knew that because I was keenly inspecting their sculpted chests. I used my stick to gesture to amber eyes.

"If you would be so kind... *actually*."

I dropped the stick and crawled on my hands and knees over to the man with the anvil jaw and plump soft looking lips. I'd never taken off a man's shirt before, but there was a first time for everything. I wouldn't mind a few firsts with the two of them.

I pulled the man's linen shirt from his pants and slowly watched the hem slide over dark honey skin dusted with dark silky hair.

"Arms up," I said playfully, and I watched his muscles flex as he raised his arms.

He had a single tattoo over his left pectoral in red and black. He watched me run my fingertips over it to circle his perfect brown nipple.

"You're gorgeous," I whispered, feeling a pull in my stomach.

I slid my hand up his chest to his hair and tugged the leather strap free so it fell just past his shoulders to his elbows. His lips were still parted as he watched me, taking slow steady breaths. My breath shuddered out as I leaned forward.

"You smell like cinnamon and spring time," I whispered as I searched his eyes.

"You smell the same. Warm spiced apples and vanilla." His voice was smooth and seductive, and I practically whimpered.

I braced my hand on his hard thigh as I leaned forward. He inhaled sharply as my lips brushed his and I gasped as his hands wound around my back, pulling me into his lap. His lips were demanding but soft, his hands gripped my thighs forcing my dress back. Our bodies were so close they seemed fused together. Suddenly, I realized I wasn't wearing underwear and I tried to imagine them back because it was a dream and I should be able to imagine anything.

My underwear didn't return. What pressed against me was very difficult to imagine but there it was. I pushed myself off his lap so my legs were still over his thighs. We both panted, staring at one another.

"She feels real," he said without taking his eyes off me.

His lips were swollen, and I licked my own wondering if I looked as wanton as he did. I certainly felt that way.

"I want to find out for myself," the other man rumbled.

I scooted back and straightened my dress. "I need a moment. What are your names?"

I asked trying to buy myself time. Even in my dreams the amber eyed dreamboat was too much for little ole me.

I ran my hand over my mouth and tried to get a grip on my reality. The two men broke their gazes from me to glance at one another.

"I'm Brass and he is Slate. Your husbands. You are Scarlett Natt, daughter of Wren and Alder," the man who called himself Brass told me.

I licked my lips again and took a better look at everything I had on. There was a diamond solar cross on my pointer finger and an emerald ring lined with diamonds on my ring finger. Was I married? No, I'd remember that. Two husbands wasn't right, was it?

On either one of my wrists were braided torques, one gold, one silver and on my ring hand's ring finger was another with a stone the color of sunset. I patted the necklace at my chest and felt a pendant of a glyph like tree. I didn't recognize any of it. I ran my hand over my hair and found feathers attached to it, one that looked like a peacock eye and a plain white one. Two silver beads that looked like Slate's were clasped to the ends of two narrow braids that held a jade canine and an ivory sunburst.

"You gave your pearls to Tawny, and I no longer wear my beads so you got rid of the ebony and bronze you used to wear. You had a tree of life carving but you gave it to Indigo. You had a wooden comb... it's gone for good," Brass explained.

"Any of those names sound familiar, Torch?"

I shook my head at Slate whose silver eyes reflected the flickering flames. "Who's Torch?"

"You are, Love," Brass said in a careful tone.

I didn't like the dream. I wasn't in control. I wanted them to stop with all their chatter and do things all *romancey*.

Maybe it was an abandoned island dream, and we were stranded there just the three of us, or maybe it was a post-apocalyptic dream. We had to repopulate the earth together.

Okay, the dream was back on.

Brass held out his hand to me, leaning forward. "May I see your left hand?”

I held it out and watched as he slid the emerald ring up to reveal an arrow pointed up, he rubbed a red fluid over it and I knit my brows as he sucked in a deep breath. Was that his blood? On the skin between my thumb and pointer finger was a greater than symbol tattooed in intricate designs.

“What are you doing? What do these marks stand for?”

I was busy looking down to notice that Brass was holding my face. He pulled down my lower lip, sliding his finger along it and I heard Slate groan before it slid back.

“Bonds,” Slate breathed.

Brass placed his palm to my belly. He made an awkward sound half-sob, half-exhale as he looked to Slate.

“Triplets, you bastard.”

Slate moved so quickly I yelped in surprise. Sitting so quietly he was hard to ignore, but he seemed to expand when he moved. He was inches taller than Brass, but Brass was a big guy. Slate was even bigger.

His touch was gentle though when he placed his hand beside Brass’s. I looked down at him, his long thick lashes fanned across his high cheekbones. He had a hard-featured face, but his full lips and girlish lashes softened him immensely. He glanced up to me and he was smiling. His smile lit his entire face. His bronze cheeks creased in what must be a rare showing of teeth.

My mouth fell open as I took in the glorious man. He smelled like sunburnt leaves and cloves and he overwhelmed my senses. I was never the kind of girl who would chase a boy, but with his lips so close and that smile blindly bright... I ducked my head and slanted my mouth over his.

I moaned as he kissed me back, the charge between our bodies pumped my blood through my veins at a rapid pace until it was all I could hear. My back hit the sand as he lowered his weight atop me. My face cooled as he blocked the campfire with his body.

The dream wasn’t making sense. I didn’t know their names; I barely recognized my own. Contemplating triplets was impossible when I had no recollection of ever having had sex. I didn’t know what a bond was and that was okay by me. All I wanted was this place and these two men. It felt right.

His breathing was rougher than mine as he bunched the fabric at my thighs and fit his hips to me. My head canted back and rubbed on the sand as he moved against me. I opened my eyes and caught sight of Brass going down to the water, he began to wash himself.

"I *need* you," Slate moaned as he planted an open mouthed kissed to my throat.

My sensibilities had fled, but it was a dream. I could do what I wanted.

"*Uh-huh,*" I breathed.

My fingers curled in his thin shirt as he breathed in my ear tickling my skin. A probing warmth came from his body into mine with the slide of his pants over roped hips and I could feel him at the apex of my thighs. *More of that please.*

I braced myself. Such big men were likely to have big... instruments.

"Scarlett?" Slate leaned back to look at me. "It is *you?*"

"I... I think so," I stammered breathlessly.

"That is not possible," he mumbled, hovering above me and licked his lower lip before shifting back.

He took my wrist so I was sitting and I straightened the white dress. Slate pulled his pants up over his hips, tucking a considerable length of himself away as he glanced up to the shore.

I'd never had a more uncomfortable moment.

Brass jogged up and stared down at me. "A maiden? That's not possible. *I* was your first lover."

I curled around my knees. "I want to wake up. Nothing you say makes any sense, and that was horrible."

Slate's brows rose to his hairline.

"Maybe it is a onetime gift. If we leave, she disappears," Brass interrupted looking down at me.

"I do not want to sleep with her if she is not Scarlett. I have made that mistake before," Slate murmured, staring at me. "Do you remember anything?"

"This is just a dream. A *sugarfooty* dream. Who wants to be a virgin with two hot guys on a beautiful star filled night on the ocean shore? I mean, *come on.* I'm going to wake up any second now," I said, resting my chin on my knees.

Brass kneeled in front of me and swept his damp hair from his face.

"I'm sorry if you're feeling used. We believe you have amnesia. Are you hungry? Thirsty? We would like to tell you about our wife. All you have to do is listen."

"I am a bit hungry still. It's... okay. I'm not offended. I'm not his wife or yours. I can understand why he would not want to cheat on her, though to be frank it seems a little late. I'm not complaining. I don't think he'd... fit." I dropped my eyes and felt my cheeks heat.

Did people blush in dreams?

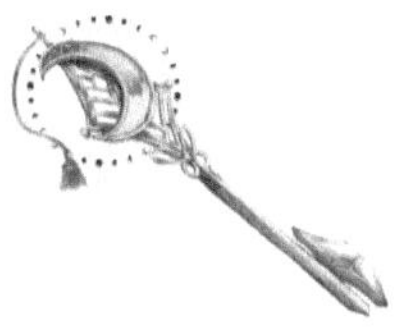

With my belly full, they told me the story about their wife. She sounded like an amazing woman, but I wasn't her. The more they talked about her impossible feats, the better I felt about the whole night being a dream.

They said they'd waited all day, unable to leave the shore out of grief. That the sun had set and there was a green flash. I was there when the light faded. I remembered all of that, but the fact that they could remember before I arrived was disconcerting. Dreams didn't exist before the dreamer.

Despite Slate's reservations, I didn't mind if they held me while we slept. I'd wake up in bed anyway and I could tell they desperately wanted me to be their dead wife. I didn't mind giving them comfort.

"This is thy hour O Soul, thy free flight into the wordless. Away from books, away from art, the day erased, the lesson done. Thee fully forth emerging, silent, gazing, pondering the themes thou lovest best. Night, sleep, and the stars," Slate whispered in my ear where he had tucked me to his body.

"That's beautiful," I whispered.

He sighed enough to shift strands of my hair over my face. "Walt Whitman. I will make sure you remember who that is."

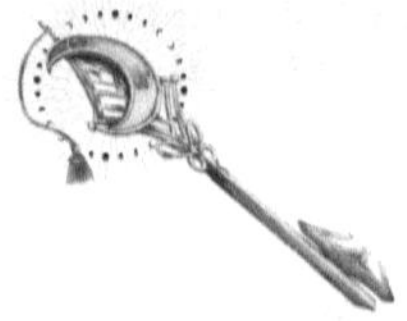

When I woke up sandwiched between the two men...I was hysterical.

They made me breakfast and pointed out that my breasts were leaking. When Slate offered to suckle, I slapped him. It was a knee jerk reaction to a complete stranger offering to put his mouth on my body as he leaned. The events of the night before, especially with Slate, replayed before my mind and I was mortified.

Not a dream.

Brass lent me clothes and forced me to wear a ring that changed my voice and he said it changed my appearance as well. He emphasized that I could not reveal my identity because a bear man named Demyan was on the loose as well as rogue tribes and fleeing Stygian Knights. I had no idea who any of those people were, but Brass and Slate did not seem like the types of men who exaggerated.

Besides, they brought up a good point. I had nowhere else to go. I had no other options. They said they could help me remember.

What if they were right?

They wrapped my feet, and we walked to an enormous white stadium that they said was built by their wife and we traveled through a magical lighted arch that brought us to a palace.

Maybe I *was* dreaming.

They led me into a dining room of the mosaic filled palace and I saw a blue morning glory vine. I remembered my mother. I remembered Pearl. I was Scarlett Natt, but I didn't remember those men.

Hawk and Sparrow ran into the dining room and memories flooded back as they held me. Freeze frames sped up of my childhood and I gasped as I was overloaded with forgotten information.

Tawny, Steel, Gypsum... I remembered my family.

Word spread fast as Brass and Slate packed for a journey leaving me in the dining room. When I saw Jett, I remembered Alder. Bee and Tree came trotting in before Indigo and I remembered her. My beautiful, once sweet now jaded, sister.

It wasn't until we were moved to the Ostara cottage before I remembered Quick. He changed into the clothing the Aves gave us and was walking past shirtless. I knew those tattoos.

They brought a portal from the Anguillan and hid it deep the Ostara jungles. I'd stayed at the cottage before with my father and siblings. My father and mother rekindled their affair there, and I had spent the night with Cory in one of the bedrooms.

I had two beautiful sons, and I was pregnant with triplets. Tawny and Indigo confirmed it. They also confirmed that I was, in fact, intact.

Gypsum was recovering his memories along with me and Indigo was coming down from her rousen addiction. Where Indigo was, so was Quick. Where my sons and I were, so were Brass and Slate. We had frequent visitors as Tidings healed itself much the same way we were after the Purge War.

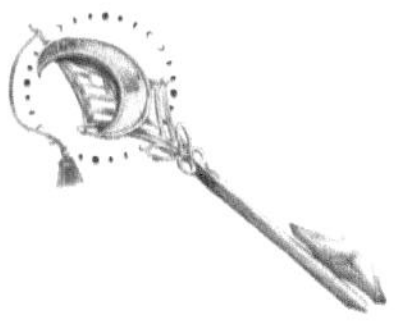

I couldn't help the smile that quirked my lips. It wasn't often I remembered things on sight. My *calling* wasn't as strong as it once was, but my abilities were trickling back to me.

"We are glad the rumors were wrong," Sky said with a smile.

"Hardly rumors when all of Tidings saw a Leshy turn her into a wight as she saved all of our lives in the gods' cursed storm clouds like nature's own projection screen." Gypsum chuckled.

"Don't tell me, let me guess. You're Crag Straumr, eldest Straumr and my uncle Jackal's lover and a battle provost at Valla U. You're Sky Tio, counter *calling* provost and eldest Tio. Your second son, Cyan, used to room with Jett and your niece is Gypsum's girlfriend.... Mica. *Oh*, I love Mica," I told them.

Gypsum sat up, scaring the skogkatts off. "Girlfriend!"

"She is not your girlfriend. Scarlett only wants to marry you off to her," Quick amended.

"She's fantastic. Just wait until you meet her," I told him with a wink.

Slate stormed over to me and I pulled myself up. His cheek still bore the outline of my hand for saying the most inappropriate thing I'd ever heard and then defended his remark by saying I used to like hearing such things. *As if!*

"You must be jesting. You remember them but you do not remember us?" Slate gestured to himself and Brass, and I rolled my eyes.

"Why didn't one of our many family members on the council join you? I see you are in your official robes; it must be a big deal for you to come here," I noted.

"We sequestered the council, so we cannot stay long," Crag admitted.

Quick laughed. "Matriarch Vetr must be thrilled."

"We voted for the Prime today. It was unanimous —"

"Absolutely not," Slate growled. "She is having three of my bairn come winter, and if she was not, the answer is still *no*."

"Congratulations, you are going to give the Tios a run for our claim on fertility," Sky interjected.

Crag continued. "You are the unchallenged Prime. Your memory loss shall not be an issue, I trust?"

"Thank you." I rubbed my flat belly, looking at them through my lashes. "Two boys and a girl. I'd like another girl, but then I think I'm done."

Slate growled and came to stand in front of me, forcing my head back in order to meet his gaze. "Who do you plan on having this other bairn with since you do not let me *touch* you? Need I remind you how it works?"

I dropped my eyes. Not because I'd been cowed, far from it, my palm itched to slap him again. I knew my pupils would have expanded with him so close.

"I haven't remembered everything, though I have recalled most. I chose this cottage because it's near the Mélange and the Jorogumo where Thre'ik took the infants and children," I informed them.

"We go once a week to help out Thre'ik and check on the Mélange."

Indigo twisted in her spot next to Quick with her hand high on his thigh, she couldn't stop touching him.

"There is no one better suited for the position." Crag stepped past Slate's back so his darkest brown eyes ensnared me.

They said that everyone saw my plight in the storming clouds. That they saw my hard choice. I remembered Ash and his haunting last words.

"I get to pick my own Second?" I asked as Slate sighed.

He moved to lean against the wall beside Brass when I folded my arms below my swollen chest.

"Naturally." Sky nodded.

"Ridge Vetr. I know he would prefer to play behind the scenes but he's perfect for the job."

"He is a Vetr. Traditionally, Primes and Seconds are Tio or Straumr descendants," Crag reminded me.

"You should have a second choice ready I do not think Ridge wants to be far from his daughter," Sky said nervously.

I smiled knowingly at them. "I'm a Natt. Names shouldn't have an impact on who is best for the job. If Ridge won't do it, then I'll ask Steel Sumar."

"You are a diabolical woman." Quick chuckled.

Ridge would do it because Steel wouldn't turn me down if I asked and Tawny wouldn't want Steel in Valla every day. Ridge or Steel would be perfect for the job, so would Hawk, but I would have a hard time delegating to the man who helped raise me.

"That will work," Crag agreed and looked to Brass and Slate. "What do your husbands say on the matter?"

Brass had kept his eyes fixed on me as I spoke — the father of my sons. There was no denying their paternity. I couldn't wait to get my memories back of the irresistible Brass Regn. Surprisingly, I hadn't had a problem resisting him for the last six weeks. I was petrified of being with either man — *any* man.

I had taken to kissing them both at night before bed, and I'd started letting them sleep in the bed with me as opposed to the floor. They were wonderful with Balas and Spinel and we did a lot of late night feedings and changes. I'd told myself in the beginning that it made sense to have them stay with me so I had help, yet at some point I couldn't fall asleep until they were both in bed with me. They were dangerous men to become reliant on.

Brass was easier. He smiled often, and I knew what he was thinking at any point of the day because he had no problem telling me. He was open and affectionate and didn't mind helping me in the garden. Brass frequently made breakfast so when I awoke he fed me.

Slate was another matter. Undeniably attractive, I still couldn't let myself relax around him. He was... too much. Then he said or did things that had an unexpected reaction in me, and I felt overwhelmed. I slapped him more days than not for doing or saying something that made me blush.

Today was no exception.

"Can we have a night to sleep on it? I can't accept unless I have my husbands with me." I licked my lips feeling Slate's gaze join Brass's on my face.

"We're with her. We're always with you, Love," Brass said in his smooth way.

"Down whatever rabbit hole she leads us," Slate rumbled.

I inhaled feeling my chest swell with pride and... could it be love? It might have been helium the way my body seemed to float from the floor boards. I may not have remembered them, but they were my men and with me to the end. I could *feel* it.

"We'll need a couple weeks to wrap things up here," I began, and started to arrange things with Crag and Sky for my official acceptance.

They left with several scrolls and dubious looks, but I felt great about the day.

Indigo and I stood side-by-side washing and drying dishes after dinner. We shared a smile, continuing our work that could be cathartic at times. Everyday monotony was underrated.

Quick strode up behind her and leaned around her as he grabbed a mug. Jett had brought troll ale with him and the men would be over indulging tonight. Our time away from it all was coming to an end. Gypsum knew enough to return to the university and with my installment as Prime, classes would begin again.

Everyday monotony would come again someday.

Indigo sighed deeply and rested back against him. He was always surprised when she paid him affection. He couldn't *feel* what I did when they were together. She drew his arm around her so his palm rested on her belly.

"Scar, you've got this?" Indigo said huskily.

"Yeah. You get out of here you two crazy kids," I teased.

I watched as Quick ducked his head to her ear with a salacious smile and whispered a number of naughty things I couldn't hear. He arched his brow at me as he turned her away from the kitchen counter.

"It would not hurt if *you* were a little crazy tonight, Prime."

I glowered at Quick as he led away my giggling sister.

With the dishes all put away, I hung the apron on the hook beside the sink and walked into the living room. Slate, Brass, and Gypsum were lounging about the couches and playing with Balas and Spinel.

"I'm going to get some fresh air. Are you guys good?" I asked, bracing my hands on the back of the couch Gypsum was laid across.

Brass lifted his head with his glittering amber eyes as he hoisted Spinel up and pressed those plump lips to his head. I may have swooned.

"We're good," Gypsum told me, peeking over the back of the couch.

"I will join you," Slate said, handing Balas to Gypsum. "Unless you prefer to be alone."

"No," I said a little too quickly, then fought not to shuffle my feet. "I'd like for you to join me," I told him awkwardly.

Slate strode over to me and took my hand from the couch then laced his fingers through mine. He wasn't the hand holding type, and the gesture caught me off guard.

Slate led me between the rows of plants and vegetables to our pond. He rolled up the legs of his pants, his hair falling over his broad shoulder as I swung my legs over the side of the pond. Across from where we sat laid a log left from a long fallen tree. I came out every night and grew the morning glory vine that not only reminded me of my first day in Tidings, but of Pearl and of my mother.

"Thank you for thinking of us before accepting the position," Slate rumbled as he leaned back on his palms as I did.

Our thighs touched as I arched a brow at him. He seldom said thanks and he never said sorry. I wondered what had gotten into him.

"I'm sorry for slapping you," I told him, looking back to the still pond that reflected the sliver of moonlight that laced through the trees.

"For today or all the times you have slapped me?" I caught a hint of amusement in his tone and let my lips quirk.

"You've deserved it plenty of times. It doesn't seem to deter you any," I joked, and rested my head on my shoulder, listening to the crickets chirp.

There was always a cacophony of noise in the Ostara jungle.

After a protracted silence, I glanced to him. His brows were drawn down as if deep in contemplation.

"You're being weird tonight. Where's your clever retort or lewd comment?" I bumped his arm with my shoulder but it didn't elicit the smile I'd intended.

"It has been six weeks. There is no one to help you retrieve your memories since Indigo lost her ability to manipulate minds after a night. What if they never return?" he asked in an inflectionless tone.

I knit my brows. "I have most of them. They come back on sight most times or with triggers."

"Not with Brass or myself." He exhaled heavily, and I slid my hand closer to his over the grass.

"What *about* you? I believe you are who you say. I don't know how things, *um*, repaired, but I know Balas and Spinel are Brass's sons and mine. I know I'm pregnant and I believe they are yours. I know we're married. My brain is all up to date on the information I just need to wait for the images to upload." I gave him a sheepish smile, but he was still focused on the pond.

"I have made..." He scoffed. "I have lost track of how many mistakes. I have wronged you, broken your heart... I did not deserve a first chance much less a second. Many times I wished it was you who had lost your memories and not myself because you were always a better person than I was, still are. Never did I imagine all the good... *great* memories that we had would be erased with all those rotten ones. Feeling how I do and not having you treat me the way you used to..." He cut off and sat up, putting his hands in his lap. "I do not think I can earn your love a third time. I do not deserve to."

I cleared my throat and faced the pond again. "I have a confession to make." He canted his head to look at me from the corner of his eye, and I continued. "I remember you."

Last night, he had earned his slap by attempting to join me in the shower. A scene had played in my mind's eye afterwards.

Slate looked wide eyed at me. "You remember me and you still —"

"I remember meeting you at the masquerade and your... exploits in the ladies' bathroom. Honestly, I can't believe I married you. You don't, *didn't* seem like the commitment kind. There is only a glimmer of Brass at the end of the memory." I sighed.

"Before you, I was not," he admitted. "Ask me to leave. I will go. You have Brass, you do not need me."

My stomach dropped. I could lose him. I had a plan when I offered my invitation to join me at the pond and it wasn't going my way.

Pulling my feet out of the water, I scrambled into his lap before I lost my nerve. I gripped his hair in my fists and tried to bring my mouth to his. Slate caught my shoulders and held me back with a stony expression.

"I do not want your pity kiss," he growled, but his body said something else entirely.

"I'm not the kind of girl who would be with a man out of pity, am I? Call me Torch. I want to remember."

My eyes flittered between his as I swallowed hard. His grip changed on my shoulders as he ran his calloused palms up and down my arms. I reached behind me and pulled the twisted tie from my hair letting it spill down my back, then yanked the straps of my shirt. The front of my halter fell to my waist, and I bit down on my lower lip as I waited for him to react.

"I did not say those things to guilt you into laying with me," he said in a low tone.

I scoffed. "You think it's *easy* keeping myself from you day in and day out? I struggle with it every second and I don't even know *why* I stop myself since we're already married."

I yanked my arms free of his hands and wound my arms around his neck as I brought my mouth to his. He didn't try to stop me. I pressed myself to his chest, skin to skin, as our chins rubbed up against one another with our tongues mingling.

I hadn't kissed him like that since the night of the ocean shore. My pulse raced, our chemistry like an energy all to itself as his hands slid behind my knees and pulled me tighter in his lap. He was not wearing anything other than his thin pants.

I jerked back his hair, and he growled low in his belly so it vibrated up through his throat as I ran my tongue along it. I nipped at his pulse. His moans came throatily as I pressed kisses along his collar bone.

"Take me. *Please*," I pleaded as I brought his head down to my chest.

Slate was too fast. In one fluid like move, he flipped me from his lap to the grass without breaking contact. His hand untied the knot at my hip so my sarong fell away. I bent my legs so my foot hooked in his waistband and pushed it over his hips as I ran my hands over his hot satin skin. He didn't waste time with pulling me up to remove my shirt the rest of the way, I felt him slice through the thin material and then I was naked beneath him on the warm grass.

Part of our actions were frenzied, but I could sense that he was trying to rein himself in. I was wriggling as I savored his openmouthed kisses over my body, trying to not grow impatient. Then he was hovering above me and I could feel him pressed firmly against the apex of my thighs.

My fear was back. Maybe I'd broken something down there and it didn't work anymore.

"You are choosing me," he breathed. "Tell me why. Why not Brass? I know you care more for him."

"By the Mother!" I groaned in exasperation. "I love you, even without the memories. Not more than Brass and certainly not less, the same but different. I want *you*."

His nostrils flared, and I felt a thrill at the look of challenge in his eyes. My thrill turned to fear in my belly.

"Wait." I stopped his wrist before he could move. "Could we, *um*, go slow. I don't remember doing this before. I —" I stammered.

His face softened, and I ran my thumb down his scar. He turned his mouth to the inside of my wrist and kissed it.

"We will do it however you wish, Torch," he promised.

Images flitted through my mind and I started smiling, my smiling turned into laughter until Slate was leaning away from me with concern etched on his all too handsome face.

"Do not tell me how to fuck you," I said in a mocking bass.

Slate's full lips parted, and I swallowed as I began to blink at tears. I could only nod as a sob tore from my throat.

"Slate. You big, knuckle dragging, Neanderthal. How could you ever think for an instant that I couldn't have fallen back in love with you?" I sobbed again as my body shook. "I'm so sorry. The Leshy made me choose between you and Brass. I saw what it did to my mother and Sparrow — leaving the men they loved behind. I never could have been happy having let one of you die."

I sobbed harder and Slate only stared in disbelief. I sobered, wiping my nose as I remembered.

"The Mother, she said you and Brass share a life. If one of you die, you both die. You have to be careful. Slate, you're not going to die." Tears blurred my vision as I cupped his jaw. "Oh! That bitch! She said she was giving me a gift, but it was really for you. What a dirty, rotten, entirely pointless thing to do!"

"No, Torch. It was letting me know you loved me despite the rousen. That you were not with me because you are my khoraz but because you want to be." His lids slid low and a smile curled on his full beautiful mouth. "Deflowering you is a bonus because I have never been with a maiden."

My Slate. My arrogant, cantankerous, dark, dangerous, barghest.

"I love you. Forever and always. Mine, yours, the world's, for all time. I would risk the world, defy the Norns, just to keep you," I promised.

"Forever is a long time," he breathed, coming back down to my mouth to plant kisses along my jaw.

"Only forever will do."

CHAPTER 52
SLATE

Indigo was more than happy to take care of the twins with Silver and Gypsum's help. Days were needed to properly reacquaint with our wife. Meals were not nearly as important and could be done while she nursed.

Healing was required after hours on end of worshipping one another. That was the only way to do it.

After deflowering Torch, we had to put the boys to bed. It was an extremely difficult twenty minutes as she tried not to reveal that she had regained her memories so she could surprise Brass and have her wicked way with him while I laid down Balas and Spinel.

The walls in the cottage were very thin even though they were made of stone. I could hear my Torch sing her torch song from the bedroom where our boys laid and Gypsum had come up to retrieve the bassinets. Tree-gold had a big mouth and had already divulged the new developments. He'd winked and brought the boys downstairs so the bedroom was ours.

What started in the garden, went into the showers, before we made it into any bed. It was agony waiting for her body to adjust, and some things could not be healed.

"Tell me this isn't the absolute most stupid idea I've ever had."

Scarlett wore a cream flowing dress with old metallic threads in the sweetheart neckline she favored. Katydid had done her makeup and hair before we left so she looked ravishing.

"Is there anything you have tried to do that failed?" Brass asked wryly.

"That's not the same. I'll take a kiss if someone is offering," she said, kneading her palms.

I ducked down, beating Brass to her lips, but as soon as I shifted he stole a kiss for himself. Her body language changed and she looked dreamily at us. We were both dressed in black and armed to the teeth. A message would be sent, and it had better be heeded.

Ridge was as nervous as Torch but was doing a better job of hiding it. He and Sparrow had ended their marriage on the best of terms. He held no ill will towards her for having moved on. I had caught whispers of clandestine meetings between him and Magnolia Rot that had been going on since the public dissolving of his marriage. It was unprecedented, but how often did someone return from the dead? I had lost track of how many times.

Heavy wooden chairs and bodies filled the hall outside the hearing room and Torch glanced down the polished floors again, smiling tightly at her co-conspirators.

"It's time, Love," Brass said in a soft tone, but she jerked to attention, anyway.

"You are a visionary. The people will love you even if the council does not. I have it on good authority that most of them do." I offered her a smirk that made her lips quirk.

Brass and I each took a handle of the double doors and swung out. The air formed the dress to Scarlett's body and gasps sounded all around.

They had kept the secret of her rebirth well.

We walked behind her as she sauntered with purpose down the center aisle between the pews. Her heels rang out with our boots. I should have been glowering ahead, but her hips had a hypnotic roll to them I could not stop myself from staring at.

When she came to a halt before the dais the council sat at I pulled my eyes off her backside with an effort and faced the greater family patriarchs and matriarchs.

Each one sat at their carved backed seat before the horseshoe desk where their sigil hung in their robes. At the bend sat Sky and Crag beside them were Tawny in her scarlet and white Vetr robes and Hawk in his reluctant Sumar royal blue and gold. There was Jett in Var green and gold, Sterling in Haust chocolate and gold. Amethyst wore the seldom seen orange and purple Geol robes, while Sparrow was content to let me be a husband to my wife and take up the sky blue and yellow robes of the Dagr.

Beside Tawny in midnight blue and black Natt robes was Willow who had been the only Natt other than Diamond to be completely absolved of her crimes. There had been a lengthy trial by Guardian standards after the funerals. Quartzite and Novaculite were under house arrest for the next year and had been able to have their children in the comfort of the Natt castle. Cassiopeia was granted leniency after a plea from Sterling and Diamond. She was sentenced to wear a nix torque for the rest of her days and forbidden to use calling. She too was restricted to the Natt castle. Ridge had volunteered to oversee them and visited his mother and nieces frequently.

Sterling had been but a footnote in the proceedings. Indigo had left the cottage only that once to offer a heartfelt plea for his acquittal. Sterling and Diamond had come back with her to offer more apologies and had seen that Torch was alive. Things had changed between the couple. That Gypsum did not recall his affections towards Diamond and Indigo no longer longed for Sterling forced the two to focus on one another.

Sterling had spoken to me privately. He wanted me to come to Mabon so we could discuss our inner beasts. He had felt the kinship when our howls had rung out in Valla. I told him once we returned, I would give it serious thought.

Crag rose. "We are here to elect the new Prime; may they bring balance and peace to the Mother."

Sky rose beside him. "As our only nominated candidate, Scarlett Natt, please approach the dais."

She took two measured steps away from us and it was too far. I shot my eyes to Brass who rubbed his lips together, no doubt thinking the same as I. We would never let her more than an arm's length away again.

"Council will put it to a vote. The candidate must have five of the nine votes to become Prime," Crag said, his croaky voice carrying to the furthest corners of the room that crowded with Guardians.

Jackal sat with the other Straumrs and Diamond. The girl had taken Indigo's advice and was trying to make the transition from cousin to birth father. Jackal was making that transition easier on them both. He had his arm around her shoulders as he gave Scarlett a wink, making her lips quirk.

Steel and Cherry sat in the front row with the children, Indigo, Quick, and Gypsum. The multitude of Tios were just behind them including a noticeably pregnant Crimson and her husband Beryl as well as Mica Rot.

"Not our secret to tell," Brass whispered under his breath.

... You must tire of knowing everyone's secrets. As long as our wife does not harbor any, I could not care less... unless it pertains to her safety...

Brass grunted in agreement.

Hands went up. Tawny was a split second faster than Jett with a broad smile on her face. All the hands went up with Willow cool indigo eyes focused on the back of the room. Her hand went up last of all with a mere flick of her fingers. She did not want to anger the new Prime, but she would make her discontent known.

She was history in the making.

Murmurs broke out in the crowd. The absence of the claviger was apparent when Crag came around the table and stepped off the dais with the black sleeveless robe of the Prime trimmed in silver and gold, the three interlocking triangles on the back. Scarlett lifted her hair as he held it out for her to put her arms through.

Crag led the way back to the table, with Brass and I behind Scarlett. I called over the chair we had specially made with all the others. Baboo had been honored with the commissioning of the chairs.

I set the valknut carved chair between the Tio and Straumr seats and Scarlett stood before it and rested her finger tips on the table top. A hush fell over the room a thousand Guardians had gathered in to catch a glimpse of our legendary wife.

"I present to you, your Prime of the Guardians, Overseer of Valla

University for Guardian Mastery, Scarlett Natt," Sky said as she raised her hands to hush the crowd.

The people rose to their feet. I could scent the mixture of those who feared her power and those who loved her. The Mother's chosen one or the khoraz seductress. In any case, she was respected.

"Thank you, Guardians for your trust and confidence. I humbly accept."

She smiled brilliantly at them and lowered her hands for them to sit. I could scent some men's desire and women's jealousy. She remained standing, and the crowd began to murmur again. The fun was about to start.

"I have had the privilege of knowing the outcome of today's vote for the past two weeks and have already chosen whom I wish to follow me as Second. May I reintroduce to you, Ridge Vetr — my Second."

She swept her hands to the doors using her calling to open them with Ridge waiting nervously behind. Crag and Sky scooted further as Brass called over a second chair with the Yggdrasil carved in the back. It matched the grey and white robe Scarlett had designed for her reign as Second.

Ridge strode between the pews wearing thick Elivagar fashion though it was midsummer. He had chosen his ensemble with care. Red for the Vetr and black for the Natt. He came around the side of the table and Scarlett set his robe on his shoulders herself.

We'd anticipated the clamoring from the crowd. We'd resurrected not one, but two long thought dead Guardians.

Ridge slid into his seat beside Scarlett and she graced the crowd with her very best smile. Jett grumbled as men shifted in their seats to puff up their chests.

"As my first order of business as Prime, I would like to make a proposal to the council. From this day forward marks a change in times. Never before have a man or woman governed this nation much less one not being of direct Tio or Straumr descent. In theme with this change, I propose we allow lesser families a vote on the council. Each of the islands lesser families would count as a single greater family vote," she said in a clear voice that projected across the room.

Willow would be her greatest adversary, but until she regained support, she would be outnumbered. She shot Scarlett an incredulous look but didn't voice her objection.

"I cannot think anyone here could deny that how things have been done is not efficient and there is a very large gap between the greater families and the common families. The lessers are only called such because of their amount of historic abilities. All those in favor of creating a lesser council?"

Scarlett looked to either side of her. Slowly, the hands went up. Tawny had had forewarning of her plan, though she was having a difficult time governing the lesser families who thought she was weak and, after being under Orion and Cassiopeia's tight fisted rule, they had begun plotting before the robe settled on her shoulders. Mabon was the only island not to have a second greater family and after generations of having free rein over the island, Sterling was reluctant to give it up. He was the last to raise his hand.

The doors had remained open. With Steel and Quick's help, Brass and I brought in the two parts of the second horseshoe-shaped table from the side room with our *calling*. The crowd gasped again when the table settled just below where the greater families sat. There had been more than enough room, it was as if a second table was supposed to be there.

Coyote strode in first floating his chair with its raindrop sigil carved on the back, he wore the navy and green robe of the Regn. Cordillera was next for the Blomi, Boa Sunna after her and so on. The lesser families who would likely cause more problems than they would solve having finally been allowed to sit at the adults' table, sat in their seats facing the stunned crowd.

"Thank you for joining us," Scarlett addressed them, and they were all smiles for her.

She had earned more allies than enemies with the risky move.

I could feel her hesitation. What she had proposed next was more than risky. There was a good chance it could start an uproar. Scarlett would not like to be hated by her people on the first day, but changes had to be made. We had all agreed. Our system was fatally flawed.

I saw the fabric of her draped sleeve shift and knew Brass had given her a squeeze of reassurance with his air. She took a deep inhale and pushed her shoulders back.

"We have petitioners and there is no time like the present." She magnified her voice with our help, there were things she was still learning. "Please, enter."

Anundr and Brusi did not have to duck to enter the large hearing room. Their burnt umber boulder like heads appraised the petrified gathered Guardians, most of which had begun to believe giants were myths. Behind them was Rikke, Vanna'ra, Vernal, Lewt, and Caolan striding down the aisle with Baboo trotting to keep up and a blue-eyed fairy on her shoulder.

Anundr and Brusi towered over the people and shed knowing smirks at those who clutched one another. People from Valla were unaccustomed to seeing the tribes since there were none on their island. Most were afraid. Fear led to ignorance. Scarlett wanted to educate the people.

"Prime Natt," Anundr said in his guttural voice.

"Risar Anundr, what have you come to be petitioned here today?" Scarlett asked in an all too sweet voice.

Brusi chuckled at her feigned ignorance. "We petition the council for a voice. The tribes wish to assemble. To have a voice as to what happens to us and to be a part of our own governing."

"And you speak on behalf of all the tribes gathered?" Sterling asked.

The Risar brothers turned to their ruler. "We do," they said together.

"We can hardly be expected to vote on this here and now." Willow could no longer hold her silence.

Scarlett simmered with excitement. Willow had taken the bait.

"I am afraid I agree with Matriarch Natt. Instead, I propose we ask the tribes to elect a representative of their choosing to plead their case. They may gather here in Valla in a housing of our choosing. I believe there is a section that has recently been rehabbed and currently has no tenants owned by Matriarch Blomi that will suit your needs until we have made our judgement." Scarlett plowed right through not letting anyone get a word in edgewise. "All those in favor of waiting to hear the tribes' proposal?" she asked.

Tribes in Valla walking the cobbled roads, getting Guardians used to treating the tribes as equals — as real people as opposed to problems to be dealt with. That was the overall goal. If they could have the assembly too, that would be better.

Willow withheld her vote as did Sterling. The lesser families from Elivagar and Mabon withheld theirs as well. There were still enough to pass the vote.

"I appreciate your willingness to bring Tidings into a new era. We will work it all out in time and patience to unify the Guardians again and put the ugliness of the past year behind us. We will go forth stronger and wiser for it."

Torch glanced back to Brass and I and we felt her love through the bond she activated the moment the hardest part of her day was through.

"If you kiss her now, it will diminish her authority," Brass whispered.

... I am going to do a lot more than kiss her. I suppose it would be inappropriate to bend the new Prime over her fine new tables and chairs...

I slid my eyes to Brass who was hiding his smirk with his hand.

"It would be while there are so many Guardians here. I did not say we couldn't *after*."

Brass and I chuckled as we plotted how to best take the new Prime as the meeting was concluded. Torch wriggled in her seat having caught overwhelming scents.

It was a good day to do things extremely well.

EPILOGUE

JETT

The world was changing. Scarlett's plotting was key to all that change. It was needed, they had all agreed. It was easier for her to find and fix the flaws in their system, not having been born and bred in Tidings.

It'd been a week since Scarlett became Prime and the Vigrid tournaments had gone off without a hitch other than the moping of their chief of staff, who would rather have been in bed with Indigo far away from the eyes of the public.

She hadn't pulled away or pushed him as she used to do. Indigo told

Quick how it was and what she intended and invited him to help her. Scarlett held marathon movie nights to introduce her to pop culture that everyone attended in the family except for Quick.

Jett couldn't blame him. He was holding onto hope that she'd change her mind.

They were all gathered to say their goodbyes under the blue starry lights of the Sumar portal room. Scarlett held Indigo tightly in her arms. She'd pulled every string at the Prime's disposal which were several spools' worth to get Indigo forged college transcripts, a social security number, and a birth certificate. What Indigo didn't know was that as soon as she passed her clinicals, Scarlett had gotten her a job at a hospital near her old apartment. A bank account was set up in her name and she'd secretly begun to refurnish the house she grew up so when Indigo's son was born she'd have a house to live in instead of her one bedroom, second-floor apartment.

"I'm going to miss you. I'm keeping the Aves ambassador position open just in case. What's the point of being Prime if you can't have a little nepotism, right?" Scarlett's eyes gleamed as she smiled. "Love you."

"Love you, too. I'll be back for our birthday and I'll have a little boy with me," Indigo said, laughing through a sob.

"Don't you dare. You had better call me the second you go into labor. I mean it." Scarlett gave her one last embrace before she let her go.

Jett held out Bee's carrier and Indigo smiled wiping her nose as she wrapped her arms around his waist. "Why do my little sisters insist on being so damn independent?" he whispered roughly into her hair.

"I love you, Jett. Have I ever told you how glad I am that I'm not your type so you never hit on me?"

Jett chuckled despite himself. "You and me both."

The light lit around the shape of a man as the portal activated and Sterling stepped through with brows drawn together as he searched our faces. His eyes landed on Indigo and he moved past us as she stepped from Jett.

Sterling lifted her off her feet as he held her, lowering his face into the crook of her neck. "Forgive me, Indi. I cannot stand you leaving and hating me forever."

She held him back only slightly less firm. Indigo's hand stroked his head as she pressed a kiss to his cheek. He set her feet back on the floor and she held his face so she could level her eyes at him.

"I could never hate you, Sterling. Part of me will always love you." She offered him a rueful smile and withdrew to take the cat carrier.

She looked past us all to the hall then swallowed hard. If Quick had seen that look on her face, he might not have been so livid about her leaving. He had won her heart in spite of herself.

She ran her fingers over the braid she wore that bespoke their last night together before she walked to the portal. Indigo waggled her fingers one last time and Scarlett stifled a sob against Slate's chest as the bright white of the portal enveloped her.

Indigo was gone.

EPILOGUE PART II
SCARLETT

I LOST myself in my two gorgeous husbands — one soft and sweet, the other hard and wild. A better combination of men had never been made.

I made a contented sound in my throat. "This is my heaven. The two of you with our children."

"Asgard... or Valhalla, if you're being true to our heritage," Brass

478

called from the other room. "This heaven business won't stand as Prime."

"One day I am going to get sick of seeing your hairy ass," Slate rumbled from where he laid against my stomach as Brass strode across the room naked as the day the Mother made him.

We both chuckled.

"Good thing your opinion of my ass doesn't matter," Brass said, climbing into our big white bed to lean against the headboard beside me. "The boys are out. They're both holding tight to the trains Slate made them."

I lifted my chin to kiss Brass's lips and felt Slate shift in my lap to run his teeth along the underside of my breast. Not very good at sharing, my Slate, but I loved him that way.

I sighed and closed my laptop after saving the email I'd have to send later when I was back at Valla. Brass took it from me and floated it over to the dresser where I'd placed the carving Slate had made of me holding two infants. If the whole patriarch thing fell through, he would open his own shop to sell his carvings. They were stunning.

"What did you tell Chris?" Brass asked.

Slate growled since he wasn't a fan of my ex-fiancée. It didn't last before he quickly returned to his nipping and suckling that prickled my skin. He was not easy to ignore.

"Remodeling is almost finished. He slept on her couch last night and she begins clinicals tomorrow. All in all, he says she's good. The gym will be done soon and the website will be up before then. I found a family in Chicago, a Guardian family with a daughter from the year of minerals from Basil's book of the families who left after the Massacre. She's been applying to hospitals; I'm going to give her a little help. She's very pretty too." I glanced at Brass who was giving me a wry look. "I want Chris to be happy. He's an insanely great guy," I said defensively.

Slate had stopped and gave me a dry look. "You feel responsible for him. I understand, Torch, but you gave him a house. Made him a co-owner of your gym with its own clothing line. I hope you mean this girl for him as well as Indigo because unlike Brass, I do not wish to see you with the myopic."

"You're jealous. You always were," I teased.

Slate narrowed his eyes, and I felt Brass shift away and Slate pulled me down the bed as I giggled. "Quiet, wench. You will wake our sons," he rumbled, pulling the sheet from between us.

Brass had moved off the bed as Slate prepared to truly make a wench out of me. Brass returned as things were heating up and chuckled as Slate attempted to shove him off the bed.

Slate growled as he rolled off me. "Go on, it is always fun to boost her mood. Dibs."

"We agreed, no dibs," Brass said, and helped me scoot back up to tuck me against his body.

I was still giggling until I saw what he held in his hand.

"No more avoiding it. I have not pressed, though I should have." Brass sighed.

ALDER was scrawled across the blood splattered letter in my mother's handwriting. I'd avoided the letter for two years. I took it from his hands and smoothed it over my thigh.

"You already know what's in it?" I asked, pulling the sheet up under my arms.

"Yes, Love. We both know. Slate does because he's always known and I know because I read it in Alder and Wren's minds."

"Is it... bad?" I asked as I opened the envelope with care.

"Perhaps for Jett. It is too late to change it." Slate sighed, scooting up beside me.

"It isn't anything you haven't already suspected," Brass murmured, kissing the side of my head.

I sighed as I unfolded the letter. It was a myopic thing to do, having a letter in an envelope instead of a scroll. I read my mother's private words to my father and prayed it wouldn't completely rip free the scar tissue that had healed over old wounds.

Dearest Tree,

I am writing you because it seems whenever I try to say it out loud, I lose my nerve. Twenty-four years ago, I didn't show up to our special meeting place. It wasn't because I didn't love you. On the contrary, I'd fallen deeply in love with you and was afraid of your rejection. I was sixteen and a greater family daughter. I thought you worked at the Var castle and that our time together didn't mean to you what it meant to me. I thought you would forget me and so I went to the Valkyries when I found out. My mother began to tell people that she was pregnant. When in truth it was me all along.

Jett is not your first-born son. Steel is not the second son of Flint and Pearl, but our first son — the true heir to Ostara. We've raised them as brothers, but they believe they are uncle and nephew. It never seemed like the right time to change their beliefs, but now that we are planning to become a family, I want Steel to know.

Help me tell our first son that we are his true parents and claim him as your own.

Forever Yours,

Little Bird

I swallowed, looking down at the letter. All my suspicions about Steel, how closely he resembled Jett and me... I'd known. Deep down, I'd always known. My father made Jett heir before he read her letter. He died before he could fulfill her wishes.

I sailed the letter and envelope back to the dresser.

I had two brothers; I should've been more excited. I loved Steel. He was already like a brother. It didn't change anything for me. It might for Tawny since she'd slept with both of my brothers — the hussy.

But Jett...

"Torch?"

"Love?"

My husband's said over one another.

"Nope," I said dryly before I took a deep breath. "It's fine. You're right. I... knew. I'm not going to be the one to ruin everything. Things are finally settling down. Everyone is happy. I'm burying that letter and it...changes nothing."

"Take it in, Love. Think on it," Brass said, slinking down on the bed.

Slate mimicked him on the other side. "You will tell Indigo."

"Right. That's it, and only after she swears a blood vow never to reveal it," I agreed as they both grabbed a thigh under the sheets. "I mean... *seriously*? We have a dragon on the loose that no one's seen, an albino barghest no one is claiming to be, and now Ostara has the wrong Patriarch? Just.... *nope*."

"All in good time. Hawk should know," Brass murmured pressing his lips to my now exposed kneecap.

I knit my brows. "He should," I agreed.

Brass trailed kisses along the inside of my thigh while Slate kissed up the small swell of my belly. I was getting bigger sooner this time.

"But that's it," I said with finality.

"Ridge has figured it out on his own, he has mentioned it to Sparrow," Brass whispered against my inner thigh.

"Stop with these underhanded acts of persuasion. I know what you're hinting at. It's only a matter of time. I *know*."

Brass pulled my thighs, so I slid lower on the bed and Slate's big hand cupped my breast. I didn't stand *half* a chance.

"Tell me of these underhanded acts of persuasion, Torch," Slate said, brushing his lush mouth over mine.

"Love-thoughts, Love-juice, Love-odor, Love-yielding, Love-climbers, and the climbing sap. Arms and hands of love — lips of love — phallic thumb of love — breasts of love — bellies press'd and glued together with love. Earth of chaste love — life that is only life after love, The body of my love — the body of the woman I love — the body of the man — the body of the earth. Soft forenoon airs that blow from the south-west. The hairy wild-bee that murmurs and hankers up and down — that gripes the full-grown lady-flower, curves upon her with amorous firm legs, takes his will of her, and holds himself tremulous and tight till he is satisfied. The wet of woods through the early hours, two sleepers at night lying close together as they sleep, one with an arm slanting down across and below the waist of the other —"

"Three sleepers, though I don't intend on sleeping for a time." Brass lifted his head long enough to interrupt Slate's poetry.

I gasped as I felt Brass's tongue against me. "*Ah,* three. Yes, that's a good start. What would Tidings think if they knew the Prime was so easily manipulated?" I said huskily.

Brass chuckled against me. "Lucky woman," Slate rumbled with a smile.

Heaven, *er*, Asgard was constantly evolving.

THE END.
For now.

AFTERWORD

Rising Ashes ends with a few questions. It is going to be at least a year (from 2024) before I work on Indigo's story. If you cannot wait to discover the paternity, I won't make you. It's a spoiler, but not one that impacts the plot in a major way.

Check out *Who's the Baby Daddy?* on the blog.

For more of Tidings's world, family trees, quizzes, events, and news from Charli Rahe, please visit www.charlirahe.com and join Charli's Devils on Facebook.

BIBLIOGRAPHY

Whitman, Walt. "A Clear Midnight." *Leaves of Grass,* 1856

Whitman, Walt. "Spontaneous Me." *Leaves of Grass,* 1856

Rossetti, Christina. "Echo." *Goblin Market and Other Poems,* 1862

Hughes, Langston. "Wisdom and War." *The Span* Vol. 5, No. 1, 1946